RUDE BUAY

VOLUMES 1-3

Original Stories ...

By

International Bestselling Author

John A. Andrews

The RUDE BUAY Series®

Copyright © 2020 by John A. Andrews.
All rights reserved. Written permission must be secured from the publisher to use or reproduce any part of this book, except for brief quotations in critical reviews or articles.

Published in the U.S.A. by
Books That Will Enhance Your Life™
Cover Design: John A. Andrews
Cover Graphic Designer: Abhai Kaul
Cover Photo: Anthony Johnson
Edited by: Pernell Marsh/ALI

ISBN: 9798627795140

RUDE BUAY

Original Story …
By
International Bestselling Author
John A. Andrews

The RUDE BUAY Series®

RUDE BUAY

... The Unstoppable

aka Rude Boy ... The Unstoppable

by

International
Bestselling Author

John A. Andrews

Other Titles Include:
Dare To Make A Difference – Success 101 For Teens
Total Commitment - The Mindset of Champions
When The Dust Settles - A True Hollywood Story
How I Wrote 8 Books In One Year
Whose Woman Was She?
The FIVE "Ps" For Teens
Who Shot The Sheriff?
Cross Atlantic Fiasco
A Snitch On Time
Quotes Unlimited
L.A. Undercover
Agent O'Garro
NYC

RUDE BUAY

Copyright © 2010 by John A. Andrews.

All rights reserved. Written permission must be secured from the publisher to use or reproduce any part of this book, except for brief quotations in critical reviews or articles.

Published in the U.S.A. by
Books That Will Enhance Your Life™

A L I - Andrews Leadership International
Entertainment Division®
Jon Jef Jam Entertainment®

Cover Design: John A. Andrews
Cover Graphic Designer: John Andrews/Abhai Kaul
Cover Photo: Anthony Johnson
Edited by: Pernell Marsh/ALI
ISBN: 978-0-983-1419-52

Table Of Contents

Chapter One..................................7
Chapter Two.................................14
Chapter Three..............................17
Chapter Four................................21
Chapter Five.................................27
Chapter Six..................................33
Chapter Seven.............................40
Chapter Eight...............................43
Chapter Nine...............................47
Chapter Ten.................................53
Chapter Eleven............................58
Chapter Twelve............................62
Chapter Thirteen..........................68
Chapter Fourteen.........................71
Chapter Fifteen............................74
Chapter Sixteen...........................78
Chapter Seventeen......................81
Chapter Eighteen.........................86
Chapter Nineteen........................93
Chapter Twenty..........................100
Chapter Twenty-One...................103

RUDE BUAY

Chapter Twenty-Two......................110
Chapter Twenty-Three....................114
Chapter Twenty-Four.....................119
Chapter Twenty-Five.....................122
Chapter Twenty-Six......................126
Chapter Twenty-Seven....................130
Chapter Twenty-Eight....................133
Chapter Twenty-Nine.....................139
Chapter Thirty..........................144
Chapter Thirty-One......................151
Chapter Thirty-Two......................156
Chapter Thirty-Three....................162
Chapter Thirty-Four.....................166
Chapter Thirty-Five.....................169
Chapter Thirty-Six......................176
Chapter Thirty-Seven....................179
Chapter Thirty-Eight....................187
Chapter Thirty-Nine.....................190
Chapter Forty...........................203

"Ask not what your country can do for you - ask what you can do for your country."
- John F. Kennedy

1

A CUPBOARD DOOR SLAMS SHUT!
"What's taking you so long to pack your bag, boy? You are going to be late for school again, the second day in a row Randy." That parental voice came screaming from the kitchen and echoing upstairs through Randy's untidy room. Randy in a state of urgency forces his tattered notebooks inside his one strap, still hanging book bag.
"Mom I got it, will you stop screaming at me?"

RUDE BUAY

"You too *rude buay!* Don't make me come up there!"
Footsteps heard coming up the stairs alert Randy, as he comes running down the stairs passing his mom who misses her swing at him. His Afro pick comb falls out of his unzipped bag at the bottom of the stairs; he turns back to pick it up.
"That's what your rudeness would do for you."
Shoeless but neatly dressed, he grabs a mango and a banana from the kitchen counter, throws them in a plastic bag, and darts through the door.
Several kids, neatly dressed, wearing designer sneakers, carrying laden book bags - speed up in an attempt to keep pace with him.
"*Rude Buay*, what's the rush we are all going to the same class." He keeps on running. Suddenly, they catch up with him going up the steep hill. The leader of the pack, Mike, tugs Rude Buay's book bag away, retrieves the afro pick and proceeds to aggressively comb his hair. Rude Buay retaliates; as a result the comb which was made from bicycle spokes bends.
Frustrated, Mike punches Rude Buay hard in the stomach. Rude Buay, now holding his stomach, falls over in the gutter. The brawl escalates as it continues. Mike lands a few more punches in Rude Buay's stomach, leaving him breathless. The other kids kick Rude Buay's bags into the street.
Suddenly, with a burst of energy, Rude Buay athletically catches up with Mike and the other kids. He fights back, throwing wild punches. Mike counter-

RUDE BUAY

attacks. Rude Buay retaliates. Mike grabs him and engages in a wrestling bout. The struggle intensifies. Mike reaches for Rude Buay's jugular. The loud exhaust of a truck "backfiring" could be heard in the distance. None of the kids seem to pay any attention to the oncoming traffic. They are focused on the two kid brawl, which has now transcended onto the street. Mike's supporters are cheering him on. The gasping Young Rude Buay manages to remove Mike's hand from around his neck and darts after his now no strap disheveled book bag and lunch sack. Mike loses his footing on the banana in the plastic sack and falls onto the street. The approaching truck unable to stop runs Mike over before coming to a complete stop. The kids on the sidelines all yell.
"You pushed him! We saw you, Randy! You killed Mike!
The truck driver JUMPS out, shaken up and flustered. The front tire left its mark on Mike's khaki shirt as he lays trapped under the buses' chassis. The truck's conductors jump out *starring* at the "whose fault is it" catastrophe. They assist the driver in removing Mike's body from under the truck. He discovers that Mike doesn't have a pulse and tries CPR. Mike responds negatively to resuscitation. Meanwhile, Rude Buay, drenched in tears, shakes like a leaf on the nearby rocky embankment.

RUDE BUAY

ONE YEAR LATER:

All lights are out except the one in Rude Buay's room. He lies on his back studying from a grease-stained book by candlelight. The Officer walks by and notices. With a vindictive look he opens up the door, and in thick patois dialect, he confronts Randy. "That is murder you know, me na know way dem ah talk bout when dem say it's only manslaughter. You wicked mon! Him ah me sister's son, her only begotten. Bend over!" He retrieves a twisted switch and whips Randy across his backside several times. Randy cries out, "I did not push your nephew. He slipped! "
Another prisoner across the way witnesses and yells out at the Officer, "Leave the boy alone, mon! The law is the law whether you live on a hill or inside tenement yard."
The Officer discontinues his brutal attack on Randy, puts out the light, confiscates the book, and extinguishes the candle.
Randy staggers to get up off the floor and onto the bed. He's bruised so badly, blood trickles down backside and forearms.

SIX YEARS LATER:

Randy's older brother Clifford on his way home was confronted by several drug dealers outside the

RUDE BUAY

perimeter of their tenement yard. He tried eluding the Uzi wielding quartet but they had him cornered. The leader of the pack yells, "This is our turf, you are hurting our revenue."

Clifford, arguably replied, "I and I live here! I sell what and where I want."

Gunshots like popcorn ring out from their weapons, as they cut Clifford down, leaving him blood-drenched on the sidewalk.

Several tenement dwellers rush to the scene as the supped up green, yellow, and black Mustang speeds away.

A woman wearing an oil-stained apron and carrying a large kitchen fork yells out. "Miss Bascombe, its Clifford! They shot up Clifford bad, mon."

Randy and his mom abort dinner at the dinner table and rush to the scene. She pushes through the gathered crowd towards her son Clifford.

Trying to comfort him, she's now immersed with his blood. His limp hands and body, indicate his lifelessness.

Randy, bathed in tears, looks on.

A Jamaican police land Rover pulls up. Two officers jump out and proceed with their investigation. Several tenement dwellers retreat because of police presence. The senior officer in his 50s asks, "Any witnesses?" as the junior officer releases Miss Bascombe's tight grasp on Clifford. Simultaneously he notices the kitchen fork in a woman's hand. The woman pointing up the street with the fork yells out in deep patois, "Mustang, the color of the flag! You all better find them..."

The officer interrupts.

"Miss, my name is officer Lent. What is your name?"

The woman now with her fork holding hand on her hip responds.

"Maude! Maude Davis."

Maude Davis, what you are holding in your hand is considered a deadly weapon."

She continues, "Worry bout me officer Lent, and let the murderers go free, instead of fighting crime you are fighting me. Shoo, fire ah go burn you." And she moseys inside the tenement yard, leaving Randy and his mother to complete the police report.

ONE MONTH LATER:

Before daybreak, a taxi pulls up outside the tenement yard and waits. The only illuminated dwellings belong to Miss Bascombe and Maude Davis. Suddenly, the light at the Bascombe's dwelling goes out. Miss Bascombe locks her door and follows Randy in tow as he knocks on Maude's door with a suitcase and a carryon bag in hand. Maude comes to the door and embraces him.

"Take care of yourself Rude Buay. I will look after your mother for you."

Randy replies gratefully, "Thanks Godmother, I'll miss you." The car horn honks. He continues, "The cab is

RUDE BUAY

waiting." He departs and enters the cab accompanied by his mom.

Later, he stands amongst travelers at Michael Manley International Airport and embraces his mom in tears. Then swiftly Randy heads towards the American Airlines departure lounge waving goodbye.

2

ARRIVING IN NEW YORK, Randy Bascombe acquired a job as a parking attendant, while he figured out exactly what he wanted to do with his life. He was determined to put the imprisoned past behind him.
Deep in his psyche, he knew that he wanted to fight crime. However, becoming a police officer, he would be a mediocre accomplishment. Plus, he tragically witnessed firsthand, the ineptness of that entity, when his brother was shot and killed by drug dealers. That Jamaican tragedy stood out like a sore thumb.

RUDE BUAY

He worked hard during the week, and on weekends, he frequented the library.

Before 1960 Americans did not use drugs as acceptable behavior. Neither did Randy Bascombe, who was born after that era. He saw it as a serious offense. Additionally, losing his brother in a drug-related incident contributed to his abstinence.

Randy gravitated to materials dealing with drug enforcement. He was very much taken aback, when he read the stats that DEA Special Agents grew from 1,470 in 1973 to 2,135 in 1975, two years later.

Retrospectively, his present, once quiet neighborhood, where he played street basketball, was now saturated with drug dealers, buyers, pimps and prostitutes.

This growing Law Enforcement entity became more and more attractive to him. Consequently, he not only studied up on what the U.S. was doing to fight the war on drugs but got so immersed in the subject that he decided to attend college.

There he earned a bachelor's degree, majoring in Criminal Justice and Police Science. Randy came clean on his background check among other requirements. Coincidentally, the Jamaican authorities had recently cleared him from manslaughter charges as a kid. Judge Hastings had revisited the case and found him innocent of the charges.

Randy Bascombe, felt like a new man when he received the phone call that he was hired as a Drug Enforcement

RUDE BUAY

Agent. Bascombe, left New York for Virginia, where he underwent basic training. Upon completing this process, he looked at several major cities where he would like to work. Miami and New York were his top choices, but to give the other cities an equal chance, he included their names in a hat, closed his eyes and drew one. He picked Miami, Florida. To him this was a perfect choice for two reasons:

(1) Miami was close to Jamaica, and it would only take a few hours to hop on a plane and visit his Mom and Maude Davis.

(2) His graduating class all wanted to work for Special Agent Bob White. Why? White, was not only highly-skilled, but he was an intuitive, motivated, and deeply committed agent.

So, Bascombe was interviewed and joined the DEA in Miami. Sadly though, after only being under Bob White's tutelage for two months, White was executed during a friendly fire incident. His assistant, Jose Mendez, was appointed to "fill his shoes."

3

MRS. BLACK, a middle-aged history teacher, collects the last batch of test papers from her students. She places the stack on her desk and reminds the students to be back in their seats immediately after the lunch break. The school bell rings.
Ray, a skinny teenager, shows his disgust with her request. He darts out of the classroom and rushes through the crowded schoolyard. Chattering kids mingle. In the distance, Ray makes a break across the street, to the local grocery store.
Moments later, dozens of kids assemble in the L-shaped cafeteria enjoying their lunch. A variety of food odors fills the air. On the outside, Ray appears. He is larger than life, demonstrative by a hard-wine

interlude. Many kids follow suit in the revelry. The revelry expands and intensifies as it progresses inside the cafeteria.

Teens, enjoying their lunch, would rather not participate in the carousing. But indulge in food tossing attack on the boisterous intruders. Fighting back, their partying turns into the displaying of their food tossing skills.

Two security guards abandon catching up on the sports scores in the Jamaican Gleaner and rush to the scene. After their intense, wielding of the batons, the kids are subdued. Many leave the scene, while the sane ones stay behind and clean up the food residue.

A few yards away, Ray and many of his partying buddies huddle. Their voices are inaudible. A chain reaction, vicious, skin scratching dilemma begins. Rashes break out on their face and hands. Uncontrollably, they begin falling onto the school grounds. Some kids tough it out.

Teachers, students, as well as increased school security personnel, rush in an attempt to investigate and comfort the ailing kids. The persistent ones are now gasping for air and eventually fall to the ground. The fallen attack the sympathetic cries of their classmates, other students, and school personnel alike. Mrs. Black emerges on the scene terrified.

Ray, lies in a fetal position, biting hard into the unpaved school grounds. His classmates and teacher, hover, puzzled; they can't believe what has transpired since the bell rang. The next bell rings, some students saunter back to the classroom; others remain to bathe in grief.

The sound of sirens can be heard in the distance. The increase in decibels indicates their closeness. Suddenly, ambulances pull up. The schoolyard is now a spectacle of flashing lights, cries, and flashing lights. Medics rush out, wheeling stretchers. The debilitated teens are placed on them and rushed inside ambulances, one at a time.

Jamaican Police vehicles emerge onto the scene. Officers jump out and investigate. They carefully collect food residue off the ground and deposit it into trash bags.

Meanwhile, inside the principal's office, terrified teachers congregate. They rummage through the backpacks of ailing kids. Contents are emptied onto the principal's desk. Tiny, neat packets in aluminum foil, along with textbooks, fall from a midnight blue backpack onto the desk bearing the name Ray C. The two overworked security guards, overseeing the search, unwrap one of the packages. Inside, one of the guards discovers a white powdery substance. He refolds it and places it along with the other unopened ones, inside a brown envelope. He seals it airtight. The on-looking teachers wail hysterically, as a result of the findings.

Two officers, wearing transparent gloves, enter and confiscate the envelope. After which they rush to their cruiser, and drive away speedily.

In the meantime, medics steer gurneys with bodies wrapped in white sheets to the morgue at the general hospital. Dozens of tagged bodies (reading Cyanide Overdose) are transported inside this small rectangular-shaped facility. Ray Collins' body makes its way in, followed by his breathless mother, bawling and engulfed in tears. Wearing a soiled dress, with an apron tied around her waist, a multi-colored head tie blowing in the wind, she carries her shoes in her hand. Other parents, in search of their kids, embrace one another in tears. The busy medics sense their grief.

RUDE BUAY

4

THOUSANDS OF MILES AWAY in Bogota, Columbia, livestock graze noisily behind a warehouse. From the hills above, clouds of dust rise from between the trees. The dust follows in tow of a moving object. That yellow hummer speeding through the bushes finally reveals itself, as it emerges and comes to a bumpy, screeching halts.
Immediately, three women jump out:
First, beautiful dark-skinned Agnes Richards. She is in her late 20s, wearing unkempt braids, and carrying two black duffel bags. Second, Asian, trophy woman, Denise Gomez. She is in her late 20s. Denise carries a duffel bag over her shoulder and a semi-automatic rifle in the other. The huge diamond stone on her ring kissing her wedding band glitters in the sun as she

kisses her wedding band. She's all business. Following Denise is a tall, feisty, WWE type, Shelly Hall. A Caucasian in her early 30s. She sports a ponytail hairstyle, and totes two larger duffel bags in one hand. On the other, a semi-automatic rifle. She proceeds in tow of her two traveling partners.

Denise gives them a wink, then leads the way to the shack. The livestock disperses as she moves up to the steel door of the shack. Denise enters a code. The door unlocks. She pulls it open. The three women enter in haste and quickly load up duffel bags with packages containing about five kilos each, labeled: DRAGON X. They load up their hummer and drives away, leaving a trail of dust behind.

Back in Jamaica, outside the general hospital, the sounds of sirens fill the air. Ambulances eventually show their presence. Now idle, with lights still flashing, the paramedics wheel gurneys out, towards several, excessively, vomiting kids. One paramedic, sporting an elongated dreadlocks hairstyle, wheels a teen, who is foaming extensively through the nose inside the ER.

Upon entering, the paramedic glances at the kid and announces:

"This one stopped breathing!"

He checks for a pulse, there is none. He quickly administers CPR. He pauses. Then echoes: 'Nothing! We lost her."

RUDE BUAY

Sirens are heard in the distance, as emerging ambulances raced to the scene. Police vehicles join the emergency response units.

Mourners crowd the ER entrance. Their cries increase in decibels, sandwiched by deep patois, transcending into an inaudible lamentation. So much, that it competes with the ambulance siren.

Jamaican police, rush from an occupied gurney after occupied gurney, with pen and clipboard, collecting data.

Meanwhile, in Columbia, a twin-engine plane taxis as the yellow hummer races towards it. The aircraft speeds up and takes off to the sky, blanketing the vehicle with dust.

In the interim, in a downtown Bogota hotel, Axel James, sits on a couch smoking a long marijuana spliff. He is of Columbian decent, in his mid-forties. Axel displays the tattoo of a dragon below his right ear lobe and has a missing index finger and expensive gold rings on the four fingers of his right hand.

Ricardo Herrera, also of Columbian decent, in his mid-thirties, robust in demeanor, sitting across from Axel James, cogitates. Behind his right earlobe, Ricardo sports the same signature as Axel.

In walks, Ian Baynes, African American, in his late thirties: he is dressed in a pilot's uniform, horned rimmed glasses. The handle of his glasses almost kissing his dragon tattoo. Ian faces Axel but dares not to look him in the eye. Instead, he looks away and addresses him.

"Boss, we've got problems."

"That's why I hired you," responds Axel James authoritatively.

"I know, but you don't understand. Boss, the X product has turned up to be very lethal in Jamaica. That last shipment was probably too concentrated. Kids are dying off like flies."

Axel stares him down in disbelief. "That is what's causing the…"

Ricardo, interrupts, "How about a recall?"

"A thousand kilos…? Too expensive…No deal. That was only one bad apple," claims Axel James.

Let's find another turf," Ricardo urges.

"Right! How about Port Antonio," commands Axel.

"That will never work," responds Ian.

"Why not?" remarks Axel James.

"Those Ministers of Parliament are going to be getting all up in our business. We might check in there but never check out." Ian cautions.

"That's bull…! We'll buy them out," says Axel James.

"How?" Ian questions.

Axel James replies, "Set up roadblocks and dominate. That's virgin territory…"

Ricardo interjects, "Boss, and the girls?"

To which, Axel responds, "Too many…questions. If they fail, we'll ship the product in the stomach of

RUDE BUAY

Columbian kids. All they have to do is take a monitored dump and we...cash in. Let's move it!"

Axel James retires the meeting. He gets up from the table with his semiautomatic in hand and exits. Ricardo and Ian follow closely behind him.

They escape the view of hotel guests and jump inside a red pickup truck. Ricardo is armed in the back, Axel is in the front passenger seat and Ian takes the wheel. Axel's gun glitters, casting its shadow on Ian. The pickup drives off.

The powdered, brown-yellow hummer arrives outside the warehouse in Bogota. Agnes, Shelly, and Denise disembark. They aggressively surround the timber warehouse, armed with semiautomatic rifles. Carefully, they scan their surroundings. Denise moves towards the door.

Un-expectantly, the red pickup truck arrives from the opposite direction. Ricardo, jumps out from the back, waving his automatic weapon. Ian Baynes exits from the driver's seat and follows suits. Axel James exits like a mad man. He releases the safety on his semiautomatic.

Shelly reacts. "It's late Axel, where...is the good blow?"

Axel James advances towards them. The women, readily perfect their deadly aim. Denise shoots at the truck's left front tire. Instead, the bullet hits and disunites the left fender *reverberantly*. The next round connects, deflating the tire.

"Calm down sisters. Let me explain," remarks Axel James.

Agnes responds, "No time for your explanation. Our clients are waiting. The last shipment was laced with cyanide. People are dying, Axel."

Ricardo creates a decoy. Denise refocuses.

"That's not the way we do business. Clients wait until the goods are delivered. X label was a glitch," states Ricardo.

'We paid in advance!" says Shelly as she aims at Ricardo's head.

Axel James interjects, "We are trying to bring in a fresh shipment into Port Antonio. One is already on its way, just give it time."

Denise eyeballs him while she caresses the trigger on her rifle.

"No one informed me about the crap you sent us. Now picking up in Port Antonio would create a nightmare. Too many sniffing MP'S." Denise states.

"That's right. You've.." says Agnes.

"Time is our money, Axel." Denise reminds him.

Looking at Denise, he responds. "Your husband's aware of the delay. His business in Miami is hurting... Meet us in Montego Bay tomorrow morning. We'll be covering all of our tracks."

Axel, Ian, and Ricardo board the red pickup truck and drive off.

The three women withdraw their arms, jump inside Hummer, and depart unhappily.

RUDE BUAY

5

AT THE DRUG ENFORCEMENT AGENCY in Miami, Special Agent Jose Mendez, in his late forties, lights up a cigar. He then hands over a set of keys to agent Randy Bascombe and departs. Bascombe, nicknamed RUDE BUAY aka "Rude Boy" is of Jamaican descent and in his early forties. He's adorned with a scorpion tattooed to his bald head, with fangs upstaging his forehead and tail extending towards his right earlobe. Bascombe familiarizes himself with the surroundings. He removes a portrait of Jamaica from a box, hangs it on the wall, and stares at it retrospectively. Next, he retrieves a portrait of his older brother. Reminisced by the picture, he fumbles. The portrait falls. He catches it before it hits the ground. He takes in a second look.

RUDE BUAY

The office phone rings. He lays the portrait securely on top of his desk, before answering.

The voice in the phone states, "Requesting DEA presence at the corner of Main and Broadway."

Bascombe picks his brother's portrait off his desk and hangs it securely on the wall. He throws on his jacket over his strapped two semiautomatics and heads out, hitting the streets.

Bascombe pulls up on Broadway and waits. A red Monte Carlo is parked on Main. A rugged-looking, Hispanic Man, in his mid-thirties, comes out of the high rise office building on Broadway. He's carrying an attaché case. Bascombe gets out of his car in a calculated pursuit. The Man gets inside the hot rod. Bascome, on foot, is catching up to him. The Man attempts to stick the key into the ignition. Bascombe sticks his left hand through the driver's window, grabbing at the keys. Bascombe fails to grab the keys, but the suspect rolls up the electronic window, putting Bascombe's hand in a vice.

The car takes off. Bascombe tries to keep pace with the speeding car. The Man looks at Bascombe's trapped hand and laughs hysterically. The Monte Carlo turns a corner, throwing Bascombe's body onto the hood. His hand is still fastened. He manages to viciously shoot at the suspect through the windshield using his other hand, at the suspect. An oncoming tractor-trailer honks, as it closes in on the Monte-Carlo, now zigzagging over the yellow line. Before the trailer could clip Bascombe, the Man shoots at Bascombe's trapped hand and blows out the driver's side window. Bascombe is thrown free onto the sidewalk. The car slams into a telephone pole.

The man crawls out on the passenger side, bloodied and shaken up, yet, he escapes on foot. The trailer proceeds, regardless.

Bascombe, incurs several lacerations to his face, head, along with minor bruises over some parts of his body. In pain, he gets up, puts two fingers in his mouth and whistles in an attempt to stop an oncoming taxi cab. His whistle is inaudible. The cab passes him by. Moments later, an ambulance arrives and whisks him away.

Meanwhile, Shelly, Agnes, and Denise embarking on their Jamaican quest board a Jamaican taxi cab, occupying the rear seat. The driver, adjusts his rearview mirror, attempting to eavesdrop.

Shelly declares, "We're going to MO BAY airport. Could you get us there in fifteen?"

Driver nods, yes.

The taxi turns in the opposite direction. Shelly notices.

"Where...are you going?" she asks.

"Shortcut," replies the cab driver.

"I don't like shortcuts!" Shelly echoes.

The driver makes another turn and swings into a driveway. The three women are frustrated, as they feel cornered.

RUDE BUAY

Immediately, the taxi stops. Abandoned vehicles create a spectacle. Axel James emerges from behind an abandoned car. He has a black bag in one hand and a gun in the other.

"Do not get out of the car," he commands.

In dismay, Shelly looks at the cab driver, then back at Axel.

"Where is our merchandise? Con Man!" Shelly asks, demandingly.

Axel inches towards the cab. The cab driver, fearing a shootout, exits the cab.

Axel is distracted. Shelly swings the front passenger door open, it hits Axel hard, and knocks the gun completely out of his hand.

The three women jump out with switchblades in confrontation, before Axel can retrieve his gun. Axel is trapped. Ian Baynes, sensing a bloody end to his boss, comes to his aid.

Pointing his gun at the three women. Ian exclaims, "Not so fast ladies."

Shelly tosses her knife at Axel James. He dodges. The knife misses him and lodges in the board behind him. Axel grabs the knife by its handle, flings it back at Shelly. She ducks. As a result, the knife sails through the taxi's rear window and lodges in the seat.

Shelly comes at Axel with a left uppercut. He ducks. She returns with a left uppercut. Again, he ducks out of it. This time, he grabs her hand and twists it behind her back.

Following up, he whacks her hard in the face. Shelly staggers and falls to the ground.

Witnessing the manhandling of Shelly pisses off Denise. Frustrated, she yells, "Where's our product, Axel?"

Axel James points to the black bag on the ground. Agnes picks the bag up, opens it. Satisfied, she throws it inside the taxi. Finally, Shelly gets up and crawls in on the other side of the cab.

Ricardo, taking no chances, keeps his gun pointed at Denise. Ian Baynes, sensing water under the bridge, returns to the car. Axel, signals "let's go" to Ricardo.

The taxi driver, observes from a distance. Axel, while departing, looks over at him authoritatively. "Take those bitches to the airport!" he commands.

The driver nervously walks over to his taxi. He gets in. Agnes and Denise get in. The taxi drives off.

Axel, Ricardo, and Ian witnessing their peaceful departure enter their car and take off in the opposite direction.

The taxi travels speedily through the potholed streets of Montego Bay. Shelly wipes her face and stares at her blood-stained hands.

"I have to piss. Driver, can you pull over?"

He complies.

"Now get out of the car,"

Shelly commands.

He tries to grab the car keys.

RUDE BUAY

Shelly opens her switchblade and stabs him once. He manages to open the door, exiting the cab. She gets out in pursuit. Shelly stabs him several times. He crouches, falls to the ground, kicks around and stops breathing. Shelly, gathers some leaves, cleans the blade. She looks at it. Noticing blood residue, she cleans it thoroughly with her red bandana, after which, she takes the wheel.

6

LATER, AGNES, SHELLY, AND DENISE dressed to the nines, all emerge from the ladies room at Montego Bay Airport. Their sensualistic physique grabs attention, as their oversized "rack" giggles. Shelly holds on carefully to that black bag recovered from Axel.

A luscious hottie, exquisitely outfitted, Jamaican style, joins them as they meander through customs all toting duffel bags. A Caucasian businessman, traveling in the opposite direction, is distracted by the estrogenic aura. He smashes into a pillar, sending his carry-ons flying. Embarrassingly he recovers but finds himself blanketed by the crowd he attracted.

Hours later, the American Airlines 747 touches down in Miami, Florida. The aircraft comes to a complete stop, but its doors remain closed.

RUDE BUAY

A U.S. Marshall steps out of the cockpit and forms a huddle with two flight attendants. Sage Ross, in her late twenties, is as sophisticated as they come. Her Ivy League status shows through in her communication skills. Sean Williams, in his late thirties, listens attentively. The Marshall glances at Agnes, who grabs his attention, in so many different ways. He compartmentalizes his thoughts and then refocuses.

"She fits the description…conveyed to us by Jamaican police," states the U.S. Marshall.

"What do we do?" asks Sage.

Meanwhile, Denise seductively applies hot red lipstick. A passenger across the aisle devours a pack of multi-colored M and M's.

"Keep the passengers in their seats. Bring in the DEA."

Sage picks up the microphone. With an air of sophistication, she announces:

"Thanks for flying American Airlines flight 1934. When the aircraft comes to a stop, we ask that you please remain in your seats for further instructions."

Sage enters the cockpit as the aircraft comes to a stop. Passengers panic, in a state of restlessness, mainly those four women in question.

The Hottie, sitting behind Denise, reaches inside her pocketbook and pulls out an object. She quickly removes the rubberized casing, revealing a "Dillinger." She shoots at the Marshall. The bullet misses him, hits a passing male flight attendant, who falls on top of several passengers. She shoots again.

The agile Marshall moves and the round grazes his shoulder, ricochets and penetrates the plane's skin. Marshall returns fire and shoots her in the face.

Passengers are screaming, some of them swearing. Denise, Agnes, and Shelly rummage nervously through their carry-on luggage under the seat. They cleverly remove a package each. Unnoticed by everyone else they place their luggage under their seats, behind other luggage. The Marshall, surveying, steps over the dead body in the aisle, then returns to the cockpit area.

Two concerned pilots, now concerned more than ever, remain seated at the controls. Sage dials.

The Marshall, somewhat annoyed with himself, exclaims,

"She's dead."

He fetches the phone in front of the cockpit and dials.

On the desk of DEA Bascombe, a pen phone rings. No one is there. In the office, the wall is displayed portraits of Jamaica. Agent Bascombe's nameplate stands out amongst the stacks of folders on his desk. The phone continues to ring.

Inside the green room, Bascombe fetches a cup of coffee and leaves the green room with a cup of coffee in hand. He accidentally spills some of the drinks on his suit and tie. Yet, he pays no attention to the spillage. He's got a more urgent task - getting to the phone.

He grabs the pen phone that's been ringing unremittingly.

"Hello, this is agent Randy Bascombe!"
In speaker mode, he listens in as he writes with his pen phone.
"Okay. No one gets off that plane! "
He dials on the device.
Agent Desmond Scott, Caucasian, good looking stud, in his mid-thirties, aborts the name search on the computer. He picks up the call.
"Scott, this is agent Bascombe. Meet me outside with the black Tahoe, ready to go."
Scott dashes out.
Bascombe dials again.
Heidi Hudson, Caucasian, in her late twenties, aborts applying her makeup and picks up.
"Agent Hudson, we need you on this..."
She jumps up, checks her gun. Satisfied, she darts out. Bascombe inspects his tie. He goes to his locker. He opens it. Inside the locker, there's a sports coat that matches his pants. He removes his jacket and tie, hangs them in the locker, puts on the sports coat, and takes off as a man possessed. He turns doorknob to Mendez's office. The door is locked. Bascombe dashes out towards the lobby. There, he bumps into Mendez, knocking the box of Kentucky Fried Chicken to the ground. Bascombe regains his balance. Mendez picks up the box of KFC.
"Yet another wild goose chase?" he asks.
"This is huge. Dade County Airport." Responds Randy Bascombe.

RUDE BUAY

"Aren't you supposed to check with me first?" asks Mendez.

Bascombe, glancing at the box of KFC in Jose Mendez's hand, replies.

"Sorry..."

Mendez, focusing on Bascombe, asks:

"Who's the informant?"

Bascombe reflects, and then replies, "American Airlines. The flight originated in Jamaica."

Heidi Hudson barges in. She stares inquisitively at Bascombe and Special agent Mendez. She readily arranges her hair into a ponytail.

"Are we going to the Caribbean?" she asks smilingly.

Bascombe is focused. He addresses Mendez.

Chief...

Mendez interrupts him.

"I know. I'll be sending you some needed backup."

Outside, the Black Tahoe emerges from the parking structure and stops abruptly. Desmond Scott is at the wheel.

Bascombe jumps in the front passenger seat. Agent Hudson scurries in the rear seat and reaches for the seat belt.

"So where are we heading?" asks agent Hudson.

The Tahoe takes off. Agent Hudson accidentally loses her balance.

Bascombe, with a delayed response.

"Dade County Airport!"

"Who's involved?" she asks.

Bascombe overwhelmed with her questions.
"Step on it, Scott. One woman, there could be more."
Meanwhile, inside the aircraft. Shelly, tries to switch another passenger's bag with hers.
Seth, a flaming guy, catches her in the act.
"Did you just move my bag?" he yells.
"I'm sorry, it looked like mine." Shelly remarks.
"Don't be sorry. Can't you read? It says SETH!"
"Bitch, I said I'm sorry." Replies Shelly.
She sits back down clutching on to her carry on.
Seth, not trusting her, gets up and examines his bag. Opening it, he discovers two pieces of silicone, stuffed with small zip-locked packages. Staring at Shelly's reduced "rack". Seth erupts,
"Help! This bitch is trying to frame me. You've got the wrong man..."
He removes both objects from his bag and holds them in his hand. Treating them as a personal object, he draws an audience.
"This is a "D" cup." Seth removes the packages from the silicone.
Meanwhile, the Tahoe pulls up outside the aircraft. Agents, armed, ready to shoot, rush towards aircraft.
Back inside, Shelly removes herself from that seat and sits in an empty seat a few rows back.
The Marshall returning from the cockpit with a log intercedes.
Seth, still obsessed with the fake breast gently lays them on Shelly's empty seat.

Agents, now on board huddle with Sage along with the Marshall reviewing the passenger's log. The Marshall points to the three women and Shelly's fake breasts on the seat. Hudson eyes the pieces of silicone, perturbed. Bascombe, commands: "My name is agent Randy Bascombe - Miami Drug Enforcement Agency. Shelly Hall, Denise Gomez, and Agnes Richards, you are under arrest for alleged drug possession. Come to the front of the aircraft with your hands on top of your head."

The women, reluctantly cooperate.

Bascombe, place them in handcuffs. The other agents swarm the aircraft collecting their carryon.

Outside the abandoned aircraft, more Police vehicles converge, including a Coroner's vehicle. The three handcuffed women are pushed inside of a police utility vehicle. The vehicle drives to outside Dade County Prison. The women are escorted inside the prison and booked by Miami police officers.

7

IN KINGSTON, JAMAICA, festive music is playing. Pedestrians crowd the busy streets in a dancing mood. Busy vendors display merchandise, enticing tourists to shop. One tourist walks up to a vendor and window shop. Every style of hat under the sun is stocked. The tourist cleverly slips him a U.S. Twenty dollar bill. The Vendor takes it in his left hand, and sticks out his right, asking for more. The tourist opens his wallet, hands him another twenty. The vendor discretely hands him a brown bag. The tourist surveys his surroundings and secures it inside his pocket. He proceeds up the street. A Teen enjoys some fresh cotton candy as he helps a blind man cross the street. Voluptuous women parade the streets, creating a "turn on" to the men enjoying the view.

A Taxi pulls up. Two Hotties with oversized tanks (breast) jump inside. The cab takes off.

RUDE BUAY

The Teen, making a B-line, dashes out of its way to avoid getting run over by the taxi.

Meanwhile, in the cab, the indulging cabby gets an eyeful in the rearview mirror.

Suddenly, he asks the passengers,

"Where do you, two bumptious women...,"

The taller of the two responds."

"University of the West Indies, West Kingston. Hurry!" The Cabby "steps on it" while he scans the radio station. He finds the right music to compliment the vibe and personalizes "Sweet Jamaica" in a sweet baritone voice.

The song ends, another starts. He searches for the right key to this ballad and gets it.

"This is our stop!" announces the Hottie.

The Taxi pulls up to the curb and stops outside a booth, with a variety of merchandise on display. Two women of less voluptuousness step out of booth, and trade places with the two Hotties. The cab takes off.

Moments later, teenagers flock the booth in droves, like flies to molasses. They are eager, to purchase the white powdery substance, in a transparent wrap. The teen, previously helping the blind man across the street, shows up breathless, pays for his packet and smilingly opens it.

One of the Hotties gets into a taxi. Later, it pulls up next to a closed grocery store. The Hottie jumps out and slides a large envelope underneath the door. She returns to the waiting taxi. It takes off.

RUDE BUAY

An approaching police cruiser with flashing lights pursues the taxi. The taxi pulls over and stops curbside. Without hesitating, the Hottie jumps out and shoots at two approaching officers. One is hit, he falls to the ground. The other officer shoots back, striking the Hottie, she collapses and falls to the ground. She dies instantly. The Officer attends to his partner, who is still breathing. Sirens in the distance accompany a blanket of pedestrians, now converged onto the bloody scene.

8

A TEACHER HURRIES through the school gate and boards the waiting airport bus, with a folder in hand. She closes the door securely, after entering. Two women disguised as tour guides emerge from the back of the bus. The Teacher hands over the folder to them. They quickly scan through the folder and conduct a careful headcount. They present the folder to the Bus Driver. His dragon tattoo behind his right ear lobe is very revealing. He conceals the folder.
The Women reach into their aprons and pull out several fist-sized aluminum foil packets resembling those recovered from Ray's backpack. These packets are quickly distributed to each kid, along with a bottle of bottled water and a sheet of instructions.
The anxious kids review the instruction pamphlets and then consume the packets, aided by water. The bus pulls into a small airport-hanger. A twin-engine jet

RUDE BUAY

with propellers turning in slow motion - waits. The kids are transferred to that waiting aircraft.

Back in Miami, at the DEA Headquarters, Bascombe paces, while Mendez sits at the desk smoking a cigar.

Bascombe, perturbed, throws the newspaper onto the desk. He composes himself, facing Mendez squarely and addresses him.

"I would like to put in my request for an early vacation."

Jose Mendez asks:

"Family...?" As if he is not up to speed on the current fiasco in Jamaica.

Bascombe, feeling as if his intelligence has been insulted, remarks,

"No one seems to be doing anything about all these kids dying off like flies in Jamaica."

Mendez reassures.

"I am sure their government is handling that situation."

Bascombe, not giving up:

"Their MP's could be in on this whole fiasco."

Mendez responds,

"They've already imprisoned the Drug Lords. That's progress!"

Bascombe reflects.

"My mom used to always say "There's more in the Marta besides the pestle""

Mendez, understanding the cliché, comments,

"Do you think there's more to it? I think you should let

the government do their job. They are ..."

Suddenly, the four eyes in that room are glued to the TV set, as a news reporter interrupts the scheduled program.

"Late-breaking news, as we continue to follow this fiasco in Jamaica. The death toll continues to rise as three teenagers died today as a result of using cyanide-laced cocaine. One drug dealer, a woman, was also shot and killed by Jamaican police. As a result of this shoot out, one officer has been hospitalized. The death toll equals ninety."

Mendez, to it all, responds.

"Everyone seems to be using the "F" word way too much - FIASCO."

Bascombe, in disbelief, (concerning his boss's attitude), goes to the window. Reflecting, he looks outside.

Bascombe retreats.

Before further addressing Mendez, he points to his brother's portrait on the wall.

"My only sibling. Lost him in a drug-related incident."

Mendez, nods, indicating that all that is old news. Then he remarks,

"My condolences..."

Bascombe has endured enough.

"I refuse to let more of relatives go through this fiasco. If not now? When? Some innocent person's kid is going to be next. That is my final "F" word." Bascombe throws the keys on the desk at Mendez and walks out of the office.

RUDE BUAY

Mendez gets up from his seat at Bascombe's desk and takes in a close up view of the portrait for the first time. Moments later, Mendez moseys up behind Bascombe in the Green Room. Bascombe, adding cream to his coffee, sees him peripherally. Mendez apologetically returns the keys to agent Bascombe. Scott and Hudson surprise them, by barging in during the reconciliation. Mendez bids farewell to Agent Desmond Scott and Agent Heidi Hudson. The three agents board a Miami Police SUV with their luggage in tow.

9

THE 747 AIRPLANE touches down at Michael Manley Airport in Jamaica. Agents Bascombe, Scott, and Hudson move briskly through the crowded Jamaican airport terminal. Outside the terminal, the agents hustle toward the blue unmarked police vehicle, waiting. A Distinguished Gentleman, dressed in white attire steps out. He hands over the keys to Bascombe, along with a folded piece of paper. Bascombe reads the address: The Villa, 23 Pine Grove, St. Andrew, Jamaica. Before getting inside, Bascombe asks.
"Is this thing GPS equipped?"
The Gentleman, replies,
"Rude Buay, it has recently been installed in our entire fleet. On the other hand, I must tell you that the Jamaican government is not very happy with your involvement."
Bascombe replies.

"I understand. Dual citizenship has its advantages. Doesn't it?"
The Gentleman continues,
"How about your team?"
Heidi Hudson, interjects.
"Where agent Bascombe goes, we go!"
"A dual name does have its disadvantage, agent Bascombe. I'm sorry, RUDE BUAY. Anyway, your brother will appreciate this homecoming." The Gentleman admonishes.
Rude Buay, looks towards heaven.
Heidi Hudson admires the gentleman. He then makes the sign of the cross and smilingly gives Rude Buay thumbs up. The Agents jump inside the vehicle. The Distinguished Gentleman departs and moseys inside the terminal as their car takes off.
It's a great distance from the airport to the Villa. Agent Bascombe takes control of the car along the winding roads of Kingston, en-route to Mandeville.
A beautiful, Victorian designed house, with an earthen extended driveway, nestles on the hill above homes of lesser value.
Rude Buay brings the car to a stop. With Hudson covering him, they move in, weapons drawn. Scott waits outside the car, armed and ready.
Rude Buay and Hudson arrive closer toward the house. They scrutinize their surroundings. Feeling satisfied, Rude Buay inches closer towards the front

RUDE BUAY

door. He kicks the door in and charges inside, with agent Hudson in tow.

Now inside, both agents proceed intensely, but with immense caution. Their entrance has them staring into a sunken living room, with a giant screen TV, a black leather couch and a huge glass center table. On the table, the neatly folded maps get their attention momentarily, but they remain focused.

Commandingly, Rude Bauy cautions.

"US drug enforcement agents! Come out nice and slow with your hands on top of your head."

There is no response. A black Cat emerges. Rude Buay releases the safety on his gun. The cat meows. Hudson, now standing over the center table, gets a closer look at the contents. She notices three separate sets of maps of the Jamaican city of Port Antonio.

Next to the maps lay syringes on a tray, straws, a crack pipe, two cigarette lighters, and cocaine residue, validating the habits of the dwellers.

Rude Buay's attention is drawn to several pieces of luggage in a corner. However, he proceeds into the room where the cat exited. Agent Hudson proceeds into the other room while covering Rude Buay from the corner of her eyes.

Rude Buay rummages through the room. He cautiously checks a closet, as he slowly pulls the door open. It's empty. He throws off the bed mattress and box spring. He checks under the bed; nothing's underneath it. On the nightstand, he notices a replica

RUDE BUAY

of "The Tempest," a beautiful yacht. Rude Buay admires it.

Hudson's voice penetrates the room.

"Rude Buay! You've got to see this."

Rude Buay, with a gun, still drawn, vacates that room and joins her.

In the second bedroom, Agent Hudson stands in front of a giant-sized closet with its door ajar. She proceeds to rid it of its contents. Packets labeled: Dragon X, attache' cases, guns, stacks of Jewish bankrolls in various currency, grenades and survival kits, put things in perspective. Rude Buay and Hudson more committed than ever to the manhunt, continue rummaging through the house.

In Jamaican prison, a rat runs across the entrance to cell number fifteen and disappears. Axel James, dressed in prison garb, stares in the direction of the disappearing creature.

In the meantime, outside the prison, a Black sedan rolls up. Ricardo and Ian Baynes, dressed in prison security uniforms, step out and hasten through a huge iron gate.

An on-duty Security Guard, sitting in the booth, acknowledges them with a nod of the head. They proceed into the interior of the prison.

Back at the booth, a new Guard replaces the on-duty guard.

Inside the prison, Axel's men hustle, as if they are heading to break up a brawl. A guard getting some snacks from the snack machine is alerted. He draws his gun, while curious inmates eavesdrop.

"Follow us, the alarm malfunctioned. There's a fight outside cells ten through fifteen," warns Ian Baynes.

The Guard remarks, "Trouble zone since fourteen went to the pit. Let's move it!"

They're now right in front of cell #15.

Ian Baynes grabs the prison guard around his neck. The Guard spins around facing Ian Baynes and Ricardo as his weapon falls to the ground. Two guns with silencers attached are pointing at him.

"Your clothes…and open fifteen! "

Commands Ian Baynes.

The Guard is bewildered until Ian Baynes quickly points the gun in his face. The Guard nervously disrobes, removes a bunch of keys from his belt, and unlocks the cell door.

Ian Baynes caps the Guard in the head, tosses his clothes to Ricardo, who hands them to Axel. Axel emerges from his cell, clothed in prison guard's uniform.

Ian Baynes and Ricardo drag the semi-nude guard inside cell # 15 and shut the door. They exit the prison interior, accompanied by Axel James.

The on-duty guard approaches the three of them questioningly.

"What is going on…with you three?"

"Going to get a smoke. We soon come back, yo hear?" Baynes, answers in patois and hands the Guard, a bag of weed. The three Drug Lords exit through the prison gates.

Outside the prison, Axel, Ian, and Ricardo get inside the black sedan and drive away, laughing hilariously.

10

BACK AT THE VILLA, A Jamaican Police Officer, armed like a SWAT member, ambulates outside the police cruiser. The Black sedan drives up, carrying the three Drug Lords. Axel barges out, followed by Ian and Ricardo. They immediately open silent fire on the police officer. His exchange is too late. Hit by several rounds, he falls to the ground while his ammunition soars. Axel pumps bullets into all four tires of his vehicle as well as the parked DEA Agent's car. Their black Sedan rolls up in the driveway. They are still oblivious of the search going on inside by the DEA.
Inside, Rude Buay and Hudson are now joined by Agent Scott, who recently aborted his surveillance duty on the exterior of the Villa. He rejoins his colleagues, with thumbs up, and assists in the assembling of the seizure, inside the living room.

RUDE BUAY

A ray of light, reflects, shining into the living room, from the sedan's headlights.
The agents, sensing pending trouble, disperse respectively.
Scott leans up behind the front door.
Rude Buay goes through the back door, while Hudson hides behind the door to the first bedroom.
Axel James, now out of the car, reacts to the moving shadow behind the door of the first bedroom.
Axel James hints at Ian and Ricardo.
"We've got more company. PIGS! (Police) "
Rude Buay, not only notices Axel but hears his voice and adjusts for the perfect aim. He would rather take out Axel, but as soon as he gets the perfect aim on him, Axel darts in through the front door.
Already engaged, the bullet from Rude Buay's gun flies towards the sedan blows out its front windscreen.
Ian Baynes and Ricardo, hiding on the ground, behind the back of the car, return gunfire, which misses Rude Buay, who dodges on time.
Behind the front door, Agent Scott and Axel James, end up in each other's space.
Scott tries to get a close-quarter shot off, but Axel "gets a drop" and the two engage in hand to hand combat. Axel out does Scott by a long shot.
Hudson emerges from behind the door and into the corridor. At the same time, Ricardo shotguns through the front door. Hudson, witnessing duel between Axel and Agent Scott gets an aim at Axel James' head. She

shoots at Axel, simultaneously Scott punches Axel in the right eye; Axel rolls over. The bullet penetrates the wall.

Bullets go flying everywhere from Ricardo's gun like popcorn.

Before agent Hudson can retaliate, a bullet from Ricardo's gun grazes by her face. She's all shook up. Axel regains his presence of mind and lands a punch into Scott's stomach. Scott catches his breath.

Axel stumbles around with blurry vision.

On the outside of the Villa, Rude Buay, engages in a shootout with Ian Baynes. Both men miss their target. Finally, Ian reacts to being hit. He goes down. Rude Buay, satisfied, dashes to the inside through the front door.

Ricardo peripherally sees Rude Buay entering the house, and dashes towards the back door.

Ricardo, whispers to Axel,

"Let's get out of here, Boss."

Axel manages to recoup. They sprint to their car on the outside.

Ian Baynes, crawls in the back seat, with blood trickling down his neck.

Ricardo takes the wheel.

Axel scoots in on the other side.

The black car, with no front windshield, takes off in reverse, down the long, extended driveway.

Rude Buay, seeing the car disappear, rushes back outside, in frustration.

RUDE BUAY

The black cat saunters across the driveway. Rude Buay aims at the animal but changes his mind.

Heavy pouring rain presents a hazard for Axel James, Ian Baynes, and Ricardo Herrera. They are not only soaking wet, but the car begins to swerve off the road. The sedan pulls over to the side of the road.

They exit. An approaching vehicle casts its light in their direction. The oncoming Mini-Van gets closer. The three men run out into the middle of the street. Their guns are drawn on the driver.

The Mini Van comes to a screeching halt, running off the road and into the gutter.

The Driver is a Rastafarian. Before he could get a word out, Axel James, shouts at him,

"Get out!"

The Driver complies and starts running for his life. Before he could escape, Axel pumps several bullets into his body.

The driver falls over the embankment. Axel follows him and confiscates his wallet.

They speedily transfer their cargo from the sedan to Mini Van, using it as their get-away vehicle.

The Mini Van pulls up outside the dock. A sailor from "The Tempest" waves in acknowledgment.

Axel James, Ian Baynes, and Ricardo step out and hurry on aboard the waiting yacht, with huge duffel bags.

The sailor lifts the yacht's anchor, while another releases the line and leaps back onto the sailing yacht.

RUDE BUAY

At the Villa, sunrise casts its rays, as the three DEA agents vacate the premises.

They look at their sedan with its deflated tires.

Scott, the first one to speak, says:

"They could have already fled to Cuba."

Heidi Hudson, responds,

"With all that rain last night, driving without a front windscreen is impossible."

Rude Buay, after radioing for help, reminds them,

"I wouldn't put it past them. For all, you know they could have driven in reverse."

"Reverse? In the rain? On these winding roads? Asks agent Hudson.

"Yep! If the desire is strong enough, the facts carry no weight," replies, Rude Buay, as they wait next to the abandoned sedan.

| RUDE BUAY

11

TWO JAMAICAN POLICE Officers show up in an SUV and a land Rover. They jump out apologetically. The officer driving the jeep, hands over his keys to Rude Buay.

"You can use this," he instructs.

Rude Buay, looking at the jalopy, certainly does not resonate with it.

"Get us a helicopter, Officer," Rude Buay responds.

"That's not my call, Mr. Bascombe."

Rude Buay stares at him more intensely.

"Time is running out," remarks, Rude Buay, as he attempts to take the wheel of the SUV.

"Hold on, this is a Government Utility Vehicle. I am

RUDE BUAY

the only one allowed to drive this GUV," says the other officer.
Rude Buay ignores him. The two other agents jump in. The officer retaliates. Rude Buay takes the wheel anyway, leaving both officers behind.
The retaliated officer, yelling in Patois, echoes,
"Don't you realize, the roads have changed! Motorists are skilled at driving in reverse. You need I and I to..."
Rude Buay, realizing, that he does need some help navigating, makes a roundabout turn. The officer hops in.
The *GUV* drives away followed by the Land Rover.
Later, a helicopter carrying Rude Buay, Scott and Hudson circles over the countryside. They spot an abandoned sedan on the roadside in Montego Bay. Moving in closer they discover the body of the car jacked Rastafarian in the gutter.
Scott, remarks, "Yep. These guys could have already fled the country."
"What if they're still here?" responds, Rude Buay.
Hudson, interjects.
"I doubt it,"
Rude Buay, unconvinced says,
"Navigating seems to be their cup of tea."
Hudson, using a pair of binoculars, notices as a tow-truck backs up to the Mini Van and engages in a tow. The name on the tow truck reads Black River Towing.
Later, the copter returns to the small Jamaican airstrip. Rude Buay and Scott step out. The accompanying

officer directs Rude Buay and his agents to a parked sedan.

During this interim, cries from mourners are heard in the city of Mandeville, as more dead bodies are wheeled into a makeshift morgue. The stench is unbearable, coming from the regular, overcrowded facility next door.

Outside the hospital, hundreds of mourners congregate, waiting in tears to identify the body of their child.

"Could this have been prevented?" one mourner asks another.

"Yes, kids ought to learn not to play with matches," the intercepting Peace Keeping Officer responds.

The agents pull up outside Black River Towing.

Inside Rude Buay's car, his Pen Phone rings. He reviews the caller's ID. By the customary look on his face, his fellow agents suspect that it's their boss on the other end. So they eavesdrop.

"Hello. Agent Mendez," Rude Buay responds.

"Bascombe, we've been monitoring the Jamaican situation. Axel James and his allies have fled the country. Possibly to Cuba:" Jose Mendez remarks.

"Apparent, how? Is Castro signed on?" asks Rude Buay.

"What goes on in Cuba, stays in Cuba. My hands are tied. I'm having all three of you brought back to Miami tomorrow:" Mendez insists.

Rude Buay, says to Hudson and Scott, "Search has

RUDE BUAY

been called off" and to Mendez, "We'll see you then."

12

IN A DOWNTOWN, ritzy, Miami hotel: Carlos, of Asian descent, in his mid-thirties, removes his blood-stained clothes and discards them in a black trash bag. Semi-clothed, he rummages through a bag, scanning through logs and other prison-related documents. He goes to a suitcase, where he retrieves a toupee, and carefully affixes it to his mask. He then removes four Warden Uniforms from a suitcase and puts them on. The name on his lapel reads Warden Richard Culligan. Carlos takes a detailed look at himself in the full-length mirror. Again, he studies Warden Culligan's picture, scotch-taped to the wall next to the mirror. He uses some paper tissue and creates padding for his biceps. He is satisfied with his new look. Carlos picks up a laden black duffel bag and departs.

RUDE BUAY

A sedan pulls up outside Florida State Prison. Carlos steps out. He passes a prison guard, filing away paperwork in the booth.

"Wide-eyed and bushy-tailed?" Carlos, greets him, signing in.

"Hi Boss! Warden Culligan," replies the Guard.

"Anything to report, Miles?" Carlos asks.

The Guard responds,

"Everything's dandy, except that my replacement is usually here fifteen minutes early and he's..."

Carlos interrupts.

"I'll look into that for you."

Carlos proceeds towards Warden Culligan's office. He unlocks the door and enters. Shedding, three layers of prison uniform, Carlos deposits them; one per paper sack.

Outside Culligan's office, Bruce, the guard on patrol, ambulates. He removes a pack of cigarettes from his pocket, it's his last one. He lights up. Carlos steps out of the office, noticing Bruce's name tag.

Carlos, greets, "Hey Bruce, you got a cigarette?"

"Sorry, I've just smoked my last." Bruce responds.

"What you smoke, Salem?" asks Carlos.

Bruce nods, yes.

"You want to pick up a pack of Salem Lights?" asks Carlos.

"Yes Mr. Culligan," Replies Bruce.

He hands Bruce the money. Bruce departs.

RUDE BUAY

Carlos makes his move, stopping in front of cell numbers one, twelve and thirty.

In cell # 1 resides Agnes Richards.

Carlos unlocks Agnes' cell and deposits a laden paper shopping bag. He hands Shelly a cellular phone along with a handwritten page of instructions. He departs.

In cell # 12 resides Denise Gomez.

Carlos unlocks Denise's cell and deposits a laden paper shopping bag. He hands her a cellular phone along with a handwritten page of instructions. He departs.

In cell # 30 resides Shelly Hall.

Carlos unlocks her cell and deposits a laden paper shopping bag. He hands Shelly a cellular phone along with a handwritten page of instructions. He leaves, noticed by other inmates and exits hurriedly. Most seem not to care. However, the Prison Guard at the booth, is somewhat confused, by all this unusual business.

"Warden Culligan, it's your off night. You're ..." he asks, inquiringly.

Carlos steps up closer to the booth and interrupts.

"Inside here your off night is always an on night. After your third month, you'll see what I mean."

The Prison Guard removes the sign-in sheet from the clipboard and sticks it in a brown manila envelope, sealing it with his saliva, then with scotch tape.

Carlos sensing the Prison Guards' strategic move to log a genuine report, eyes the clock inside the booth. The clock shows seven minutes to midnight. Carlos pushes the door open.

"So you're covering for him?" Carlos asks, and pulls out a semi-automatic from the duffel bag, with a silencer attached. He aims it at the guard.

Surprised, the guard remarks,

"You don't want to do that! I'll keep everything confidential. I swear..."

Carlos pumps several bullets into the Prison Guard's body. He falls outside of the booth, to the ground, to his death. Carlos PICKS up the handheld radio and radios. Three guards sitting in separate towers tune in. Carlos, announces:

"The next shift will be coming in five minutes early."

The Guards, respond,

"Good deal!"

Carlos picks up his cellular phone, and speedily, dials. Shelly, dressed in prison guard's attire, holding Automatic with a silencer attached and emerging from within prison compounds, answers.

"We are coming out!"

Shelly is oblivious, and steps on a line in the pavement. Immediately, the prison grounds floodlights come on all over the compound. The three women, attired in the Warden's uniform, disperse. They rush towards an individual, separate towers.

Now situated, they proceed to trade place with the three on-duty guards.

The guards, before completing their decent are shot simultaneously. They fall precipitously to their death.

RUDE BUAY

The women race to the prison exterior, dash towards the sedan and enter like greased lightning. Carlos drives away.

Back at the State Prison, Bruce returns with the cigarettes but notices three empty cells as well as Warden Culligan's empty office. He's dumbfounded and confused.

Inside the car, Shelly, Agnes, and Denise rid themselves of the Warden's garb, revealing their true identity.

Suddenly the reflection of red and blue flashing lights stream inside the sedan. Sirens accompany the kaleidoscopic illumination.

Shelly, Agnes, and Denise reach for their gun simultaneously, in readiness.

The Miami police cruiser aggressively tails the sedan. The Sedan reduces its speed and moves to the right shoulder of the road. The Police cruiser stops closely behind. The Officer barges out, proceeds towards the driver's side of the sedan, and draws his gun.

Inside, the women, with guns still drawn, are poised, ready to shoot.

The officer proceeds with caution, trying to look through the rear tinted windscreen.

Instantly, three sets of bullets storm through the rear windscreen, laying the Officer flat onto the street.

The women return guns to the original position. Broken glass everywhere creates discomfort. The sedan speeds away and merges with the flow of traffic.

Moments later it drives into an underground parking lot where the limo waits.

Shelly, Agnes, and Denise exit. Still armed, they survey before getting inside the limo. The limousine door closes. It speeds off and merges into the flow of traffic, and subsequently arrives at the dock.

Carlos, Shelly, Denise, and Agnes join Alberto, already aboard his yacht, "Gomez".

Inside the other yacht, "Tempest," the phone rings. Axel, on deck, picks up.

"Axel, let's go to plan B." commands Alberto.

Axel reaches for and reviews the city of Port Antonio. He glances at his watch and responds.

"Okay, Boss! All the lights are green. Port Antonio by midnight."

13

THE "TEMPEST" SAILS BY Port Antonio's Peninsula. Axel James, Ian Baynes, and Ricardo dressed in wet suits, plunge into the water. Each carries a bag strapped to their back. The ship continues sailing towards Port Antonio, where it docks. A customs official boards the vessel. He inspects thoroughly. The captain of the Tempest over accommodates. Content the customs official returns to his booth.

In the wooded area of Port Antonio, shrubbery provides privacy, as Axel James, Ian Baynes, and Ricardo remove their water suits, dry off and get into street clothes retrieved from waterproof bags. They remove and open their duffel bags. Retrieving their

RUDE BUAY

weapons, they rush through the bushes.

They hit the streets of Port Antonio. A minivan designed to seat twelve passengers pulls up at the bus stop. They jump in. The door closes and it drives off.

The van, almost full to the max, with seats aligned theatre style and very little leg room between them, takes on the treacherous hillsides.

Ian Baynes, after finding a seat, takes out a wad of mixed currency and pays the conductor upfront. The locals, noticing the U.S. currency, eye him enviously. One man even sticks his hand out. Ian ignores the beggar's plea.

The Van stops. Axel James, Ian Baynes, and Ricardo exit and board another van.

This Van is filled mostly with Rastafarians wearing massive dreadlocks. The driver's dreadlocks are wrapped up in a knitted tam, black, yellow and green. Axel James studies the passengers, but mainly, two high school kids with untied shoe strings grab his attention.

Ian, eyes the driver, an Afro Asian.

"Central Port Antonio?"

"We just passed it!" replies the driver.

"Really?" asks Ian.

"Yes *mon*!" assures, the driver.

The Van stops. They get off.

Ian and Ricardo travel back on foot towards Avis and rent a white van. Axel and Ricardo await Ian's arrival. Ian pulls up in a white van. Axel and Ricardo jump aboard, duffel bags in hand.

Inside the Van, Axel unzips a duffel bag and admires his gun extensively. Finally, he utters,

"When do we return this vehicle?"

Ian, turning up the music, responds,

"All we have to do is call them at Avis if we need an extension. My brethren rule that joint, and besides…"

Axel James interrupts Ian,

"Where's your weapon?"

"My bag's behind the back seat. Where's base camp?" He answers.

Ricardo, interjects,

"Hope Bay! Close enough."

Ian replies, very sarcastically,

"Is that close to agent Banks?"

Ricardo eyes Axel questioningly.

Ian continues,

"Don't worry. We'll find Banks. First, we'll take out the government."

Axel, comments.

"Banks? He's small fry. If we could get the MP on our side…They wouldn't have a problem giving us the 411 on a former MP."

| RUDE BUAY

14

A SMALL DIMLY LIT HOUSE overlooks the city of Port Antonio. Lights from ships in the harbor create a picturesque subterranean backdrop.

Inside, maps, radios, headsets, binoculars, microcassette players and miscellaneous gadgets contribute to the ambiance. Walter Banks, an African American in his late fifties, with salt and pepper hair, sweats. He is fiddling disparately with his spy tech gadgets. An intermittent sound from his Pen Phone gets his attention. Banks retrieves it from his desk and listens in. The sound comes in and out, muffled; finally, he loses it.

On top of a mountain in Columbia, camouflaged between some trees, nestles a tiny shack built from wood and painted grass green. Chelo, a Colombian, dressed in a straw hat, ruffled clothing, and shoe-less, runs out of the shack. He tiptoes and adjusts the dismantled wire antenna on the roof. Like a champion, he hurries back inside.

The computer screen reveals a parked airplane at a Bogota location with a huge vacant cargo area. Scanning further, he notices several crates loaded with sacks of Dragon X Cocaine, destined for Port Antonio, Jamaica. He's possessed, like a kid in a candy store. The way he handles the mouse device, says he is hungry for this information. His screen reveals and captures an airport bus, registered to Bogota. Inside the bus, twelve teens take time to review instructions and small packets.

Walter Banks, sitting in his living room in Port Antonio, Jamaica, is enjoying the live feed. Suddenly, the computer screen goes blank. Banks desperately adjusts the picture via Tivo. He tunes in and replays.

Over the blank computer screen, he hears Chelo's voice.

"Come in Banks!"

"Go ahead Chelo." Banks replies.

Chelo, exclaims, "A huge shipment of contaminated Cocaine is being prepared. Destination, Port Antonio - Jamaica. The Dragon Drug Cartel has got it all lined up."

Banks, sharing Chelo's hunger for the info, reviews the

RUDE BUAY

entire video.

Jumping up from behind his desk, he echoes, "Bastards! Never!"

Banks goes to the window, pen phone in hand, taking in the harbor view. Nothing is visibly unusual, so he returns to his desk. Using the pen phone he writes on a slip of paper. He sticks the paper in an envelope and seals it with his saliva. Then he grabs his keys, along with the envelope and his Pen Phone.

He dashes outside to his car, turns it on and drives away.

An hour later, he arrives at the Ministry of Tourism and Culture Office in Kingston.

A red-eyed, Jamaican security guard, patrols the premises. Banks turns off the headlights. He travels on foot, eludes the guard and slips an envelope under the door, before exiting.

RUDE BUAY

15

THE FOLLOWING MORNING, inside the Ministerial Building across the street, a meeting's in session. Five men dressed in suits, sit, facing each other, around a huge mahogany table.
Dalton Castello, the deputy Prime Minister, who is African American in his late forties, presides.
Michael Young, Caucasian, is in his early forties.
Vince La Borde, a bald African American, is in his mid-fifties. Bazil Taylor, African American, also is in his mid-fifties. William Russell, an African American, with salt and peppered hair.
This quintet of think tanks waits anxiously, ready to write.

Dalton Castello, addresses:
"The Prime Minister has asked me to preside over this meeting."
He searches through a stack of documents and continues.
"As you know he returns from CARICOM next week. The Jamaican economy is..."
The door opens. A drop-dead gorgeous, sophisticated, Mildred Simms, the desire of any man's heart, in her late twenties, enter.
Five pairs of eyes pierced her soul, questioningly.
Mildred, though slightly embarrassed for interrupting, radiates, "Excuse me!."
She hands the envelope to Dalton Castello and exits hurriedly. Castello opens the envelope and reads its contents.
"Gentlemen, it seems as if a Colombian Drug Cartel "The Dragons" is about to infiltrate our country with a shipment of over $25M worth of "cyanide-laced" cocaine. Our shores will now need to be guarded twenty-four-seven. Starting with Mo Bay. He EYES the clock on the wall and continues reading.
"They're known for taking out governments, they did in Grenada a few years ago. Watch your backs. Let's reconvene tomorrow."
Unnerved, they shut their folders and exit speedily.
 Outside, a Mini Van stops, abruptly. Axel, Ian, and Ricardo jump out, armed with automatic weapons. The men are masked, with their tattoos covered up. A

Minister of Parliament standing outside acknowledges Axel and walks briskly ahead of them. As soon as they catch to the MP, he hands Axel a piece of paper. It's a blueprint. Axel, "crash studies" document.

They enter RAMBO STYLE. Two guards are jovially conversing inside the lobby. The guards, called to action, attempt to un-holster their uncompetitive weapons. The unwarranted visitors, quickly tie up the guards and throw them inside a closet. Proceeding, they meet the government ministers coming down escorted by a Police Officer. Before he could draw his gun, Axel shoots him in the chest. The Government Officials, scared out of their wits, try reversing upstairs.

Axel, commands:

"All we need is your cooperation. Your choice, resistance or termination? Extinction?"

Dalton Castello stares at Axel James with surprise.

Axel continues:

"Just do as you're told. Place your hands on top of your heads."

The five Ministers comply.

Axel, commandingly, directs:

"You are boarding the minivan across the street. Come on, move it!"

They are now on the outside, unnoticed, Ian Baynes opens the door to Mini Van.

Dalton Castello, Vince La Borde, Basil Taylor, Michael Young, and William Russell are forced inside. The

RUDE BUAY

Mini Van speeds away.

RUDE BUAY

16

INSIDE THE COMMISSIONER'S office, sits Commissioner Richard Baptiste, a tall, slim, kingly man in his forties. Sitting across from him is the governor-general Dr. Bradford Wiley, intellectually sound and in his sixties.
"We have no choice but to bring in **Rude Buay**," suggests, the commission.
Bradford Wiley, agitatedly, responds.
"Might as well sell our souls to the Devil."
"People like Rude Buay, get hired to find the Devil. Plus he has a vendetta - his brother. Make it happen...no matter what the cost," Advises the Commissioner.
The governor reminisces:

"We're still in a deficit from the last time, commissioner. Why should we have to pay for him? He's the son of our soil. JFK said, "Ask not what your country can do for you - ask what you can do for your country."
Richard Baptiste, explodes,
"This is Jamaica in crisis! The death toll has reached 150."
Bradford Wiley, shaken up and prayerfully composed, responds:
"Calm down Richard. Ask, and it shall be given you; seek, and ye shall find; knock, and it shall be opened unto you:
Matthew 7:7"
The Commissioner picks up his phone and dials.
At DEA Headquarters in Miami, the stone-faced Jose Mendez walks into the ringing of his office phone. He picks it up after the first ring.
"Jose Mendez!"
The Commissioner, responds,
"Mr. Mendez, this is Richard Baptiste the commissioner of police in Jamaica. As you know we've inherited Axel James and his allies from the U.S., as well as a huge epidemic; our kids are dying by the minute. We don't want to run our government using interns. Plus we're still recovering from the effects of that devastating hurricane. We need to broker a deal for Rude Buay's services.
Mendez replies,

"He's already headed back to Miami, and let me be clear...Rude Buay is the United States Drug Enforcement Agent, not a mercenary."
Baptiste, reminds him.
"You didn't have a problem taking a fee when his services were required prior..."
Mendez, matter-of-factly.
"Twenty percent increase and wire my handling fee to the same account as before. Happy hunting, Commissioner."
The Governor-General and The Commissioner shake hands and depart, accomplished.

17

A TAXI PULLS UP OUTSIDE the Michael Manley Airport departure terminal. Rude Buay, steps out followed by agent Hudson and Agent Scott. Rude Buay's cell phone rings. He answers.

"Bascombe, you've just been hired to put out Axel James' trash in Jamaica. It's a sizable raise from your last trip off of the reservation," commands, Jose Mendez.

Rude Buay, responds,

"According to Benjamin Disraeli: 'Nothing can resist the human will that will stake even its existence on its stated purpose."

Mendez, instructional replies,

"The Commissioner has already made arrangements for you and the team to meet him tomorrow in Montego Bay."

"There could be a conflict in the schedule as Mr. Banks is also expecting to meet with me tomorrow in Port Antonio."

Instructs, Rude Buay.

Jose Mendez responds sarcastically,

"What could a former MP do for you? That old racehorse is tired."

Rude Buay, disagreeing, remarks.

"The greatest tragedy in America is not the destruction of our natural resources, though that tragedy is great. The truly great tragedy is the destruction of our human resources by our failure to fully utilize our abilities, which means that most men and women go to their graves with their music still in them.' So said Oliver Wendell Holmes."

Hours later, the plane touches down at Montego Bay Airport. Rude Buay, Agent Scott, and Hudson deplane. Jamaican police patrol the grounds, armed with automatic weapons forming an impediment.

Mildred Simms is sandwiched like a rose between two sharp thorns, the commissioner to her left, Banks to her right.

Rude Buay emerges, followed by the agents. The commissioner greets.

"Welcome. Meet Mildred Simms, the eyes, and Banks, the ears, of Jamaica."

Rude Buay, replies,
"Meet my partners Agent Scott and Agent Hudson, if it moves he can drive it. If it's there, she can find it."
Glancing at Banks, he remarks.
"Mr. Banks, thanks for readjusting your..."
The Commissioner intercepts,
"Welcome Agent Scott and Agent Hudson."
Banks, announces.
"Jamaica? One Love!"
They walk over toward a waiting black Hummer.
Mildred Simms, states,
"In less than an hour, you'll be briefed on the current situation involving Axel James."
Banks, suggestively,
"Tonight we'll be partying Jamaican Style at the Beach Resort in Montego Bay. Sam's Taxi Tours will pick you up.'
Hudson, echoes,
"I love this place!"
Rude Buay, replies,
"I'm here to work, Mr. Banks."
To which, Banks responds,
"You have to assimilate into your environment, no?"
Hudson, wastes no time, securing the seat belt around her. Rude Buay and Scott throw the luggage inside the Hummer, they climb in as the hummer departs.
In the meantime, at an Airfield in Port Antonio, a small aircraft touches down. Passengers of Colombian decent rush from the aircraft and onto a waiting bus.

RUDE BUAY

The bus drives away.

Additionally, on top of an Ocho Rios hillside, Jamaican police comb through the bamboo trees with dogs in search of Axel, Ian, and Ricardo Hererra.

In a Mandeville park, a posted sign reads: PARK CLOSED UNTIL FURTHER NOTICE.

Outside a Vegetable Market, in Kingston,

Produce is off-loaded from trucks. Desperate shoppers bid for supply in quantity, fearing a scarcity.

At a tenement yard in Kingston, where Rude Buay once lived, a couple stack up on food supply of corned fish, starch, canned foods, rice, peas, flour, sugar, and cooking oil.

Over the airwaves, the breaking news continues. One announcer throws himself into it. He reports:

"Power 106 FM. Radio Jamaica on the go. Gas prices continue to soar. While several vehicles wait in line at the pumps. The Jamaican coast guard cutter aggressively patrols the shores. Helicopters fly at low altitudes to find Members of the Dragon Drug Cartel. Meanwhile, the death toll continues to climb as several adults have also lost their lives as a result of using contaminated drugs. Sources close to the Prime Minister's Office claim that American DEA agents are expected to be briefed shortly regarding this fiasco, as five Government officials are still missing."

On several drug trafficking streets in Port Antonio, MP's oversee the setup of roadblocks. In particular, those leading towards the airfield. Several locals wait

RUDE BUAY

in line with parked vehicles, as individuals displaying Dragon tattoos, exchange sacks of cocaine for cash.

| RUDE BUAY

18

OUTSIDE THE CROWDED Port Antonio Hospital E.R., many patients lay waiting on gurneys. Despite her medical garb, stunningly eye-catching, 25-year-old, Attending Physician, Dr. Tamara Ross, draws applause - mainly from the male gender. She is focused as she enthusiastically watches over the growing life and death drama of the ill-fated children.

In Kingston, outside the police barracks, the streets are lined with early morning vendors, flanged by carnival demonstrators. The Jamaican and U.S. flags wave in the breeze. Steve, in his 50s, shirtless, establishes the tune on his steel pan.

Steve, in a rugged falsetto, sings:

"Don't stop the carnival. Down with the criminals. We

want Steel band, Calypso, and Mardi Gras."

The black Hummer pulls up, sandwiched by Jamaican police on motorbikes. Rude Buay, Agent Scott, and Hudson step out and enter through the police barracks.

Jamaican policemen gait excessively. Seated behind a long desk are the Governor-General Dr. Bradford Wiley, Deputy Police Commissioner Winston Davis, and the honorable, Pete Bacchus. Seated in front of the desk are Prison Warden, Ralph Bullock, Mildred Simms, and five distinguished officers of the Jamaica police force. Rude Buay, Scott, and Hudson walk in, occupying the front row seats. Police Commissioner Richard Baptiste, emerges from the back room and sits next to the Governor-General. They shake hands. Jamaican police officers close the door. The Commissioner stands and addresses:

Good morning. I'd like to introduce, The Governor-General of Jamaica, Dr. Bradford Wiley.

Applause! The Commissioner sits.

Dr. Bradford Wiley stands up and removes an index card from his breast pocket. He puts on his reading glasses, and after glancing at the index card, addresses the working group.

"Rude Buay, Agent Scott, and Agent Hudson welcome to Jamaica."

He continues,

"Our collaborative efforts in finding the missing and

ensuring that justice is served will certainly protect the lives of our future generation: THE KIDS."

The gathering applauds.

Dr. Wiley removes his reading glasses, puts them inside the case, and sits down. The projector light comes on. Police Commissioner, Richard Baptiste stands. He points to the screen.

A picture of exhibit #1: Axel James.

Baptiste, continues,

"Axel James, mid-30s, Columbian decent, scarred, and stone-faced. Axel a fugitive, murderer, drug lord, sailor and con artist."

Next, a picture of exhibit #2: Ian Baynes

Baptiste, continuing:

"Ian Baynes, mid-30s, African American."

Followed by a picture of exhibit #3: Ricardo Herrera.

Baptiste states,

"Ricardo Herrera, early 40s, Colombian descent. Both are known associates of Axel James and equally have extensive rap sheets throughout the Islands and several of the Southern States. They are known also as gang members of the notorious Dragon Drug Cartel."

Next, a picture of exhibit #4: Dalton Castello.

There is silence, you can hear a pin drop.

The Commissioner, echoes,

"Dalton Castello, Minister of National Security (Police, Prisons, and Seaports)! The Public Service and Airport Development. Missing!"

A picture of exhibit #5: Michael Young, follows.
Baptiste, echoes,
"Michael Young, Minister of Tourism and Culture. Missing!"
A picture of exhibit #6: Vince La Borde, follows.
Baptiste, continues.
"Vince La Borde, Minister of Telecommunications, Science Technology and Industry. Social Development, the Family, Gender and Ecclesiastical Affairs. Missing!"
A picture of exhibit #7: Bazil Taylor, appears.
Baptiste continues.
"Bazil Taylor, Minister of Transport, Works and Housing. Missing."
Followed by, a picture of exhibit #8: William Russell
He continues,
"William Russell, Minister of State in the Ministry of Education, Youth and Sports. Missing!
The projector light goes off.
The Commissioner engages the podium. All eyes are focused on him as he expounds:
"Those ministers of government were kidnapped at the Economic debate... The carnival celebrations are still on hold for security reasons. Agents, your assistance in this crisis is invaluable."
He shakes hands with the Minister of Health and Environment, Honorable Esther Graves. Then he exits briskly on heels of the Governor-General.

RUDE BUAY

Rude Buay, stares at prison Warden Ralph Bullock, a man of East Indian descent, with displeasure. His name tags glitter in the dimly lit room of aggravated government officials.
Mildred Simms moseys out from the briefing room, and connects with Rude Buay.
"Rude Buay, the Governor-General wants to see you in his office."
Rude Buay leaves Bullock an eye full of "it's all good." Inside the Conference Room, the Governor-General and Commissioner sit face to face.
Mildred Simms enters, followed by Rude Buay.
Wiley greets them and remarks,
"Rude Buay, whatever you need. The Commissioner and his team are here for you."
Rude Buay, without batting an eye, replies,
"I need maps containing every street, track, river, stream, gutter, sewage line, mountain, hill and valley, blueprints of buildings, homes, huts, outhouses, and every dog house and "pig pen" in Port Antonio. Plus, I need Helicopters, speedboats and fast automobiles."
He pauses, and then continues:
"If a hammer hits a nail on its head there after today I want to know who did it and where."
The Commissioner responds,
"Why our police barracks?"
"Because you never know who is rolling in the **mud**."
The Commissioner, eyes Wiley and Mildred, then focuses on Rude Buay.

RUDE BUAY

"And how soon do you need these?"
Rude Buay, responds,
"Tomorrow by sunset."
Mildred Simms looks at the Governor-General.
Baptiste eyes Rude Buay with concern.
Wiley ponders before responding.
"Rude Buay, we don't have enough manpower. We have access to one extra helicopter, which we borrow from Haiti only on Sundays…Two coast guard cutters and they've been working around the clock, since…We have one Hummer, the next shipment has been delayed…"
Rude Buay, says to Scott,
"Get on the phone. We have a few favors to call in. Ask Banks to show up half an hour earlier."
Scott, questioningly,
"Am I in this meeting?"
Rude Buay, responds, sarcastically,
"Only if you speak Patois."
Rude Buay shake hands with Baptiste and Wiley. Mildred Simms escorts him to the door. She waves goodbye.
Mildred returns to the room. The Commissioner walks over to Mildred and addresses her in Patois.
"Keep a close eye on Mr. Rude Buay and his partners. Don't lose them out of your sight. This isn't his show. He's our… "

RUDE BUAY

Mildred senses his trend of thought and trails Rude Buay.

| RUDE BUAY

19

SAM'S TAXI TOUR bus arrives at the dock in Negril. Rude Buay, Agent Scott and Hudson step out dressed to the nines.
A short Jamaican Police patrolling, carrying semi-automatics, approach the agents. Five additional officers, observe.
The officer confronts the agents.
"May I take a look at your ID's?" he asks.
Like clockwork, the three DEA agents flash their badges.
Police continue,
"I'm sorry, but you're not allowed."
Rude Buay, replies,

"Looks like you boys didn't get the memo."
The Police replies,
"What "memo" would that be, Mr. American tourist?"
Rude Buay, lashes out at him after that comment.
"The "memo" that this "tourist" is here to save your country from the bad guys."
The other five policemen advance. Six weapons are now pointed at Rude Buay, but before they know it, Rude Buay, Scott and Hudson have swiftly disarmed and subdued two of them. The remaining Police train their weapons on the two Agents. Five additional police officers draw closer towards the agents with guns cocked.
There's radio transmission. The Policemen, listen in. Mildred's voice echoes,
"Send Rude Buay and Scott and Hudson in. Over."
Rude Buay and Scott release their captives and are promptly escorted inside.
An Elderly man yells from the crowd in Patois.
"Yardy Buay come home to roost with Yankee gal!"
Rude Buay ignores the welcome.
A Police Officer escorts them inside Negril Beach Hotel.
Mildred is sitting alone at a table.
Rude Buay rambles in her direction, with agent Scott and Hudson tailing him. Banks is at the bar drinking a beer. Rude Buay, pulls up a stool next to Banks.
"Pardon my tardiness. What can I say about some of these locals?"

RUDE BUAY

Remarks, Rude Buay.
"They see you as a sophisticated American, who has a vendetta against them. But it's all good. Now, how can I help you?"
Says, Banks,
Rude Buay, takes a beer and responds.
"Your commissioner wants me on this case but their resources are so limited."
Banks' very diplomatic. Ponders, then states,
"I still have some Cuban ties."
Mildred gets up from her seat at the table and walks over to the bar.
"Mr. Rude Buay. Your agents are waiting for Sir,"
States Mildred.
"Let's talk later, Mr. Banks,"
Says, Rude Buay, excusing himself.
Rude Buay, joins the others at the table.
Mildred, observing him closely, states,
"Welcome to NEGRIL Resort."
Maitre D steps up and seats them and leaves.
Agent Scott scans the room discreetly. The dance floor is crowded. Booze is everywhere. The DJ plays a slow song.
Rude Buay and Mildred exchange glances.
Hudson, jealously, clues in.
Mildred continues,
'Would you like to dance Rude Buay?"
Mildred Simms gets up and leads Rude Buay to the dance floor.

RUDE BUAY

Scott notices a hot woman sitting alone at another table. She winks at him, and touches her neck, on the jugular vein. Scott clues in, that's how the women in that clique introduce themselves. Scott strolls in her direction. Her added smile says to Scott, "we belong." Scott leads her to the dance floor. Hudson is left alone at the table.

Hudson scouts, looking for someone she could lead to the dance floor. She notices Scott, as he departs with the woman.

Shelly, Agnes, and Denise, all wearing bandanas, arrive at the dock. They huddle with Jamaican police officers. The Officers point them in the direction of the resort.

Inside, Rude Buay and Mildred pass by the bar, en route to a busy dance floor.

Banks, full of man talk, cautions.

"Easy now, Rude Buay!"

Rude Buay smiles.

Banks resumes,

"Enjoy the music "Reggae Style."

The Bartender serves Banks another beer. A Local joins Banks with "cheers".

Banks asks the local,

"Are you participating in the festivities?"

The Local, responds.

"Not this year, Banks."

Banks, follows up.

RUDE BUAY

"Burnt out?"
The Local replies,
"Drug lords are seeking refuge here. On top of that, cops get shot down like flies and five government officials... Who wants to venture out and get shot?"
Banks looks at his beer, takes a calculated sip.
Banks encapsulates,
"It used to be Jamaica "One Love" until..."
Rude Buay and Mildred Simms return to the table. Banks' eyes are fixed on them, wishing it was him in pursuit of the Jamaican beauty, Mildred.
Banks turns to leave.
"So, tomorrow we'll continue our manhunt?"
States, Rude Buay.
Banks returns to the bar.
Mildred addresses Rude Buay.
"Yep. You find Axel first or I will."
The Waiter brings another round of drinks. Mildred removes the cherry from her drink and dangles it in front of Rude Buay's face. Finally, she puts it inside her mouth and chews the life out of it.
Rude Buay feels like Mildred has thrown a ninety mile an hour curveball.
Adjusting, he asks,
"How much does Banks know?"
Mildred, responds.
"His grey hair speaks for itself, Mr. Rude Buay."
Rude Buay, remarks.
"You've called me that name twice tonight. Are we

going to be able to keep this on a business level?"
To which, she responds,
"All I can say is, 'what is to be will be.' Sir."
Rude Buay excuses himself from the table and moves into Banks' space. Mildred pursues. Hudson remains at the table writing in her journal. She sees the three all familiar women. Before she could respond in self-defense, they offensively, have invaded her space.
Shelly whacks Hudson in the head with her automatic weapon. Hudson falls to the ground and struggles to get up. Shelly whacks her again. This time, she falls to the ground hard. Denise grabs her, blindfolds her, and escorts her through the back entrance.
BANG, BANG, BANG. GUNSHOTS.
People run for cover. Beer bottles, from aroused locals, are hurled in direction of the bar, accompanied by gunshots from the three women. Rude Buay and Scott, struck by beer bottles, hit the floor. Getting up they give chase, trying to get an aim in through the dense crowd.
Agnes sticks a rag inside Agent Hudson's mouth, seals it with duct tape, and quickly binds her with rope.
There's a huge crowd of people trying to get out. Agent Scott exits through the side doors.
Mildred Simms follows close behind.
Banks notices an unclaimed lady's purse on Mildred's table. Next to it lies a napkin, drawn on it, in red ink, a dragon.
He yells,

RUDE BUAY

"Miss Simms, you forgot something."

Mildred turns around, goes back to retrieve it. She notices the Dragon tattoo drawn on the napkin. Mildred reflects. She had seen the same signature worn by agent Scott, earlier at the table.

Outside the resort, the three women rush Hudson aboard a speed boat.

Rude Buay pursues on foot. He runs into two Jamaican police officers. Rude Buay pushes his way through, slightly brushing against one of the officers who loses his balance in the process. Several Officers respond in retaliation.

Mildred rushes out and sedates Rude Buay. Meanwhile, the boat speeds off. Leaving Rude Buay along with white water waves at the vacant dock.

Agent Scott returns. Rude Buay notices. Not pleased about his absence during a manhunt of this magnitude addresses Scott.

" You missed it huh? Did she French kiss you on the brain?"

Agent Scott claims,

"Too many double-crossers."

Rude Buay responds,

"Welcome to the real WAR, Manhunt in the Caribbean"

| RUDE BUAY

20

INSIDE THE NEGRIL HOTEL, Rude Buay, sits at a desk conducting a database search of names on the computer. His Pen Phone rings. The caller ID reveals Mendez's number.
Rude Buay takes the call.
"This is no good. Bascombe, what did you find out on Hudson?" remarks Mendez.
Rude Buay responds,
"Nothing so far."
Mendez replies,
"Rude Buay, it's clear that you failed to cover her."
Rude Buay, getting straight to the point, responds.
"Hold on! Are you accusing me of... Chief, this had to have been a..."
Mendez questions,

'By who?"
Rude Buay, replies,
"I'm still gathering info. Possibly the three female fugitives."
Mendez responds,
"Are you trying to say that they escaped from prison in less than twenty-four hours and are already raining on your parade?"
Rude Buay states,
"They showed up in Jamaica. How did they know where to find her?"
Says Mendez,
"No idea! Bascombe, you've left me with only one choice... I'm going to have to bring you back to The U.S."
Rude Buay responds,
"Never! Why? So that the drug Lords feel that they've won? We're flirting with the possibility of having Hudson's body returned to us in a body bag. Never! I will never concede!"
Mendez continues to break him down.
"You begged to have her and agent Scott join you. We don't want to have their bodies returned to us in caskets."
Rude Buay states,
"I need time...as well as resources. Plus there are too many probabilities."
Mendez reminds him.
"We don't have much of it."

RUDE BUAY

Rude Buay, cogitates, then responds.
"48 hours?"
Mendez replies,
"When and if you get into my seat, you can run things your way, but until then, in this department, what I say goes. This case is going to be... reassigned. Rude Buay, you begged for this assignment. Plus, her son calls you Uncle Rude Buay. You're not even..."
Rude Buay, senses not only the racist overtone but for the first time, his boss called him by his local name. Could his boss be in on this also? He ponders before responding.
"Too many cooks spoil the broth."
Jose Mendez persisting,
"That's all you have 47 hours 59.30 minutes."
Rude Buay replies.
"I'll take you up on that mandate, but from here on in, I am going to run things my way. This is my soil."

RUDE BUAY

21

INSIDE THE HOTEL ROOM, Rude Buay engages in a set of pushups. His hotel phone rings. The thought occurs. Could this be his boss? He grabs it.

"Rude Buay, this is Alberto. I can tell you that you are not a good swimmer. Anyway getting down to business, I have your partner. In exchange for her, I want you out of the Caribbean for good. For Good! In 24 hours I'll have a jet waiting to fly you back to Miami. My peeps will contact you."

"How much?" asks Rude Buay.

Alberto, responds,

"I don't need the cash. I just want you out of Jamaica."

Rude Buay, replies:

"This is the land of my birth. I will not give up this

RUDE BUAY

right to... I will fight in the hills, in the valleys, on the seas, in the air, underground. If I go down I will go down fighting!"

Alberto, responds.

"A very poor rendition of Winston Churchill..."

Rude Buay, hangs up the phone and researches on his computer. The name Alberto Gomez surfaces. He double clicks on the profile. An error message comes up: INFORMATION NOT AVAILABLE. He inputs the name for a second time. Same result. Rude Buay picks up the phone and dials.

On Walter Banks' wall, there's a portrait of Banks and Chelo. The red phone, sitting on his desk keeps ringing. No body's there. Rude Buay dials a different number.

"You've reached 876-322-7171. Leave a message after the beep."

He does not leave a message.

On the beach, Banks lies on the sand. He's cuddled up next to a hot babe sharing a beach towel. Waves wash up against their feet.

Rude Buay dials in desperation.

At the office of Tourism and Culture, Mildred Simms picks up the phone.

"This is Mildred Simms!"

"Mildred, this is Rude Buay. An assignment has been thrown at me. What do you know about...Alberto Gomez?" Waiting for her response, he gets ready to write.

RUDE BUAY

Mildred responds:
"Nothing. I've never heard of him. Banks should have more of the inside scoop on him."
Rude Buay asks,
"Where's he?"
Mildred, licks her lips before responding.
"It's a sunny day, try the beach. He likes playing Casanova. It's the Island in him"
Rude Buay, asks.
"Which beach?"
Mildred responds.
"It's 96 degrees in the shade and the water stays warm all night long."
Rude Buay informs her.
"I've got a big fish to deep fry. If you hear from Banks, tell him to call me ASAP."
Mildred replies,
"It's apparent that you are going to have a fish frying party before this whole thing washes out. Huh??
Rude buay, responds, "Thanks. I need a 20 on Scott."
Mildred replies,
"To the best of my knowledge, he's with that woman from the party. They both display similar tattoos."
Rude Buay cautions.
"No one gets my whereabouts except Mr. Banks.
Rude Buay hangs up. "
Rude Buay's phone rings.
He picks up.

RUDE BUAY

"This is Bascombe".
Banks, voice comes in.
"Rude Buay..."
Banks' on the phone.
Rude Buay enthusiastically,
"Walter Banks! The man of the hour. Banks, I know that you're a beach bum, but I've got something that might interest you. How would you like to team up with me?"
Banks asks,
"Why?"
Rude Buay responds.
"I've got a big fish to fry. The agency is trying to hold me responsible...for the kidnapping of Heidi Hudson. All I have to go on is a name... Alberto Gomez."
Banks, asks with concern:
"How do I come in?"
Rude Buay answers.
"I need a guy who knows them inside out. I understand that you've spent several years working underground in Bogota and an MP for the Jamaican government."
Banks replies,
"I let sleeping dogs lie."
Rude Buay states,
"I'll protect you exclusively."
Banks asks,
"What about your guys?"
Rude Buay replies.

RUDE BUAY

"You know how shafted these guys are. I need someone who can deliver. Someone with a destiny and a passion and purpose to fulfill it.
Banks replies,
"I believe in priorities."
Rude Buay, interrupts.
"God, family, job..."
Banks interrupts,
"Country! You don't identify with us."
After a beat, Banks continues.
"It was Kennedy who said: Ask not what your country can do for you - ask what you can do for your country."
Rude Buay informs,
"So said your commissioner."
Rude Buay, reflects, then continues,
"Except that he forgot that: A man without vision shall perish."
Banks, has had enough. He responds.
"Rude Buay I've been there, done that. Don't need your third party tactics. How much?"
Rude Buay responds,
"Half a mil..."
Banks inquires,
"Who picks up the tab?"
Rude Buay assures,
The PEPI account.
"I'm in."

RUDE BUAY

Says Banks.
Banks hangs up the phone and immediately surveys the coastline using his binoculars. He reaches into his pocket, retrieves his Pen Phone and dials and makes contact.
"Come in Chelo."
Chelo responds,
"Come in Banks."
Banks replies.
'Go ahead Chelo. What you got?"
Chelo, always excited when he discovers a plot:
"A blue ship operated by the dragon cartel bearing the name "Tempest" has dropped off a shipment last night in Mo Bay. It could be heading your way, pronto.
Banks responds,
"Thanks. I've got it on the radar as we speak. By the way, I need everything on Don Alberto Gomez."
Chelo, not sure.
"I don't know...Maybe..."
Banks demands,
"Everything!"
Banks hangs up and dials.
Rude Buay answers.
"Rude Buay, this is Banks. A blue ship named "Tempest" has stepped into our radar. Destination: Negril. Mildred will meet you onboard "Hairoun" at the Negril's Dock. The coast guard ship will be tailing you."

RUDE BUAY

Rude Buay exuberantly,
"Good. Very good."
Rude Buay get up from his chair, STRAPS a gun to his left leg and summons agent Desmond Scott.

22

NEGRIL OVERLOOKS A VAST body of blue water, a variety of ships nesting on it. White sand beaches, hilltop houses, and trees provide a paradisiacal backdrop. Sounds of horns and engines from ships on the go drown out the sound of waves washing up against the shoreline. The water reflects the rays from the sun.

Rude Buay scans the harbor through binoculars. He zooms in for clarity. He spots the "Tempest." But notices that its country of origin is missing.

Rude Buay adjusts the focus and notices the transferring of cargo from yacht to yacht.

Mildred's hair blows in the wind. She looks through

RUDE BUAY

her binoculars to catch that view..
Rude Buay says to Scott.
"Do you see what I see?"
Scott responds.
"No. Not really."
Rude Buay indicates,
"Straight ahead to the left."
Agent Scott fires up the engine.
Their ship Hairoun picks up speed, heading in direction of the suspected ship. It drops anchor. Rude Buay and Mildred climb aboard the Tempest.
Rude Buay and Mildred proceed with weapons drawn; they amble closer.
There's a shadow.
Rude Bauy, yells.
"Freeze! DEA."
The sailor hastily releases the anchor chain and dives into the water. Three men wearing masks emerge on deck, with guns drawn.
Rude Buay continues.
"Drop your weapons! Now! "
Ian Baynes comes out from the hull of the ship, wearing a blue expensive business suit and dark sunglasses. His gun is drawn.
Ian yells.
"You're trespassing! Private property."
Ian is distracted by two Jamaican and one Cuban coast guard, cutting water, heading in that direction. Three Jamaican coast guard officers and one Cuban aim

towards the Tempest with a drawn semi-automatic.
It's now a standoff. The Jamaican coast guard officers concentrate their aim on the masked men. Meanwhile, a Haitian Helicopter circles overhead.
Rude Buay commands.
"Drop your weapons!"
They hesitate.
Rude Buay shoots. The bullet hits the "made-over" Ian Baynes in the chest. He falls overboard.
Scott remarks,
"Maybe he'll listen next time."
Coast guard officers dive into the water and fish out Ian, who happens to still be alive. They drag him aboard the coast guard boat. Blood is pumping out of bullet hole in his chest.
Jamaican Police place cuffs on the other three men: Michael Cox, Sebastian Perez, and Nigel Davis.
Rude Buay and Scott proceed into the hull of the ship, with Banks in tow. Mildred guards the deck. They cautiously enter.
Rude Buay stops abruptly, listen, and then moves a few steps, with ears cocked. He hears a squeaky sound. He draws up behind the door and opens it. The way looks clear so he beckons Scott in his direction.
Scott ambles up close to him. Banks follows in tow. There's another door. They try to open it but it's locked. The sign on it says: ENGINE ROOM DOOR MUST BE KEPT CLOSED.

RUDE BUAY

Rude Buay glances back at Scott. Moves to the other side of the door and begins to grasp the handle. He checks his gun, grabs the doorknob, swings it open and charges in with Agent Scott and Banks on his tail. They scan the room hastily.

Rude Buay notices some canvas draped like a table cloth. He grabs it in disgust, throwing it on the floor. There's a lid. Rude Buay lifts it off.

INSIDE: Stacks of twenty-dollar bills in Jamaican currency, binoculars, hammocks, blankets, and survival kits and grenades and a huge gun collection. Another lid gets Rude Buay's attention.

Inside: Dalton Castello's body, bound with ropes, wounds to the head; he's still breathing. So they carry him up to the deck, to be transported to the hospital.

RUDE BUAY

23

THE AMBULANCE PULLS UP in front of the E.R. entrance at Port Antonio Hospital. Medics wheel out a gurney with Castello on it. Simultaneously, a Taxi pulls up to the gate. Out steps, Tamara Ross, she's dressed in blue scrubs, a stethoscope hanging from her neck. She hustles through the entrance to the E.R. and assists in treating Mr. Castello.
A pot of coffee is brewing in the kitchen at Banks' house. Steelpan music is playing in the background. Rude Buay is admiring the view of the Port from the window. Banks returns with a huge roll of blueprints. Rude Buay, looking out the window, exclaims,
"Great View!"
Banks replies,

RUDE BUAY

"Like a basin decorated with toy boats."
Rude Buay returns to the dining room table, now cluttered with blueprints.
Rude Buay follows up on his comment.
"Yep! Do you sail, Banks?"
Banks, enjoying the conversation:
"I love yachts."
Rude Buay feeds his ego.
"You must have captured some great pictures from this location."
Banks responds,
"Oh yes, but most of my pictures come from Bogota'.
Rude Buay asks,
"Great place?"
Banks, replies,
"I spent five years there, working undercover for the U.N."
"What was it like?"
Asks Rude Buay, with concern.
Banks replies,
"Scary. One moment you're alive knowing that the next moment you could be eaten by vultures flying overhead."
Banks shows him a stack of pictures. One has a man wearing the dragon tattoo. Rude Buay clues in.
Banks, continues.
"The night they caught Chelo taking pictures of their operation, they captured him and decided to hang him."

RUDE BUAY

Rude Bauy, likes what he hears, plus, being able to build such a bridge with his new sidekick, is invaluable, so he asks.
"Really?"
Banks relays.
"I rode into their camp strapped to the chassis of the truck driven by the guy who was commissioned to hang Chelo. When the truck stopped, I untied myself and waited underneath. The Driver stepped out, I grabbed him by his feet, took him down, crawled out, grabbed his rifle, wasted him, put his clothes on, drove Chelo to the gallows site and shot the men waiting for "the Kill." Chelo and me been buddies ever since."
Rude Buay enquires further.
"How did you learn about their plan?"
Banks, full of wisdom, responds,
"When your ear's to the ground you learn many things, my friend."
Rude Buay, feeling as if he had just received some food for thought, responds,
"Tell me about Alberto Gomez."
Banks, opening up.
"Man's like a sealed case. He's not your average Czar."
Rude Buay inquires,
"Who funds him?"
Banks responds,
"Your agency hasn't...?"
Banks phone rings. He answers.
Chelo's voice is like music to his ears.

"Banks what I know you already know..."
Rude Buay eavesdrops.
Banks replies,
"Thanks!"
Banks realizes that there is nothing new on Alberto. So he continues informing Rude Buay.
"They claim that he has billions in Swiss accounts, yet nothing has turned up in his name. He posted record profits in the last two years. He controls most of the traffic up and down the coast. Axle James' former boss, he's married to Denise Gomez, whom you busted last year."
Rude Buay reminisces.
'No wonder she's broken out of prison so easily." He ponders, then continues his series of questions.
"Where does he reside?'
Banks replies,
"Every agent who has met with him in person is already dead or on his waiting list. His home address is never published. No landline telephone. His ships are not registered. He owes the IRS over $2.8 Million in back taxes. They can't bring him down. The man's untouchable."
Rude Buay, asks.
'How do we get him?"
"Make contact with his wife Denise; hold her as ransom. We could start there,"
Banks says.
Rude Buay questions.

RUDE BUAY

'Could she be our doorway to Heidi Hudson?"
Banks remarks,
"They work independently at times but they could have teamed up on kidnapping of this magnitude."
Rude Buay's cup is full.
"Where there's a will there's a way."
Banks says sarcastically,
"I thought that your Mom practiced..."
Rude Buay, with limited knowledge of the craft, replies,
"She never taught me the tricks. Said it will make me mentally lazy. Neither did she leave a catalog in her WILL."
Banks, continuing like a runaway train, declares.
"When the Philistines wanted to take out Samson, they went through Delilah."
Rude Buay ponders that gesture, then immediately thereafter, picks up the pen phone and dials. He receives a busy tone. Meanwhile, Banks phone rings in the other room. Banks leaves to get it. Rude Buay redials.
Rude Buay reaches Mildred.
"Mildred, I am having a challenge getting through to the commissioner. He's not..."
Mildred replies,
"It's 2:00 a.m Rude Buay, I'll get him for you."

24

THE PHONE RINGS inside the Commissioner's bedroom. Commissioner Richard Baptiste and his wife Christine are asleep in bed. He snores like a freight train. She rolls over, pokes him in the ribs, then grabs the phone.
Mildred echoes.
"Richard! Richard!"
Christine responds.
'He's..."
Christine jealously looks at the clock, and continues.
"Mildred he's fast asleep after a steamy night. I'll tell him that you called. Is there a message?"
Mildred responds,
"Police business."
Christine is about to hang up.
Richard rolls over and tugs the receiver from her.

RUDE BUAY

She removes the handcuffs from bed-head, opens the night stand's draw, deposits them, and meanders towards the bathroom - semi-clothed.
Richard, occupied with the phone call, says,
"Hello?"
Mildred responds,
"Commissioner, I have Rude Buay on a 3-Way call."
The Commissioner senses serious business by this 2:00 a.m. call.
Rude Buay informs,
"Commissioner, Rude Buay here. I didn't mean to wake you."
The Commissioner, still half asleep,
"Rude Buay, didn't you get them?..."
Rude Buay informs,
"If we, meaning, U.S. Government personnel and equipment were to guard the shores tomorrow, would you have enough manpower available to piggy-back our effort?"
Commissioner responds,
"That's a rather hypothetical question."
The Commissioner composes himself and continues.
"Why do we need to guard the shores?"
Rude Buay, wishing the Commissioner gets his concept, replies,
"It's a possible escape route that Axel James and his men could use. If he rejoins Alberto we could have more trouble on our hands. Agent Hudson could be

history."

To which the Commissioner responds,

"Do you have any idea as to how much it's going to cost the government of Jamaica to carry out such a feat? On top of that our police force is already working over time."

Rude Buay goes for the jugular.

"Let me put it like this...for a few extra dollars, you can either help save your country from the tyranny of the Axel James' of the world or become pawns under the weight of their oppressive cartels?"

Commissioner Baptiste responds,

"We're already over budget on you Mr. Rude Buay. That Cuban helicopter drinks up a lot of fuel."

Christine returns all dolled up and crawls in bed.

The Commissioner continues,

"Plus, that's not the way we do things here."

"This is your baby. Plus you couldn't pay me if you wanted to." replies Rude Buay.

Baptiste looks over at Christine and says.

"I'll have a word in at sunrise,"

and hangs up.

RUDE BUAY

25

RUDE BUAY, LOOKS across at Banks, who is head-bopping frequently. Rude Buay picks up his phone and dials.

At The DEA office in Miami, Mendez walks out towards the door, attaché case in hand. His phone rings. He returns to his desk. Picks up. Looking at the caller ID, he sees agent Bascombe's number displayed. "This better be good," he says under his breath.

Picking up, Rude Buay, addresses him.

"Mendez! Bascombe here."

Mendez expecting great news:

"Lay it on, Rude Buay!"

Rude Buay responds.

What are the chances of rescinding the offer?

RUDE BUAY

Mendez replies.

"Which offer?"

Rude Buay reflects and feels like he's now in a vice. He wants to save his country, but trust is waning in these critical moments. His existing team of U.S. agents is down to the rather untrustworthy, Desmond Scott. His sidekick, Banks, wakes up and pours two cups of coffee. He hands one to Rude Buay.

Rude Buay, responds to Mendez's question.

"The one that you've made with the Commissioner."

Mendez looks at his Rolex. Admiring it, states,

"Why? What's the hurry Rude Buay?"

Rude Buay responds,

"Everyone seems to be in on this including the man who brokered the deal with you."

Mendez replies.

"Are you saying that you don't trust your countrymen? Is the doctor in on this also?"

Rude Buay would rather not discuss his love interest.

"You know as well as I do that in a war like this one ... no one can be trusted. Not even..."

That went over Mendez's head.

Mendez asks,

"Yeah, but how can you help me help you."

Rude Bauy advises.

"Let's take out the Commissioner. Run this operation as we see fit. We can bring in the tanks, the whole infantry...Then it becomes our war and not theirs."

Mendez, liking where this conversation is going, says,

"You're thinking on your feet. Go on."
Rude Buay follows up.
"Pressure these guys to come out of hiding."
Mendez asks,
"What's the payoff?"
Rude Buay is deep in thought. Mendez senses this. He makes his chess move and continues.
"Yes Rude Buay, the payoff? We're in it...to win it."
Mendez aborts that call and dials. He talks into the phone.
"Commissioner, this is Jose Mendez. I must let you know that I'm going to need a substantial increase or I'm pulling my agents out within twenty-four hours."
Baptiste responds.
"Wait a minute..."
Mendez reminds him of this fact:
"Rude Buay works for us. I repeat ...Twenty-four-hours!"
He hangs up.
It's sun up, outside the Commissioner's home, but Richard Baptiste's not happy. He dials Rude Buay.
"Mr. Rude Buay!"
He answers.
"Rude Buay here."
Baptiste, knowing that he can't win this without Rude Buay replies,
"I'm here for you."
Rude Buay, feeling some local support, says.
"Good deal, Commissioner.

RUDE BUAY

If Axel James tries to leave tomorrow, he'll have to get through reinforced surveillance."

Christine strides in. Make-up and hair in place. Commissioner notices her enhanced sensuality. Baptiste hangs up and chases Christine around the room.

26

BANKS, REFRESHED BY THAT CUP of coffee, paces back and forth in the kitchen. The sunlight beams through the glass window. Horns resonate from ships leaving and entering the harbor. Banks discontinues his ambulating and joins Rude Buay at the table, uttering.

"You remember the guy you shot in the chest during the arrest, search, and seizure in Negril?"

"Yes. What about him?"

"Sources close to the Axel team claim that he was the driver involved in the kidnapping of those government officials. He changed his identity after fleeing from Jamaica with Axel. His real name is Ian Baynes." Banks informs Rude Buay.

"Information left out at the briefing don't you think."

"Don't think it was done purposefully. Late Breaking

RUDE BUAY

News, that's all."
Rude Buay reflects on growing up as a kid, always being *late* for school.
He says to Banks,
"Get me the number for a taxi."
"Where to?"
Rude Buay, in an exasperated huff,
"Port Antonio Hospital."
Rude Buay's Pen Phone rings. He picks up.
It's agent Scott.
"Any leads?"
Rude Buay, looking for possible reform in his fellow agent, advises,
"Meet me at the Hospital. I need someone I can trust!"
Banks says.
"Call Sam's Taxi!"
Rude Buay dials.
"Will be here in five minutes," says Rude Buay, as he departs.
Rude Buay sees a display of Rastafarian hats with wigs attached inside an illuminated Vendor's Booth. He purchases one. The Vendor puts the hat in a shopping bag. A taxi pulls up. He gets in, with the bag in hand.
The Taxi runs into a roadblock. Several vehicles are held at bay. Boisterous and angry locals protest in a thick Patois dialect. Drug dealers conduct business amongst barricades as if it is highly legal to do what

they do. One man, no doubt, fed up with the disregard for the up-keeping of the law, holds up a sign: I AM RUNNING FOR MP.
Rude Buay, sensing trouble, retrieves the hat and puts it on his head. He sticks his finger in his throat and pukes up outside through the window. That outside door gets plastered... Then he lays flat, face down on the rear seat. An MP walks up towards the taxi and asks the driver,
"Where are you heading to?"
He responds in Patois,
"Port Antonio Hospital. Sick patient. The man sick bad, could be poisoned."
The MP covering his nostrils, signals a policeman to let the cab proceed.
The taxi takes off speedily.
Later, the taxi pulls up outside Port Antonio Hospital. Rude Buay removes the hat. Before exiting, he hands the Driver a U.S. $100.00 Bill. The Driver smiles. Rude Buay exits and enters the hospital.
 Baynes is wheeled out of E.R. to a room nearby, accompanied by Tamara. Rude Buay notices her but remains unaffected. Always the professional, she is focused on her patient. Agent Scott, just arriving, observes from close by.
Rude Buay moves into Dr. Tamara Ross' space.
"Hello, Doctor."
She glances up and quickly returns towards the E.R. Rude Buay, continuing,

RUDE BUAY

"When he wakes up, I need a word with him."
Tamara, very curt,
"When he awakes, Rude Buay."
Agent Scott is bewildered. Did they introduce themselves?
Tamara continues,
"In my professional opinion, he might not wake up, period. The bullet to his chest came out through his rib cage, barely missing his aorta. It's also possible that he could have suffered considerable memory loss due to a decrease in the blood supply flowing to his brain."
"Memory loss. Sounds like someone else I know," asserts, Rude Buay.
Scott eyes Rude Buay, surprised.
Tamara continues her work.
Meanwhile, in the hospital room, Ian Baynes holds his breath and assumes the dead fetal position.
Scott, oblivious, draws closer inside the huddle with Dr. Ross and Rude Buay.
"So you don't think there's any chance...he asks.
A nurse walks out, and echoes.
"TAMARA, TAMARA the patient just died."
"Sorry."
Tamara says to the agents and departs.
Rude Buay steals a backside view of the doctor. He goes in one direction, while Scott meanders contrariwise.

27

LATER, RUDE BUAY, driving through the streets of Kingston in a Hummer, reaches in glove compartment for his Pen Phone and calls Mildred.

"Miss Simms, this is Rude Buay. Ian Baynes died while we were at the hospital."

"Did you get any info from him?" she asks.

"Not a thing. I know he worked with Axel back in Jamaica. He shot at me during the shootout at the Villa. Also, he was shot during the sting in MO Bay"

He pauses, then continues.

"Plus my source claims that he could have been in the van when the government officials were kidnapped."

"Who's your source?"

"Why didn't you guys provide us with that information?"

"If you did not receive it through the... commissioner's

office, it could be a setup; in an attempt to create a decoy."

"If I'm going to continue on this manhunt, I need an entire profile on Baynes. Who he knew, who knew him, where he hung out, everything!" Rude Buay states, bluntly.

"I'll see what I can do. It's up to the commissioner."

"Is he...?" asks Rude Buay.

She responds.

"You're walking a thin line Rude Buay."

Inside the hospital, an African American man wear-ing scrubs and a mask prowls. He is carrying a doctor's bag. He opens the door to Ian Bayne's room, deposits the bag, and disappears.

Ian Baynes, turns in bed and looks around the room. He retrieves his iPhone from under the mattress. Then he pulls out the top drawer. Baynes, slips on a doctor's uniform, along with a stethoscope around his neck. He throws his iPhone into the doctor's bag. Picks up a syringe and dispenser off the night table, and injects himself in the arm with morphine. He disposes the utensils in the trash, and sneaks out of the hospital.

A Taxicab pulls up. Ian gets in. The Taxi drives off.

Meanwhile, Agent Scott and Rude Buay are reviewing maps. Rude Buay, looks preoccupied but tries to mask it.

Scott asks.

"What's going on?"

"Those three Crooks who were arrested during the

RUDE BUAY

Cold hit on the Tempest. I'll bet that they've got the info that we need to wrap up this manhunt."
Agent Scott responds.
"I don't think you'll get it out of them."
"Why not?"
"Fear. Fear that they and their family are getting killed and fed to vultures."
"What if I offered them protection and the chance to live."
"They know that there's nowhere for them to hide."
Rude Buay, measures Scott.
"I'll have to do this solo."
"Why?"
"I've got a hunch, my friend."
Scott, feeling like he and Rude Buay are now full cohorts, asks.
"What's that?"
"Strike, while the iron's hot. Find a Stool pigeon."
Rude Buay, turns to leave.
Scott remarks.
"I thought we were in this together."
"Time will either promote or expose..."
Responds Rude Buay, as he picks up his gun and exits.

RUDE BUAY

28

AFTER ENTERING THE KINGSTON Police Barracks, Rude Buay hands over a document to the Desk Police. He reviews it, gets on the phone and announces, "Bring out Michael Cox!"
Rude Buay comes to an office, with a small desk, a computer, filing cabinets, and some chairs. Cox is seated on a chair in the middle of the office.
Rude Buay surrounds him, the Police look on.
Rude Buay proceeds.
"Michael, my name's Rude Buay. I'm going to ask you a couple of questions. I ask that you be truthful in your answers."
Michael rubs his nose, unsure what Rude Buay wants.
Rude Buay continues,
"Your name's Michael Cox. Born in Bogota' Colombia?"
"I don't speak English."

RUDE BUAY

"Como se llama?"

"Sorry, I don't understand."

Rude Buay, in disbelief, removes his gun, pointing it towards Michael's head.

"Yesterday, when you were arrested on the 'Tempest' in Negril, what were you doing on that yacht?"

"Kill me, I no tell you nothing!" responds Michael Cox.

Rude Buay looks over at the desk police.

Bring in, Sebastian Perez.

The police, remove Michael from the room and speedily return with Sebastian.

Rude Buay wasting no time -

"Sebastian, what's your affiliation with Michael Cox?"

Sebastian replies,

"Who is that?"

Rude Buay punches him hard in the face. He bleeds.

Sebastian whimpers,

"He's my boss."

"How long has this boss-employee relationship been in force?"

'I don't remember."

"Answer the question. How long?" demands Rude Buay.

"As long as I could remember!"

"And how long ago was that?"

Sebastian nervously responds,

"I don't remember."

Rude Buay gives his last words a digestive interlude.

"What were you doing on the 'Tempest' on the day of

your arrest?"
Sebastian is tight-lipped.
"I..."
Rude Buay punches him again.
Rude Buay restates,
"What were you doing on the "Tempest" on the day of your arrest?"
"Sorry, I see nada, hear nada."
Rude Buay says to the desk police,
"Bring in Nigel Davis."
The Police escort Sebastian out of the room and re-enter with Nigel.
Rude Buay shows Nigel a picture of Ian Baynes and asks Nigel,
"Do you know this man?"
"No. It's my first time seeing him."
"Do you know who Ian Baynes is?"
"I've never heard of him."
"What's your affiliation with Ricardo?"
Nigel responds,
"I don't know him."
Rude Buay is pissed. He grabs Nigel by the collar and throws him up against the wall.
Nigel continues,
"Sorry."
Rude Buay punches him mercilessly. Nigel spits out blood.
"He's my boss."
"For how long?"

RUDE BUAY

"I forgot."
Rude Buays' cup of avoidance is filling up.
"How long...?"
"Sorry, I don't remember."
"You've seen a gallows before?"
"Yes."
Responds Nigel,
"Could you see yourself hanging from one?"
Rude Buay gaits.
"How long since you've been an employee of this...?"
"Long time!"
Replies Nigel,
"And how long ago was that?"
"Since..."
"Since when?"
Nigel deliberates.
"Since he bought the yacht."
"Which yacht?"
Rude Buay pressurizes.
"I'm not a snitch"
Rude Buay sensing a victory moves in closer to Nigel-
"Which yacht...?"
"The blue one."
Responds Nigel.
"Was it the "Tempest"?"
Nigel, showing signs of fatigue, says,
"I'm really tired."
Rude Buay not giving in -
"Was it the...Tempest?"

RUDE BUAY

Nigel responds,

"He had two yachts. Yes."

The Police hand a passport to Rude Buay. He reviews it.

Rude Buay asks,

"Nigel, is this your passport?"

Nigel gives it a good look.

"I think so."

Rude Buay discloses.

"This Columbian passport was recovered at your home. It has not been stamped by Jamaican immigration. How and where did you enter the country?"

Nigel hesitates.

Rude Buay punches him hard in the already bloodied right eye. Nigel's vision becomes blurred.

"We came in by airplane at Runaway Bay, and then took a bus."

Nigel pisses on himself. Urine trickles down his trousers.

"You never got this from me, okay."

"Who else was on the flight?"

"I don't remember."

"Think, recall!"

Nigel ruminates and then comes clean.

"Rebecca Herrera."

Rude Buay inquires,

"Ricardo's wife?"

"Yes sir," retorts Nigel

RUDE BUAY

"Where did she get off the bus?"
Nigel reluctantly answers,
"Ocho Rios."
Rude Bauy meanders away from Nigel. He mulls over and then asks pointedly.
"What else was on the plane?"
"Fifty kilos," replies Nigel.
Rude Buay returns the passport to the Police and exits like a man on a mission.

29

THE BLACK HUMMER pulls up in Ocho Rios. Rude Buay arms himself strolls out and hastens outside to a large wooden house. With the use of his gun, he blows out the lock and kicks the door in.

Ricardo, dressed in pajamas, emerges from the bedroom with a gun. He shoots at Rude Buay. The bullet misses him. Rude Buay get a few shots off at Ricardo, who jumps through a window in an escape. Rude Buay takes off on foot, in pursuit.

The Foot RACE continues through a dark alley. Coming around a bend, Ricardo cuts through the bushes.

Rude Buay approaches the bend; there's no Ricardo insight. So Rude Buay proceeds with caution.

RUDE BUAY

Ricardo sees Rude Buay go by and shoots desperately at him. Rude Buay dodges the bullet and lies face down, then rolls over on his back, shooting randomly through the bushes. A bullet hits a wall close to Ricardo. The sound deafens him. He grabs his ears with both hands. His gun falls to the floor.

Ricardo recollects himself. Scrambling for his gun, he locates it, picks it up, off-balanced, discharging several rounds, at the now standing, Rude Buay. He misses his target.

Rude Buay returns fire, hitting Ricardo in the chest and uprooting several plants in the process. Rude Buay get a close up look at Ricardo's blood saturated corps.

He returns to Ricardo's house and opens his closet and rummages. He discovers and confiscates twenty kilos of coke. Rude Buay, sends Scott a text message, via Pen Phone, notifying him about Ricardo's massacre.

A Taxi pulls up outside a mansion overlooking Montego Bay Airport. Ian Baynes ambles out. He proceeds inside the mansion.

Axel opens the door and embraces Ian.

Ian hands over the bag. Axel opens it, removes items, and lays them on the table. The living room is packed with Dragon X cocaine.

"Are you ready for battle?"

Asks Axel.

"I've got enough morphine in me."

Observing the cargo, Ian replies,

RUDE BUAY

"Where's Ricardo?"
"At his house. We'll sail tomorrow,"
Responds Axel.
At Banks' partially lit house in Port Antonio, a man dressed up as a black man steps out of a car. He surveys. Then he moves closer towards the house. He removes a gun from under his coat and gets a perfect aim at Banks, who is at his desk reading blueprints.
Maps and high lighters clutter the table, where he sits. Banks' phone rings. He moves away from his desk and picks up the phone on the wall.
Vehicles drive by, casting beams of light onto the house.
The Man crouches and lies on the stomach.
Banks returns to his desk.
The Man gets up and recaptures his aim.
He discharges several rounds through the window. Banks ducks too late and gets shot in his left arm. All he sees of the intruder is his disappearing shadow. The man rushes back to his car and disappears.
Banks rolls over onto his uninjured side in pain.
Later, Ian Baynes and Axel James meet with Banks' *failed* assassin. He's still masked, however.
Axel hands over an attaché. He opens it, counts the money. Nods. Departs.
Rude Buay's driving back to the hotel. His cell phone beeps. He tunes in and reads this congratulatory text message from agent Scott.

RUDE BUAY

"Glad you got him before I did. Cause I had a bullet in my gun for him." D.S.

Rude Buay savors the moment and scans the radio for a great music station. He catches the fading of *The Harder They Come* by Jimmy Cliff. The RADIO ANNOUNCER breaks in:

"The weather outlook for Port Antonio calls for clear skies, brisk winds of 10-25 knots, with a high of 86 degrees and a visibility of 30 miles. The high tide is at noon. News just coming into our newsroom: Jeff Cyrus aka "Walter Banks", a former Minister of Parliament and broadcaster here at WE FM was shot at his home in Port Antonio earlier this morning. Banks was rushed to Port Antonio Hospital. He remains in critical condition."

Rude Buay calls Banks from his cell phone and gets a busy signal. He turns the steering wheel to the left and U-Turns, burning rubber in the process. The Hummer merges with the flow of the early morning traffic. It later arrives outside Port Antonio Hospital. Rude Buay hurries inside.

He sees a sign reading: NO VISITORS ALLOWED. Rude Buay, ignores the sign and approaches Banks' bedside. Banks' eyes are closed, tubes attached to his arm.

Tamara enters.

Their eyes meet.

She eyes the sign.

Rude Buay forces a smile.

RUDE BUAY

She smiles.
He leaves.

RUDE BUAY

30

AT BANKS' HOUSE, Jamaican police are busily collecting evidence. Blood is splattered everywhere. Rude Buay approaches and engages a plainclothes Officer.
"How did they get inside?" asks Rude Buay.
The Officer points to a shattered glass window.
"Any leads?"
"No one claimed responsibility," answers the Jamaican Police.
"If anything turns up, give me a call,"
Says Rude Buay, who gives the officer a business card, and heads back to his hummer.
Rude Buay answers his Pen Phone.
"Where are you a partner? You heard the news?" Scott asks.
"Yes, looking for answers," Rude Buay responds as he contemplates.

"I'll be trying my luck tonight at the dock. Feel like catching a few Jacks?"
Agent Scott responds.
"I'm in the area. I'll meet you there."
Rude Buay, arrives outside Agent Scott's hotel room. He knocks on the door; no one answers. He breaks in using the screwdriver part of his Pen Phone. Rude Buay rummages through the room and discovers an attaché case. He opens it. There's an African American Man's mask on top, underneath, stacks of Jamaican dollars. Rude Buay takes possession of the attaché case. Soon after, Rude Buay leans up against an iron rail at the Negril Dock, leisurely, viewing the coastline through binoculars. A Taxicab pulls up. Agent Scott gets out and steps into Rude Buay's space. Scott extends a hand. Rude Buay accepts. They shake as good buddies do.
Scott observantly asks,
"No fishing gear?"
Rude Buay answers,
"The bait shop has plenty available."
Scott sensing an intensity in his voice asks.
"Any new information on our manhunt?"
"Very little, since Banks' accident,"
Replies Rude Buay.
Scott, sarcastically,
"Yep. He helped us out a lot."
A small ship sails by in the distance. Rude Buay reaches for binoculars and surveys.

Rude Buay remarks,
"Somebody is trying to double-cross us, Scott."
Scott responds.
"Really?"
"Yep." replies Rude Buay.
"But why? We're here to clean up the mess."
'You think it could be Mildred?"
Rude Buay, asks.
"I thought that she was on our team," remarks agent Scott.
"Everyone seems to be until... "
Scott interrupts.
"They say you can never trust a woman."
Rude Buay ruminates.
"Not even Delilah."
Rude Buay resumes.
"You wouldn't sell out... would you?"
Scott, without hesitating, responds.
"You've known me since the first day of training. I wouldn't sell out on you or the administration."
Rude Buay punches him hard in the face. Scott loses his balance.
"Well you just did, partner," reminds Rude Buay.
Agent Scott struggles to get up and does. He successfully lands a punch into Rude Buays' stomach. Scott replies,
"You have no proof, Rude Buay."
Rude Buay gasp for air. Coughs and spits out blood. Scott comes at Rude Buay with a left hook and misses.

RUDE BUAY

"Proof? You've been gone for most of the time. Ever since that shoot out at the Villa, your time card has missed a lot of ink. Your tattoo is the signature of the Dragon Drug Cartel. I've got more."
Rude Buay, punches him in the face.
Scott retaliates.
"You are not my boss. He's..."
"The Cartel?" asks Rude Buay.
Rude Buay, hits him hard with a right uppercut. Then a left jab. Scott falls to the wooded dock thunderously. The attaché case now lays flat on the dock.
Agent Scott looks at the case suspiciously, then at Rude Buay. Rude Buay kicks attaché into Agent Scott's space.
"Open it, Scott." Commands Rude Buay.
Scott hesitates. Rude Buay reaches for his gun and resumes.
"That's all they paid you to be a rat?"
Rude Buay throws a left uppercut at Scott and misses. Scott with a resentful look to that name comes at Rude Buay swinging the attaché. Rude Buay ducks and the attaché' tumbles to the ground behind him. On impact, it opens up, displaying the mask and stacks of Jamaican currency. Scott gets that final look at the contents as Rude Buay shoots him, in the chest.
Scott falls to the ground and kicks several times to his death. Rude Buay picks up attaché, closing it, he heads towards his Hummer.

RUDE BUAY

On his way there, a car approaches, creating a roadblock. Ian Baynes jumps out.

"Put the attaché' down nice and slow, and drop your weapon Rude Buay."

"How convenient. I could not have planned this," states Rude Buay.

Ian releases safety on his gun.

"You've overstayed your welcome, agent Bascombe.

"Says who?"

"Alberto," replies Ian.

Rude Buay hesitates. Ian shoots at him. Rude Buay ducks to the ground. Laying flat on his back, he fires and shoots Ian in the groin. Ian, in pain, tries to get up. Another car pulls up. Axel jumps out from that vehicle and corners Rude Buay.

"Drop your gun and hand over the attaché! Who's paying you to be a pain in my ass, Rude Buay? The U.S. Government? I know that the government of Jamaica cannot afford too," States Axel.

"Why, because you put the brakes on their economy for your benefit and continue to kill innocent kids with contaminated Cocaine?"

Axel releases the safety on the gun. Rude Buay proceeds to comply.

Ian, regaining his composure, demands,

"Your gun, Rude Buay."

Rude Buay, drops the attaché case, spits out blood onto it. He aims the gun at Axel's head. His gun's jammed.

RUDE BUAY

Axel James whacks Rude Buay in the face with his gun. Rude Buay, falls over, then staggeringly gets up. Axel James not trusting him, asks,
"Who's picking up the tab?"
Rude Buay, refuses to enlighten. Axel hits him again. This time, he falls over thundering to the ground. He remains there. Axel removes a rag from his back pocket and sticks it inside Rude Buays' mouth. He removes Rude Buay's shirt and ties his hand behind his back with it.
Axel picks up the attaché' and Rude Buay's gun. He opens the rear door, throws them inside the car. He returns with some rope, which he uses to tie up Rude Buay. First, he ties the rope in his mouth, like a bit in a horse's mouth, then he ties his hands and feet. He drags Rude Buay to the back of the car and throws him in the trunk. He closes it and gets ready to drive off.
Ian heads to his car. Axel, yells out,
"Join me for the Kill!"
Ian accelerates towards his car and opens the rear door. A few blocks away, a white car, speedily approaches, pending a head-on collision with roadblocks. The car stops. Banks gets out with his bandaged left arm and removes the roadblock. He gets back in and drives away. Further up the street, he encounters the same scenario. This time he drives through clearing the obstacle. This time the car spins around with him almost losing control of it. He continues driving,

avoiding all traffic signs. Pedestrians dash out of the car's way.

Ian finally locates his bag of weed and then retrieves an Uzi from the rear seat of his car and jumps in the front passenger seat.

Banks car pulls up at the dock.

Walter Banks jumps out. He's just able to get a few rounds off at Axel's disappearing car. He gets back inside his car, and engages in a chase, unable to match the speed of Axel's automobile.

31

A HUMMER PULLS UP outside the Kingston Police Barracks. Mildred jumps out and scurries inside the building. A Jamaican Police Officer pushes his cup of coffee aside and hands Mildred an envelope marked fingerprints report. Mildred enthusiastically breaks the seal and examines the contents.
She says, "Thanks!" and leaves in a hurry.
The informed officer, with his eyes, stuck on her, yells. "Aren't you going to need some backup?"
"Thanks but I've got it under control from here on in." She darts outside.
Mildred, meets the Commissioner coming in. She hands him the folder. He opens it and reviews the fingerprints report. He cautions.
"You know as well as I know now, that we can't trust Agent Scott."
"I assure you that I'll get to the bottom of it." She

promises.

Richard Baptiste, appreciative of her commitment, declares,

"My job is on the line, Miss Simms! "

Mildred picks up folder and exits.

Mildred jumps inside the black Hummer and drives away.

Banks, previously noticing Rude Buay's car at the dock, maintain a suspicion that Rude Buay is inside that getaway car and continues in pursuit. He reaches into his breast pocket and pulls out his Pen Phone. He radios.

"Rude Buay come in. This is Banks."

There's no answer.

He continues,

"Rude Buay where the hell are you? We've dis-covered the Snitch."

Still no answer.

Banks aborts that call and dials Mildred's number.

Inside the hummer, Mildred picks up. She knows it's Banks.

"Mr. Banks, give me the good news!"

"News? The bad, the good or the ugly? The bad: Agent Scott's body rests at the dock. The Ugly: My car is in shambles after going through two separate roadblocks. The good: I am still looking for him, after having a shootout with Axel and Ian. Rude Bauy's vehicle was there but he wasn't there. I have a strong hunch that they took him captive."

Mildred asks.

"Or where else can he be?"

Banks replies.

"With the doctor."

Mildred is peeved.

"That's impossible." She declares.

Banks, mockingly,

"I'll bet you..."

Mildred responds.

"Did you call him on his pen phone?"

Banks states,

"No response."

"Let me call you back. If you hear from him before I do. Please ask him to call me." demands Mildred

Mildred aborts that call and dials. She is more peeved. She gets no answer and goes on a tirade..

"Rude Buay you need to pick up...You're a ... a disgrace to this country...the U.S. Government, the Deceiving Evil Administration. If this manhunt goes sour, your ass will rot in a Jamaican prison. Pick up or else...You flake."

Mildred stops outside a coffee shop. She gets out and goes inside.

MOMENTS LATER, Mildred sits at a table sipping coffee. Her Contractor walks in. He's dressed in Jamaican police uniform. She motions him to a seat at her table. Mildred surveys, and waits for privacy, then hands him an attaché' case. He opens it. It's loaded

RUDE BUAY

with stacks of E.C. Bills. He closes it. Mildred, eyes her Contractor as he leaves and commands.
"Finish her!"
Her Contractor takes off with it in a hurry.
At the Port Antonio Hospital, A tall Jamaican police officer parades the corridor. Dr. Tamara Ross, dressed in blue scrubs delivers a chart to the Nurse.
"Give this medication to Mr. Castello in an hour. Absolutely no visitors are allowed," The doctor admonishes.
The Nurse asks.
"That Baynes guy didn't wind up at the Morgue, huh? Could this be Voodoo?"
Tamara, informs her that:
"The Jamaican police are conducting their investigation."
She smiles deceitfully as Dr. Ross exits.
Crickets are creaking, as Tamara sits on the grass, next to the old breadfruit tree. Burning candles form a periphery around her. She holds up pictures of Mr. Castello towards the heavens. With eyes closed, she meditates.
The Contractor, disguised as Jamaican Police Officer shows up. He surveys. There's no sign of Tamara. He departs.
Back at the hospital, the Nurse is on the phone with Axel. She informs him.
"The doctor has just left for the Botanical Gardens."
Axel is ruffled, he can't stand the thought of the doctor

RUDE BUAY

escaping. He yells at the Nurse.
"Find her and finish her!"

32

WITH NOT MUCH SPACE to move around in the trunk of the car, Rude Buay uncomfortably tosses and turns, trying to break himself free from the ropes.
Tamara instantly receives an epiphany of her purpose in Rude Buay's life. She expediently blows out the candles and gets into her black BMW, driving away speedily. An Unmarked sedan pulls up. The contractor steps out. He surveys for the second time. He returns to his car and drives away.
A White van appears. The Nurse exits, gun in hand. She notices the candle's residue. Upset, she KICKS them over, returns to the white van, and makes a swift U-Turn.
Tamara glances in her rearview mirror as she senses being tailed. She is, so she speeds up.

RUDE BUAY

The Sedan with the contractor tailgates ferociously.
She nervously speeds up as panic sets in deeper and deeper.
The white Van turns a corner. It proceeds illegally in the opposite direction at high speed, focusing on a head-on collision. The Sedan is still in pursuit of the Tamara. Her BMW veers left speedily. The Van crashes head-on with the sedan, killing the Contractor and Nurse instantly.

INSIDE AN UNNAMED SHIP, in a black armchair, wrapped in a white sheet, sits agent Hudson. She has many bruises and concussions to her face and head. Her feet are tied together, with hands tied behind her back and duct tape, fastened over her mouth.
She tries desperately to PRY herself loose. Finally, she manages to break loose of the rope around her legs and makes baby-like steps as she drags the chair she's attached to, closer towards the door. Shelly enters from the deck and notices that Hudson has moved somewhat. She slaps Hudson in the face.
Denise and Agnes run down into the hull of the ship. Shelly slaps her again, grabs her by her hair, and tugs viciously. Hudson's head rocks back and forth complimenting the movements of Shelly's hand.
Shelly warns her:
"Don't even think about it, Bitch. If this happens again, we'll pluck out your ten fingernails, one every morning until..., and then we'll work on your toenails. We'll call

it the "Mani-Pedi-vicious-extract." You hear me?"
Agnes re-ties Hudson's feet tighter. She winches. Agnes pulls the rope tighter, thus adjusting her stance. She looks Hudson dead in the eye and declares boisterously:
"Do you have any idea what it's like living in jail? Bitch! "
Then she slaps Hudson, twice in the face, and continues.
"FYI, it stinks like hell; just like your feet.
They drag the armchair with Hudson on it, back to its original location. This time, Shelly ties agent Hudson's hair around a pole.
Denise stands to her left, Agnes to her right and Shelly, facing her, asks,
"Who is paying, to keep Rude Buay in
Jamaica?"
Hudson, surprised to be asked this question, says.
"I don't know what you're talking about."
Denise disagrees.
"She's lying!"
Agnes insinuates.
"You've worked with him for six years. You know how he squeezes his toothpaste."
Shelly, trying to break her down:
"Tell us. You know he sleeps around."
Hudson responds,
"I'm not seeing..."
Shelly, inquisitively asks.

RUDE BUAY

"Where does he live in Miami?"
"I'm afraid that I don't have the answer to your question," replies Hudson.
Outside on the deck, a lassoed rope dangles from the ship's mast.
Denise reflectively calls Hudson's attention to the rope.
"How would you like to be hung from the mast of this ship tonight?"
Hudson shudders.
A Blonde Woman walks in and hands over a stack of pictures to Shelly.
Shelly browses through the unique collection, asking,
"Who feeds information to Rude Buay from Colombia?"
To this question, she answers,
"I don't know."
Agnes not believing her asks,
"What do you know?"
Shelly agitated by Hudson's avoidance of supplying information, goes into her deep past -
"Bitch, who did your dad pay to take out my MAN in Bogotá?"
"I don't know what you're talking about."
Denise insinuates,
"You got this job based on nepotism, didn't you?"
"Let my dad rest in peace. I've paid my dues."
Shelly shows Hudson a Polaroid.

RUDE BUAY

"Who's this standing next to you?"
Asks Shelly.
"Ross! Dr. Tamara Ross."
Shelly removes a picture of Hudson, Hudson's daughter, Hudson's dad, and Rude Buay from the stack. She shows it to Hudson inquisitively.
"How old is she?"
Hudson refuses to answer.
Agnes fetches the tray with a pair of pliers and lint on it. She lays it on the table in front of Hudson. Agnes looking at Hudson's daughter evokes,
"We can use her as a Mule. Her granddad will tell us."
Agnes gets ready to extract Hudson's nail on her right index finger.
Alberto walks in. Shakes his head.
Agnes changes her mind and slaps her instead.
The three women untie her hair from the pole. They remove Hudson from the chair, bind her from head to foot with a rope, and attach weights to her legs.
Shelly hands a piece of paper to Alberto with Dr. Ross's name on it.
Alberto reminisces,
"We financed her education at the medical school in Grenada. The best in her class."
Then he looks at the clock, reaches for his cell phone, and dials, he's oblivious that Rude Buay is inaccessible.
Rude Buay's Pen Phone rings in the car trunk. He frantically tries prying himself loose.

RUDE BUAY

His Phone rings several times then stops.

33

MILDRED SIMMS GLIDES IN. Her office phone rings. She answers on the first ring. It's The Commissioner.
"Mildred Simms."
She senses something different in his voice.
"Oh, hi Mr. Baptiste."
He reports,
"The curfew's lifted. Tomorrow the carnival celebrations will begin under strict supervision."
She jumps up out of her chair. The phone's still off the hook. She is euphoric -
"Yes! Yes! Yes!"
(singing and dancing)
"It's carnival time again."
The streets of Kingston are teeming with trucks, carrying steel bands and masqueraders. Buses and minivans drop off passengers and make U-Turns to

accommodate those waiting to be brought into the city. The sound of steel pan music and calypso fills the atmosphere. People dance and wind up under the heat of the blazing sun. Steve, standing on top of a truck, plays music from his steel pan as a man possessed. Calypsonians and Reggae artists are singing their hearts out. It's masquerading galore! People dance to the calypso beat. The procession continues for several blocks. Music and more music fills the air.

ALBERTO DIALS FROM HIS CAR. Dressed in faded blue jeans, muscle shirt, ostrich boots, and a red bandanna, Salvador, in his mid-forties, of Colombian descent, picks up the phone.
Alberto commands,
"Hold the shipments for seventy-two and a half hours."
Salvador enlightens,
"Boss, too much traffic. Can't get through."
Alberto recommends,
"Instruct the truck drivers to postpone their pick up until after we dock."
Salvador whimpers,
"This cause mucha problema. The police, the police...You know?"
Alberto disapproves,
"What do I pay you for?"
Salvador butters up,
"You know I got your back boss...I fix it."

"Maricon! That's what you said when you used "Cyanide" to cut it."
Alberto chides before hanging up.

A CADILLAC DRIVES UP and stops in Compton, Los Angeles. Several customers rush out into the street, like passengers fighting for a yellow cab on a rainy day in New York City. One bargain hunter gets in and slams the door shut. The Cady takes off.
That Buyer drooling says,
"Can I get a kilo, Holmes?"
The Dealer ponders,
"Only half a kilo, dawg. It's going to cost you the same price as a regular kilo. You know that, right?"
"When is the rain going to fall?" asks the Buyer.
"Who knows? El Nino could be seriously delayed."
"If it doesn't soon, this place could turn into an inferno. Thanks!" he shouts.
He gives the cash to the Dealer. The Dealer hands over his last bag to the Buyer. The Cady stops, the Buyer opens the car door and exits in a hurry. The Cady continues on its way.

SEVERAL WOMEN DRESSED IN SCRUBS, masks, and surgical gloves, holding on to bed-pans wait in line in front of the restrooms at a Jamaican hotel. Teenagers join a line in front of the restrooms. The women serve them a pill and a glass of water. One by one, teens are escorted into stalls by an attendant carrying a bed-pan. Individual flushes follow minutes after each teen's exit. Women exit later carrying a covered bedpan.

Outside the hotel, the jaded kids re-board the bus, accompanied by two tour guides and a Hispanic woman, carrying an attaché case.

The Bus departs.

34

INSIDE THE CAR TRUNK, Rude Buay with his ear to the ground is still lying on his back. He battles against time, as he vigorously rubs the ropes that bind his hands against the metal hinge. Strands of frayed rope increase with the continued rubbing. Beads of perspiration running down his face, and into his mouth. Tirelessly, Rude Buay, keeps trying.

Finally, the rope severs. He rolls over from his back and onto his right side. Rude Buay reaches into his jacket pocket and pulls out his Pen Phone gadget. He proceeds to scan the trunk with it. A diagnostic Light flashes from the gadget. He then uses hands to grope in that direction. The agent tugs on the wire harness and peels away the sealed black electrical taping. He eyes the wires, so many of them; now he's confused.

The car gains altitude, going up a precipitous hill.

Rude Buay clicks on the pen section on the Pen Phone,

and out comes the screw driver portion. He utilizes it, stripping away the blue and then red wires on that wire harness. Now, he's more confused as he tries to decide which wires to unite. He closes his eyes then opens them.

The Car comes to a stop on top of the steep hill. Axel dials Alberto's number, envisioning a "Three Man Execution" of his kidnapper. Rude Buay, unites two wires. The car trunk pops open. He JUMPS out and scuttles down the mound.

Axel James opens the car door, upon noticing the shadows of the split-second movement of the car trunk. He and Ian Baynes release the safety on their guns and rush cautiously towards the back of the car. They look inside the trunk and over the embankments on either side, but there's no sign of Rude Buay. They get back inside the car peeved and speeds away.

Laying beneath the thick shrubbery over the mound, Rude Buay radios from his Pen Phone.

"Banks come in."

He dials from that phone in a hurry. There's no response.

Rude Buay sees a donkey tied to a stake. He unties the animal and gets on for a ride. The donkey begins to gallop and kicks him off. He gets back on, again it gallops kicking him off. He grabs the donkey by its right ear twisting it and forces a rope into its mouth creating a bit. Now controlled, he briskly rides *it* to a distant shack.

RUDE BUAY

At the shack, he notices a wrecked Land Rover parked in the yard. Rude Buay, jumps off the donkey's back and DASHES inside the jalopy. He hotwires it with his gadget. It cranks up. The noise attracts several barking dogs embarking on the property, in investigative pursuit. Rude Buay hit the road inside the vehicle.

RUDE BUAY

35

INSIDE THE UNNAMED SHIP, Alberto waits, staring at an unopened bottle of champagne in front of him on a table. Axle and Ian arrive empty-handed.
Alberto demandingly inquires –
"Where is our MAN?"
Axel James apologetically retorts,
"Boss, we've lost him."
Alberto advocates,
"The girls would not have..."
Axel challenges,
That guy is very slippery...
Ian Baynes interrupts,
That guy is unstoppable...
Alberto vetoing their incompetence -
Shoots Ian Baynes in the head.
"The girls don't think so, pieces of...

RUDE BUAY

INSIDE THE REARVIEW MIRROR, Rude Buay sees a black Hummer approaching. He stops the Land Rover abruptly on the side of the road and jumps out.

Rude Buay quickly removes his jacket, waves it in the air at the oncoming vehicle. The Black Hummer comes to a SCREECHING halt. He retrieves a gun from under his trousers foot and pulls the gun on the female driver. Surprisingly, it's Shelly Hall. The rear doors open. Out jump Agnes and Denise, with guns drawn. Shelly peers into his soul seductively. He feels the penetration but compartmentalizes in exchange for an aim at Shelly's head.

Rude Buay commands,

"Give up Hudson. End this ordeal!" Agnes, previously preoccupied with the white Mini Van parked several yards away, inches up closer toward Rude Buay in protest.

"Not a chance Rude Buay!"

"Stop this drug trade. You are destroying..."

Shelly proposing,

"We need your little Mildred Simms and Banks."

"Why?"

Asks Rude Buay.

Shelly declares,

"They are impeding traffic."

"They're the property of the Jamaican government."

Retorts Rude Buay.

"Help! Help!"

RUDE BUAY

A Voice echoes, from the vicinity of the white Mini Van.

Rude Buay's attention is drawn peripherally to the abandoned Mini Van. The three women's guns remain focused on Rude Buay.

Shelly, goes to the rear of her vehicle and fetches a five-gallon container. She opens it and immediately creates a broad wet gasoline trail leading towards the abandoned vehicle. On purpose, she pours some on Rude Buays' lower trousers and his shoes.

The cry for help coming from the abandoned vehicle intensifies. Denise releases safety on her gun. Rude Bauy, aims at Denise but gazes at the wet trail on and in which he stands.

Agnes moves into Rude Buays' space and whacks him behind the head with her gun. He falls to the ground. Before he could reciprocate, Denise whacks him with her gun. Rude Buay gets up, staggers. His gun is now wet after touching the ground. With one continuous kick, he sends their rifles sailing into mid-air. Their weapons fall back to the ground. Unfortunately, for them, their guns are now wet with gasoline. All four of them scuffle for the wet weapons. The scene turns into an impasse; everyone cognizant of the deadly effects triggered by a little spark.

Inside the Mini Van, Bazil Taylor, one of the tied-up government officials struggles to set himself free. He finally slips his right hand out of the noose.

Meanwhile, Rude Buay inches in closer towards the

abandoned vehicle. He slips, as a result of the incline and gasoline drenched surface. He regains his balance and knocks the pursuing Shelly to the ground. She gets back up. It turns into a fist fight, with Rude Buay gaining the upper hand.

Bazil Taylor is now out of the abandoned vehicle and comes crawling towards them on all fours. His feet are still tied to his right hand. Denise unties the malnourished Taylor and throws the rope to Agnes. Shelly is still engaged in hand to hand combat with Rude Buay.

Agnes catches the rope and twists it into a lasso. She throws it towards Rude Buay's neck and lassos him. She DRAGS him towards the hummer. Despite his fighting tactics, they manage to subdue him and throw him inside the SUV.

Denise grabs the three rifles and puts two in the Hummer. Shelly grabs one from her, dries it off with her red bandana, and jumps out. She gets ready to waste Taylor.

A white car pulls up and makes a swift U-turn. Every second count, realizing that they have Alberto's Man. So she aborts shooting Taylor and boards the hummer. Inside the white car, is the bandaged left arm man, Walter Banks. His eyes connect with the disappearing hummer, driven by Agnes. Taylor steps into view. Banks is not only breathing gasoline but the mud on his shoes is saturated with it.

Banks yells out,

"Mr. Taylor! Mr. Taylor! Mr. Taylor! You are alive! Those idiots."

Banks puts Mr. Taylor in the rear seat of his car. Before leaving the scene he rummages through the abandoned vehicle and discovers the other three ministers of government all tied up, yet still alive. He unties William Russell, Vince Laborde, and Michael Young. He puts them in his car. With a mixture of joy and sadness, he drives away from the scene.

ALBERTO SITS ON THE SHIP'S DECK, across from Axel. Axel focuses on his boss's gun pointing towards him. Alberto removes safety and perfects his aim. Two men, PEDRO and RAPHAEL, dressed in expensive business suits, white gloves, and sunglasses observe.

Agnes, Denise, and Shelly emerge, dragging Rude Buay. Alberto takes away his deadly aim,

Alberto signals Pedro and Raphael. They lift Rude Buay into a semi-upright stance. Rude Buay regains his presence of mind and realizes that he's now faced to face with ALBERTO.

Their eyes lock. The captive audience made up of Axel, Shelly, Denise, Agnes, Pedro, and Raphael looks on.

Alberto interrogates,

"Rude Buay. You've been a thorn in my side. You didn't keep your promise. OUT means I want you OUT."

Rude Buay inquires,

"Where's Hudson."
Alberto retorts,
"Her funeral? You wouldn't attend, Rude Buay."
Rude Buay recaps,
"You've killed innocent people including kids."
Alberto does not bat an eye.
Rude Buay continues,
"You are a menace to the Caribbean and all that it stands for."
Alberto reduces the effect -
"You killed that teenager when you were a kid. Sin is sin. Right? How's the doctor? Are you aware Rude Buay that I've funded her education."
Rude Buay surprised; he does not want to believe what he just heard.
Alberto continues,
"When you think pleasant thoughts of her you should always think of me."
He gets up, circles and punches Rude Buay hard in the face. Rude Buay falls over. He shakes it off and gets back up. Alberto hits him again. This time he stays down. Pedro grabs him and drags him down the steps into the hull of the ship.
There's no one there in the hull, except for tiny droplets of blood, scattered on the hardwood floor. Rude Buay stares at the bloodstains. Before he could bathe in his pain and sorrow, Pedro and Raphael quickly strap him into the same black armchair, previously occupied by Agent Heidi Hudson. Axel and Alberto enter.

RUDE BUAY

Alberto's cold as ice. Stands erect.
Alberto commands,
"If he moves, kill him."
He smilingly says,
"Goodbye Rude Buay! "
Pedro looks at Raphael in agreement. Nods, yes. Axel and Alberto head off in a hurry.

36

AXEL JAMES GIVES Alberto a tour of the city of Port Antonio. He looks across at his boss, sitting in the passenger seat.
"Boss, Shelly, and Agnes are anxious to join Denise if she would like to traffic again."
Alberto responds,
"Every agency is looking for them by now."
Alberto looks at his watch.
"When does our intestinal shipment arrive?"
Axel informs,
"The LA and Miami shipments have already cleared customs. No word yet on our next local shipment."
Alberto instructs -
"I need an update."
Alberto's phone rings.
Denise Gomez, sitting in her car outside Michael Manley Airport, bites her fingernails. She's not happy.

RUDE BUAY

"Hello," replies Alberto.
Denise reports,
"Pappy! Those three kids got sick and are held in custody at Michael Manley airport,"
"Conyo!" yells Alberto.
Continuing he questions,
"Where are you?"
"Waiting in my car outside the airport."
She replies.
Eavesdropping Axel James discloses,
"Salvador blew it!"
Alberto dials again.
Inside a tent filled with empty seats in Bogota, Columbia. Salvador answers his cell phone.
"Hello!"
" Salvador! I'll kill you and your whole... family,"
Threatens Alberto.
'Que pasa senor?"
"You're selling me out."
"No senor!"
"The kids got busted, Sal."
"I no tell nobody."
"How much are they carrying?"
Inquires Alberto.
"Two kilos senor."
"Overweight! Only one... kilo! "
Alberto frustratingly hangs up the phone, screaming out -
"Maricon! Maricon! Maricon!"

A few blocks away at the hospital, Dr. Tamara Ross, accompanied by her medical team of two Nurses, cuts through Junior Carlos' stomach wall. They remove several tiny packets of cocaine and lay them on a tray. The Commissioner walks in, stares at the tray and then at the patient. He's concerned. Junior Carlos begins to slip in and out of a coma.

One of the nurses checks the intravenous equipment attached to his forearm. It is secured. Tamara checks his pulse. Once, twice, three times. All eyes are focused on the heart monitor. The heartbeat is irregular. It continues to worsen. Finally, he stops breathing.

Tamara looks at the tray and exclaims,

"Tough kid!"

Commissioner Richard Baptiste shakes his head and walks out of the room.

37

BANKS AND MILDRED pull up outside the hotel. Mildred is driving an SUV and Banks is in his banged-up wreck. Several vehicles are double-parked, blocking the narrow street. They jump out and ZIGZAG their way through the cars, in a mad rush towards the hotel lobby.

Patrons mingle, some with drinks in hand. The music reverberates from the room close by. Banks and Mildred push through the crowd. They push open a door leading to the stairway. The intoxicated patrons react to their intrusion. A woman staring at them pulls out her cell phone and makes a call. Then she rejoins the party.

Mildred knocks on Rude Buay's door. There's no response. She fires and blows out the lock. Banks kicks in the door.

An open, half-empty suitcase is on the bed. There's no

sign of Rude Buay. Banks looks in the bathroom, while Mildred looks under the bed. He's not there. On the dresser is a framed portrait of Clifford, Rude Buay's brother, nestled alongside pictures of two ships - "The Tempest" and "Gomez." Banks clues in. They exit and rush through the exit door leading downstairs.

Shelly, Agnes, and Denise drive up. They enter the hotel in haste.

The already frazzled patrons are shoved out of the way by Denise, Agnes, and Shelly. They get onto the elevator, armed to the maximum. The elevator door closes. Simultaneously, the exit door opens. Mildred and Banks exit and rush outside.

They race to their vehicles and depart.

Patrons have gradually vanished, anticipating a showdown. Denise, Shelly, and Agnes get off the elevator, survey, and anger turns into fury. They rush outside. Banks and Mildred are nowhere in sight. They jump into their SUV and travel in the same direction.

Banks and Mildred arrive at the dock. They survey. Banks notices the ship "Ambassador" with a fresh coat of paint. They climb aboard with guns drawn.

Raphael is alerted. He reaches for his Automatic weapon. Just before he can get one-off, Mildred blasts him. He soars overboard.

Denise, Shelly, and Agnes' SUV arrive at the dock. They see Raphael fall overboard. They enter the ship with their weapons drawn.

Inside the hull of the ship, Pedro, responding to the

RUDE BUAY

sound of gunfire, leaves Rude Buay unguarded and goes to the ship's deck.

Pedro encounters Mildred and Banks. He shoots at them and misses. The three women, now on deck, are inching closer on Banks and Mildred's tail.

In the hull, Rude Buay tries hard to pry himself loose.

On deck, Denise, Agnes, and Shelly are now shooting furiously at Banks and Mildred. Banks returns fire, Shelly gets hit and goes down.

Banks turns around and shoots at Pedro, he misses. Denise shoots at Mildred, who goes to the floor, rolls over and shoots back at Denise. The bullet grazes her right leg.

Denise, falling to the ground, shoots back at Mildred, and misses. Mildred gets up in an attempt to get a shot off at Denise.

Denise shoots at her again. Mildred ducks, return to the floor and lies flat on her stomach. Mildred fires and shoots Denise in the leg. Denise accidentally falls overboard.

Rude Buay finally slips his leg out of that noose, with his tied hands.

Banks, at the duel with Pedro, eludes him. Pedro shoots back at Banks, and then at the emerging Mildred in a flash. He misses.

Banks and Mildred reposition themselves, aiming at Pedro, who positions himself in front of the entrance to the hull of the ship. Losing that aim Pedro searches for the perfect one.

RUDE BUAY

Rude Buay cuts his way out of the ropes. He picks up the armchair with both hands and heads towards the steps leading to the deck.

Pedro's attention is focused on Mildred, who continues to rain bullets in his direction. Rude Buay, now nearby, hits Pedro in his back with the chair.

Pedro falls backward into the hull of the ship. His gun falls out of his hand in the process. Rude Buay stands over him with the hoisted armchair.

"Where's Hudson?" Rude Buay inquires.

Pedro looks at him and doesn't reply. Rude Buay strikes him again with the chair.

"Where's she?"

Once again he does not reply.

Rude Buay, hits him again with the chair.

Pedro rolls over, this time he grabs Rude Buays' two feet, attempting to bring him down. Rude Buay stumbles. In the process he picks up Pedro's gun, and shoots him in the chest, killing him.

Rude Buay notices a door to a closed room in the hull. He turns the doorknob, swinging the door ajar. Inside, he discovers dozens of guns, stockpiled, a huge assortment of bullets, along with stacks of grenades in a corner. Additionally, there are two shelves with stacks of cash in various currencies. He grabs two of the guns, checks them to see if they're loaded with bullets. They are. He hurries to the deck, with guns in hand.

RUDE BUAY

Banks and Agnes exchange gunfire. Mildred reloads.
Shelly gets back up, staggering.
Rude Buay EMERGES. Both guns were drawn demanding -
"Drop the gun, Agnes. You're under arrest."
"Says who?"
She responds.
Rude Buay aims at her head.
"Where's Heidi Hudson?"
"I'm not your Bitch's keeper."
"Lead me to her and you'll go free."
"I'm not for sale Rude Buay."
She reaches for the pulley attached to a rope overhead and SWINGS it in Rude Buay's direction. He ducks.
She jumps overboard. Rude Buay dives into the water after her.
Shelly staggeringly regains her presence of mind and challenges Mildred into a fistfight.
Mildred drops her gun and takes her on.
Shelly shows her the "snake". Mildred shows her the "eagle". Banks observes as they go at it "karate style."
One kick from Mildred finally lands Shelly overboard.
Meanwhile, Denise does not resurface.
Rude Buay swims viciously in pursuit of Agnes. He sees her. Agnes somersaults and eludes him.
Shelly dives under, goes after Rude Buay.
Agnes emerges and grabs at Rude Buay's legs.
He senses her move and punches her in the face.
Her head rocks backward, she goes under.

RUDE BUAY

Rude Buay comes up for air and spits out a mouthful of water.

Shelly pursues him. He grabs her by the head and pushes her under. She kicks hard, gasping for air. Agnes resurfaces, and grabs hold of Rude Buay around his neck. He fights her off, thereby releasing his hold on Agnes, who at this point is drinking water like a fish. Shelly resurfaces, fatigued. He PUSHES her under; after she takes in many gulps of water, he releases her.

Jose Mendez, smoking a Cuban cigar observes from the dock. His eyes lock with Rude Buay's.

"Rude Buay, we've got bigger fish to fry. Who's left on board?" Mendez asks.

None of the women resurfaces. Rude Buay considers them drowned. So he climbs up out of water. He notices Mildred carrying two guns. He grabs one of the guns, and points towards the ship. Mendez tips his cigar, releasing some ash.

Mendez commands,

"That wouldn't be a good move Rude Buay."

Rude Buay is preoccupied.

"Still no word on AGENT HUDSON, huh? Rude Buay ignores him and SHOOTS viciously into the ship. Blowing it up into pieces. Mendez looks at Rude Buay with concern and continues.

"Hudson's not on that ship. Is she?"

Rude Buay does not respond. Instead, he looks around and realizes that he has a choice of who he rides with,

RUDE BUAY

Banks or Mildred. He gives both of them thumbs up. He chooses to ride with Banks in his banged-up car.

They take off, leaving Mendez standing at the dock with Mildred proceeding in tow.

Rude Buay begins rubbing his nose.

"Thanks. Is your car leaking fuel? And, how did you find me?"

Banks responds,

"I'll answer the second first."

"Banks, what if someone cut your...fuel line?"

Rude Bauy gets ready to open the car door. In the rearview mirror Banks notices, as Mildred takes a detour.

"Relax Rude Buay. You are safe. It dried from your feet but mine are still wet."

"Fill me in. Enough of the parables. 'When the student is ready the teacher appears.' "

Banks reciprocates,

"Well, your footprints were at the scene. And if they finished you off they had to be heading back to sea and this was the nearest port of escape. Plus Mildred and I, trying to find you, had to break into your hotel room. We saw your brother's photo on both ships owned by the cartel."

"Really... and Mr. Taylor?"

Retorts Rude Buay.

"I took all four of them to the hospital. They were treated and discharged."

"Four?"

RUDE BUAY

Inquires Rude Buay .
Banks fills him in -
"Russel and La Borde and Young were also in the back of this vehicle."
"Nice work...horse. I mean bloodhound. Great instincts! Dinner is on me. But first I need to stop at the Haddon Hotel."
Banks pulls up outside the hotel.
Rude Buay receives a text message on his waterproof cell phone.
TEXT READS: Received a tip - Alberto is at Sunset Shores. M.S.
Rude Buay says to Banks.
"Wait here. See who shows up. I'll be at Sunset Shores Hotel!"
Rude Buay get out of the car and catches a Taxi.

38

THE SOUND OF THE WAVES creates a musical ambiance for the oceanic backdrop at the Sunset Shores Hotel. Alberto and Axel, sitting in a suite, are joined by Carlos dressed in an expensive suit and dark sunglasses, along with a Blonde Woman. They sit around a table, drinking. Axel takes out a pack of 555 cigarettes from his pocket. He opens it, withdraws five from the box, lays them on the table.
Carlos strips the tobacco out of the five cigarettes, creating a heap.
Axel takes some cocaine from off a plate on the table, sprinkles the base onto the tobacco, creating half and half. He then feeds the cocaine laced tobacco back into the empty cylinders of paper until the cigarettes are

three-quarters packed. He twists the unfiltered end creating a closed valve.

Carlos lights a match and holds it under the cigarette to heat it. The cigarette is toasted gradually, as the oil from the base shows through the white paper. Carlos lights the cigarette and passes it first to Alberto. He takes a toke, passes it to Axel, who takes a toke and passes it to the Blonde, who takes a toke and burns her finger while she passes it to Carlos, who takes a toke.

Carlos feeling the buzz looks up at Alberto and asks,

"Don Alberto when do we sail?"

Alberto doesn't respond.

Carlos inquires -

"Manana?"

Alberto finally pays him some attention asking -

"Did you tie her down properly?"

Carlos is high as a kite.

"Si don Alberto."

The Blonde Woman intercepts -

"I didn't see him put holes in the ship."

Alberto winks at Axel. Axel pulls out his gun and shoots Carlos in the face.

The place becomes a bloody mess.

"Let's get out of here!"

Commands Alberto Gomez.

"Where too?"

Asks Axel.

"Hudson knows too...much,"

RUDE BUAY

Responds Alberto.

Alberto's phone rings. He answers,

"Hello!"

It's Shelly and Agnes.

"Alberto, the Ambassador has been destroyed. Rude Buay has once again escaped. He was last seen at the dock with Banks and Mildred. Your wife Denise is missing. She could be feared dead."

"Where are you?"

"Heading to Sunset Shores,"

Responds Shelly.

Alberto hangs up. He is not happy.

39

A TAXI DRIVES UP at Sunset Shores Hotel. Alberto, Axel, and Blonde Woman get in. The taxi drives to the Port Antonio dock. Alberto JUMPS out of the cab. He's FURIOUS.

Axel and the Blonde Woman exit the cab staring at the remains and simultaneously at their boss. Alberto sees a Catamaran speed boat docked on the other side. He heads in its direction. Axel and the Blonde Woman follow in Alberto's tracks.

With guns drawn, Alberto, Axel, and the Blonde Woman climb aboard. Three people: Tommy, Margaret and their teenage daughter Niki sit around a table enjoying a lobster dinner.

Alberto, Axel, and Blonde Woman move in. Before the family could take flight, bullets start raining on them.

RUDE BUAY

Bullets hit Tommy and Margaret, who soar over-board from the impact. Niki runs for cover. Axel follows Niki.

Alberto reminds Axel -

"Spare her, she's a hot commodity!"

Axel refrains from shooting her but maintains his aim. Axel heads into the cabin and cranks up the engine.

The Blonde Woman, playing team, runs ashore, loosens the rope which ties the ship to the dock, and makes her way back on deck. The Ship sails.

The Blonde Woman seeks out the teary-eyed Niki. Axel releases his aim on her and throws her a Snicker bar. Niki, scared, but deprived of her dinner, take a bite. The Woman reaches into her pocketbook, retrieves a hairbrush, and gently styles Niki's hair into a ponytail. Niki dries her tears. The Woman grabs some rope, attaches it to Niki's hair, and ties it to the mast.

Alberto is busy scanning the shores through a pair of binoculars.

Catamaran KICKS up white water.

SHELLY, DRIPPING WET at a phone booth,
dials in a hurry.

"I need a taxi at Hope Bay Terrace."

Momentarily, a taxi drives up. Shelly pulls the driver out of the taxi and places him under a chokehold, and pops his neck. The Cabbie falls to the ground to his death. Agnes comes out from behind the tree and takes the wheel, while Shelly accesses the front passenger seat. The Taxi drives away.

Shelly calls on Cabbie's cellular phone which she found inside the taxi.

Alberto's cell phone rings. He picks it up.

Agnes responds.

"We're heading to the Sunset Shores Hotel. Is our man there?"

"He's waiting for you. Hurry,"

Replies Alberto.

BANKS ENCOUNTERS PROBLEMS as he tries to get a signal on his laptop, outside The Haddon Hotel. Finally, he does, as he picks up video of Shelly and Agnes getting inside the taxi. He discovers that it was not in real-time. He catches up to speed and overhears their phone conversation.

Banks gets Rude Buay on the phone.

"Rude Buay, Shelly and Agnes just left the beach. They are heading to the Sunset Shores Hotel."

Rude Buay replies,

"Cover the Sunset Shores Hotel. I'm heading there too."

Banks arrives and waits in his car. A taxi pulls up. Shelly gets out and enters the hotel. Agnes continues the ride.

Banks picks up his phone and dials Rude Buay.

"Rude Buay, Agnes dropped Shelly off in a taxi."

"Did you get the tags?

"Yep. The license tag is H 29562. She's driving that thing like a maniac."

Rude Buay responds,

"Keep an eye on Shelly. Do not let her leave the hotel."

Rude Buay's car accelerates through the crowded night street. The Cab in question, leaves, heading in the opposite direction.

Rude Buay's SUV immediately makes a swift U-turn, in pursuit. Shooting at the taxi, he deflates the rear tires. The taxi slows up. Rude Buay hit it again, shooting Agnes in the neck.

The car collides into the wall, bursting into flames.

Rude Buay departs.

His Pen Phone rings.

Banks, on the other end, discloses,

"Rude Buay, Shelly just walked into the hotel. She's alone."

"Great! Hold on."

Rude Buay reviews a text message which he received earlier from an informant. On that list is the name Carlos Chavez, a guest at Sunset Shores Hotel.

"Banks, I need the profile on... Carlos Chavez."

Banks goes to work and pulls up the info from his laptop's database.

Banks discloses,

"A Former DEA, worked alongside two of your superiors, Bob White and Jose Mendez. He moonlighted as a prison guard, busted for cocaine possession in 2002, a master in disguise. He has a

RUDE BUAY

Miami address. Do you need it?"
"No. Awesome! Call the commissioner, ask him to send in backup."
Rude Buay responds as he pulls into the Hotel's parking lot.
In the hotel room, Shelly, almost unclothed, bruises on her body, rolls out of bed. She glances at her lover in bed, lying on his stomach. She strides to the bathroom.
Before getting out of the car, Rude Buay radios Banks.
"Banks I want you to stay put. I'll call you if I need you."
"What's up with that, are you a loner?"
"DEA business!"
Rude Buay meets his informant in the lobby and gives him a wad of cash. He hands Rude Buay a slip of paper with the room # 122.
Rude Buay moseys up to door. Disregarding the hanging no disturb sign. He aims at the lock with a silencer attached to his gun, and fires, blowing out the lock.
He kicks in the door.
On impact, Shelly darts out of bed, and grabs a gun from on top of the dresser, along with her lover's bulletproof vest. The man turns over in bed. A close up reveals him. It is Special agent Jose Mendez. Rude Buay is oblivious. He scuttles out of bed, turns off the lights and seeks refuge in the adjoining vacant suite.
Shelly hides behind the dresser. She pulls her blouse over the vest.

RUDE BUAY

Rude Buay enters, gun in hand. Shelly accidentally bumps into the dresser.

Rude Buay fires, a bullet penetrate the dresser and grazes against Shelly's gun holding hand. She loses control of it. The gun hits the floor. She's off balanced and tries to regain her presence of mind while lying on the floor. She succeeds and retrieves gun. Getting up she shoots at Rude Buay. He returns fire.

The bullet misses her as she hits the floor behind the dresser.

Meanwhile, bullets from other room come flying at Rude Buay. He turns in wonderment. Shelly shoots again. Rude Buay dodges and fires back at Shelly as he gets up. The bullet strikes Shelly in the chest, knocking her to the ground.

Rude Buay stares at her in admiration but shoots her again in the chest. She kicks a few times. Rude Buay thinks that he has taken her out with that last shot. Rude Buay hears the front door to the adjacent room open. He rushes through the front door to the hotel room.

He locates a light switch, turns on the light and peeps inside the adjoining room. It is empty. Peripherally he notices a shadow. He turns and gets a glimpse of a man's shadow going around the corner.

Rude Buay pursues the shadow, still ignorant of the performer's identity. As Rude Buay carefully grazes the wall, you can HEAR a pin drop.

Suddenly, he hears the sound of a gun reloading. It sounds just like his. Rude Buay checks his gun and proceeds with caution.

Mendez is now moving closer towards Rude Buay, in the same proportion as Rude Buay is moving towards him. If it wasn't for the 90 degree wall between them they would be shaking each other's hand.

Rude Buay gets off a random shot. So does Mendez. The shadows of their outstretched hands on the wall alert them to the tiny distance existing between both of them.

Rude Buay hugs the wall with the gun in his right hand and fires. The Bullet misses Mendez's ducking head.

Mendez purposefully goes flat on his stomach, gun in hand as he aims, waiting for Rude Buay to turn the corner.

Walter Banks, coming up the stairs, darts through the exit door, with gun in hand. He sees the perpetrator's backside. The man is lying flat on his stomach with his gun pointed in the opposite direction. The Exit door closes after Banks's entry. Rude Buay is alerted. Banks yells out,

"Rude Buay! Hold your fire. I've got him cornered!"

Mendez, responding to both sounds, rolls over on his back and shoots at Banks. The shot misses him. Rude Buay appears around the bend and yells,

"Banks, don't shoot! He is mine!" Mendez is still facing Banks with his back turned to Rude Buay. Rude Buay, still uncertain of the man's identity, commands -

RUDE BUAY

"Turn around you... prick!"

Mendez, sensing that two guns are now pointing at him, turns slowly. He is now facing Rude Buay, who castigates -

"Suit? Lies! Deception! Duplicity! Sabotage!"

"We're on the same team, Rude Buay."

"We are?" asks Rude Buay.

"We've always been."

"Really? Where's Hudson?"

"You should be answering that question, Rude Buay... You turned her over to Alberto. She stood in your way." Mendez responds.

"Which way?" inquires Rude Buay.

"Your promotion. You brought her to the Caribbean so that you could orchestrate her kidnapping." responds Jose Mendez.

Banks eyes Rude Buay and then Mendez. Not trusting anyone, he's aiming at both men. Is this what I came out of retirement for? He reasons.

Mendez continues,

"How much did Alberto pay you and how much more did you agree to pay Carlos Chavez for all of this?"

"Nice try. You know what, Boss? You stand in the way of my promotion. So I'm going to have to cap you. Then I'll find Alberto and cap him. Then..."

"Do you think that Alberto is going to fall into your trap. You'll never catch him. He's invincible," Interrupts Mendez.

Rude Buay aims at Mendez's head, motioning him to

get down on his knees. He does.
"If you kill me, the parasites that devour my body will tell me. You'll never catch Alberto."
Rude Buay retorts,
"The record states that You've killed off several Colombian Officials in the 1990s and gave Alberto Gomez control of the most vicious Colombian Cartel. Etched his name and signature. Claiming that it will be so hot. All five oceans wouldn't be able to cool it."
Rude Buay continues,
"Off the record, I'm about to release that DAM, Jose. Drop your weapon!"
Mendez shoots at Rude Buay, and misses. Rude Buay fires, shooting Mendez in the head. Mendez kicks and stops breathing. Rude Buay confiscates his gun. Looking at it, he declares,
"In every arena, there's a need for great teams. Men and women would become champions if they committed to playing team."
Rude Buay and Banks make a B-line to inside Shelly's hotel room.
They rummage through the room. Rude Buay discovers an attaché case with the initials: JM. He pries it open and throws everything out on the bed. He delves through the contents, while Banks observes.
List of recovered items:
1. A shotgun
2. A pair of binoculars.
3. A miniature camera.

RUDE BUAY

Pictures of:
1. Rude Buay and Tamara cuddled up on the beach.
2. Rude Buay struggling with Shelly in the water at the dock.

Rude Buay notices Axel's name on the back of one of Mendez's business cards with phone number 876-362-0800 Ext. 27.

He hands it to Banks.

Banks responds instantly,

"This Hotel!"

They throw the evidence back inside the attaché. Toting it along, they leave in a hurry.

Rude Buay and Banks approach room # 27. A no disturb sign hangs from the doorknob. Rude Buay blows out the lock with a bullet. He enters, followed by Banks in tow. They react to the strong stench. Lying on the ground soaked in blood is Carlos Chavez. There's a gunshot wound to the head. Rude Buay rolls him over and discovers the dragon tattoo behind his right ear. A flashing infrared light directs Rude Buay to a cell phone inside Carlos's breast pocket.

Rude Buay removes the phone. Their attention is then drawn to the four-chair dining table. On it lies the residue from a free-basing session. Banks collects the leavings.

Rude Buay toys with Carlos' cell phone. First with the camera wallet. Several thumbnails exist. Rude Buay searches through the pics.

Pic # 1: A close up of Warden Culligan's corpse.

Pic # 2: The Ambassador.

Pic # 3: Warden Ralph Bullock's house.

Pic # 4: A close up of Warden Ralph Bullock.

Pic # 5: Agent Hudson bound with ropes in a dinghy.

Rude Buay goes to a full screen on the thumbnails. Next, he accesses the phone book. Two phone numbers for Alberto Gomez pops up. Rude Buay dials the first one. There's no answer, so he tries the second number.

"Hello, this must be good news!"

Answers Alberto.

The sound of a boat's engine and that of waves splashing against a huge object is heard in the background.

Rude Buay quickly hangs up. He exits, departing with Walter Banks.

An SUV pulls into the driveway, followed by Jamaican police. Mildred steps out, almost colliding with Rude Buay and Banks.

Mildred articulates,

"The hotel called saying that you were on the premises. Where's Axel? Is he finished?"

"We're about to find out," Replies Banks.

Several Jamaican police cruisers with flashing lights have blocked the entrance to the driveway making it a hazardous exit.

Mildred jumps inside Banks' jalopy. It is fully loaded with wiring and gadgetry. Jamaican police officers, already having entered the building on foot, return, responding to tooting horns. They clear the entrance of

RUDE BUAY

parked police cruisers. Rude Buay manages to turn his car around speedily. They drive away at top speed to the dock.

The two cars pull up parking precariously. They jump out, proceeding hurriedly on foot.

A Native administers some serious elbow grease as he polishes a blue and white 400 SuperSport speedboat.

Rude Buay demands,

"DEA, we need to use your boat."

The Native looks at him like he's crazy.

Mildred supplicates,

"Come on! We'll return it."

The Native, checking out Mildred's physique articulates,

"Not even my wife gets behind this wheel..."

Rude Buay pulls out his gun on the native exclaiming "This is a rescue mission. We don't have time to explain. Don't make me have to force you to..."

The Native disembarks.

Rude Buay, Mildred, and Banks jump in.

Banks grabs the wheel. The boat takes off careening between other ships at the dock.

Native yells,

"You return it one scratch...mon you'll be...dead meat!"

In afterthought, he continues,

"It's almost on empty! "

Rude Buay asks,

"What did he say?"

RUDE BUAY

Mildred holding on tightly to the rail answers, " Something like…don't bring it back on empty. His patois is awful."

RUDE BUAY

40

THE 400 SUPERSPORT picks up speed as it travels through the waters of Jamaica's north coast. A Jamaican police helicopter follows overhead.

Inside this speedster, Rude Buay and Mildred scan the coast with aid of binoculars. Rude Buay answers to the ringing of his Pen Phone.

It's The Commissioner.

"Rude Buay, we've given you all that we've got available. "

Rude Buay looks up in the distance, acknowledging the helicopter.

"The man found dead at the dock was identified as sailor Tommy Clarke and his wife Margaret, owner of the missing Catamaran. Autopsy results indicate that they could have been killed less than thirty hours ago," Informs The Commissioner.

Rude Buay rejoins Banks who's enjoying the machinery.

"They could have already made their escape to Colombia. They have got a huge head start on us. How fast can this thing go?

Banks looks at the gauge meters, showing signs of uneasiness.

"What's the fuel capacity on this...?"

"It says, two hundred and fifty gallons," Indicates Rude Buay, after which the fuel gauge grabs his attention.

" It's on empty. So is the reserve tank."

He continues,

"Where can we refill?"

Mildred walks in, binoculars in hand, comments,

"Are we really on empty?"

"We're eight miles from land,"

Indicates Walter Banks.

A ship heading in the opposite direction passes nearby, leaving a trail of water, causing a huge undercurrent. The SuperSport gets caught up into that current, creating maneuvering problems for Banks. Rude Buay and Mildred grab onto the rail to avoid losing balance. Mildred informs,

"Making this stop is going to cause us to lose those bastards. I want Axel's head served up on a... platter."

Rude Buay responds,

Would that make them the property of the Colombian

RUDE BUAY

government?"

"They could refuse to release them to us,"

Banks cautions.

"How much faster can this thing go?" Banks asks, with Cuba now close-in view.

Rude Buay replies,

"The faster we go. The more fuel this rocket consumes. Inside the Jamaica Helicopter overhead, the pilot adjusts his binoculars stating,

"We've spotted the Catamaran off the coast of Cuba."

"There's not enough time for us to refill in port,"

States Rude Buay.

Banks radios,

"400 SuperSport heading south, five miles off the Island Cuba, requesting assistance! Running low on fuel. I repeat: We're running low on fuel."

Suddenly the engine stops and the boat begins to drift. In Port Antonio, a Pickup truck pulls up at the wharf. The Jamaica Helicopter, circles overhead. Two natives hurriedly secure the laden gas container inside of the helicopter's lowered net. The Copter takes off in assistance.

The Copter attempts to lower the container unto the 400 SuperSport. Rude Buay tries to grab it. High tide creates treacherous waves causing the ship to drift from underneath the descending net.

Copter flies right, making another attempt. Another wave rocks the ship further right, making that drop off more difficult.

RUDE BUAY

Meanwhile, the Catamaran picks up considerable speed heading north. Axel helms the ship, while Alberto and the Blonde Woman engage in a free-basing session on deck. Niki observes. Two Automatic weapons resting in the men's arms extend onto the table. Looking through his binoculars, Alberto spots a dinghy adrift in the distance. His curiosity increases as he zooms in for clarity.

"That could be Hudson!" he remarks.

The dinghy's passenger continues waving a portion of a sheet to the distant, rapidly approaching Catamaran. The 400 Super Sport continues to drift briskly further as the waves continue to rise higher and higher. The Copter comes in for its third attempt. Before the depositing of the container on board the 400 SuperSport, the Co-Pilot notices the catamaran, up ahead, traveling at runaway speed.

The Pilot unites the net with the 400 SuperSport. Rude Buay fetches the container and immediately starts the refueling process.

The Helicopter's Co-Pilot reaches for his pair of binoculars. He sees not only the Catamaran in the lenses but the dinghy, sailing away, with someone in it, waving a large piece of fabric.

He reports -

"We've spotted the missing Catamaran cutting water towards Cuba. There's someone in a dinghy ahead of it, waving for help."

RUDE BUAY

Rude Buay FIRES up the engine and takes over the wheel.

Mildred joins Rude Buay in the helm seat. She is armed with her 350 magnums.

Banks survey the coast from the cockpit, binoculars in one hand and gun in the other.

The SuperSport begins CUTTING water at an increase of speed.

The Catamaran continues sailing at a step it up speed. The Helicopter up above progresses with increased velocity.

Axel draws Alberto's attention to the dinghy still drifting at sea. A woman's image is now visible. The Blonde Woman onboard the catamaran grabs a pair of binoculars and zooms in. Realizing that it's Heidi Hudson she exclaims -

"That bitch is still alive?"

The sound of the approaching helicopter, changes the mood, as three binoculars are tossed aside in exchange for automatic weapons. Alberto, Axel, and the Blonde are now engaged in a shootout with (a) the helicopter pilots, (b) firing simultaneously at the dinghy. Niki tries desperately to untie herself from the mast. The Blonde Woman notices her planned getaway and aims at Niki yelling,

"Don't you dare."

Niki retreats. The Catamaran's engine is *turned* off.

The tide favors it and it pulls away from the 400 SuperSport still trapped in its rapids.

RUDE BUAY

The Dinghy continues to drift. Gunshots begin to rain down onto the Catamaran from the Helicopter overhead. The exchange of firepower continues. Axel and Alberto retreating with several rounds. None of these bullets make contact with the helicopter though. Moving full speed, the 400 Super Sport's gaining momentum on the Catamaran.

The Catamaran is now in a comfortable shooting distance from the supersport. Rude Buay, Mildred and Banks proceed with the onslaught. Several bullets ricochet onto the Catamaran.

A Bullet from Mildred's gun hits the Blonde woman, explosively. She hits the deck hard. Her breath dissipates from her body.

Axel and Alberto return fire onto the 400 SuperSport, missing everything but the water.

The Dinghy with the lone, tired, sunburnt agent Hudson, is now in close view.

Alberto shoots at her. The Dinghy rides the huge wave causing him to miss, but puts a gaping hole into its left side.

Water begins to seep through, filling up the dinghy. Hudson is discombobulated.

A helicopter swoops down, lowering its net for agent Hudson. She reaches the net like it was the last straw, amidst the continued shooting between the DEA agents and the two drug lords. She is unsuccessful.

Axel gets back to helming the Catamaran, speedily.

He desperately tries to create some distance between it

and the SuperSport.

Rude Buay returns to the helm seat.

The 400 SuperSport picks up speed, in pursuit. The swift movement of the water, enhanced by the water current caused by both ships, washes away the dinghy, as soon as Hudson successfully grabs onto the net. The Helicopter briskly departs from the area with agent Hudson holding onto the net. Alberto shoots excessively at the rescued agent Hudson. He misses his target as he competes with the wind's trajectory. Rude Buay continues to shoot at Axel and Alberto from the helm seat. Banks moves to the bow, in an attempt to secure his stance. He is off-balanced but shoots desperately at Alberto, who's stationed in the Catamaran's cockpit.

Several bullets from Alberto's gun intended for Banks strikes the 400 SuperSport, damaging it. Banks retaliates with several rounds.

Bullets severely penetrate the Catamaran. One of the bullets brushes against Alberto's leg. He's off-balanced. More bullets rain, hitting the Catamaran's mast, grazing close to Niki.

"No. Please! No!"

Screams Niki.

Niki's screams aren't heard. Rude Buay, Mildred and Banks are oblivious that she is aboard. They continue to shoot aggressively at Alberto and Axel.

A huge wave pushes the Catamaran out of focus. Bullets from the 400 SuperSport miss that ship. Alberto

returns fire. A Bullet from his gun hits Banks in his left upper arm. He goes down. Mildred runs to his aid. He's still breathing. But aching severely.
Rude Buay evens the score, blowing out several portholes. A series of waves rock the punctured Catamaran. Pushing it closer to a "run ashore" collision on the Island of Cuba.
Axel emerges with Niki as his human shield. A huge wave hits the Catamaran.
Niki screaming hysterically,
"Don't kill me! You son of a bitch!"
Mildred eyes Rude Buay as he aims for Axel's head. The movement of the boat makes it tough to maintain the focus of the bullet's trajectory.
Axel points his Automatic weapon towards Niki's head. Her screaming intensifies.
Rude Buay emerges closer on deck. He, eyes Mildred assuredly. He shoots. Instead, a bullet from Axel's gun hits Rude Buay in his chest. He falls onto the deck.
Mildred keeps dodging Axel's bullets. Rude Buay with blood on his vest, rolls over onto his stomach and gets a good aim at Axel. Discharges.
The bullet HITS Axel right between his eyes. He falls backward thunderously onto the deck. Niki falls forward into the deep.
A mountain-like wave beckons. It hits the Catamaran viciously. Alberto, dressed in a wet suit jumps over board into the wave, unnoticed by everyone on the other ship. The Catamaran sails speedily towards an

RUDE BUAY

unavoidable collapse onto the island of Cuba.

Mildred dives into the deep, and clutches Niki around her neck. Rude Buay throws out the life rope. Mildred catches it. Rude Buay reels them in.

Another mountainous wave hits the Catamaran, it slams into Cuba at full speed, bursting into flames, debris, spikes, and fragments of lumber.

THE HOSPITAL LOBBY IS CROWDED with Jamaican police officers. Banks is pushed around in a wheelchair with his left arm in a sling. The Police commissioner, Mildred, and Rude Buay admire compassionately. Rude Buay walks up to Banks and hands over an attaché. Banks opens it. He smiles upon seeing the stacks of crisp C notes. He closes the attaché, gives Rude Buay a thumbs up and departs. Agent Hudson walks out from the discharge room, accompanied by Tamara. Rude Buay greets agent Hudson smilingly. They turn to leave.

Richard Baptiste steps into their space, and utters -

"Thanks, Rude Buay."

"My pleasure,"

Says Rude Buay.

Tamara rushes past the commissioner, right into Rude Buay's space. Their eyes become locked momentarily. Mildred moves closer towards Rude Buay, scrutinizing her.

"Rude Buay, you forgot something," says Tamara.

"My vest!"

She flies into his arms. Mildred eyes them enviously.

ALBERTO STANDS OUTSIDE the Medical School in Grenada dressed in an expensive business suit and dark glasses. Clipboard and pen in hand urging -
"Sign up for educational funding!"
Several enthusiasts form a line in response.

SHELLY AND DENISE JUMP INSIDE a waiting Jamaican taxi.

ABOUT THE AUTHOR

John A. Andrews, screenwriter, producer, and author of several books, founded Teen Success in 2009. Its mission statement: *To empower Teens in maximizing their full potential to be successful and contributing citizens in the world*. As an author of books on relationships, personal development, and vivid engaging stories, John is sought after as a motivational speaker to address success principles to young adults. John makes an impact in the lives of others because of his passion and commitment to make a difference in the world. Being a father of three sons propels John even more in his desire to see teens succeed. Andrews, a divorced dad of three sons ages 14, 12 and 10, was born in the Islands of St. Vincent and the Grenadines. He grew up in a home of five sisters and three brothers. He recounts: "My parents were all about values: work hard, love God and never give up on dreams."

Self-educated, John developed an interest in music. Although lacking formal education he later put his knowledge and passion to good use, moonlighting as a disc jockey in New York. This paved the way for further exploration in the entertainment world. In 1994 John caught the acting bug. Leaving the Big Apple for Hollywood over a decade ago not only put several national TV commercials under his belt but helped him to find his niche.

His passion for writing started in 2002 when he was denied the rights to a 1970's classic film, which he so badly wanted to remake. In 2007, while etching two of his original screenplays, he published his first book "The 5 Steps to Changing Your Life" Currently he's publishing his fifteenth volume, while working on empowering teens worldwide.

In 2008 he not only published his second book but also wrote seven additional books that year, and produced the docu-drama based on his second book, *Spread Some Love (Relationships 101)*.

See Imdb: http://www.imdb.com/title/tt0854677/

RUDE BUAY

"Ask not what your country can do for you - ask what you can do for your country."

- John F. Kennedy

www.famousquotes.me.uk/speeches/John_F.../5.htm

FOR MORE ON
BOOKS THAT WILL ENHANCE YOUR LIFE ™
Visit: **A L I**
www.AndrewsLeadershipInternational.com
EMAIL US
www.JohnAAndrews.com

*Rude Buay is a drug prevention chronicle about teens caught up in the war on drugs and contains content for adults; parental discretion is advised for children.

A 2010 Books That Will Enhance Your Life. All Rights Reserved.

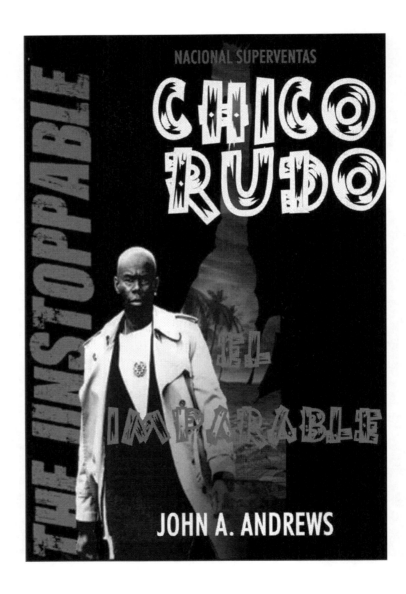

RUDE BUAY

RUDE BUAY ... THE UNTOUCHABLE

RUDE BUAY

RUDE BUAY

... The Untouchable

An Original Story
By
National Bestselling Author
John A. Andrews
Creator Of:
The Rude Buay Series

| RUDE BUAY VOL. II

Copyright © 2011 by John A. Andrews.

All rights reserved. Written permission must be secured from the publisher to use or reproduce any part of this book, except for brief quotations in critical reviews or articles.

Published in the U.S.A. by
Books That Will Enhance Your Life™

**A L I - Andrews Leadership International
Entertainment Division®
Jon Jef Jam Entertainment®**

Cover Design: John A. Andrews
Cover Graphic Designer: A L I
Edited by: Prof. Harminder Kaur
ISBN: **9780983845775**

| RUDE BUAY VOL. II

Other Titles By:

John A. Andrews

Dare To Make A Difference – Success 101 For Teens
When The Dust Settles - A True Hollywood Story
Total Commitment - The Mindset of Champions
How I Wrote 8 Books In One Year
Whose Woman Was She?
The FIVE "Ps" For Teens
Cross Atlantic Fiasco
&
Quotes Unlimited

RUDE BUAY VOL. II

TABLE OF CONTENTS

CHAPTER ONE 8
CHAPTER TWO 12
CHAPTER THREE 15
CHAPTER FOUR 19
CHAPTER FIVE 22
CHAPTER SIX 28
CHAPTER SEVEN 33
CHAPTER EIGHT 38
CHAPTER NINE 43
CHAPTER TEN 51
CHAPTER ELEVEN 56
CHAPTER TWELVE 61
CHAPTER THIRTEEN 65
CHAPTER FOURTEEN 69
CHAPTER FIFTEEN 74
CHAPTER SIXTEEN 78
CHAPTER SEVENTEEN 83
CHAPTER EIGHTEEN 87
CHAPTER NINETEEN 92
CHAPTER TWENTY 96
CHAPTER TWENTY-ONE 103
CHAPTER TWENTY-TWO 107
CHAPTER TWENTY-THREE 112
CHAPTER TWENTY-FOUR 115
CHAPTER TWENTY-FIVE 120
CHAPTER TWENTY-SIX 124
CHAPTER TWENTY-SEVEN 129
CHAPTER TWENTY-EIGHT 136
CHAPTER TWENTY-NINE 142
CHAPTER THIRTY 147
CHAPTER THIRTY-ONE 151
CHAPTER THIRTY-TWO 154
CHAPTER THIRTY-THREE 158
CHAPTER THIRTY-FOUR 162
CHAPTER THIRTY-FIVE 167
CHAPTER THIRTY-SIX 172
CHAPTER THIRTY-SEVEN 175
CHAPTER THIRTY-EIGHT 179

RUDE BUAY VOL. II

"I firmly believe that any man's finest hour, the greatest fulfillment of all that he holds dear, is the moment when he has worked his heart out in a good cause and lies exhausted on the field of battle - victorious"

- VINCE LOMBARDI

http://thinkexist.com/quotation/i_firmly_believe_that_any_man-s_finest_hour-the/173395.html

The RUDE BUAY Series

RUDE BUAY VOL. II

Vol. II

1

A dense mixture of blackened and gray clouds open up to sparse streaks of lightning, followed by severe and intense intermittent thunderstorms. Torrent rain showers burst out of those sporadic illuminated clouds as a follow up to the rumbling fiery interlude. Meanwhile, trees sway noisily, splitting into halves at their trunks, sending splinters of timber flying in the distance.

Additionally, the downed power lines, and the uprooting of multiple plants, seem to indicate that whatever is about to happen in Port Antonio, Jamaica, on this mid-Friday afternoon is more than just a severe rainstorm.

It could equal or top the destruction of Port Royal back in 1692.

"Could this be *Déjà Vu* or what some may call voodoo? These inclement weather conditions are not felt elsewhere, not even in another parish on the Island. Weather conditions have not been this severe since Mount St. Helens blew its top sending trees downstream or since the destruction of Port Royal in 1692." One enthusiastic yet subdued radio announcer with a sophisticated British twang, candidly remarks.

Patrons at a Port Antonio restaurant, not only hear and watch the news but feel the earth tremble continually and intermittently for several minutes, while the sea roars like a hungry lion, adding to mother nature's audio effects.

Meanwhile, at sea, high magnitude waves boisterously crash against protruding rocks and the battered shoreline.

Small crafts sway as they get tossed back and forth by the wind. Some crafts under duress, even sever the ropes which ties them to the small wooden dock. HUGE waves, forms in succession. Sand, gravel and the last waves' deposits are removed from the shore, and then viciously REDEPOSITED on the debris saturated beach.

Nervously and securely docking his boat, a frazzled American Sailor senses futility as the dock which held his forty-foot *Casper* collapses. The raging storms eventually and hastily send his small vessel and others alike into the now tsunami-like waves of the ocean.

While watching his boat tossed away in the current, the Sailor; like the enthusiastic famous crocodile catcher from Australia; fights the treacherous waves as he swims back to shore in an investigative pursuit of the human carcass which just washed ashore.

The sailor rushes to the beach as the waves drawback. With his hand covering his nostrils, he runs over to the mostly decomposed body in investigative pursuit. The body is motionless. The sailor gets a close up of the man's corpse. In the corpse's left hand tightly clenched, he bears the leg portion of a multicolored wet suit. The Sailor, not only drenched but remains startled by the dramatic unfolding toxic scene.

In the subsequent moments, the rain recedes as a long extended rainbow decorates the flustered, angry, still overcast cloudy sky.

The Sailor embraces the opportunity to call 911 using his rubber cased protected cell phone, retrieved from his seat pocket.

He enthusiastically yells into the device, drowning out the sound of the waves. His voice echoes in the distance.

"...My boat *Casper* is gone! All the boats have been pulled out to the ocean. A man, a dead man! I swear, so dead he filthy rots. The corpse sports a dragon tattoo behind his almost decomposed right ear lobe. He looks multi-ethnic-mixed, could be of Hispanic descent, in his mid-forties. He has a missing index finger and expensive gold rings on the four fingers of his right hand. In his tightly clenched left fist is a wet- suit. His grasp on it is so tight not even the rough seas had a chance to dislodge this object from his lifeless hands. What an ... eclipse!"

MOMENTS LATER, FLASHING LIGHTS accompany the coroners' vehicle, with Jamaican Police vehicles in tow. It races to the scene. The medics quickly place the "washed ashore human body" in a body bag and haul it away aboard coroner's transport.

2

In the interim, retrospectively over a thousand miles away, it is a beautiful sunny day in St. Georges, Grenada. The local TV weatherman takes his reporting to another level by boasting the clarity of the sky and the warm water beaches in and around the capital city. This much smaller Island to the south is nestled between St. Vincent and the Grenadines a group of 32 Islands, neighboring Trinidad and Tobago, two Islands in the Greater Antilles.

In the meantime, the brisk wind coupled with the heat extracts the spicy aroma from a variety of produce. In particular, those been transported to the market by late vendors in pickup trucks.

The savory spicy fragrances saturate the air. Ships, arriving and departing toot their horns as they signal their mix with the sailing traffic.

A few blocks away, several people including a priest and other dignitaries congregate. ALBERTO GOMEZ, drug Czar, and leader of the Dragon Drug Cartel emerge. The man who was once assumed dead after a most recent *high-seas* shoot out with DEA agent Rude Buay, back in Jamaica.

Alberto is dressed in an expensive business suit and dark glasses. He is the mid to late 30s, and Colombian descent. The Drug Czar is poised with a pair of scissors in hand.

"Ladies and gentlemen today we celebrate a new landmark in the history of the Caribbean. This library stands as a cornerstone to the men and women...of tomorrow. What good is a man if he ducks ... his education? Worthless! Your children's future has never looked brighter."

Alberto addresses,

He cuts the ribbon to the sound of a standing ovation, and applause, accompanied by a brief interlude of steel band music.

The librarian, a Caucasian woman in her early 50s, wearing spectacles, and proudly displaying her name tag: VERONICA TOWNSVILLE, saunters across and proudly shakes Alberto's hand.

DAVID LEE, Entrepreneur and Asian Drug Czar, wearing an expensive suit and dark sunglasses, AMBLES through the crowd.

David hands Alberto a slip of paper.

Alberto reads the handwritten note and accompanies David back to his car.

They embark.

The car driven by Lee takes off SPEEDILY.

3

Just a few blocks AWAY, at the Grenada Medical School, the car pulls up.
Alberto Gomez steps out of the car.
The car continues.
With a clipboard and pen in hand, Alberto urges the students charismatically
"Sign up for educational funding! The future of your country, rest in your hands, not in your government."

It's not long before he attracts an enormous crowd. Amongst the gathering, several enthusiasts line up and eagerly sign up in response to his plea.

In the crowd, AMANDA KINGSLEY stands out. Amanda is African American, in her late 30s. Amanda softens her stern demeanor as she looks out at the growing line of candidates, all waiting to benefit from her boss' financial aid program. Alberto makes eye contact with her. She evolves and with sophistication handles the dense crowd.

After satisfying the many would-be students Alberto and Amanda depart.

Smiles from that upcoming medical fraternity sweeten the two organizers goodbye.

Alberto and Amanda board a waiting taxi.

A black limousine pulls up moments after the taxi drives off.

Agent Randy Bascombe, nicknamed *RUDE BUAY* - aka "Rude Boy" is of Jamaican descent. He exits the car from the rear seat on the driver's side. He's, in his early forties, adorned with a scorpion tattooed on his bald head, with its fangs upstaging his forehead, and a tail extending towards his right earlobe. Dressed in street clothes, he steps out.

The agent is oblivious that Alberto Gomez and his team have left the building. So he waits in anticipation of Alberto's exit from the medical compound. Alberto is a no show.

To Rude Buay, from the way things look on the outside, everything indicates it's a normal day at any school. Even so, he enters the compound.

A Guard meets and greets him.

"Are you looking for someone?"

The guard asks.

"Where is your restroom?"

Rude Buay inquires.

The guard accommodates nonchalantly.

Rude Buay visits the facility, noticing nothing rather unusual he departs and re-boards the waiting limousine. The limo waits. Rude Buay dials DEA headquarters in Miami.

MICHAEL ORTIZ, in his early 50s replacing the snuffed out Jose Mendez Rude Buay's former boss picks up the phone.

"This is Rude Buay,"

"How are things in Grenada?"

"Nothing to report on Alberto's whereabouts just yet," Rude Buay responds.

"Well, we need you back in Miami... seeing that the dead man has not shown up yet."

Ortiz says sarcastically.

Feeling like the last statement is seasoned salt in his wound,

"Why? What is going on in Miami?"

Rude Buay asks double questioningly,

"We can always use good DEA in Miami. One who can afford to let sleeping dogs lie."

Rude Buay ponders and ends the call. The Limo makes a hard U-turn and later arrives outside the airport.

Rude Buay hurries inside the terminal where he boards a plane bound for Miami.

4

One day later. Outside the dock in Montego Bay, a taxi pulls up with two women seated on the rear seat. Alberto saunters from one parked taxi to one with the occupants. He boards on the front passenger seat. On the rear seat, seated is his wife DENISE GOMEZ and SHELLY HALL. Denise is an Asian, trophy woman, in her late twenties. Her engagement ring, touching her wedding band, is to be greatly desired by any woman. The blinding rock speaks for itself. Additionally, Denise's new hairstyle gives her a much sophisticated younger look. Alberto is happy to see her alive and vice versa.

SHELLY HALL, on the other hand, is Caucasian, tall and feisty, WWE type. Shelly is in her 30s, wearing a red bandana which color schemes with the healing bruises on her face. Both women are armed with semiautomatics.

Night falls. The taxi pulls up outside the Blue Lagoon Hotel. Alberto and Denise exit the taxi and enter the hotel. Shelly continues the ride to MO BAY airport.

Inside the hotel room, Alberto's newly acquired outfits are still lying on the bed. Among them are nicely tailored suits, and a wetsuit. He goes to the bathroom and discards the upper portion of another wetsuit in the trash and passionately reacquaints himself with Denise.

Alberto's cell phone rings. He answers it.

"*Don Señor* Alberto, the shipment is ready to be picked up, *pronto*,"

The voice of SALVADOR, his Colombian counterpart assures.

Sal, as he is better known, is a Colombian, in his late 30s, and stationed in Bogota. He is overseeing the day to day operations of cutting and shipping cocaine to Miami, The Caribbean, and Asia. His inaccurate cutting was responsible for the glitch in the lethal

Dragon X which caused the death of many Jamaican kids a few months prior.

Salvador hangs up the cellular phone and drives off in his beat-up white pickup truck.

"*Gracias,*"

Alberto says.

Alberto dials another number,

Shelly Hall rushing out of the shower with a towel wrapped around her picks up the phone from her hotel room.

"I need you on the plane in the morning heading to Miami. I need a clean job, no flaws."

Alberto demands.

"I'm on it!"

Shelly responds.

5

Later that evening, a private airplane touches down at Dade County Airport in Miami and parks at a hangar. Shelly deplanes, under disguise and dressed to the nines. Shelly's demeanor says she is anxious to be back in Miami.

A RASTAFARIAN, wearing a green, yellow and black tam, the colors of Jamaica, with his dreadlocks hairstyle almost touching his butt, greets Shelly. The Rastafarian, hands over a set of keys and an envelope.

Shelly opens the envelope. She pulls out the white sheet of paper, on it is written instructions. She reads it and departs inside the airport terminal en-route to the parking lot. Shelly presses the remote, a black on black Jaguar answers. She hurries to it, gets in and drives away. This automobile is quite her style.

ON THE FOLLOWING MORNING, the sun, after many failed attempts shines some tiny rays of sunlight on the Dade County Prison. This enormous structure nestled in the suburban area of Miami, Florida is a landmark to many. It is public knowledge that the walls are over twenty-five feet below the ground as they are above the ground. They boast a diameter of over three feet in thickness. Built over a hundred years ago, no one has ever escaped those walls. This penitentiary has housed many non-celebs as well as celebrities.

A midnight blue van pulls out from the facility's underground parking area. It exits the compound and merges with the steady flow of morning traffic. Inside three guards: the driver RAYMOND PEREZ of Cuban descent. Raymond is armed to the max.

In the rear: TONY CLINTON Caucasian and DARRELL WEEKS of African American descent. Both men are also armed to the hilt.

Darrell Weeks looks across at his co-worker who has a gun pointed at the prisoner en-route to Miami's maximum-security prison. Their man is JOHNNY, alias *"Too Bad."*

Johnny is Jamaican of African American descent, who was recently captured in Jamaica and extradited to America by the U.S. Government. It was claimed that Johnny was one of the most notorious Drug Lords to ever operate on the Island of Jamaica outside of ALBERTO GOMEZ leader of the Dragon Drug Cartel. Johnny ruled Tivoli Gardens. Looking across at Clinton, Johnny remains stone-faced while shackled hands and feet.

The Miami Prison Official blue vehicle approaches the Miami Bay Bridge as traffic begins to thin out. A black Jaguar tailing it for more than half a mile speeds up from behind and passes the moving van, slicing its way directly in front of it to avoid a head-on collision with a tractor-trailer. The two guards in the back of the prison transport are discombobulated as they grab on to the vehicle's seat for support.

Johnny is shaken up. Even so, he remains poised and stoned faced.

"That is a sick ...! Where the heck did she get her driving instructions?"

Raymond the driver mutters.

"She must have bought it in South Beach."

Responds Darrell Weeks.

The correction officers share a jovial laugh in regards to the South Beach allusion.

"BTW, did any of you watch that repo show about South Beach?
Clinton states in gesture.
There is silence as no one seems to get what he is talking about.
He answers his question by saying,
"It's sick."
Moments later, along the mid-point portion of the bridge, the Jaguar comes to a complete stop.
Before the van could complete its unavoidable rear-end collision with the Jaguar, the driver of this chic, luxurious vehicle, Shelly Hall, opens the door. Shelly jumps out of the car and over the bridge, plunging into a frigid body of water.
The airbag in the prison vehicle malfunctions. The no seatbelt wearing Perez sails through the front windscreen and out onto the bridge's roadway, head first. Perez's weapons and most of his warden accessories disperse as he crashes hard onto the metal and concrete pavement. He tries to get up but is unable to make it solo. So he falls unconscious back to the ground.
Flustered and in a state of panic Tony Clinton jumps out to assist Perez.
Johnny seizes the opportunity and with a full force he "head butts" Darrell Weeks.

The severe blow and impact cause Weeks' head to crash hard against the longitudinal interior of the van. Knocked out, Weeks collapses onto the floor.

Johnny, still chained hand and legs, sits on top of Weeks, now in the fetal position. Johnny seizes the opportunity and searches through the Warden's pockets and retrieves the keys which he uses to set himself free.

Prowling, Johnny darts outside and finishes off Raymond Perez and Tony Clinton, one round of bullets per officer.

Johnny speedily returns to the van, discharges one round of bullets inside Weeks' mouth finishing him off.

Before making his escape, Johnny pulls out a plastic bag of weed from inside his underwear. It is a large *Ziploc* bag.

He empties the contents on the driver's seat. One whiff of that deposit is enough to get one high and sustain it for hours.

Johnny secures his gun inside the bag, seals the bag, and slides the package inside his waist. He plunges into the frigid water of Miami Bay.

Traffic is at an all-time standstill as the bridge is only now accessible by foot traffic.

The early arrivers seem to want to dive in after Johnny, but they dare to carry out such a feat from so high an altitude and pursuing an armed criminal.

RUDE BUAY VOL. II

Rescue teams finally press their way through, they plunge into the deep with bloodhound dogs. News reporters converge onto the scene. Rescue teams come up empty, as neither Shelly nor Johnny are recovered from the Bay.

HOURS LATER, AND MILES AWAY from the scene, a 75 feet long submarine, made of fiberglass and wood, surfaces and picks up Shelly and Johnny *Too Bad*.

6

Back in Jamaica, a Caucasian woman named BEVERLY HASTINGS, adorned with a lengthy dreadlocks hairstyle, almost touching her butt is bottle feeding her toddler. Beverly is in her mid-thirties, and at a younger age looked like she could have been a runway model if she wanted to. She aborts feeding her five-month-old son, Andrew. This kid has just finished sucking on the residue in that eight-ounce bottle.

Before she could adequately burp Andrew, her three-year-old daughter Leticia, once seen sucking the residue from her bottle falls off the high chair and onto the floor below.
Beverly puts the toddler in his crib and rushes to her daughter Leticia's aid. Three other kids, two boys, and one girl, all under the ages of five rush out of the bedroom to the scene.
Beverly picks up Leticia who is now limp, and in a daze. Leticia's vital signs are almost nil save only for little visual movement in her upper torso.
Beverly tries comforting the little girl in her arms. Finally, Leticia collapses with the climax of one last breath while lying in her mother's arms.
Beverly is not only flustered but mortified. She desperately tries CPR. That doesn't revive her three-year-old Leticia.
Beverly screams out. So do the other kids, except for baby Andrew who lies innocently in his crib playing with his hanging toys.
Beverly calls 911 and thereafter huddles with three of her kids. They are all sobbing, engulfed in tears.
Moments later, the Medics arrive.
Inquiring Neighbors also show up. The Medics enter the house and return with Leticia on a Gurney. Leticia has been rushed away aboard the Medical vehicle earlier.

THE FOLLOWING MORNING, two middle-aged women from Child protective Services arrive at Beverly's door. They are officially escorted by Jamaican Police in a squad car. One of the women carrying a clipboard knocks on the door.

Beverly answers. The police officers introduce themselves as Officers Bailey and Carter.

Bailey addresses her,

"Miss Hastings, my name is officer Bailey with the Jamaica Police Department and this is Officer Carter. Based on autopsy results it was determined that your daughter Leticia died as a result of a drug overdose. We have been authorized to assist in the removal of four kids: Andrew, Michael, Max and Sherunda Hastings from your custody; pending an investigation."

The officers round up the kids and carry them through the door.

Beverly sheds tears as she witnesses her kids escorted inside the Child Protective Services vehicle.

The officers return to the house. Bailey once again addresses,

"Miss Hastings, I am afraid that we are going to have to take you down to the station for further questioning."

They escort Beverly outside. The two Jamaican police officers shove Beverly inside the rear seat of the squad car. The car departs.

A FEW DAYS LATER, Beverly returns to the house but the kids don't. Maintaining her innocence; Beverly in her mind's eye knew that she was framed and just couldn't understand why and by whom. Even so, she is determined to solve this gruesome mystery.

Beverly sits on the side of the bed smoking Hookah. It poses an enormous challenge for Beverly to recall everything relating to her five orphaned kids, mainly in those moments before the mishap. So she decided to calculatingly retrace her steps.

In her mind, she relived the entire meal preparation process for little Leticia. Starting with the washing and sterilizing of the feeding bottle to the putting of the eight-ounce bottle of milk in Leticia's hand.

Beverly's intuition leads her to the milk can container from which she scooped the milk to make Leticia's meal. Upon opening the can she recalled sensing nothing abnormal. Yet, for some reason she can not-leave the milk can alone. She read up on the contents, preparing instructions, and even where it was packaged.

Beverly frustratingly turns the can upside down emptying all the powdered milk onto the kitchen table. To her surprise, there is a plastic *Ziploc* bag on the top of the milk pile. The size of the bag averaged at least one eight of a kilo of a white substance. While removing it, the powdered contents continuously seep out and onto the heap. Using her pinky finger Beverly takes a taste test. The sordid look on her face indicates that inside the milk container there wasn't all milk. Saddened, her scream alert the neighbors.

Some neighbors abandoning their chores in an investigative pursuit. Some of them show up barefooted.

One woman, in particular, shows up wearing her bathrobe along with a pair of house slippers. Another woman arrives with one half of her hair styled and the other half still in rollers.

In tears, Miss Hastings immediately called 911. Minutes later, her house is now not only filled with visitors but the same two police officers who orchestrated her arrest. They showed up. The officers trying to mask their apology confiscate the contaminated combination of milk and cocaine.

They put the can inside the trunk of the squad car and drives off.

7

A light blue sedan pulls up outside the Miami Drug Enforcement office. Before the driver agent Rude Buay, could slam the car door shut, the car built in agent's radio transits.

The voice states, "Requesting DEA presence at Milky Way Warehouse, at the corner of Providence and Dixie Highway. Rude Buay gets back inside his car. Making a swift U-Turn his sedan merges, tires squealing, with the intercepting traffic.

Rude Buay speedily pulls up in front of the warehouse. He jumps out armed but with caution. He notices a man's body, bloodied laying in the gutter. The man's face though bloodied looks familiar.

Rude Buay goes to his car and retrieves a pair of gloves. He rolls the man over for a close up look. Rude Buay shakes his head. He knows him. Rude Buay releases him.

The victim's badge falls out of his jacket pocket along with a Polaroid picture.

Rude Buay confiscates the two pieces of evidence along with the victim's wallet. He puts them in a plastic bag and lodges the bag inside the car trunk. Rude Buay notices the agent's car across the street. He investigates the agent's car for additional evidence. Moments later, Paramedics arrive and remove the body from the scene. Medics place the body inside a body bag. Miami Police Officers intervene and yellow tape of the area.

Before the dispatch call and agent Rude Buay being dispatched to the scene. The victim, undercover agent MARK JONES showed up outside the Milky Way Warehouse and purchased two kilos of cocaine from Shelly Hall.

After the deal was made, FRANKIE O'NEAL, a Colombian in his early 40s, pulled up in a black limousine to fetch her and Johnny. *One Arm Frankie-* as he is nicknamed decked out in a suit and tie, wearing an artificial left arm with a stub and a clip at the end of it is all business.

Shelly and Johnny board the black limo, while the undercover agent walks towards his vehicle. Johnny seated on the limo's front seat rolls the window down, and blows the man's brains out with the stolen warden's gun.
Shelly getting inside the rear of the limo asked,
"Why did you shoot him?"
Johnny responded,
"Just another PIG, who deserved to die. Every pig ought to be dead; they get in the way of business."
Johnny retrieved the narcotics from the undercover agent and threw it back inside on the rear seat of the limo.
Frankie drove away taking the back roads and side streets, heading towards the Manor on top of the hill.

Back at DEA headquarters, agent Rude Buay tries to glean more detailed information about the Polaroid photo recovered at the crime scene. So he searches the web for all the elite homes in Dade County. He comes up empty. Flustered, he goes to the office next door. No one is there except for a box of Crispy cream doughnuts. He indulges.
Rude Buays' new partner MILES TATE, a Caucasian in his early 30s, whose youthful demeanor says I am a rookie. He walks in with a soda in hand. On his other hand, he is carrying a copy of the chronicle *Rude Buay ... The Unstoppable* along with a yellow highlighter.

Tate looking at Rude Buay states,
"I thought you didn't like chocolate,"
Rude Buay replies,
"It looked so good, I couldn't resist."
Rude Buay continues,
"The first day on the job, you seem to study people's preference a lot. Plus only overzealous students read with a dual-colored - high-lighter."
Tate responds,
"I was in the Greenroom and noticed that only chocolate donuts were left in the box. So I assumed you..."
Rude Buay looking at the book in Tate's hand for a second time remarks,
"Reading, killing time or studying?"
Tate replies,
"Digesting and assimilating."
"Have you ever seen this house before, Miles?'
Rude Buay asks pointing to the Polaroid.
Tate responds,
"Never. No sir."
"Who owns this ...?"
Rude Buay questions,
"Your guess is as good as mine, and as well as Mark Jones'."
Tate replies.
"Look it up see what you find."

RUDE BUAY VOL. II

Rude Buay finishes the doughnut. He picks up the Polaroid and exits from Green Room.

Tate yells,

"Do you need me for backup?"

Rude Buay responds,

"I got this. Call me if you find something."

Rude Buay hits the streets in his sedan. The car tires burn rubber upon take off.

8

Rude Buay pulls up in his sedan outside of a *REMAX* real estate office and barges inside. A tall, peerless woman, looks like she's straight out of *Desire Magazine,* and wearing a nametag which reads ROCHELLE HUNTER, answers the buzzer. Rude Buay saunters into her office. She's Real Estate person of the week adept, although unraveled by Rude Buay's presence,

"I'm Rochelle Hunter. Who do I have the pleasure of finding their dream home today?"
Rochelle states while directing Rude Buay to a seat.
"I'm Randy Bascombe."
"What brings you to *REMAX*, Mr. Bascombe?"
She asks,
Rude Buay responds,
"I'm very intrigued by your properties. I am looking for something very chic."
Rochelle responds,
"What's your interest? Mr. Bascombe, and what can we help you to move into within the next ninety days?"
Rude Buay is captivated by her beauty. Even so, he tries to conceal that desire.
Rude Buay replies,
"I'm looking for something Colonial with much privacy maybe. I'd like to be able to entertain my friends, well, ... *there*."
Rochelle replies,
"We're out of those colonials but there's a nice Victorian on the market right now. It's an entertainer's dream and privately tucked away in one of the chicest locations in Dade County. This impressive 3-acre new estate will have you staying for a long time. Private and gated entrance, sprawling lawn areas for volleyball, basketball, and adjacent tennis court, organic gardens, an artist retreat, and detached guest house. Mr. Bascombe, the ground floor plan offers 5

bedroom suites, great natural light, his study, her study as well as a craft room. A professional theater, billiards room, an extensive wine cellar, full-size gym, and much more. Fit for a King!"

Rude Buay removes the Polaroid from his jacket, walks over to her desk, sits on its edge and lays them out in front Rochelle. She browses through.

Rude Buay says,

"I'd like one just like that or similar."

Rochelle reflects on that particular sale, as she scans through the database.

Rochelle states,

"Six months ago. Three million dollars! That's a rare one."

Rude Buay asks,

"Who's the proud owner?"

Rochelle responds,

"That's strictly confidential Mr. Bascombe."

"Really?"

Rude Buay inquires.

Rochelle informs,

"We are not under obligation to give out confidential information to potential buyers."

Rude Buay remarks,

"Could you have the owners give me a tour, just in case they ever decide to sell?"

Rochelle replies,

"Not on this one! We could have one like that built for

you. It will take years..."
Rude Buay insists, still sitting on the edge of her desk.
Have you ever been...?
Rochelle questions,
"Why did you ask?"
Rude Buay pulls out his gun, pointing it towards her head.
She's trembling.
Rude Buay continues,
"I need a name and the address."
Rochelle retrieves the data from her Rolodex.
Alberto Gomez. 712 Palm Grove.
Bang! Bang! Bang!
Bullet shells scattered throughout the office.
 Several rounds of bullets through the glass window strike Rochelle.
Meanwhile Rude Buay ducks for cover. Lying on the ground he gets a few rounds off at the perpetrator. The villain Frankie is unhurt, as nothing connects owing to his agility.
Frankie speeds away from the scene inside the black limousine, his gun occupying the front passenger seat. Rude Buay get up, dusts himself off, darts outside boards his sedan, and follows aggressively in the pursuit of *One Arm Frankie.*
The fast driving *One Arm Frankie* eludes Rude Buay as his limo disappears in the distance.

RUDE BUAY VOL. II

Agent Rude Buay radios DEA Headquarters for backup while he continues in his pursuit of the culprit, Frankie O'Neal.

9

On top of a hill Rude Buays' vision is suckered into the much sought after Colonial Manor. Its grandeur is a majestic sight to behold. He is poised for this dream come true and the grand tour. Except that now it's *officially* DEA business. Finally, the most desired house is now less than a half-mile away. His adrenaline rush is at an all-time high.

Rude Buay reaches inside his breast pocket and retrieves the blood-stained Polaroid. He very quickly discerns that it's a perfect match. He radios DEA Headquarters for backup.

Miles Tate responds.

"I am coming up the hill. After you left I went to work and found the info on the house you were looking for. It is owned by Alberto Gomez. It is one of a kind. Very rare..."

"Enough! Tate. Just meet me there ASAP."

Says Rude Buay,

Tate speeds up. His sedan swerves as it careens through the narrow uphill streets. The Manor is now in sight. Tate, realizing that it's his first day on the job he *Man* up for the task ahead.

MOMENTS LATER, RUDE BUAY steps out of his car. Tate pulls up behind him and follows suit.

Rude Buay is confronted with multiple gate entries inside the Manor. He presses the buzzer outside the huge Iron Gate to the manor while Tate covers.

There's no response.

So he tries again, unfortunately to no avail. Rude Buay relocates. He detects a switch box behind the Iron Gate. He squeezes his hand through between the gate and the wall and PRIES open the box. The device: harnessed with not only multiple colored wires but an excess of black, blue and red wires.

Rude Buay is puzzled by the sophisticated wiring of the switch box. However, being occupied with bridging the buzzer with his device takes precedence. While Tate focuses on keeping any possible retaliation at bay. Immediately, two Guards march out from the house toward the gate trigger happy.

Tate is alerted and ready. While they train their weapons, Tate counterattacks.

Tate CAPS both of them before they could accomplish their objective. With the two guards dead Rude Buay gives more of his attention to bridging the connection to the intercom. Yet, he remains unaccomplished.

The Black Limo PULLS up from the opposite direction, with full beamed illuminated headlights. Out of the limo RUSHES, Johnny *Too Bad*, and his partner Frankie O'Neal.

They immediately discharge multiple rounds at Tate and Rude Buay.

The agents retaliate trying to MATCH Frankie's onslaught and Johnny's firepower.

A smaller adjacent gate opens as if by its own accord.

Johnny and Frankie swiftly make their way through that gate while dodging the bullets from the agents' onslaught, as if they were the size of an NBA basketball. The gate closes abruptly behind them.

Rude Buay, peripherally notices the infrared on the surveillance camera up ahead. He aims, and SHOOTS at the camera, dismantling it. With the camera now out of commission. Johnny and Frankie's shooting intensifies as they REFUSE to let up.

Tate in the meantime, hides, and shoots from behind the left wall pillar which supports the huge Iron Gate.

Rude Buay does the SAME from behind the right pillar.

Rude Buay, in an effort to limit the Drug Lord's possible getaway tactics, SHOOTS up the black limo, deflating all four of its tires with his rounds of fire.

Tate single-handedly manages to keep Johnny and Frankie at bay, during a fierce, fiery, DEBRIS FLYING exchange caused by a sequence RAINING bullets. Bullets, sailing through and over the iron gates from all the parties involved. Yet nothing connects.

Suddenly Frankie realizes that his guns out of bullets.

Rude Buay clues in and aims for Frankie's head.

Frankie turns to flee.

Rude Buay aims for his head and SHOOTS.

Frankie somersaults. The bullet ricochets and catches Frankie in the left leg.

Frankie falls to the ground and gets back up limping and tossing rocks at the agents.

Johnny hurriedly reaches under his coat and with his right hand BRINGS out a semi-automatic. Now two gun - equipped, he does a 360-degree turn while he UNLOADS on Tate and Rude Buay.

The gun in Johnny's left-hand goes CLICK, CLICK. He THROWS it to the ground and BRINGS out another with his left hand from under the left side of his coat as he continues to shoot with the one in his right hand.

During the swift exchange of this gunfire interim, Tate DARTS through flying bullets. He SPRINTS towards the limo and opens the rear door. Johnny sees the move made by Tate but he concentrates on TAKING OUT Rude Buay who is still attacking with a vengeance.

The wall pillar begins to sag as the Iron Gate moves a few inches horizontally, leaving a wider gap.

Rude Buay senses the pending collapse of the Iron Gate but RELOADS and continues shooting at Frankie and Johnny.

The Limo is penetrated with multiple bullet holes. Tate searches inside and discovers a collection of Uzis, grenades and other weaponry, in addition to several milk cans. Tate exchanges his semi-automatic for two Uzis and EXITS like *Rambo* in full force.

Tate DISCHARGES from both Uzis. Still, he's no match for Johnny's experience and firing power, although unscathed by Johnny's onslaught.

Johnny yells out,

"Catch me if you can, Rude Buay!"

Rude Buay emerges from behind the twisted pillar and gets a glimpse at Frankie's and Johnny *Too Bad's* backside. He aims for Johnny *Too Bad*. However, they immediately disappear inside the interior of the Manor. The two agents with enough room barely SQUEEZE their way through the partially opened gate. They enter the grounds very cautiously in pursuit.

The agents enter the gigantic living room by way of the front door. The ceiling's almost twelve feet high. A gigantic fire place with ash residue greets them. The Living room's decorated with oriental rugs and other chic furniture. A large glass screen door leads to the pool area. There seems to be no current activity on the part of the dwellers, except for the incongruent display of bloodstains.

Moving through each room in a "take-down" style, looking for a trace of consistency, they wind up in the dining room. Next door is a bathroom.

They search inside the bathroom, no one's there. The table inside the dining room catches their attention. So they revert to it.

Entering the dining room, they careen by the huge dining table, with twelve disheveled arranged chairs, and a bar secluded in the far corner. On the table: two huge partially fresh mounds of cocaine with two straws and two razor blades reside, refilled cigarettes, a pile of laced cigarette extracts, a crack pipe, syringes, and several Polaroid shots with groups of Asian kids.

Next to those pictures are opened milk cans. The agents complete their sweep of the house room by room but they still come up empty-handed as the dwellers have left the premises without any obvious exit trail. The agents, puzzled by their exit strategy, rummage through the Manor a second time in collecting evidence and hoping for a blunder on the part of the Drug Lords, so they could *roast* them.

IN THE MEANTIME Alberto, Shelly and Johnny *Too Bad* vacate the premises using a trap door leading to the underground beneath the building's foundation.
The trio boards a black limo. Frankie is in the driver's seat. A trail of blood leads to the driver's door. Frankie who had stopped the bleeding at the house is unaware that he is bleeding again as blood continues to trickle down his trousers' leg.
The limo departs and arrives at a small dock. There, a 75-foot submarine surfaces and docks. Alberto, Shelly, and Johnny *Too Bad* exit the limo and board the ship. Meanwhile, Frankie oversees as the Sailor unloads several kilos along with laden milk cans onto the waiting limo. Frankie O'Neal gets back inside the limousine. The limo drives off. The Sailor re-boards. Moments later, the submarine submerges and departs. Frankie in pain drives to Milky Way. He gets out of the limo. He unlocks the back door to the building and unloads the milk cans into the warehouse. Blood droplets still accompany his every move. He is hurt but skillfully masks the pain. He gets back inside the limo and retrieves a milk can off the front seat. He opens it, takes out the *Ziploc* bag of cocaine from underneath the powdered milk. Now powdered milk is all over the

front seat. In a sense of urgency, he opens the bag of coke, creates a few lines on the dashboard and snorts them up as if to ease the pain. In added desperation, he places some on the wound and whimpers as the substance unites with his flesh. Anyway, he feels like there has been some relief to his pain. Even so, he is high, in a daze and now unable to drive. So he parks the car curbside.

10

Back up DEA agents arrive swarming the exterior of the Manor. They, yellow tape the premises. Sensing no need to stay, they depart. Meanwhile, deep in the interior of the Manor Rude Buay hears a sound coming from the pool area. So he conducts another sweep of the premises with Tate covering him. Exiting through the rear door towards the pool they encounter a caged PARROT, too quiet for its good.

Rude Buay entertaining the bird asks,

"You want a banana?"
The articulate Parrot yells,
"Thieves! Thieves! Thieves!"
Rude Buay convincingly,
"No, we're not."
The Parrot not believing a word he says argues,
"Liars! Liars! Liars!"
Rude Buay questions,
"Undercover?"
The Parrot argues,
"Same thing! What's with the gun? Who'd you shoot, Osama? Bang, Bang, Bang, Bang!"
Rude Buay probes,
"Self-defense, that's all. Where's Alberto, Johnny and the rest of the gang. Where did they go?
TATE is enjoying the exchange.
The Parrot responds,
"That's confidential!"
Rude Buay urges,
"Come on stud, I'll give you a peanut."
Parrot dances.
After the imaginary curtain, the parrot unveils,
"Sailing. Sail away."
Rude Buay feeds it another peanut and asks,
"How they do that?"
Rude Buay inquires.
Parrot responds,
"Trap door opens up! Ship sails!"

Rude Buay removes the cage and its occupant. Suddenly, the alarm for the building goes off. The sound of a siren fills the air. Even so, Tate leads the way holding on to the bag of confiscated evidence. Rude Buay exits the house with the caged bird.

The Miami Police arrive in response to the alarm. Police cruisers swarm the grounds. Tate flashes his DEA badge.

"Miles Tate. DEA business."

Rude Buay in confrontation,

"Where the hell you were when we needed you?"

One of the Officers responds,

"Better late than never."

Rude Buay and Tate jump into their respective vehicles. Rude Buay, carries the caged bird. The vocal Miami Police Officer eyeing the caged parrot warns.

Officer continues,

"That's stolen property agent Rude Buay."

Rude Buay argues,

"He's a witness."

Parrot addresses,

"Where's the subpoena? I no see nada nor hear nada.

The vocal Miami police officer, somewhat amused, reaches for the bird. Could the parrot have been the witness to a getaway, knows the escape route in the house or just possess a vivid imagination? These thoughts lingered in Rude Buay's mind.

Anyway, he reluctantly hands over the bird to the Miami Police Officer.

Rude Buay feeling a hunch says,

"You can hold onto the bird but cover the exterior or your A... is mine."

The Officer doesn't seem to get it.

Rude Buay continues,

"I have some unfinished business to complete on the inside. We will call you if I need you."

Rude Buay returns to the interior of the house with Miles Tate following in tow.

Inside the Manor Rude Buay eyes every square foot of the floor looking for anything that resembles a crack in the rug and carpet. From room to room he surveys. Inside the master bathroom which they previously visited, they come up upon a rectangular crease in the rug. The rectangular outline in the carpet indicates that a door, the size of a trap door is concealed in it. The agents tug on the carpet. A door opens up in the floor of the bathroom floor. Engaging the descending steps, with their guns cocked the two agents wind up inside the partially lit tunnel.

Descending inside the tunnel agent Rude Buay and Miles Tate discover several luxurious, expensive automobiles. In an investigative pursuit, they notice cars are parked on one end. The other end leads through a thoroughfare with a fork. The two agents

RUDE BUAY VOL. II

walk the full length of the small tunnel which opens into a small dock.

11

Rude Buay notices the fresh tire marks left in the mud next to the dock. Additionally, bloodstains create a trail at the scene. Rude Buay "rolls up his sleeves" and calculates the measurement of the vehicle's chassis based on the impressions of the tire marks most dominant and resident in the mud. Based on his calculations he estimates that this vehicle had to be at least 120 inches or more in length.

Staring across at the blue watered horizon, he adds yet another piece to the getaway puzzle.

"So this is where they made their escape."

Rude Buay declares,

Miles Tate responds,

"Sure looks like it!"

Rude Buay nods yes.

Miles Tate inquires,

"So what's next?"

Rude Buay, thinks long and hard as if he is not quite up to it. Then looking at Tate with direct eye contact he responds,

"The Caribbean! If it's going to be up to me."

Miles Tate responds,

"Lies, corruption, deceit, and sabotage. Some trip huh?"

Rude Buay looking across the horizon responds,

"You've got to be in it to win it. Before the Caribbean though, I need to pick up some milk."

Miles Tate questions,

"Really? Milk?"

Rude Buay answers,

"Yep! Milk!"

IN SEPARATE DEA CARS the agents drive through Miami, passing several supermarkets.

Tate doesn't get Rude Buay's epiphany so he radios Rude Buay.

"You forgot to get the milk?"
Tate asks,
"No, I didn't. Just stay on my tail and don't shoot unless I say so."
Rude Buay advises,
Moments later the duo pulls up at Milky Way.
The Black limousine driven by Frankie pulls away from the curb. Rude Buay recognizes Frankie and vice versa. Rude Buay is in pursuit followed by Tate.
The race proceeds through the streets of Miami.
Frankie tries to make a getaway before the entrance to Interstate 95 Freeway. Rude Bauy is tailing him closely so he changes his mind and opts for the highway's ramp. The two agents pursue resolutely.
Rude Buay radios Tate.
"Get ready, I rather have him alive than dead."
Tate questions,
"What's his value?"
Rude Buay informs his rookie,
"He didn't lose that one arm for nothing. I am sure."
Rude Buay tunes to his favorite reggae station. The DJ is playing his favorite. The vibe soothes.
Rude Buay instructs Tate via other radio,
"Call Headquarters and request a search and seizure at the Milky Way Warehouse, will you?"
The Limousine merges with traffic as it enters the HOV lane. The two agents' vehicles follow suits.

RUDE BUAY VOL. II

They are now keeping pace with the limo. That dancehall music is still playing as if it's an extended version. Frankie, sensing being tailgated, exits the HOV lane illegally and merges to the right, thus causing a multi-vehicle collision while making his getaway. Rude Buay skillfully avoids the mayhem, while Tate is boxed in because of the related accident.

Rude Buay continues in pursuit of Frankie. The chase escalates through city streets, where the maneuvering of this 120-inch stretch limo is now problematic at such a high speed, thereby posing a problem for other motorists as well.

On-lookers see a fatality brewing as pedestrians and motorists use their cell phones to videotape the happenings. Catching Frankie alive would appease Rude Buay but in his mind, not at the expense of the lives of other motorists.

Suddenly, bullets from the limousine begin to rain in the direction of Rude Buay's sedan. Rude Buay aims for the right rear tire and connects.

The limo swerving from side to side, careens slams into a retaining wall, lands on its roof and bursts into flames.

Rude Buay get out of his vehicle in an attempt to observe the demolition. Meanwhile, Tate pulls up, gets out of his sedan, and stares at the flames and then back at Rude Buay.

Tate asks,

"I thought we wanted him alive."

Rude Buay replies,

"In life, you go after what you want, but there is nothing wrong about accepting what you get. The thrill lies in the effort."

Tate looks at Rude Buay while assimilating that thought. He begins buying into Rude Buay's positive mental attitude.

Rude Buay asks,

"Are you still up for the Caribbean?"

Tate smiles and responds,

"I wouldn't renege on the Caribbean for anything in the world."

They board their vehicles and depart back to DEA headquarters. Agent Tate is excited and enthused about going to the Caribbean.

12

Rude Buay is in his office typing an email. He later submits it addressed to Michael Ortiz. Walking out of the parking garage, Ortiz retrieves the email via his cell phone. He senses the importance, knowledgeable of the fact that it's not Rude Buay's style to send him an Email.

Ortiz mulls over the contents as he knocks on Rude Buay's office door. Rude Buay answers the door. Ortiz barges in and looks squarely at Rude Buay in the face.

Immediately, two junior agents enter through the still open office door. Both agents are laden with part of the seizure recovered from their Milky Way drug bust. One of the agent's remarks, while focusing one of the milk containers:

"That place has recently turned into a narcotics depot. I don't think any place in Asia, Colombia, Canada, Mexico or even the Caribbean has been this busy lately when it comes to narcotics trafficking. We just lost agent Jones, he was a good man. It is going to be necessary to put Milky Way under surveillance 24/7."

Ortiz responds paying attention to the email and then to Rude Buay.

"Rude Buay, you've been there before. The U.S. did them a huge favor by extraditing Johnny *Too Bad* from Jamaica. That should have helped. It's about time the locals fight their own narcotics war."

Rude Buay responds,

"So said your predecessor the deceitful agent, Jose Mendez. This is our war. If we lose this one, we could be in for one of the most tragic recalls this world has ever encountered – Milk.

The prison authorities did the locals a disfavor by setting Johnny free.

With a menace of that caliber on the loose, who knows what will happen next? Who knows what his next target will be?

Our freedom gets eroded every day. Mainly, because we fail to be all we can be.

To know something is wrong and not do anything about it is worse than not knowing that thing is wrong."

Agent Rude Buay looks over at the junior agents and continues.

"Let me set the record straight. If you feel so sentimental about Milky Way, maybe you should step out of your comfort zones: by honing your skills so you could protect your love interest."

They both make their exit feeling agitated regarding Rude Buays' sentimentalism statement.

Ortiz saving face,

"Rude Buay, give me until tomorrow to come to a decision. You understand that we are short-staffed. Who knows when agent Heidi Hudson will be well enough to return to active duty?"

Rude Buay reminds,

"Boss, the clock has been ticking since that submarine sailed from the Miami dock.

Let me remind you: The most notorious Drug Lord since Alberto Gomez is on the loose.

Not only that, he has also linked up with Alberto and his name is Johnny *Too Bad*.

Who knows what the two politicians could be concocting?

I will be packed and ready to go in the morning.

This is my country and they are my people.
If not Me?
Who?"
If not Now?
When?"

13

It's late evening in Shanghai, China. *Femme Fatales* Denise Gomez, Shelly Hall, and Amanda Kinsley show up outside the Shanghai Karate School. The women are all dressed in karate gear, accessorized by luggage including duffle bags. They, survey and wait. Suddenly, David Lee gets off the elevator. The women are alerted as he turns the corner inside the lobby.

They unzip the duffel bags and remove their semi-automatic weapons. The dark alley behind them adds to the grittiness and the pre-nightfall.

David steps onto the sidewalk and is confronted with three women and three weapons pointing directly at him as they sucker him inside a portion of the dark alley.

In high flying Kung Fu style David single-handedly disarms all three women leaving them defenseless. Even so, they remain verbally confrontational.

"This is not right, David...!"

Denise yells,

"Don't blame me, blame Sal. He cuts and packages..."

David responds.

"What does Sal have to do with this? This is a tough economy. Recession is eating away at our profit margin. Thankfully we've got milk, that's our only conduit. Your packaging is horrendous that's why we...."

Denise explains.

"Do you know what could happen if milk gets recalled?"

Shelly interjects.

"Kids will starve."

David Lee replies.

"So would we!"

Denise responds.

"How many containers were in your last shipment?"

Denise asks.

"One thousand cans..."

David responds,

"One Thousand Cans?"
Denise, Shelly, and Amanda questioningly interrupt.
"That's what I said. One Thousand Kilos,"
David restates.
"We are going to have to use a different vendor for our containers, bags, and cans. That's not our style. It is all about quality. That is our entire existence."
David continues.
"Too late. Too ... LATE! No wonder you flunked out of high school, you bozo. What else have you fallen short on? Those *Ziploc* bags are defective."
States Shelly Hall,
Denise reminds David.
"My husband pays you well. Not for a botch job."
"This is my living. Yes, I flunked High School. If there is no me you don't eat. Plus wear that expensive jewelry."
Shelly attempts to retrieve her gun from the ground.
David senses her move.
David remarks,
"You touch that gun and I will break your jawbone."
Denise looks across at Amanda. The Boss Woman Amanda clues in. Amanda shows David the snake.
He responds with the crane.
They go at it hand to hand combat, Kung Fu style, with Amanda gaining the upper hand. When it was all over, David lies on the sidewalk not only exhausted but badly hurt, "licking his wounds and embarrassed."

His lady, CHU LING, an Asian model in her late 20s, pulls up in her fully loaded BMW. She steps out, glides across and onto the sidewalk peering inside the dark alley.

As a result of the humiliation and the pain endured by her man, the take-out order of Chinese food Chu's carrying, falls out of her hands and onto the paved sidewalk in decorativeness.

Denise, ignoring Chu's presence, responds sarcastically as the three of them leave the scene,

"Take that! Get your act together or next time or you will experience a threesome."

14

The following morning, Michael Ortiz walks inside Rude Buay's office and notices he's all packed with Tate's luggage aligned next to his. Tate walks in and in acknowledgment of his superiors, he smiles accompanied by a slight nod of the head. Ortiz addresses:

"Your return to Miami is very much anticipated gentlemen. Who knows where the next tunnel will be constructed. Our city needs you now more than ever."

Rude Buay and Ortiz shake hands. Rude Buay and agent Tate leaves in a sedan. Tate takes the wheel.

On the drive to the airport, Rude Buay catches up on making some phone calls.
He dials.
Inside the gadget-filled living room WALTER BANKS, an African American man with salt and pepper hair and in his fifties is on the phone. On the other cell phone, in Bogota, Colombia, is a barefooted CHELO, in his mid-30s and of Colombian descent. Chelo secures a newly constructed ladder to a tree overlooking the village, and mainly its long stretch of dusty unpaved roadway.
"What is next for him and Johnny, nobody knows. I am sure if matters get worse Rude Buay will respond."
Walter Banks states,
"Did he ever pay you from that last...?"
Chelo asks,
Banks interrupts,
"Hold on Chelo, talk about the devil and here he is. I have to grab this call. Let's talk later."
Banks aborts that call with Chelo and facilitates Rude Buays'.
"Man after my own heart, Mr. Rude Buay! Chelo and I were just talking about you. When are you going to visit the homeland? So we could enjoy some roast breadfruit, with *Ting*, ackee, and salt-fish."
"Don't tempt me with that finger-licking food, Banks. You know how this black man loves to feed his stomach. I will be there on the first flight from Miami

in the morning. Why don't you, Mildred and the Commissioner meet my partner Tate and me for a midday debriefing at the hole in the wall?"

"I don't foresee a problem with Mildred attending; you know how that woman feels about you. On the other hand, the General Election talks are heating up, not sure about the Commissioner, but one never knows if he will be able to meet with you on such short notice."

The sedan pulls up at the airport parking lot. Rude Buay is still on the phone.

"Banks, 9:00 a.m., see you then."

Banks calls MILDRED SIMMS a Caribbean beauty in her late twenties. She is a drop-dead gorgeous, sophisticated African American beauty, every man's heart desire. Mildred is filing her nails at the office. She picks up on the second ring.

"Mr. Banks ah whey yo ah deal with?"

She answers in deep *patois*.

Banks took aback as he had never heard Mildred drop some *patois* before.

"Rude Buay will be in tomorrow. He wants to meet at noon at the hole in the wall. Are you available…?"

"Is that doctor going to be there?"

Inquires Mildred,

"It's a debrief…"

Banks responds.

"Okay, will you come to get me?"

Mildred suggests.

"Will do!"

Says Banks.

RICHARD BAPTISTE, the commissioner is sitting across from the Governor-General Bradford Wiley. The two men are casting light on the Beverly Hastings situation. Wiley suggests that Beverly be reunited with her four kids. Based on the fact that she was oblivious the milk was contaminated with cocaine.

On the other hand, Baptiste feels that the situation should not be rushed. Additionally, he argues that Beverly should be retested for any possibility she was under the influence at the time of Leticia's death or has recently been a narcotics user.

Baptiste's office phone rings. He gets it.

"Mr. Commissioner, it's Walter Banks!"

Baptiste accommodates.

"I know you are a busy man. Mr. Rude Buay will be coming in tomorrow. He will be arriving at 9:00 a.m. Rude Buay would like to meet at noon, to catch up on old times, and the current crisis, if you are available."

"Oh Really? You mean that he did this on his own accord. What a changed man! Tell him I will oblige. By the way, do you know if that scorpion he had on his head is a temporary fixture or a permanent one?"

Baptiste inquires,

"You may want to ask him about that yourself. I am sure he will fill you in. See you at the hole in the wall, Commissioner."

RUDE BUAY VOL. II

Banks replies.

The Commissioner returns to his discussion with the Governor-General.

While Walter Banks aborts the call and continues to enjoy the sunset view of the harbor

15

The shadows lengthen as the sun sinks beyond the horizon in Montego Bay, Jamaica. Late workers enjoy the light flow of traffic as they leave their jobs for their respective domiciles. A few vagrants hang out at the corner streets. Some are getting high while others are just chilling listening to music via earphones on their iPhones. A cargo van displaying U.S Diplomat licenses tags pulls up and parks on the outside next to the Ministry of Tourism building. Inside under the wheel is Shelly Hall, Denise is upfront on the passenger seat, while Amanda is in the rear seat with her gun in hand.

A security guard notices the vehicle but fails to investigate; taking those diplomat plates for granted. In his mind, it could be nothing more than a UN diplomat, conducting official business. Workers continue to file out of the Ministerial compound, some pedestrians and motorists, carpoolers as well.

Mildred Simms steps out of the building and travels towards her car. That stud of a security guard steps out of the booth and walks over to her. He sneakily indulges in walking her to her car. She gets inside. He closes the door behind her. The car takes off.

Mildred drives out of the parking lot. Suddenly, her car is sandwiched by three other cars one in-front and two behind.

The diplomat wearing tag van is now several cars behind Mildred's car and tailing it.

Approaching a small street, Shelly Hall notices the right indicator light blinking on Mildred's car up above. Mildred pulls up next to a hair salon. She parks the car, gets out of her car. She is heading towards the salon.

The van speeds up and stops parallel to Mildred's car. Mildred is sandwiched. Denise and Amanda jump out while Shelly completes the parking of the van.

Denise immediately stalls Mildred as she steps out. Amanda, with a gun in one hand, wraps a huge bath towel continuously around Mildred's head. Tying a knot where the fabric ends.

Mildred's scream is almost muffled under the towel.

They drag her to and inside of the van.

The van takes off as they finish binding her with ropes. They remove the towel and duct tapes over Mildred's mouth.

Simultaneously, Johnny is positioned in a cube truck a few hundred feet away from the Commissioners' home in MO Bay. Johnny *Too Bad* waits.

Secluded in a chic suburban neighborhood, not only very little evening traffic, but the chirping noise of crickets accompanies Johnny's' linger.

The Commissioner's car pulls up. Richard Baptiste, always a sharp dresser. He is suited with a nice shirt and tie. He looks suave and debonair. No doubt happy to be home after a long day at the office. His car stops, waiting on a lounging cat to clear its stroll across the street. Baptiste prepares to pull into the driveway.

Johnny takes off in the cube truck and intentionally rear-ends the Commissioner's car.

The Commissioner gets out peeved, as he evaluates the damage done to this car.

Johnny steps out as if to console the Commissioner and possibly exchange some vehicular documental information. Instead, Johnny displays his gun. He puts Commissioner Baptiste under a chokehold, sticks a rag deep in his mouth, escorts him to the rear of the truck, opens it, and shoves him inside. Johnny duct-tapes the Commissioner's mouth, closes the door, returns to the driver's seat and takes off.

Now underway, Johnny radios Alberto.

"Mission accomplished, Boss!"

Albert responds,

"Let's meet up in Port Antonio close to the MPs blockade. Stay put once you get there. I will drive to meet you."

Johnny responds in *patois*,

"Scene, Rasta! I love those Ministers of Parliament to ... *rarted*."

16

Outside Walter Banks' Port Antonio home a taxi pulls up and waits. Under the wheel sits Drug Czar and leader of the Dragon Drug Cartel, Alberto Gomez. Meanwhile, inside Walter Banks' house, the house phone rings. Banks answers it on the second ring.

On the other end is Chelo his Colombian understudy. He's sitting on his living room floor in Bogota, Colombia toying with his espionage gadgets. He picks up a video signal from Walter Banks's neighborhood in Jamaica.

"Banks there's a taxi waiting on your block. Did you call a blue taxi cab? Are you going someplace? Did Rude Buay show up earlier than planned?"

Chelo is now affixed to the TV monitor, and images of the blue cab. He zooms in for more clarity.

Finally, the monitor goes blank.

Chelo fiddles with a few gadget antennas while he's still talking on the phone.

"I saw that taxi outside your home. The driver just sat there waiting. Your house lights were on. So I figured you were at home. Now I lost that ... signal. I don't see it anymore. Let me try fixing the signal router. I will call you back."

Banks' phone rings again.

It's Chelo,

"Sorry Banks no more picture. I lost it. I saw it a few minutes ago. Conyo! The blue taxi cab was there. I did not get the driver's profile though. He looked ... It happened so fast."

"Is he black? What does he look like?"

Banks inquires as he grabs his gun.

"Not sure. I didn't get a close up of the driver. The image was just a flicker"

Chelo responds.

"Darn, if Rude Buay changed his itinerary, why didn't he inform me? He knows where I stand with surprises. I hate them. He better not ... pulling one on me. I'll blow his brains out."

Banks states as he ensure that his gun is fully loaded.
"If he did, that's a big NO. Even if he offers you a bonus, you just never know with those Americans."
"Got picture! Got Picture!"
Yells Chelo.
Continuing,
"It looks like the Don. Don Alberto it is. He just stepped out of the taxi."
Banks finally gets picture. It reveals Alberto coming toward the house, and carrying a sack large enough to house an UZI.

FLASHBACK:

Rude Buay calls a taxi and leaves. Later, Banks is sitting at the table at home having coffee while he reviews blueprint. Suddenly, a bullet coming through his glass window pane strikes him. He blacks out.

BACK TO PRESENT:

Seeing this, Banks, knowing that an UZI will outmatch his arsenal of weaponry, he turns off the light and exits through the back door, carrying his cell phone and semi-automatic gun in hand.

Alberto shows up outside the house. He removes the UZI from the sack, attached with a silencer. He knocks on the front door. There's no answer. He blows out he lock and enters the house. He switches the light on and rummages from room to room. There is no Walter Banks.

Noticing Banks espionage gadgets, he kicks most of them over in addition to unplugging the multiple TV monitors.

Meanwhile, Banks dials 911 for emergency backup before returning to the house, just in case he confronted Alberto. Don Alberto sees Banks' shadow entering the yard. He unloads several rounds on the Jamaican agent. Nothing connects. Banks fires back also missing the agile Alberto. The neighbors are alerted by the sound of firearms. Suddenly, the once quiet neighborhood except for the sound of ships is awakened to the sound of gunshots like popping corn. Alberto gets inside the taxi and drives away before the community could converge on him.

Moments later, late-arriving Jamaican police flood the area in squad cars. They are too late. Alberto has already fled the area.

Chelo, losing signal once again in that satellite unfriendly community of Port Antonio is unable to capture Alberto's getaway.

Alberto Gomez later abandons the car in a ravine and joins forces with his partner in crime, Johnny *Too Bad*.

Together they drive away with the Commissioner, taking him hostage.

17

The shook up Walter Banks, nevertheless shows up solo and on time to meet with Rude Buay and Rude Buay's partner Miles Tate. Rude Buay greets Banks and then introduces him to agent Miles Tate.
"Glad to know you've escaped."
Says Rude Buay.
"Thanks to Chelo, and his high tech gadgets. His work will no doubt be in the Smithsonian Institute someday."
Banks replies,

"The Dragon Drug Cartel's MO indicates that they were planning a clean sweep operation. By kidnapping Mildred, the Commissioner and then you, they would not have only left us ill-equipped to compete effectively - short-staffed to combat their onslaughts."
A waitress seats the three men at a table.
Rude Buay asks,
"Which of the locals do you confide in, and can be made ready soon?"
"Not sure about that. Most are still upset about how America handled the extradition of Johnny *Too Bad*.
States Walter Banks,
"Ah, they should let sleeping dogs lie. The man is a menace, always has been."
Interjects agent Tate,
"Banks we will find the kidnappers along with the members of your team. 'We may lose some battles but rest assured we will win this war.'
Rude Buay cleverly responds.
The waitress serves up some roast breadfruit *ting* and saltfish with ackee. Tate looks as if he is not sure about the food.
Rude Buay in confidence,
"Eat up man it's all good. *Ital* food! Don't bite your fingers when you are finished."
Tate obliges and is relishing the savory dish.
Banks interjects,

"Maybe the doctor will, seeing she knows so much about our last mission."
Rude Buay responds,
"I am afraid it's not her thing. They said if little Leticia was able to get to the hospital on time her life might have been spared."
"The doctor is that good huh?"
Tate responds.
"Yes, Tamara is great at what she does."
Claims Rude Buay,
"Do we get to…?"
Tate interjects as he is interrupted by Banks.
"Yes, there is a great spot we can go after sunset."
"I haven't had a chance to talk with DEA head-quarters about these kidnappings along with other new developments. By sunset, the kidnappers could be asking for ransoms,"
States agent Rude Buay.
"You think?"
Tate replies,
"… and after sunset no partying?"
Says Banks.
Rude Buay responds,
'I'd like to ask for a rain-check on that one."
"You could invite TAMARA. Its Jamaica got to mix business with a little bit of pleasure. You never know who is connected to…"
Rude Buay reflects.

"Agent Tate is too wet behind the ears to deflect."
Banks inserts,
"Plus he is missing his tattoo."
Tate looks across at both men in response,
"I must say that I have read the entire account. I love it!"
"Good! I don't want to have to take you fishing for Jacks."
"Is Jacks, your favorite fish?"
Tate asks.
"Every snitch finds out the hard way."
Rude Buay states as he excuses himself from the table.
Tate follows Rude Buay.
While Banks stays behind.

18

At the Crows' Nest, an upscale restaurant nestled between the coconut trees and the beach in MO BAY. Rude Buay, Tate and Banks are at a table having a few drinks. There is one vacant chair across from Rude Buay. The soulful Reggae artist performs a combination of dancehall favorites and ballads.

The three men are enjoying the ambiance of the revelry.

TAMARA ROSS, the stunningly eye-catching, 26-year-old beauty walks in. She has never looked so hot publicly. Eyes in the semi-lit room are focused on her, multiple double-takes, indicated by the turning of the necks from all genders. If a massage therapist was present, that individual was about to cash in big time with some deep tissue and double sessions.
Rude Buay acknowledges Tamara while admiring her sensuality.
Rude Buay gets up from his seat, pulls out her chair.
She sits.
He slides that chair in a little closer to the table.
Tamara is flattered.
He pats her lightly on the shoulder area.
She smiles.
He responds in kind.
Rude Buay introduces her,
"Glad you could join us. This is my partner agent Miles Tate. Agent Tate, meet Dr. Tamara Ross."
Tate, drinking Guinness Stout, possibly for the first time could not contain himself. The bottled drink slips out of Tate's hand and spills in the direction of Walter Banks, some splattering on Banks' evening attire.
"Sorry, my gosh. I am so sorry."
Banks responds,
"Hey, calm down, you only had half of the bottle. What is the matter…?"
Rude Buay interjects,

RUDE BUAY VOL. II

"I don't think it's the drink. Maybe..."
The *Maître D.* darts in with a mop and wash rag. He begins cleaning up the spill.
The waiter aids him while he evacuates the guests to a table close to the stage.
The artist delivers another hot number. Tamara wishing Rude Buay will do this dance.
Even so, all eyes at the table are focused on Miles Tate. Tamara, the lady she is, has been somewhat taken aback by Tates' naivety.
Banks looks at the ruin caused to his "Threads."
Rude Buay jesters,
"Tate is so on top of his game he memorized our last account verbatim in less than a day."
Banks stares at Tate in amazement.
Rude Buay continues,
"He said if he was going to be efficient he needed to prepare himself by learning from those who have gone through the minefield against the Dragon Drug Cartel. But he still has a lot to prove...'
Tamara interjects,
"Don't be so hard on him Rude Buay. Tate you are going to love it here in Jamaica. Watch out for those *Hotties!*"
Tate regains his presence of mind and addresses Dr. Ross,

"Thanks. So how does that voodoo works? Is the lighting of the candle and creating a periphery a part of the ritual? Or that is just something you do? "
Dr. Ross responds,
"It doesn't matter, light or no light a circle or a square, it's all in the belief mechanism. You can if you believe you can."
Tate focuses in on Rude Buay, who responds:
"Never practiced, don't care for its workings."
The artist takes a break and the DJ spins some vinyl.
Suddenly, a woman in her late 50s, wearing a head tie shows up at the table. She interrupts. In Rude Buay's mindsight he visualizes Maude Davis, his long-gone godmother.
The woman hands Rude Buay a folded piece of paper and departs. Rude Buay opens it. The others are oblivious concerning what's contained therein.
It says:
"Your friends are in Tivoli Gardens, West Kingstown. Seek and you shall find. Knock and it shall be opened unto you. Ask and it shall be given onto you."
Immediately, Rude Buay's phone rings.
He answers.
It's his boss Michael Ortiz.
"Rude Buay, I have some great news, Heidi Hudson has been reactivated. She will resume active duty tomorrow, and team up with you and Tate in Jamaica.

Now promise me one thing. All three of your asses will be coming back alive to Miami when this is all over."
Rude Buay responds,
"Great move! That second part I can't promise though. It has much to do with the playing of the hand versus the one that's been dealt."
All eyes at that table are fixed on agent Rude Buay. They all anticipate him breaking the news.
He does,
"Hudson will be joining us in the morning!"
"That is awesome!"
Says Tamara.
She continues,
"Now I don't have to spend my night at the shooting range."
Banks jokingly,
"I won't be surprised if you are strapped right now."
They all celebrate with cheers.
Moments later, they wrap the event.
Rude Buay takes Tamara up on a much-celebrated nightcap.

19

Outside the small airport hangar at Kingston Airport, agent HEIDI HUDSON, Caucasian, in her early thirties, wearing dark sunglasses and street clothes deplane. Two full-size minivans wait. Agent Rude Buay and Tate step out from the black minivan and Banks steps from the gray minivan. The three men greet agent Hudson. After which Rude

Buay directs her to Walter Banks' vehicle. She gets inside.

The hatch of the aircraft opens up and with the aid of the pilot, the three men load eclectic assortments ammunition including UZIs and AK 45s into the rear of both minivans.

The black and gray vehicles step into their low rider modes and take off in "rhythm and soul through Kingston."

Inside the gray minivan, Banks, under the wheel is poised for battle. Hudson in the front passenger seat though buckled in, she holds on for her dear life.

Banks reiterates,

"Welcome back agent Hudson."

Hudson replies,

"I love this place! I must say that things have changed since our last visit. Do you think we are going to be able to find Mildred and Baptiste with all the going on?"

"Where there is a will there is a way."

Banks continues,

"That's what agent Rude Buay believes."

Hudson responds,

"He is so resilient, charismatic and at times untouchable. Rude Buay cares about his people so much. It is contagious."

"We so appreciate him,"

Replies Banks.

Both vehicles are approaching West Kingston. Rude Buay tunes the car radio to 100.9 FM Radio Jamaica. The reggae music fades abruptly. The crisp articulate announcer says: "We continue to follow information regarding the death of the three-year-old Leticia Hastings who died of a cocaine overdose last week." Rude Buay presses the transmit button on the stereo, the gray minivan picks up the timely audio feed.

"News just in states: that over one million cartons of powdered milk are feared being recalled around the world, according to the FDA. This happened after a three-year-old girl lost her life as a result of being accidentally fed contaminated milk. It was alleged that a *Ziploc* bag containing almost one eight kilos of cocaine ruptured in a container of milk. Leticia was innocently fed the milk by her mother Beverly Hastings. Leticia died later as a result of that drug overdose.

In other related news, police commissioner and his one-time partner in crime Mildred Simms have still not been found after they were both kidnapped by alleged members of the Dragon Drug Cartel last week. Walter Banks a member of their team, it was reported survived kidnapped attempts by the cartel. Stay tuned for the weather forecast when we return."

With a mountainous backdrop, the street sign reads Approaching Tivoli Gardens.

RUDE BUAY VOL. II

Moments later, the two minivans roll into Tivoli Gardens. Gunmen on multiple rooftops are alerted. Even so, they are mesmerized by the hydraulic movements displayed by both vehicles. As a result, the vans proceed unscathed and with celebrated applause. Rude Buay addresses his colleagues in the gray minivan via stereo.

"Our objective is to rescue the kidnapped. If blood is to be shed, let it be that of the kidnappers and not ours. We are a team. 'United we will stand. Divided we will certainly fall.' Our only burning desire is to win. Whatever it takes, remember, we all come out of this alive. Welcome to TG better known as Tivoli Gardens."

20

Back at the Commissioner's house, a Fed Ex package arrives. Christine Baptiste signs for it. The senders' address seemed ineligible to her. Anyway, she opens it and discovers Richard's wallet. Inside the package, she finds a note which reads: RB - RIP.

Christine rushes for her cell phone. She immediately calls Rude Buay, he answers the cellular phone call.

Rude Buay, this is Christine, Richards' wife. I know you are very busy but I was asked to update you about the kidnapping of my husband Richard. A package was just delivered to me by Fed Ex. In it were Richard's wallet and a note which reads: RB – RIP. Have you heard anything from the kidnappers? Did they mention anything about a ransom as yet?"

Rude Buay responds,

"We have not heard anything as of yet. As soon as or when we do, we will inform you. Mrs. Baptiste, are those hidden cameras installed at your home working efficiently?"

In tears, Christine says,

"Yes! Thank you for making that possible."

The four agents continue on their quest through Tivoli Gardens.

Rude Buay asks agent Tate,

"What would you say are the three things that make you tick as a DEA?"

Miles Tate responds,

"Search, Seizure and Arrest, I'm still waiting for the latter ... "

Many teens line the streets, buyers and sellers, alike.

Rude Buay pulls up to the curb.

Banks follow suites and corners of the sellers.

Hudson jumps out to assist.

Rude Buay chases after the Buyers.

Tate catches up and grabs one of the teens and confiscates several marijuana *spliffs*.

Rude Buay senses the potential buried inside the more than a dozen teens.

He addresses them,

"My name is agent Rude Buay and these are my colleagues. Don't ever let us see you all out here again."

The youths are released by the agents and immediately vacate the area.

The agents return to their car. Tate is mesmerized by the giant size of these confiscated rolled in newspaper marijuana joints. He is tempted. Rude Buay looks across at him.

Rud Buay cautions:

"Not on my watch."

Tate changes that mindset.

Banks keep up with Rude Buay. Agents Tate and Hudson get an eyeful of the weaponry displayed by some guards standing outside a wooded house. Rude Buay pulls up and stops in front of the battalion. Tate is terrified.

"Are you okay?"

Asks the veteran agent - Rude Buay.

Without waiting for an answer Rude Buay says,

"Follow me,"

Banks and Hudson wait inside their greatly admired minivan.

Rude Buay asks the armed guards:

"Where is Levy? Need to see him."

One of the guards responds,
"Nobody sees Levy."
Rude Buay flashes his badge and pushes the guard out of the way, and barges in followed by Tate.
LEVY, is a bearded man in his 50s, wearing a knitted hat in the colors of the flag. His dreadlocks are rolled up underneath the black, yellow and green. There is a wide assortment of narcotics and money in the now entered living room of the house.
Levy greets.
"Hey Rude Buay, not because you are wearing a badge, it doesn't give you the right to barge in on I and I like that. *Chua*? Anyway, let's get down to business. What can I do for you, *mon*?
Rude Buay responds,
"I am looking for Mildred Simms and the Commissioner. I heard that Johnny has them."
"Who told you that?"
Asks Levy.
"Come on, you know that the commissioner helped in having him extradited to the U.S. If you were in his shoes: Who would be one of the first people to exercise vindictiveness upon? Plus his fingerprints were found on the commissioner's vehicle after the kidnapping occurred."
"America has given Johnny a bad rap. We run things in Tivoli Gardens, and he might be referred to as Johnny *Too Bad* but he doesn't have your people. Plus

you just touched my door with your bare hands on your way in. If I wanted to plant your fingerprints at the scene of a crime, I can hire the experts to do so. Money is power and when you don't have any it not only stinks, it sours,"

Says Levy,

Rude Buay doesn't believe a word he says. Even so, he notices the AKA 45 sitting on Levy's table.

Meanwhile, the guards on the outside of Levy's establishment focus on the waiting gray minivan with Banks and Hudson inside.

Rude Buay turns to leave.

Levy says,

"Happy Hunting!"

Rude Buay eyes Tate.

Tate draws and points his gun in Levy's face.

Levy asks,

"What is this Rude Buay, you didn't get what you wanted? You afraid of what the Jamaicans will do to you, so you are going to have the White Man shoot me."

Rude Buay responds,

"No, I am not. I want answers."

Rude Buay grabs Levy in a chokehold. Drags him to the restroom and sticks his head deep down in the unflushed toilet.

Rude Buay demands,

"Now are you going to tell me where my people are or do I have to make you drink first?"

Levy replies in hardcore *patois*,

"That is I and I piss. No problem if *me* drink it. That would not resurrect your brother Clifford. Is harden him been hardened!"

Rude Buay again demands'

"Give me a location. Do you want to live or you want to die?"

Rude Buay submerges Levy's head a second time into the toilet bowl and then releases him.

Levy spits out a mouthful on Rude Buay.

Rude Buay punches him hard in the face. Levy rocks back. He launches a fist at Rude Buay. The agent ducks out of it and shoots Levy in the face.

Levy's *Posse* on the outside is alerted by the gunshot. In their mind, they are thinking that Levy shot Rude Buay.

Rude Buay barges out with Tate behind him. The surprised guards try training their weapons on the agents. Banks and Hudson jump out of their vehicle in assistance to Rude Buay and Tate in the onslaught of the guards.

The death count at Levys' establishment equaled eleven, ten guards and Levy.

An old man, looking out his window from across the street, sees the body count. He yells from his window in some hardcore *patois*,

"You looking for Johnny? Him up at Chin Chins Bar and Grill, on Friday nights. Right up on Mannings Hill Road. *Me* hope you speak Chinese."

Rude Buay steps out put a Hundred dollar bill under a rock.

The old man clues in and hurries down to get it.

The four agents proceed to Chin Chins Bar and Grill.

21

The agents merge onto Kent Street and pull up next to Chin Chins. Rude Buay and Tate barge inside the bar and grill restaurant. Banks and Hudson wait outside in surveillance mode. It's dinner time inside Chin Chins. Some people are dining, some drinking, some just listening to music, others are shooting pool.

The agents, survey there is no glimpse of Johnny. Rude Buay walks up to the bar. The bartender, his name tag reads JIM and is busy tending. So Rude Buay waits his turn.

"Hey, Jim I am looking for Johnny, seen him lately?

"No *mon* sorry."

The bartender returns to his duty.

Tate yells at him,

"Seen or heard anything about the two people he kidnapped?"

"I wished I could help you guys! I mind my own business around here."

Says uncooperative Jim,

One man at the pool table getting ready to shoot for the eight-ball overhears and responds.

"The Americans took him out of here months ago. Then he escaped to China. He must be … loving those Chinese women. Try Beijing!"

Rude Buay and Tate head out to their vehicle. They wait and survey.

Rude Buay notifies his other agents in the accompanying minivan through the stereo system.

"Nothing there, everyone is so tight-lipped. Except for one drunk who said he's in Beijing."

Hudson asks,

"So what do we do?"

Rude Buay responds,

"We will persist until we find him. Even if he is under a rock we will scratch him out like… crayfish.

Hudson responds,

"I've never been to China before. I am all in!"
Tate looks over at Rude Buay and asks,
"Is that the same as shrimp?"
Rude Buay answers,
"Close!"
Tate continues,
"You did say China? Do you think Ortiz would Greenlight such an expedition? Why aren't these locals leading us to him?"
Rude Buay responds,
"In West Kingston, no one trusts anyone. Johnny is like a politician. He has been so good to those people; no one wants to bring him down."
Tate responds,
"But he is wanted. Why don't they?"
"He performs his dirty work. Then treats them like a modern-day Santa Claus would. He has learned a lot from Alberto in that regard…."
Rude Buay says.
Banks and Heidi Hudson overhear this conversation between Rude Buay and agent Tate as broadcast through the van's stereo.
 During this interlude, two local men fully armed, come up towards Banks' minivan and addresses Banks.
Banks rolls down the window to hear them.
"Got to move these supped up minivans, can't park them out here."

They both focus in on Heidi Hudson. Rude Buay and Tate are alerted and are poised to assist if necessary.

"Is that your pimp…?"

One of the men asks,

Hudson acts as if she isn't sure what he's talking about. Looking at Banks they continue,

"If he is pimp daddy I would like to…"

One of the men grabs on Hudson's arm while aiming his gun on Banks.

Hudson blasts the gun-carrying man who falls dead onto the street. Before the other man could release Hudson's arm and reach for his gun, Banks caps him in the head. He too falls onto the street a dead man. Meanwhile, Rude Buay and Tate stand erect and ready to unleash. Both agents return their guns in holster and hops inside the minivan.

Banks and Hudson follow suit and drive off.

22

The following morning, the agents continue combing through West Kingston for the hostages.

Hudson notices a gathering as they cross an intersection. She notifies Rude Buay through the stereo system.

"Rude Buay, pull over, these kids are way too young…"

Banks parks and Hudson rushes out leaving the door ajar.

Rude Buay complies.

Rude Buay's vehicle makes a quick U-Turn. Heidi Hudson is already out of the car in pursuit of the teenage crowd. Now the other three agents are on foot heading in agent Hudson's direction.

Agent Hudson is catching up to a 14 - 15-year-old Afro-Asian girl, Tasha.

In one hand the almost subdued Tasha carries two Milky Way cans and a switchblade in the other.

Hudson catches up with her.

She confronts Heidi Hudson.

Hudson kicks the opened knife out of Tasha's hand. Tasha rolls over on the ground. The two cans hit the pitched road and open revealing a *Ziploc* bag with at least one eight of a kilo of cocaine underneath the powdered milk.

Banks covers Hudson, while Tate confiscates the narcotics.

Rude Buay looks on.

Agent Hudson addresses Tasha:

"What is your name, young lady?"

"Tasha Ching,"

"How old are you?"

"I am almost 15,"

"Why aren't you in school?"

"Please don't tell my parents, they will kill me."

"How long have you been doing this?"

"One and a half years,"

'Why"

RUDE BUAY VOL. II

"The money is good,"
"How did you get involved?"
"Johnny introduced me on my 13th birthday. He said I would get rich doing the streets like him,"
"What is your address?"
"I don't have one,"
"Where do your parents live?"
"I can't tell you."
Rude Buay walks over into Tasha's space.
"Tasha, my name is agent Bascombe, some people call me Rude Buay.
"You mean like in Rihanna's song?"
Tasha immediately begins to sing and dance to the hit song by *Rihanna*.

Come here rude boy,
boy Can you get it up Come here rude boy,
boy Is you big enough Take it,
take it Baby, baby Take it,
take it Love me, love me.
Tonight I'mma let you be the captain
Tonight I'mma let you do your thing,
yeah Tonight I'mma let you be a rider
Giddy up
Giddy up
Giddy up, babe

"The name is the same. We are here to help you and will handle this intelligently."

"You don't know my parents, they will KILL me."

Hudson interjects,

"We will ask them not to."

"I don't know why you all want to help me I am nobody…"

Rude Buay interrupts,

"That' what society makes you think. You are filled with potential, Tasha."

"My parents are not together,"

Hudson questions,

"You live at home, mom?"

"Yes,"

Tasha replies,

"Where is Johnny now?"

Rude Buay asks,

"I have not seen *Too Bad* in almost a week. They said that he went to China."

Tasha says,

"How did you get here?"

Rude Buay inquires,

"I took the bus from Kingston."

Tasha responds,

"Okay, we will give you a ride,"

Says Rude Buay.

"You all promise. This is not some kind of kidnapping, right? I don't want to end up in Bermuda…"

Tasha says.

The four agents give Tasha a reassuring look.

Hudson leads the way.

Tasha follows Hudson and boards the gray minivan. The two minivans take off. The gray van leads the way towards Kingston.

23

The agents arrive in Kingston. Tasha points out the house on the hill inside a cul-de-sac. Both minivans pull up and park. Rude Buay and Tate get out and head up the hill towards the house. Rude Buay knocks on the door. A dark-skinned Jamaican woman answers. My name is agent Bascombe, this is my partner Miles Tate. Agents Heidi Hudson and Walter Banks are inside the other van. We are here on a matter which we feel concerns you.

"The man and the woman who got kidnapped are not here, agents Bascombe and whatever your name is, Tate? And we are sure not hiding Johnny *Too Bad*."

"May we call you Miss or Mrs...?"

"You may call me Mrs. Ching. It doesn't matter he is gone. I sang him hit the road, Jack. Don't come back any more... when he decided to walk out on Tasha and me."

Rude Bauy continues,

"Mrs. Ching, it is about your daughter. We found her at a location where she doesn't belong."

"Where is Tasha? I thought she said that she was going to live with her father. That..."

"We found her on the streets of West Kingston dealing narcotics."

States Rude Buay,

"I will KILL Tasha..."

Mrs. Ching responds,

Rude Buay interjects,

"That's what she told us."

Rude Buay continues,

"But we assured her that if she would cooperate by letting us bring her home, you wouldn't hurt her. Additionally, we would make sure that this is handled intelligently."

"Where is Tasha?"

Agent Heidi Hudson, overhearing the conversation via the "wired" Rude Buay, with Banks and Tasha listening in, steps out of the gray minivan and hands over Tasha to her mother."

"Thank you very much agents, Hudson, Bascombe, Tate and will you let Mr. Banks know that I say thanks. Is he the one who escaped getting kidnapped?"

Banks steps out of the minivan to deliver Tasha's forgotten sweater.

Mrs. Ching gets a closer view of the Jamaican agent Walter Banks.

"I am sure I heard about him on the news last week. Yes, that's him. You all be careful now. It is like a jungle out there…"

Tears well-up in Tasha's eyes.

"Thanks and goodbye."

Tasha says.

The agents depart.

24

Meanwhile in Shanghai, China a submarine surfaces at an abandoned dock. There are no on-lookers, so the five individuals get off undetected: Denise, Shelly, Amanda and Johnny *Too Bad*, and a blindfolded woman. They escort the blindfolded to a waiting van, seats her inside, the van takes off with David Lee at the driver's wheel.

The van pulls up outside the *Torture House*. They exit and remove the previously blindfolded Mildred from her seat and amble towards the interior of the house.

The move descends to the desolate basement. Nothing there except for the four walls a chair in the middle of the room and a noose from a rope dangling from the extended roof. With her mouth still covered with duct tape, Shelly removes the blindfold which clothed Mildred's eyes. On Mildred's face, there is a sense of frustration of wanting to speak and not being able to.

The three women bind Mildred's hand as well as her feet to the chair with ropes. Johnny overseeing grabs the slow-moving extended noose and slips it around Mildred's neck. He adjusts the chair downwards, so the rope around her neck tightens just a bit.

They feel satisfied with the proper functioning of their mechanism. They depart and board the waiting van. The van drives off.

Rude Buay checks in with the Chinese immigration authorities but they are unable to verify that Johnny along with other members of the Dragon Drug Cartel had entered the country.

MEANWHILE, VULTURES FLY LOW over a small reservation, as the morning sun begins to cast its rays on the outskirts of Tivoli Gardens. In the interim, in TG, Rude Buay, Miles Tate, Heidi Hudson, and Walter Banks continue their search for the kidnapped. Even so, they are still oblivious regarding Mildred's whereabouts.

RUDE BUAY VOL. II

The four agents continue to comb through huts, houses, tenement yards, bars along with other buildings. They are now joined by Jamaican police in the search with dogs.

Rude Buay pulls up at a Barber Shop. He gets out of his car followed by Tate.

In the meantime, Hudson and Banks visit the restaurant across the street.

Inside the barbershop: Some men are getting their hair cut, while others wait their turn.

Rude Buay, surveys, and then addresses: "My name is agent Bascombe and this is agent Tate. We are with the Drug Enforcement Agency. We are looking for Johnny *Too Bad* along with the kidnapped Mildred Simms and Baptiste."

One man who is baldheaded and certainly not there to get a haircut says nonchalantly,

"We heard about you Rude Buay! You have bigger issues in America, like Child Care, Recession and Abortion. I hope that the Prime Minister of Jamaica isn't paying you out of our hard-earned tax dollars. That man Baptiste deserves to get what he received. The woman Simms, her past is what got her in trouble. Nobody in Tivoli Gardens is going to help you, *mon*. You came to the wrong place."

Rude Buay continues,

"Has anyone seen any of the hostages or know of their whereabouts?"

Everyone is mute.

"And for you sir,"

Rude Buay looks directly at the "smart mouth" local.

"Empty all your pockets and place the contents on this table."

Fritz hesitates in fulfilling agent Rude Buays' request and finds himself suddenly looking down the barrels of two guns, Rude Buays' and Tates' semi-automatics. Out of his pockets come a switchblade knife, vials of crack and packets of cocaine.

Tate immediately cuffs him and waits for the Jamaican police to arrive in their squad car and take him away. Two officers who previously abandoned the search return and take Fritz to jail.

In the meantime, at a restaurant across the street, Hudson confronts the MANAGER on Duty.

Heidi Hudson addresses,

"Good morning! My name is agent Hudson. I am looking for Johnny *Too Bad*. Have you seen him lately? Or heard about the whereabouts regarding the kidnapped Simms and Baptiste?"

The Manager serving beef patty and cocoa bread to a customer responds,

"Fire!"

Hudson asks,

"What do you mean?"

The woman reiterates in *patois*,

"Fire ah go burn them. Them, hurt poor Johnny's feelings."
Banks responds,
"Does he have feelings?"
Leaving that for the woman to massage and marinate Banks and Hudson unfortunately leave the Jamaican restaurant unaccomplished.

25

Rude Buays' phone rings. He answers it on the second ring.

"Hello, agent Rude Buay,"

The female voice echoes,

"This is Christine the Commissioners' wife. Has there been any word yet on Richard's whereabouts? If no ransom has been requested as of now, the chances of him still being alive are pretty slim, don't you think? It has been a few days now."

"Mrs. Baptiste we are doing everything possible to try and locate your husband Richard, as well as his kidnappers.

We hope that we'll find Richard alive. So far I hate to inform you but nothing has turned up positively except that the Jamaican police, a short while ago claimed that they were able to trace the FedEx package which was sent to your home as being sent from Tivoli Gardens.

However, as you had seen on that package, the sender's name was ineligible. I am very optimistic that we'll find him. We will notify you as soon as we locate your husband."

Christine hears agent Rude Buay but doesn't believe a word he says. In tears Christine continues, this time talking to herself.

"I don't know what they want my husband for. Whatever political party gave power to this drug cartel, is putting our country to shame. We used to be one love, now it seems like one hate. Innocent people, including kids, die for nothing. Who gave drug dealers power over civilians? The government and their MPs! Richard always believed in ONE Jamaica. Now the same team he assembled to protect and serve. They all are sitting on their butts, so vultures can devour his body and ants his bones. The country he has worked

so hard to defend has allowed the oppressors to continually oppress…Like Bob Marley said: 'Who the cap fit to wear it.'
Those wicked politicians!"
Christine aborts her call to agent Rude Buay.
Suddenly her house phone rings. She tries catching it on the second ring, misses it but grabs it on the third.
"Hello, Hello, Hello!"
Christine addresses.
There is no answer.
The only sound she hears is "Click. Click"
Terrified, Christine bolsters herself and rushes to the bedroom. She removes one of the pillows and pulls out her husband's automatic weapon. She checks to make sure that it's loaded. Satisfied, she sits on the couch facing the door and waits.
Up the street, oblivious to her, and out of view by her property's surveillance cameras, two Jamaican police officers hideout.
These watchers, dispatched earlier after the tracking location of the FedEx package was determined by a Government Official and ally of Johnny and Alberto Gomez, continue to wait.
Already tapped into Christine's phone line they gather information.
On their TV monitor, the police could see Christine waiting for the kill.

RUDE BUAY VOL. II

It's dawn. The policemen look at each other, none of them dare to become a casualty, so they unwillingly vacate the area.

26

Back in Tivoli Gardens, Rude Buay not giving up continues to follow his instincts. Driving further along Mannings Hill they come upon a blockage in the street. The blockade made up of abandoned iceboxes, car tires, tree trunks, bed mattresses, old furniture, tree branches, a skeleton of stripped vehicles and oil drums. Rude Buay, Miles Tate, Walter Banks and Heidi Hudson get out of their vehicle and make a clear path. They re-board their vehicle and proceed along the same street.

At an undisclosed location in Tivoli Gardens, Alberto reclines the black leather chair and sip on the almost full cup of that black robust coffee. He reaches for his phone and dials.

Rude Buay and his agents are combing the streets looking for evidence that could lead them to the finding of the hostages.

Rude Buays' cell phone rings, he answers:

"This is Rude Buay."

Rude Buay realizes its Alberto Gomez's number and goes to full circuit stereo. The two agents in the other minivan listen in. The voice on the other end greets.

"Rude Buay, this is Albert Gomez. You and your agents will not take a back seat by letting me do my thing as I see fit. First I must inform you that the man you are looking for is sitting under my thumb. And very soon you could be accompany-ing him if you continue to be in pursuit of my enterprise. Don't forget we do not only control Tivoli Gardens, We are global..."

Rude Buay interrupts:

"All that you are saying is old news. Understand that every seed you've planted can sprout but that doesn't mean that it will. I am interested in the two hostages, not what you and David Lee have put together globally."

"That won't happen unless you and your agents are willing to comply with our demands."

Alberto says,

"Try me!"

Rude Buay answers courageously.

"You failed at living up to demands back in Port Antonio. Not sure you are capable of keeping your word."

States Alberto.

"You are nothing but a prick!"

Rude Buay responds.

"You have one hour to withdraw your antagonistic pursuits of the Dragon Cartel. I have a private jet waiting at a hanger outside the Kingston airport and a van, plus a motorcade waiting to escort you to it if you so desire. After you and your peeps clear Jamaican airspace en-route to America, I would be happy to release Simms and the Commissioner, one at a time."

"Why are you doing this? If you have gotten your wish, why drip on the releasing process of the hostages?"

Alberto continues,

"You don't ask questions at this point Rude Buay, you fulfill demands. That's the way I choose to lay my safety net. Additionally, I am sending a message to Washington, that if they mess with us any further we will not only expand across the five oceans but will cause some of the most devastating recalls that country has ever experienced."

Alberto continues,

"As for you? If you screw up, vultures would enjoy fresh meat of you and your agents."
Rude Buay weighs the consequences and asks,
"Where is that van located?"
"You are thinking on your feet."
Alberto's coffee cup is refilled by a tall Jamaican woman. His UZI is present and close to his reach. Money and milk can create a decorative aurora of drug dealing spectacle. Alberto snorts two lines of coke, one per nostril. Alberto fetches his gun and car keys. He leaves. Even so, he continues his phone conversation with Rude Buay.
Alberto continues,
"It's located at the entrance of Tivoli Gardens, on the Southwest corner."

BACK AT THE ENTRANCE TO TG, the van waits, along with a pair of motorbikes and two men standing guard.

ON ANOTHER TIVOLI GARDENS STREET, the agents park their cars.
Rude Buay puts Alberto on hold and commissions his other agents via the stereo.
"Banks and Hudson I need you to cover on the outside of this property while Tate and I engage on this investigative pursuit."

Rude Buay releases the hold button and continues his conversation with Alberto.

Rude Buay replies,

"Alberto it's a deal. How soon will we be able to take custody of Baptiste and Simms?"

Alberto responds,

"They belong to the Jamaican Government. You have my word that they will be released simultaneously to their government."

Rude Buay not believing a word Alberto says.

Alberto continues,

"Good! That private jet flies in 48 minutes."

The agents continue their search of West Kingston.

Rude Buay sees a house with an outdoor sign saying "beware of dogs." He pulls over. Banks follow suites. Alberto's guards are unaware of the agents' entourage forming outside the front door.

Upon noticing the black and gray vans parked outside the house. The guards release a few rounds from Uzis in the direction of the vehicle.

The vans are empty as the four agents had already dispersed and taken up position on the other side of the house. One of the guards' fires at Rude Buay. He misses and takes a bullet from Rude Buays' gun instead. That guard hits the ground, dead.

27

Heidi Hudson enters the house through the already opened front door amidst the sound of barking dogs. The tall Jamaican woman attempts to escape. The agile Heidi Hudson pushes her back inside with vengeance.

Heidi Hudson asks,

"Where are Simms and Baptiste?"

The Woman does not respond. So Hudson handcuffs her.

"You are going with us."

Says Hudson as she pushes the woman in front of her like a human shield proceeding through the house's interior.

In the interim, Rude Buay and Tate are still engaged in an exchange of firepower with the other guard. Rude Buay shoots. The Guard runs for the parked car. A bullet catches the guard disconnected and cuts him down.

MEANWHILE, OBLIVIOUS TO the agents, Alberto boards a waiting submarine from an abandoned dock in Kingston.

Back at the House in Tivoli Gardens, Rude Buay, Tate and Banks catch up with Heidi Hudson as they penetrate deep inside the interior of that house. Rude Buay observes the handcuffed woman. Like a man possessed he asks,

"Where are Baptiste and Simms?"

The woman now hearing this asked of her by two separate agents. Yet, she still refuses to cooperate.

Inside the living room, money and milk can create a decorative and auroras drug dealing spectacle.

The agents move deeper inside the interior of the strange house. Walter Banks is already leading the way followed by Rude Buay, Tate, Hudson, and the Jamaican Woman.

The barking sounds of multiple dogs alert the agents to open a locked door. Rude Buay blows out the lock with a bullet from his gun.

As they enter in take-down style, three chained bloodhounds forming a periphery plunge in desperation towards them.

The starving, chained dogs intermittently salivate at their prey that is chained to an electric wired chair. Bones and blood residue adds to the presence of recent carnivorous activities.

When the dogs plunge fully forward the extent of the chains, place their mouths at least three feet in front of the chained victim.

Walter Banks recognizes the victim and yells out,

"It's the Commish!"

Rude Buay advises,

"Let's get him out of there swiftly."

Four guns are pointed on the three dogs. As the agents get ready to take the drooling dogs out of their misery, the Jamaican Woman yells,

"Cease fire!"

The animals lock eyes with the Jamaican Woman and retreat. Not leaving anything up to chance, the agents maintain their aim on the three bloodhounds. Heidi Hudson sizes up the situation.

"I got it!"

Hudson marches in the midst of that "dog's den." She notices the Commissioner wired to the max.

Walter Banks senses trouble and says,
"Be careful Hudson, I hear a ticking sound. Any wire you touch could send us all up in smoke."
Banks gets on his cell phone and dials Chelo in Bogota, Colombia.
Chelo is fast asleep. He jumps up and grabs the phone.
"Chelo! I am sleeping."
Says Chelo,
"Wake up man we are under a time crunch. I need your help. We found the Commissioner. He is wired to the max, multiple red blue, and black wires."
Relays Walter Banks,
Chelo asks,
"What is the address?"
Banks replies,
"No address, a great big house in Tivoli Gardens off Mannings Hill. Come on Chelo, give us your best shot."
Chelo fumbles around with various monitor screens. He claims,
"I got it! Wait."
Ticking decibels increase.
Heidi Hudson responds,
"There is no… time to wait, we could all get killed."
Chelo replies,
"Banks, tell Hudson not to touch anything on that man not even his clothing. The only way out is to turn off the power switch located at the circuit breaker."

RUDE BUAY VOL. II

Banks looks over at the Jamaican woman and asks,
"Where is the darn circuit breaker?"
The Jamaican Woman reluctantly points towards an adjacent room across the hall.
Chelo assures,
"She is right! Move quickly. Time is running out!"
Rude Buay pulls out another automatic from under his trousers. He points it on the dogs where Banks' aim was directed.
Banks tugs the woman to that room where she indicated the power turn-off switch is.
In the interim, the dogs plunge forward at Agent Hudson with the full length of their chain.
Tate yells,
"Cease fire!"
There is no response from the dogs. Rude Buay and Hudson follow up using the same command to no avail.
Total darkness now engulfs the room, mixed with sounds of barking dogs and the mumbling of the agents.
Banks and the woman return with the aid of his mini-emergency flash-light.
The Jamaican woman again yells,
"Cease Fire!"
The dogs retreat. With the aid of Banks' flashlight, he and Hudson remove the Commissioner, who is still

wearing the clothes he did when kidnapped. Together the agents make their getaway from inside the house.
Rude Buay asks the woman,
"Any information on Mildred Simms whereabouts?"
The Jamaican woman replies,
"Try Shanghai."
As the agents make their exit on the house's terrace, Banks pulls out five U.S one hundred dollar bills and attempts to hand it over to the woman, who is still handcuffed.
Hudson grabs the cash and sticks it inside of the woman's bra. Meanwhile, the agents quickly remove the duct tape from the Commissioners' mouth.
The Commissioner now vocal,
Thank you Mr. Rude Buay and…
Rude Buay assists,
Tate, My partner Miles Tate.
The Commissioner,
"Tate. This so great seeing all you good people once again. I missed the de-briefing. Thanks, Hudson, great intuition. Banks we appreciate you!"
Rude Buay states,
"No problem we got you out of there safely. Now we've got to go and find Mildred Simms."
The Commissioner asks,
"Where is Mildred? They got her too?"
Rude Buay expounds,

"Yes. Also kidnapped by the Dragons on the same evening as you ..."

They load up, place the Commissioner inside the gray minivan and depart from the premises, leaving the woman behind still in handcuffs.

28

It's nightfall. At the Tivoli Gardens entrance, the cube van waits. The agents get ready to board. A RASTAFARIAN GUARD accompanied by the driver ushers in Rude Buay and his crew.
The Rastafarian Guard says to the driver.
"Overload!"
Driver asks,
"What you mean overload?"
The Rastafarian Guard answers in deep *patois*,
"Me, say overload, one too many *mon*."

The Driver and Guard stare at the Commissioner, who is bearded and outfitted in street clothes, wearing a Rastafarian wig and dark sunglasses. His chic tie is hanging out from his side pocket.
Rude Buay argues,
"We've got to take him or we don't go."
The driver continues staring at the Rastafarian Guard and Baptiste.
The Rastafarian Guard responds,
"That man is not getting inside this van. I was told four people now five show up. Not another thug!"
The driver and the guard continue arguing, creating a stand-off against the agents and the Commissioner. The Guard senses trouble not knowing what to expect at this point from the agents. So he commands,
"Drop your weapons!"
The agents comply.
While the Guard moves the four guns to the side and out of the way. Rude Buay kicks him hard in the stomach. The Guard falls to the ground gasping for air. The Guard quickly regains his presence of mind. He aims at Rude Buay and shoots.
Rude Buay dodges out of his onslaught and reaches for the gun under his left trouser leg. He gets a successful shot off, which caps the Rastafarian Guard. The driver swings at Rude Buay. His swing is blocked by Rude Buay using his left hand and his right hand to punch him hard in his face, as a result, knocking him out.

The four agents and the Commissioner swiftly load up ammunition and luggage from the minivans onto the cube van. They board the van. The Commissioner, under Rude Buays' instruction, takes the wheel.
The van departs through the streets of Kingston.
Suddenly, Rude Buays' phone rings. He answers.
"My pilot flies in ten minutes."
Says Alberto.
"Blame it on your drivers."
Rude Buay responds.
"We'll make it anyway."
Rude Buay continues and then hangs up.
Later they arrive at the airport hangar in Kingston. The Cube van pulls up next to the waiting Jet aircraft. They disembark and come face to face with the Pilot and his co-pilot.
The Pilot's eyes are focused on the Commissioner. Something doesn't seem right to him. Looking at Rude Buay he says,
"You are late Rude Buay, this plane should have flown five minutes ago, David Lee wouldn't be very happy with this."
Says the Pilot.
Richard Baptiste, the Commissioner responding to the name drop, asks.
"I thought it was ... Alberto?"
The Pilot answers as a matter of fact,
"On his way to ... Asia! Got to move it ...!"

RUDE BUAY VOL. II

Looking over at the Co-Pilot, the Pilot instructs, "Frisk them down and get those bastards on board."
The Co-Pilot complies.
They are clean except for Rude Buay still carrying that gun in his left trousers' leg.
The Pilot takes away Rude Buay's gun, removes the bullets and tosses it away.
The Commissioner attempts to get on the Jet last.
The Pilot is alerted.
"We are not taking you. Trying to get into America illegally?"
He continues,
"Not going to happen. Plus we don't have an extra seat anyway. You could ride on the wing."
Says the Pilot.
In protest the four agents deplane headed by Rude Buay. The Pilot is confused. He commands.
"Get your asses back on that plane. I'll take you to Miami dead or alive. It's your choice."
He aims his gun at them.
The Co-Pilot's back is turned against the aircraft. Rude Buay grabs him behind his neck, lifts him off the ground while his feet dangles. He drops him hard to the ground, takes away his weapon, caps him several times and then aims gun at the pilot.
The Pilot has a change of heart.
"It's okay we will take your friend if that's what you want."

Rude Buay commands,
"Drop your weapons!"
The Pilot is flustered but he complies.
Tate and Banks check the Pilot for additional weapons. There is none.
Rude Buay shoves the Pilot aboard the Jet and commands,
"Open up the hatch."
The Pilot does as commanded.
Rude Buay keeps an aim on the pilot, while the Commissioner and the other agents load up their weapons and luggage onto the aircraft.
Everyone is now on board.
The pilot sits at the control of the Jet.
Rude Buay announces,
"Change of plans! We are going to Shanghai, China."
The Pilot remarks,
"Never been there before. Navigation could be problematic. Plus I don't speak their language."
Rude Buay weighs his options.
Richard Baptiste gets up from his seat,
"Don't worry I got this! I've taken off and landed in Shanghai on numerous occasions."
The pilot gets up, relinquishing control to Baptiste.
Rude Buay grabs the pilot and pushes him through the door and off the plane.
He tries to get away on foot. Several rounds from Rude Buays' gun cut him down as he collapses to his death.

RUDE BUAY VOL. II

The plane taxis and then takes off.

29

It's a crisp busy morning. The hustle and bustle of the white-collar workforce resemble that of New York's Wall Street, before the sound of the big bell and the Wall Street protests. Retrospectively, across the way, an African American freestyler draws a crowd of Asian supporters like a vacuum in motion. Chu Ling joins the mesmerized audience.

Up the block, two Chinese Police Officers converse, while looking in the direction of the crowd. Their eyes

are now fixed on Chu, who seems to be mesmerized by the artistic performance. The officers proceed toward the gathering and confront Chu Ling.
The senior Chinese police officer questions,
"Miss, what are you carrying in that bag?"
Chu Ling replies,
"Groceries!"
The Junior Officer is "gun-happy" while his partner continues the investigation.
The senior CHINESE POLICE OFFICER asks,
"Do you mind if we take a look?"
Chu Ling reluctantly hands over the bag.
The senior officer opens it. He sees a full container of milk nevertheless, he looks at Chu, and asks as he approaches the trash can.
"If there is nothing but milk inside, we will replace it."
The senior officer pours the milk out into the trash can. A *Ziploc* bag with a powdery substance falls out on top of the milk. He retrieves it and asks,
"Miss what is your name?"
"Chu Ling."
"Chu - Ling!"
He continues,
"I am afraid this is not all milk. We are going to have to arrest you for cocaine possession."
The junior officer handcuffs Chu Ling and escorts her to their parked cruiser.

The crowd, as well as the freestyler, scatter as the arrest is conducted.

Moments later, on that same street, the Drug Czar David Lee meanders his way through a dense crowd of pedestrians looking for his wife Chu.

In the meantime at a prestigious law firm in downtown Shanghai, on the top floor in a high rise building, twelve lawyers of the Chins Law Firm engage in their early morning free-basing ritual. Some free-base while others chip away from the cocaine mound. Others assemble and snort. Consequently, severe vomiting and giddiness sets in later. The Law Firm's Green Room is now full of panic and pandemonium.

Less than an hour later ambulances arrive whisking all twelve lawyers to a downtown Shanghai hospital. Several blocks away the news is live on a big TV screen regarding the recent Chinese Drug Bust. People standing outside a bus station are glued to that early morning news in various languages around the world. *ONE AMERICA TV* station delivers the following newscast along with footage:

"This is your early morning late-breaking news from *ONE AMERICA TV:*"

A female American TV announcer sinks her teeth into it.

"Earlier this morning at least a dozen lawyers from Chins Law Firm in downtown Shanghai were rushed to the hospital after an apparent free-basing session.

Chinese Police discovered two milk cans containing cocaine residue under the table of the office where the alleged free-basing session occurred.

Meanwhile, over ten thousand cans of milk believed to have been packed with *Ziploc* bags of uncut cocaine were discovered in a submarine down the Chinese River bound for the Caribbean. The estimated street value of the cargo is over $10M. A Colombian Drug Lord, Salvador, was arrested and detained by Chinese Police in conjunction with the drug bust.

Meanwhile, the FDA in Washington, DC has scheduled a meeting for next Monday to discuss the possibility of a recall to all powdered milk products including **baby formula**. According to analysts, if this recall goes into effect millions of kids around the world could die of scurvy and malnutrition.

Many mothers are resorting to breastfeeding to protect their young ones from death or malnourished related diseases.

China, now emerging as one of the largest industrial nations is now under pressure; as anything shipped from that country is subject to search by Chinese authorities.

Besides, random searching of packages on all public transportation is now in effect in China. This morning Chinese police also arrested and detained Chu Ling, the mistress of the Drug Lord and Entrepreneur David Lee on drug trafficking charges. It is believed that Ling sold narcotics to the Chin Law firm earlier this morning."

Many mothers around the world are stunned by these latest revelations:

One woman in Utah rushes to her bedroom just to see if her four kids all under the ages of five years old were okay. She is satisfied as they are all playing with toys. She overlooks the powdered milk products on the kitchen counter and instead grabs the youngest and prepares to breastfeed the infant.

One woman in Hollywood, California wishing she had kids breaks out in tears upon viewing the news.

On the other hand, one starving writer in Seattle takes copious notes with the hope that he could someday cash in on the story.

30

Inside David Lee's house an intense free-basing, get high interlude unfolds around the dining table involving David Lee, Alberto Gomez, Denise Gomez, Shelly Hall, Amanda Kingsley and Johnny *Too Bad*. Johnny methodically rolls a giant-sized marijuana *spliff* on the cover page of the local Chinese newspaper which covered the drug bust. He lights up, partakes and passes it off to Alberto, who takes a huge toke before passing it along to his associates.

Everyone partakes except for David Lee, who is busily separating his upcoming dosage from the huge mound of cocaine with the use of a razor blade. Then with a straw, he attacks and snorts that entire line, like it was clean air.

David is now relaxed.

He addresses his associates,

"We have got to do something about Rude Buay. That jet still has not arrived in Miami."

"Orders must be carried out. Once again he reneged on..."

Responds Alberto.

Johnny interjects,

"It should be clear to him in the note from me that I want him out of TG."

Shelly chimes in,

"Out of Jamaica. Period!"

David Lee states,

"That private jet left Jamaica with two sets of casualties behind. One at the ground transportation pick-up site in Tivoli Gardens, and the other at the airplane hangar in Kingston."

Shelly reaffirms,

"Rude Buay doesn't know how to fly an airplane."

Alberto responds,

"I don't think that any of the others do ..."

Johnny interrupts,

"The Commissioner attended aviation school in China. That's where he met his wife."

Eyebrows are raised.

Johnny *Too Bad* asks,

"Boss, enough respect but how did you let that PIG getaway? I thought that we had him inside the net."

Alberto responds,

"Blame it on those ... guards. Too many loose ends!"

David opens his loaded wallet. He removes Chu Ling's picture and reflects. He has a moment, pondering as if in that mediatory event with his wife, she would be released from within the prison walls. Everyone in the circle up is now silent.

David Lee continues,

"Guys we need to figure out where that plane landed. There has been no communication from that pilot as of yet."

Johnny in deep thought.

Johnny *Too Bad* states,

"They took Tasha back home to her mother. I wonder if she told those bastards that I went to China."

David Lee questions,

"Who the heck is Tasha?"

Johnny *Too Bad* replies,

"She worked for me."

Amanda Kingsley is peeved.

"Risking our lives with a minor ...?"

She asks.

Alberto picks up his gun and car keys off the table in preparation to depart. Getting in his way is his wife Denise.

"Where are you going to *Papi*?"

Alberto responds,

"Let's go to the airport!"

They all look at each other as if Alberto's decision was the expected magical wand that needed to be waved to conclude the Rude Buay saga.

The get-high session escalates into a massive conclusion.

They make their exit…

31

The Jetplane arrives in Shanghai, China. The agents and Commissioner deplane. With the newly acquired cell phone from Walter Banks, Baptiste dials his wife Christine for the first time after being kidnapped. Christine Baptiste answers,
"Hello, who is this?"
"This is Rich, Richard. I am free Chris! Free at last. Meet me in China. I will text you the exact location when we check-in."
Christine Baptiste asks,

"WE?"

Richard Baptiste responds,

"I am with Banks, Rude Buay and the rest of their team. You remember telling me that you wanted to fly with me someday. I may consider taking up piloting … you and me Chrissie."

Christine Baptiste responds,

"Please send me your location soon. I can't wait … !"

A distinguished Asian Official dressed in white attire interrupts the celebration.

He meets and greets them at the airplane hangar. He bows in acknowledgment and points to a van in a parking spot. Rude Buay ambles towards the vehicle and looks it over.

The Official hands over the keys to Rude Buay, along with a folded piece of paper. They load up their luggage and weaponry. Rude Buay reads the address: The Lounge, 17 Chamber Lane, Shanghai.

The distinguished official looks at Rude Buay with concern.

Distinguished gentleman asks,

"Mr. Rude Buay, how is your Kung Fu?"

Rude Buay thinks it through, and replies,

"What I lack in skill I will make up inactivity. And where there are no roots, sprouts will appear."

The Asian Official gives him thumbs up and smilingly departs.

The agents board the van. The Commissioner takes the wheel.
The van departs.

32

Rude Buay and his entourage arrive outside David Lee's house. Covert and desolate *The Lounge* sits on a hill. Rude Buay, Walter Banks, Heidi Hudson, Miles Tate, and the Commissioner Richard Baptiste jump out. They are instantly alerted by the pacing guards on the grounds of the property, as well as the roof of that house. It's now nightfall, so Rude Buay and his men disperse and manage to surround the house. Even so, one of the patrolling guards notices the five intruders.

A patrolling guard yells out,
"We are under attack, Americans! Americans! Jamericans!"

Other guards jump off the roof. They emerge running through the back door as well as the front door in confrontation.

The agents all armed including the Commissioner unload several rounds on the guards.

The skilled guards retaliate and dodge out of the agent's firepower until there are no more bullets left in their guns.

Sensing their vulnerability, one petite guard viciously approaches them Kung Fu style. No one dare take him on except for Rude Buay.

Moments later Rude Buay leaves the elfin martial artist on the ground paralyzed.

Another agent realizing the affliction rendered to his coworker comes violently at Rude Buay with the "crane" move, before Rude Buay can even compose himself. Rude Buay quickly unravels that guard and gets confronted by yet another. This agile guard quickly shows up the agents' Kung Fu deficiencies.

Witnessing, the manhandling of Rude Buay his team rushes to the parked van down the hill to acquire more bullets.

Upon returning, the guard has Rude Buay held upside down and about to smash his head on top of the paved concrete driveway.

Agent Heidi Hudson gets a shot off from her reloaded the gun and shoots the guard directly in his forehead. The guard topples over, with Rude Buay falling on top of him.

Rude Buay get up, steps on top of the guard en-route to the interior of the house with his team in tow. The other guards failing miserably to make a comeback, try fleeing past them. They all get capped by Rude Buay's team.

Rude Buay reloads his gun upon entering, thanks to the generosity of Walter Banks who supplied him with bullets.

The agents, along with the Commissioner are now inside the living room. A maid wearing an apron comes flying out of the ceiling through the manhole. Hudson sees her and instead of shooting her changes her mind and engages in hand to hand combat.

As they go at it, Hudson asks the maid,

"Where is Mildred Simms?"

Instead of getting an answer the maid engages in more Kung Fu action. Hudson hones her skill of the craft on the maid via on the job training.

In the meantime, other members of the agents' team rummage through the house.

In a room adjacent to the living room they discover: stacks of Jewish bankroll, millions of dollars in U.S. currency, Chinese currency, hundreds of *Ziploc* bags with at least one eight kilo of uncut cocaine each,

American passports, grenades, survival kits, along with a massive gun collection.

Inside the next room, they enter the take-down style. There is no one there, but numerous milk cans arranged like on an assembly line. Rude Buay, Walter Banks, Miles Tate, and The Commissioner enter another room in search of Mildred Simms. She is not there. Another room beckons, so they enter, in search of Mildred.

33

In the interim, outside the airport hangar, a convoy of cars pull up led by David Lee's BMW. Alberto's Mercedes Benz follows. Shelly, Denise, and Amanda follow in their Hatchback and Johnny *Too Bad* in his Escalade. They, survey for a while trying to determine if the Jet, arranged to take the agents back to Miami was flown to Shanghai instead. It's tedious as most of the jets look alike. Finally, they stumble into it. Alberto opens the door and enters. The others wait outside.

Inside the cockpit of the Jet, Alberto discovers the tie Commissioner Baptiste wore at the time he was kidnapped. He alerts Johnny *Too Bad* along with his other associates. They clue in.

Shelly, Amanda, and Denise take off speedily in their Hatchback. The others board their vehicle preparing to leave.

However, before the men take off a van pulls up. Four Henchmen jump out. David Lee gets out of his car with his gun aimed at the four men.

David Lee yells,

"You are late! ...Late!"

The men bow apologetically. David Lee hands a wad of dollar bills which he retrieved from his pocket along with an address on a sheet of paper. The Henchmen take off speedily. The Drug Lords take off in the opposite direction.

MEANWHILE BACK AT LEE'S HOUSE. Oblivious to Hudson's partners, agent Hudson is now confronted by Amanda Kingsley her newly arrived combat. The tired maid whimpers, bloody in the corner as a result of Hudson's spanking.

Outside Shelly and Denise wait with the car door still open after Amanda's exit.

Amanda Kingsley outdoes agent Hudson with her Kung Fu skills.

Finally Shelly yells out,

"Let's take that ... to *Torture House*!

Amanda puts the agent in a chokehold and drags her outside to the waiting car.

Upon arriving, Amanda with the help of Shelly and Denise, bind Hudson with ropes, tie her hands behind her back and throw her in the back of their tinted windows vehicle.

Shelly takes the wheel. Looking in the rearview mirror she addresses agent Hudson:

"Welcome back, bitch you never learn, huh? You had your chance to be free. Stay in America with your son. Instead, you are determined to mess up our livelihood."

Heidi Hudson asks,

"What do you want from me?"

Shelly responds,

"You will find out at the *Torture House*."

The car continues on its way.

Meanwhile, back inside *The Lounge*, one of Lee's other houses: the agents and the Commissioner return to the living room and notice the maid on the floor coughing up blood.

Additionally, to their surprise, they realize that agent Hudson is missing.

Looking outside, the fresh tire marks leave an imprint on the dust-laden pavement. The men hustle to their vehicles to embark on a search for the missing agent Hudson.

Meanwhile, the Hatchback carrying Hudson turns the corner up the street.

Denise, never seen smoking in public before. She turns to Amanda and asks for a cigarette. Amanda grants her request. Denise lights up stating:

"I'll put that bitch out of her misery."

34

Located in the hills of Northern Shanghai on a Cul De Sac is *Torture House*. The grounds are fit for entertaining with several barbeque pits and a large swimming pool.

The three women drag Hudson inside and tie her up just like they did to the kidnapped Mildred Simms. Creating a huddle around Hudson, they continue to terrorize the agent. Shelly could have addressed any other issue to open her interrogation process of Heidi

Hudson, but she chooses to go back to the last question she asked of agent Hudson during the interrogation session back in Jamaica on the previous mission.

"Who did your dad pay to take out my man in Bogota?"

Heidi Hudson responds,

"Will you just let my dad rest in peace?"

Shelly responds,

"No *Bitch*, he is not going to rest, neither are you until I find out who snuffed out Mike."

Heidi Hudson replies,

"Dad had nothing to do with your boyfriend's death."

Shelly states:

"That's what you said the last time. Your dad had every reason to hurt him. Mike decided not to split his cocaine profits with your deceptive, corrupt, deceitful dad. Therefore your dad, one of the wealthiest DEA to ever work in Miami, hired someone to kill Mike."

Heidi responds,

"I am not my father's keeper, just his daughter. You are asking me questions I can't answer."

Denise steps right into the frame. She hands over a journal to her counterpart Shelly.

Shelly removes the bookmark and begins to read silently at first.

Shelly continues,

"You wrote in your journal the day Mike was killed: 'My dad did what he had to do to get where he needed to go.' Did you not?"

Hudson feeling like she is being put on trial responds, "My dad was paid to do a job as a DEA. Like every loyal agent he was obligated to report the facts to his superiors. Your man was a Drug Lord and dealing drugs was, and still is, against the law."

Denise interjects,

"Is that the eleventh commandment because I never saw it in the *Ten*?"

Heidi replies,

"Everything wrong was not included in those two tablets of stone…"

Amanda interrupts,

"Alright, Hudson enough of that Bible stuff. This is not Sunday school. Besides, my sister went way too easy on you the last time."

Amanda continues,

"May … Agnes Richards R.I.P."

Hudson reflects on the torture she encountered by Agnes and Shelly on the previous operation.

Amanda locks eyes with agent Hudson,

"FYI, I will be pushing the button for your hanging on the Sabbath. You can pray all you want. There won't be any miracle."

RUDE BUAY VOL. II

Amanda approaches the chair in which Hudson sits, and slaps her twice, hard in the face, and then tightens the noose hanging around the agent's neck.

The women open a closet filled with an eclectic assortment of weapons. They arm themselves to the massive.

Shelly looking back at Hudson threatens,

"We will be back! Your countdown begins right now."

BACK AT THE LOUNGE in Shanghai, Rude Buay, Miles Tate, Walter Banks, and the Commissioner all race to their vehicles. Before the men could board their van, Rude Buay notices that all four van tires have been slashed as the van sits on its rims. Rude Buay kicks the tires in disgust. Thinking it through, he then advises,

"There is an option! I am going to check that parked car in the back driveway."

Rude Buay leaves the other men and departs in that direction.

He breaks inside of a parked car and tries to start it. The car does not respond so he opens the hood only to realize that the battery is missing. Rude Buay leaves searching for options.

In the meantime, a van pulls up next to the van with the slashed tires. The four Henchmen jump out. They surround Banks, Tate, and Baptiste.

The three men are no match for these four henchmen. So the quartet captures the trio, strip them of all their weapons, and throw them inside their van. They jump inside the van.

The van departs up the hill, following in tow of the femme Fatales.

Moments later, Rude Buay, after locating no other form of transportation, returns down the hill to the scene of that abandoned van. There is no one there. Even so, he surveys but in vain. The smell of hay and the neighing of a horse alert him to a nearby barn. He rushes to the horse shed. There he finds a horse kicking up its heels. He takes it for a ride through the village in search of Tate, Banks, and Baptiste.

35

Tate, Banks and Baptiste are escorted inside an office. For the first time, they are face to face with Alberto Gomez and David Lee.

Alberto, staring at Banks states:

"Walter Banks, I knew you would show up voluntarily."

Banks pleads the fifth.

Alberto continues,

"Commissioner, you can run but you can't hide. How do you like your *Déjà Vu?*"

Alberto shoots at the Commissioner. The bullet misses his head. The Commissioner can't believe what he has been drawn into for the second time in less than a month.

Alberto looks across at his Henchmen and commands, "Take them to the *Torture House* and leave the white guy."

The four men comply.

Tate is now on center stage in front of David Lee and Alberto Gomez.

Alberto asks,

"Agent Tate, how long have you been an agent?"

Tate responds,

"Less than one month!"

Alberto continues,

"Someone suckered you into interrupting the flow, huh? You sure handle yourself like a pro."

Tate responds,

"Thanks, I've always wanted to be a DEA. A great one!"

Alberto questions,

"How much they pay you?"

Tate answers,

"I am not really in for the money."

Alberto says,

"You are such a deceitful bastard. No wonder you always wanted to be a DEA. What are you in for, Drugs and *Hotties*?"

Tate responds,
"None of those things matter!"
David goes inside of the closet and retrieves an attaché case. He brings it out, displays it on the table in-front of agent Tate. He then opens it. Inside the attaché case: Stacks of crisp U.S. one hundred dollar bills.
Tate's eyes light up.
David Lee addresses,
"Tate, we are expanding rapidly and need someone like you to head up operations at the U.S/Canadian Border. You are the right complexion and the perfect age."
David Lee hands over the attaché and encourages,
David Lee encourages,
"This is a "draw."
Tate counts the money. He is excited but confused.
David Lee states,
"If you change your mind, just return the cash as-is. Here is my business card."
Tate accepts the bribe.
Alberto says to Tate,
You are free to go agent Tate.
Tate departs.
Shelly, Denise, and Amanda bring in Heidi Hudson who is bruised, battered and tied up.
Alberto addresses:
"Agent Hudson, it is good to see you again. I must say that you are either stupid or Rude Buay must have

brainwashed you, hypnotized you or... Is it your resilience or do you get your high from being abused?" Hudson maintains her silence.

Alberto interrogates,

"I desire to get you out of this situation that you have locked yourself into. You had so many opportunities to be free. Yet, you won't leave the DEA business. It seems like you are trying to cash in."

David goes to the closet and returns with an attaché case. He opens it on the table in-front of agent Hudson. The case is stacked with U.S. one hundred dollar bills.

David Lee argues,

"Agent Hudson here is what we can do for you. We are expanding and need your expertise at the Nogales border in Arizona. You fit the profile of who we are looking for to head up that operation. We don't want to use one of *us* just not yet."

Agent Hudson stares at the loot.

"No thanks, I will not be bribed."

Says Hudson.

Alberto continues,

"Agent are you sure you want to pass this up with bonuses and incentives added? We would be also willing to bury the hatchet - your dad's."

Alberto looks across at Shelly Hall for validation.

Heidi Hudson reiterates,

"I am not interested even if it cost me my life."

Alberto looking across at Shelly.

"Take her back to the *Torture House*! We'll hang her tomorrow."

Denise asks,

"What do we do with Mildred Simms?"

Alberto responds,

"Leave her for Johnny, along with Banks and Baptiste. He wants them for Jamaica. Bring us Rude Buay alive. Hudson?... We'll hang her ass tomorrow."

36

The three female Drug Lords, Shelly, Denise, and Amanda rough up agent Hudson excessively as they take her to the car. They push her inside and drive off back to the *Torture House.*
In the meantime, Rude Buay continues riding briskly through the villages of northern Shanghai; in search of the other members of his team. He dials Banks, Baptiste, Hudson and Tate in succession. There is no

response from any of them. So he dials Chelo, and gets a busy tone.

Back in Bogota, Chelo is on the roof-top busy rewiring his equipment and misses that call.

Rude Buay hangs up and redials as the horse gallops along the narrow streets. Still, no one picks up his call. From the streets, he can see Chinese kids playing at the park. They are now focused on him. Somewhat thrilled to see a man riding on a horse through their neighborhood.

One kid yells out,

"Holy Grail!"

Finally, Chelo aborts the rooftop equipment renovation and re-enters his shack. He sees the blinking light and responds to the missed call.

Rude Buay picks up.

"Rude Buay, I have been working all day on the roof installing a new antenna, *señor*. Now I have video for you."

Rude Buay replies,

"I am not in a vehicle right now, Chelo. You are going to have to describe the visuals for me."

Chelo asks,

"What is your location, agent Rude Buay?"

Rude Buay responds,

"On a horse Chelo, in northern Shanghai, give me what you got Chelo."

Chelo replies,

"I have some recent footage from inside a building known as the *Torture House*. Shelly, Denise, and Amanda were viewed as terrorizing agent Hudson. Walter Banks, the Commissioner, and Mildred Simms and Hudson are possibly awaiting their hanging. I was able to track Johnny *Too Bad*. He just left the dock and boarded a taxi. He could be heading to the hanging or pursuing you."
"Where is that house Chelo?"
"In a *Cul De Sac* in Northern Shanghai, no address listed. That is a very remote location."
Says Chelo.
"Thanks. Anything on agent Tate?"
"Nothing, Zip, *Nada*. He could have been kidnapped, and sent to a different location or already killed by the Dragon Cartel."
Rude Buay respond,
"Thanks, Chelo …"
Rude Buay hurries through the remote village. His phone rings, he gets it.
"Rude Buay, Johnny just made a stop a mile east of your location at a place called the *Wood House*. It is situated one mile north of your location."
Chelo advises.
Rude Buay challenges the horse to speed up and proceeds to ride in that direction.

37

RUDE BUAY pulls up on the horse outside the *Wood House*. The street is swamped with expensive automobiles. He enters the house armed in search of the DRAGONS. Johnny makes a transfer of cash with two drug dealers earlier, who now leave, oblivious to the agent. Johnny proceeds towards the door with the attaché case filled with money. He unexpectedly runs into Rude Buay waiting for him on his way in.

Johnny shoots at Rude Buay and darts back to the office where that transaction was made. Rude Buay pursues and is confronted by Johnny's bodyguard.

In the interim, Johnny loads two guns and sticks them in his waist. While additional BODYGUARDS hurry to the roof-top and position for battle.

Rude Buay, in *Terminator*-style, eliminates the first body-guard.

There's movement on top of the building. The fast-paced footsteps on the roof alert Rude Buay that he is about to be cornered and possibly terminated by such an entourage.

Johnny emerges from the office. He opens fire on Rude Buay. Rude Buay eludes Johnny's onslaught and makes his way to the roof of the building to gain an advantage.

Rude Buay confronts one of the roof-top bodyguards. They engage in a massive shoot out at each other.

The bodyguard searches for a perfect aim and settles after succeeding. Yet, he misses as Rude Buay dodges out of it. Rude Buay finally gains the upper hand when he caps the bodyguard between both eyes.

Suddenly, Johnny emerges on the rooftop. Just before Rude Buay fires, a hail of bullets rain from Johnny's gun and ricochet behind the wall protecting Rude Buay.

In the heat of battle, Rude Buay shoots several rounds and hits Johnny in his right upper arm. Johnny's gun,

previously in his right-hand falls to the ground. Johnny *Too Bad* quickly engages in the continued attack on Rude Buay using the gun in his left hand. He fires off several rounds, nothing connects. The gun is now empty, unknown to Rude Buay.
"Come, Johnny *Too Bad*. Show me what you got."
Rude Buay says,
"I and I rule, Rude Buay."
Says Johnny in *Patois*.
While shooting with the left hand, Johnny kneels and retrieves the fallen gun.
Meanwhile, Rude Buay reloads his empty guns amidst the dodging of bullets.
Johnny is now holding two guns once again but shoots using the gun in his right hand. Rude Buay clues in. Rude Buay continues shooting at him.
Finally, Johnny's gun is empty. Rude Buay senses Johnny's vulnerability and shoots Johnny in the forehead. Johnny falls off the building and onto the ground two stories below. Rude Buay retrieves the note from his breast pocket. He folds it many times creating a paper airplane. He later shoots it in the direction of Johnny's corpse. The object falls on top of the wasted Johnny.
At the same time, back at the *Torture House*, Shelly, Denise, and Amanda continually terrorize agent Hudson. Upon learning of Johnny's death though, the three women rush to their Hatchback and depart

speedily towards the *Wood House* to meet the Drug Queen.

They notice Johnny's body in the street.

"I will take on Rude Buay."

Says Denise.

"This is my turn, Shelly. You faced off with him last time."

Amanda says,

"I have a spanking for his ..." She continues.

Rude Buay comes down to the ground level of the *Wood House*. The three women confront him. Realizing that his gun is out of bullets, Amanda decides that she will take him on in hand to hand combat. She envisions taking Rude Buay alive after the serious spanking she's about to give him.

"Go, girl! Show him what you got!"

Shelly and Denise yell out to their female counter-part. Sensing that Amanda has the upper hand, and not aware that agent Rude Buay has honed his martial arts skills they depart, leaving Amanda to humiliate agent Rude Buay before taking him hostage.

38

Inside the *Torture House*, Heidi Hudson wrestles with the rope that binds her hands and feet. Using her teeth she gnaws away at the remaining strands. Finally, she manages to break herself free. She hustles over to the next room where Mildred Simms is tied up on a chair. She sets Mildred free, and together they try making their getaway.
In a room on their way out, agent Hudson notices Walter Banks and the Commissioner also tied up.

While Mildred also notices something: three guns on the table. She grabs two and Hudson grabs the other.
Suddenly, the Hatchback carrying Shelly and Denise pulls into the driveway.
Inside the house, Mildred frees Walter Banks, while agent Hudson frees the Commissioner. All four of them exit the building in haste, passing by the four dangling nooses.
Shelly and Denise are now inside the house, entering through the back door, they miss the quartet.
Heidi Hudson shoots at the multi propane tanks in the Barbecue pit. While Mildred blows up the Hatchback with several rounds. The house goes up in flames progressively.
Back at the *Wood House* Rude Buay and Amanda are still going at each other, Kung Fu style. Amanda is putting a whopping on Rude Buay, she is taking him to *101* Kung Fu school. Just when it seems like her vision is close to becoming reality, the sound of a speeding vehicle summons.
On the outside, David Lee is racing in his BMW towards the SCENE. His car pulls up outside. He darts out and heads to the interior of the *Wood House*.
David Lee notices as Rude Buay sends Amanda to the ground with a flying kick to her upper rib-cage.
Wasting no time, David Lee sees this as an opportunity to capture Rude Buay. So he joins in for a possible two on one takedown of the agent. Though, before he can

make a go at Rude Buay. Amanda gets back up but succumbs to a broken neck by another kick from the agent, landing her on the ground. This infuriates David Lee as he attacks Rude Buay with a vengeance. His first kick sends Rude Buay flying. The agent artfully lands on his feet like a cat falling on all fours.

David Lee continues his flying kick tirade on Rude Buay. The agent shows signs of exhaustion like a boxer resting against the ropes. There is no bell so the duel continues anyway.

There is a sudden crash, and like the effects of an earthquake, the building rocks back and forth. The cube truck fully loaded with cans of milk and driven by Alberto Gomez slams into one of the main pillars supporting the *Wood House.*

Finally, the truck comes to a complete stop. As a result, not only is the *Wood House* lodging the penetrated truck but David Lee's attention gets diverted by the crash.

Rude Buay seizes the opportunity and lands a variation of flying kicks and jabs into David Lee's body. One kick strikes David Lee in his groin area. The drug czar is shaken up and hobbles to the corner foaming through his mouth.

Rude Buay, not letting up comes at him again with an arsenal of hits. The final of which puts David Lee's head into a fix. The drug czar falls over with a broken neck.

Rude Buay, not taking any chances delivers a series of kicks into David Lee's stomach, finishing him off.

Alberto Gomez hurries out of the wreckage and center stage, just in time to witness the demolishment of his associate David Lee. He is peeved. Not sure if he should confront the agent in hand to hand combat, he resorts to shooting at Rude Buay although he would rather take him alive.

CLICK! CLICK! CLICK!

Alberto realizes that Rude Buay's gun is now empty. So he takes him on in hand to hand combat.

The brawl ensues as Rude Buay lands on top of him and knocking Alberto Gomez to the ground. The two men go at it for a while attempting to punch each other's daylights out.

The exhausted Rude Buay begins attacking Alberto with a vengeance. Suddenly, there's a creaking sound as the *Wood House* begins to give way. Alberto wants Rude Buay alive but the agent is too much for him to handle, plus sensing the mayhem Alberto runs for the side door's exit. Rude Buay is exhausted and staggers around the room. He goes back in time.

FLASHBACK:

MILDRED KEEPS DODGING Axel James' bullets. Rude Buay with blood on his vest rolls over onto his stomach and gets a good aim at Axel. Rude Buay

Discharges. The bullet, HITS Axel right between his two eyes. He falls backward thunderously onto the deck. Niki, the 14-year-old falls forward into the deep. A mountain-like wave beckons. It hits the Catamaran viciously. Alberto, dressed in a wet suit jumps overboard into the wave, unnoticed by everyone on the other ship. The Catamaran sails speedily towards an unavoidable collapse onto the island of Cuba. Mildred dives into the deep and clutches Niki around her neck. Rude Buay throws out the life rope. Mildred catches it. Rude Buay reels them in. Another mountainous wave hits the Catamaran, it slams into Cuba at full speed, bursting into flames, debris, spikes, and fragments of lumber.

BACK TO PRESENT:

Entering the *Wood House* through the front door is agent Miles Tate. Rude Buay, exhausted more than ever senses a sigh of relief, upon Tate's entrance.
Rude Buay yells to agent Tate,
"Shoot him! Shoot the Philistine, don't give him another chance."
Miles Tate shoots, but instead of shooting Alberto Gomez, he shoots Rude Buay. The bullet lodges in Rude Buays' upper left leg. Rude Buay falls to the ground. Simultaneously, the *Wood House* caves in on Rude Buay while agent Tate makes his escape.

Outside the *Wood House*, two vehicles raced to the scene. First, the taxi pulls up, out jumps Walter Banks, Mildred Simms, agent Heidi Hudson and the Commissioner (Richard Baptiste).

Right behind it, a black limousine pulls up. Dr. Tamara Ross steps out, followed by the all dolled up Christine Baptiste.

Noticing the collapse, many tears are shed at the scene.

THE HORSE AUTOMATICALLY released from its post grazes on the other side of the street.

About The Author

John A. Andrews hails from the beautiful Islands of St. Vincent and the Grenadines and resides in Hollywood, California. He is best known for his gritty and twisted writing style in his National Bestselling novel - Rude Buay ... The Unstoppable. He is in (2012) releasing this chronicle in the French edition, and poised to release its sequel Rude Buay ... The Untouchable in March 2012.

Andrews moved from New York to Hollywood in 1996, to pursue his acting career. With early success, he excelled as a commercial actor. Then tragedy struck - a divorce, with Andrews granted joint custody of his three sons, Jonathan, Jefferri and Jamison, all under the age of five. That dream of becoming all he could be in the entertainment industry, now took on nightmarish qualities.

In 2002, after avoiding bankruptcy and a twisted relationship at his modeling agency, he fell in love with a 1970s classic film, which he wanted to remake.

Subsequent to locating the studio which held those rights, his request was denied. As a result, Andrews decided that he was going to write his own. Not knowing how to write and failing constantly at it, he inevitably recorded his first bestseller, Rude Buay ... The Unstoppable in 2010: a drug prevention chronicle, sending a strong message to teens and adults alike

Andrews is also a visionary, and a prolific author who has etched over two dozen titles including: Dare to Make a Difference - Success 101 for Teens, The 5 Steps To Changing Your Life, Spread Some Love - Relationships 101, Quotes Unlimited, How I Wrote 8 Books in One Year, The FIVE "Ps" for Teens, Total Commitment - The Mindset of Champions, and Whose Woman Was She? - A True Hollywood Story.

RUDE BUAY VOL. II

In 2007, Mr. Andrews a struggling actor and author etched his first book The 5 Steps to Changing Your Life. That title having much to do with changing one's thoughts, words, actions, character and changing the world. A book which he claims shaped his life as an author with now over two dozen published titles.

Andrews followed up his debut title with Spread Some Love - Relationships 101 in 2008, a title which he later turned into a one hour docu-drama.

Additionally, during that year Andrews wrote eight titles, including: Total Commitment - The Mindset of Champions, Dare to Make A Difference - Success 101 for Teens, Spread Some Love

RUDE BUAY VOL. II

- Relationships 101 (Workbook) and Quotes Unlimited.

After those publications in 2009, Andrews recorded his hit novel as well as Whose Woman Was She? and When the Dust Settles - I am Still Standing: his True Hollywood Story, now also being turned into a film.

New titles in the Personal Development genre include: Quotes Unlimited Vol. II, The FIVE "Ps" For Teens, Dare to Make A Difference - Success 101 and Dare to Make A Difference - Success 101 - The Teacher's Guide.

His new translated titles include: Chico Rudo ... El Imparable, Cuya Mujer Fue Ella? and Rude Buay ... The Unstoppable in Chinese.

Back in 2009, while writing the introduction of his debut book for teens: Dare To Make A Difference - Success 101 for Teens, Andrews visited the local bookstore. He discovered only 5 books in the Personal Development genre for teens while noticing hundreds of the same genre in the adult section. Sensing there was a lack of personal growth resources, focusing on youth 13-21, he published his teen book and soon thereafter founded Teen Success.

This organization is empowerment based, designed to empower Teens in maximizing their full potential to be successful and contributing citizens in the world.

Andrews, referred to as the man with "the golden voice" is a sought after speaker on "Success" targeting young adults. He recently addressed teens in New York, Los Angeles, Hawaii and was the guest speaker at the 2011 Dr. Martin Luther King Jr. birthday celebrations in Eugene, Oregon.

John Andrews is from a home of educators; all five of his sisters taught school - two acquiring the status of school principals. Though self educated, he understands the benefits of a great education and being all he can be. Two of his teenage sons are also writers. John spends most of his time writing, publishing books and traveling the country going on book tours.

Additionally, John Andrews is a screenwriter and producer, and is in

(2012) turning his bestselling novel into a film.

See more in: HOW I RAISED MYSELF FROM FAILURE TO SUCCESS IN HOLLYWOOD.

RUDE BUAY VOL. II

"I firmly believe that any man's finest hour, the greatest fulfillment of all that he holds dear, is the moment when he has worked his heart out in a good cause and lies exhausted on the field of battle - victorious"

- VINCE LOMBARDI

http://thinkexist.com/quotation/i_firmly_believe_that_any_man-s_finest_hour-the/173395.html

RUDE BUAY VOL. II

FOR MORE ON
BOOKS THAT WILL ENHANCE YOUR LIFE ™

*Rude Buay is a drug prevention chronicle about teens caught up in the war on drugs and contains content for adults; parental discretion is advised for children.

A 2010 Books That Will Enhance Your Life. All Rights Reserved.

How I Wrote 8 Books In One Year

JOHN A. ANDREWS

Author of
TOTAL COMMITTMENT
The Mindset Of Champions

RUDE BUAY VOL. II

RUDE BUAY ... THE UNSTOPPABLE

| RUDE BUAY VOL. II

QUOTES UNLIMITED II

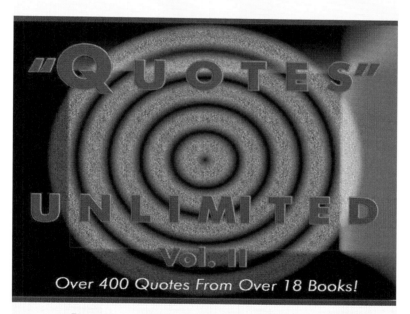

| RUDE BUAY VOL. II

DARE TO MAKE A DIFFERENCE – SUCCESS 101

RUDE BUAY VOL. II

TOTAL COMMITMENT

RUDE BUAY VOL. II

WHOSE WOMAN WAS SHE?

CHICO RUDO ... EL IMPARABLE

RUDE BUAY VOL. II

RUDE BUAY ... THE UNSTOPPABLE CHINESE EDITION

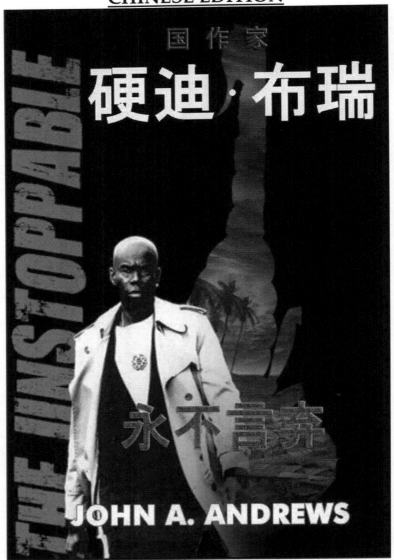

CHICO RUDO ... El INTOCABLE

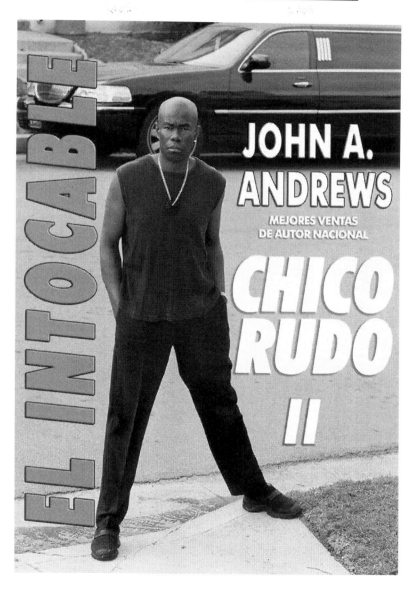

| RUDE BUAY VOL. II

CROSS ATLANTIC FIASCO

| RUDE BUAY VOL. II

RUDE BUAY ... SHATTERPROOF

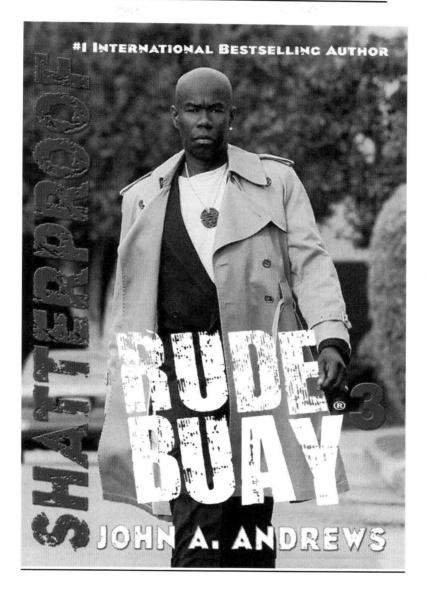

RUDE BUAY VOL. II

RUDE BUAY VOL. II

A JOHN ANDREWS FILM

DEAD MEN TELL NO TALES

BASED ON
WHO SHOT THE SHERIFF?

WRITTEN BY: JOHN A. ANDREWS   PRODUCED BY: PATRICK MCINTIRE, MICHAEL W. REID, DANIELLE E. CAMPBELL, JOHN ANDREWS
EXECUTIVE PRODUCERS: SELENA SMITH & JANIS PHILLIP
DIRECTED BY: JOHN ANDREWS. AN A L I PICTURES PRODUCTION

| RUDE BUAY VOL. II

WHEN THE DUST SETTLES

A True Hollywood Story

starring
John A. Andrews

RUDE BUAY VOL. II

RUDE BUAY

... Shatterproof

An Original Story
By
International Bestselling
Author
John A. Andrews
Creator Of:
The Rude Buay Series®

| RUDE BUAY VOL. III

Copyright © 2012 by John A. Andrews.

All rights reserved. Written permission must be secured from the publisher to use or reproduce any part of this book, except for brief quotations in critical reviews or articles.
Published in the U.S.A. by
Books That Will Enhance Your Life™

A L I - Andrews Leadership International
Entertainment Division®
Jon Jef Jam Entertainment®
www.JohnAAndrews.com

Cover Design: John A. Andrews
Cover Graphic Designer: A L I
Edited by: Prof Harminder Kaur
ISBN: 978-0-9848980-1-5

RUDE BUAY VOL. III

RUDE BUAY

... Shatterproof

by
National Bestselling Author
John A. Andrews

Other Series

RENEGADE COPS
&
The **WHODUNIT CHRONICLES**

RUDE BUAY VOL. III

TABLE OF CONTENTS

CHAPTER ONE..7
CHAPTER TWO...13
CHAPTER THREE...17
CHAPTER FOUR..21
CHAPTER FIVE...31
CHAPTER SIX..38
CHAPTER SEVEN...42
CHAPTER EIGHT...45
CHAPTER NINE..50
CHAPTER TEN...54
CHAPTER ELEVEN..58
CHAPTER TWELVE..63
CHAPTER THIRTEEN..66
CHAPTER FOURTEEN...69
CHAPTER FIFTEEN...73
CHAPTER SIXTEEN...78
CHAPTER SEVENTEEN..82
CHAPTER EIGHTEEN...89
CHAPTER NINETEEN...96
CHAPTER TWENTY..102
CHAPTER TWENTY-ONE..107
CHAPTER TWENTY-TWO..112
CHAPTER TWENTY-THREE..118
CHAPTER TWENTY-FOUR...123
CHAPTER TWENTY-FIVE...128
CHAPTER TWENTY-SIX..133
CHAPTER TWENTY-SEVEN..138
CHAPTER TWENTY-EIGHT..144
CHAPTER TWENTY-NINE...149
CHAPTER THIRTY..153
CHAPTER THIRTY-ONE..161
CHAPTER THIRTY-TWO..165
CHAPTER THIRTY-THREE..169
CHAPTER THIRTY-FOUR...175
CHAPTER THIRTY-FIVE...180
CHAPTER THIRTY-SIX..184
CHAPTER THIRTY-SEVEN..188
CHAPTER THIRTY-EIGHT..191

The RUDE BUAY Series

Vol. III

RUDE BUAY VOL. III

"The things I've been through give me fortitude. I'm not easily broken. Not only have I seen too much but I've been through too much. Selling **out** is not **in** my character. You may hang my body tomorrow but you will never hang my character."

- Rude Buay

1

In a chic Cul De Sac, located in the covert hills of Northern Shanghai, smoke, debris, fire, and ashes continue to rise from what's left of the sweltering *Torture House.*

Less than 24 hours ago, this domicile had housed some high profile hostages, four of the most efficient agents the world has ever seen. Fighters against narcotics, these adept drug enforcement agents who hailed from the U.S. and Jamaica have been tortured immensely by the invincible *Dragon Drug Cartel*. A descendant of a former special drug enforcement agent, HEIDI HUDSON: she's Caucasian in her late twenties. Hudson steps off the plane in Miami. Jamaican born, MILDRED SIMMS, in her late twenties. She is a drop-dead gorgeous, sophisticated African American beauty, every man's heart's desire and employed by the Ministry of Tourism in Jamaica. WALTER BANKS, a Jamaican born African American in his late fifties, with salt and pepper hair, and a veteran D.E.A. who served for many years in Colombia. The Commissioner of Police in Jamaica, RICHARD BAPTISTE, a tall, slim, kingly man in his forties.

These agents miraculously and cleverly not only made their escape before two *femme Fatales* of the *Dragon Drug Cartel* returned to kill them but were also instrumental in setting the house on fire. Agents Heidi Hudson and Mildred Simms were the ones who pulled the detonating gun triggers which set this *Torture House* ablaze, sending fumes of *Ganja* and mahogany wood into the universe as soon as those two women entered through the garage.

Later that day, fire trucks with idle engines and flashing lights continue to pour water on the remains of the burning building. While they dowse a room filled with sacks of weed: suddenly as if by a stroke of luck, an enthusiastic Chinese fireman notices some movements nearby in the large outdoor swimming pool.

The pool is partially covered with fallen burnt roofing and mahogany scaffolds, some of which are still falling into the body of water and extinguishing in the process.

In haste, multiple firefighters extend a ladder into the pool between the scaffolds while concentrating the water hose in that vicinity.

Two exhausted women accept the invitation of the aluminum ladder and begin climbing out in what's left of their street clothes amidst the burning inferno.

First on the ladder is DENISE GOMEZ. Denise is an Asian, trophy woman, in her late twenties. Her engagement ring, still touching her wedding band, is to be greatly desired by any woman. The blinding rock speaks for itself, despite her partially covered, with ash, appearance. The first firefighter rescues her. This agile fireman grabs her and escorts her to the sidewalk. They're a team of firefighters emerge and proceeds to pump water out of Denise Gomez's lungs.

Another agile firefighter quickly grabs the ascending WWE type SHELLY HALL and also pulls her swiftly to safety before the roof of the building caves in on top of the pool. Shelly Hall, partially covered with ash is a tall Caucasian woman in her 30s. Soon she is lying on the sidewalk. With the aid of mouth to mouth resuscitation performed by a firefighter, water pours out of her mouth and nostrils like a spurt as she coughs up some more intermittently.

Soon thereafter, both rescued *femme Fatales* are placed on separate gurneys and rushed into idling ambulances. The ambulances depart speedily while the fire trucks continue to dowse water on the smoky remains of the almost diminished *Torture House*.

MEANWHILE, IN A NOT TOO DISTANT Shanghai village, a white car cruises down the street. Inside, the driver MILES TATE navigates while surveying through the narrow Shanghai roadsides. Tate is Caucasian in his early 30s. Next to him on the front seat is a half-closed attaché case.

Meanwhile, ALBERTO GOMEZ, drug Czar and leader of the *Dragon Drug Cartel,* is on foot going down that same street. Alberto Gomez is dressed in a tattered expensive business suit and dark tinted sun glasses. He's in mid to late 30s, of Colombian descent. Alberto Gomez is bruised and bloodied over most of his body. It is evident he's been involved in a big fight or scuffle. Miles Tate stops the car and pulls over to the curb. He puts the attaché case on the rear seat and opens the front passenger door to accommodate the drug, Czar. Alberto Gomez boards on the front seat soon as the passenger door swings open.

"Thanks! Always on time, huh?"

Says Alberto Gomez.

"Like they say in Jamaica: No Problem. No problem *mon!*"

Says Tate.

Alberto Gomez seems focused.

Tate continues,

"He almost ate your lunch, huh?"

Alberto Gomez keeping it all business, questions,

"So you finished him off, yeah?"

"One shot straight for the bull's eye. He went down and that *Wood House* subsequently caved in on him."

Tate responds.

"Nice finish to that pain in the A…!"

Says Alberto Gomez.

The two men high five each other as they wait for the stoplight to go green.

"What about the hostages?"

Asks Tate.

"Without Amanda…I'm sure Denise and Shelly Hall have them bound and ready for tomorrow's hanging."

Alberto Gomez responds:

"Our first order of business will be to affix your Dragon signature as soon as I find me some new *gear* and a local tattoo shop. We have to make you official for that group hanging."

Later, Alberto Gomez pulls up at a tattoo shop. They enter the establishment run by the Tattoo King who is extravagantly tattooed all over his body. His lavish tattoo décor states clearly: I am tattooed on hands, tattooed in heart and tattooed on the brain.

RUDE BUAY VOL. III

2

In Montego Bay, Jamaica, investigators, along with the news media ambitiously converge on the Ministry of Tourism building. They swarm around Mildred Simms gleaning for every bit of news regarding her escape. The Caribbean beauty has just returned to the office at the Ministry of Tourism for the first time after being kidnapped by members of the high ranking *Dragon Drug Cartel*.

While the gathering media pry the information relevant to her capture and escape from the *Torture*

House, sends shockwaves through the hearts of her coworkers, awaiting their opportunity to console Jamaica's Mildred. TV cameras keep rolling, camera lights flashing, and boom mikes extending, as eager reporters recapture this remarkable hostage recovery story. They lament on her bravery for pulling the trigger which set the *Torture House* on fire.

A few blocks away at the Police Barracks, a similar scenario unfolds: the overzealous news media glean information from ex-hostage and Jamaican Police Commissioner Richard Baptiste. Standing across from the commissioner is his wife CHRISTINE BAPTISTE. Christine, a stylist in her own right is dressed to the nines. Additionally, she glows basking in the happiness of being back in Jamaica and by the side of her ex-hostage husband, Richard.

Standing next to Christine is the Governor-General Dr. Bradford Wiley, intellectually sound and in his sixties. He beams with joy to see Richard alive and well. The two men have been responsible for making multiple important decisions for fighting the war on narcotics not only in Jamaica but in the other Caribbean Islands, Asia, the U.S as well as Mexico.

The news media continue to garner information while the TV cameras roll excessively. One Spanish reporter from a Mexican affiliate radio station steps up and begins to etch notes on a yellow pad.

RUDE BUAY VOL. III

At home, many Jamaicans are glued to their TV sets soaking up the news.

At the Police Barracks, a microphone extends on a boom towards The Commissioner. One reporter asks: "How did you survive this ordeal and come out of it alive after being kidnapped by the *Dragon Drug Cartel* twice in *one* month?"

"I don't know. It was more than a miracle. I must say that it was ... thanks to Rude Buay and his awesome team or else we would be..."

"And ... where is Rude Buay now?"

Another reporter asks as the camera zooms out.

"Not sure. According to reports, he is feared dead. After the building; in which he single-handedly eliminated several members of the *Dragon Drug Cartel* including Johnny *Too Bad;* collapsed on top of him.

How would you categorize the presumed dead, agent Rude Buay?"

Asks the reporter.

"We owe a sincere debt of gratitude to agent Rude Buay. He wanted to create a better world for all. We were happy to be part of his mission."

Says Richard.

Before another reporter could quiz the Commissioner, two double-breasted jacket attired police officers escort him and his wife out of the room, and inside a waiting limousine. Microphones attached to booms are still against the limousine's window. The vehicle drives off leaving them hanging.

MEANWHILE, IN KINGSTON the capital city of Jamaica, drug lord MARCUS RANKS, wearing his dreadlocks hairstyle is on a tirade. Ranks an ally to the *Dragon Drug Cartel* has ordered his men to block off all streets east, west, north and south of Kingston. The Jamaican Drug Lord vowed that he would avenge the U.S., not only for extraditing Johnny *Too Bad* to America but for setting *pigs* on Johnny like a pack of dogs to snuff him out.

With water dowsed on the *Tivoli Gardens* riot, the extradition of Johnny *Too Bad* and, the Drug Lord's death, the Jamaican Law Enforcement had lapsed back into their comfort zone regarding *TG*.

Ranks, on the other hand, was planning a major comeback for the *Dragons* in *TG*, moving their new drug methamphetamine in large quantities into West Kingston. Therefore, Ranks ordered those streets heading into Kingston to be blocked off. If the police were to ever join forces and enter into *Tivoli Gardens* they would be slowed down, robbed of their weapons and then beaten to death.

The Jamaican Police Department, somewhat shorthanded at this point had to cool it somewhat when it comes to apprehending drug smugglers in *Tivoli Gardens*.

3

Alberto Gomez and Miles Tate are still at the upscale Shanghai tattoo shop. Alberto admires as the petite, in stature, attendant affixes the signature of the dragons behind Tate's right ear. Miles Tate is elated as he now sports the signature of the Dragon Cartel. Alberto Gomez, now neatly attired looks clean again except for multiple facial bruises. He is always the businessman; suave and debonair, sporting his dark sunglasses. He is focused like a man on a mission.

"So where would I be stationed, Vermont or Vancouver?"
Asks Miles Tate.
Alberto Gomez's cell phone rings in the meantime, he gets it.
"*Papi...!*"
Exclaims Denise Gomez.
Denise is lying on a Shanghai hospital bed, sadly affected by second-degree burns over most of her body as a result of the *Torture House* fire. Across from her is her partner in crime Shelly Hall. With multiple burns to her body. Shelly Hall is in the same uncomfortable condition. Overwhelmed in pain, the veteran *drug lady* tries masking it. Denise Gomez is *dying to report*.
Sensing the somber tone in Denise's voice, Alberto Gomez questions,
"Why? Where are you, at the *Torture House*, planning those hangings for tomorrow?"
"No, we are at the hospital and badly burned up. The *Torture House* burned down last night. However, thanks to the swimming pool, Shelly Hall and I are still alive but badly burned up, Al."
"You got to be kidding! The Hatchback caught on fire? What happened to the ... hostages?"
Asks Alberto Gomez.
"Too Bad! When we arrived from the *Wood House*, several bullets fired out and the building exploded in flames. They got away. All four of them! Those ...

bastards escaped. It seems like it was a collaborative effort. Don't know how they pulled that one-off. Where is Rude Buay? Did you get him?"
Denise asks.
"Escaped huh? They may run but they cannot hide. They are such a minority in this city. They ought to know that. Those agents won't have a ... chance. When we catch them we will hang their ... high!" In regards to Rude Buay, we finished him off at the *Wood House*. States Alberto Gomez.
Tate eavesdrops and reacts negatively to the survival story of the hostages. He can't wrap his mind around it. Tate had envisioned joining the *Dragon Cartel* with a major advantage over its opposition - the D.E.A. and its allies. This would be his first big celebration after deflecting back in Shanghai. He so wanted to witness the hanging of agents Mildred Simms, Walter Banks, Heidi Hudson, and the Jamaican Police Commissioner Richard Baptiste. Being disappointed is an understatement.
"We are heading to the hospital ... We'll be there soon." Alberto Gomez says.
The two men look at each other in total disbelief. They reluctantly digest this latest breaking news from Denise and Shelly Hall. Distasteful as it has been, finally, Tate is the first one to speak:
"How the heck did they get out of there alive? It's like a miracle! I mean Denise and Shelly Hall. Are they half

fish, half-human? Sounds like *Déjà vu* to me. Are they mermaids?"

"They met in swim school. They handle water situations well."

Says Alberto Gomez.

"No wonder, they could have *boiled* in that swimming pool."

Says Tate.

"Who knows what condition they are in? It could be more serious than they are claiming…"

The car with the two Drug Lords on board pulls up at the hospital ER entrance and comes to a halt. Tate puts the car in park. Tate and Alberto Gomez step out and hurriedly enter the hospital compound like men on a mission.

4

Meanwhile at the hospital, after looking at their grossly burnt bodies, Alberto Gomez, Miles Tate, Denise Gomez, and Shelly Hall embark upon laying plans for a massive comeback. They envision capturing all the DEA agents and hanging them one by one from the gallows. Additionally, they also discuss plans of setting up the *Dragon Drug Cartel* headquarters in the sister-cities of Nogales in Mexico and Arizona. This would mean, however, truncating themselves from Colombia after 5 years of narcotics operation on its soil.

About 60 miles south of Tucson lie the sister-cities that share that same name - Nogales. One is in Arizona, the other in Old Mexico. Many years ago, groves of walnut trees covered the mountain pass that bridged the two, leading to the name Nogales, derived from the Spanish word for dark walnuts. Today, not only do many Americans cross the border into Nogales to acquire less costly medical care and over the counter drugs, but drug smugglers experience much ease trafficking narcotics from the Mexican border city across to the American side. The *Dragon Drug Cartel* by now was beginning to feel the need not only to capitalize but to dominate in Mexico as well. Even so, they had to move swiftly as other drug cartels also wanted to take advantage of this narcotics trafficking accessibility.

Alberto Gomez pulled out the stops as he addresses his team at the hospital double room briefing:

"Tate, as was requested by David Lee, you will be set up at Vermont, in the U.S. Canadian Border. Shelly Hall, when you return to active duty will monitor those operations.

Denise and I will handle the Nogales Border between Mexico and Arizona until we can find a competent replacement. Our priority will be to expand trade between Mexico and California as well as Mexico and Arizona. This new venture is going to be very challenging, as we will not only have to deal with other D.E.A. agents but competing cartels as well."

Alberto Gomez continues,

"I have already contacted Johnny *Too Bad*'s protégé Marcus Ranks. He will head up the Tivoli Garden operation, thus putting it back on the map. We cannot leave Jamaica out of the mix. It is still our breadbasket our bread and butter. We miss Johnny *Too Bad* but we have to move on, that is the trend of this business."

SAMMY CHIN an ally of David Lee will head up China along with the rest of Asia.

GRACE McCLOUD will replace Amanda Kingsley and monitor our Miami operations. SALVADOR will be ready to start shipping soon. We may need him temporarily in Bogotá at this point."

"I thought Sal was in…"

Questions Miles Tate.

"I have a connection with some of the authorities over there at the Shanghai prison. We stand a very good chance of getting him out of there. You are in good hands with us, Tate."

Responds Alberto Gomez.

"We could be back in the trade in less than two weeks. Denise's and Shelly's wounds would heal soon and we will be back in business for good."

"I can't wait to get out of here guys, can't wait to join you."

Chimes Shelly Hall.

"You and me both of us,"
Adds Denise Gomez.
Before that brief emergency meeting of the drug-smuggling-minds is about to be adjourned, a piece of late-breaking news; far too coincidentally close to their train of thought; from the *ABC News* channel, catches their attention. They all glue in on to the two small TV sets inside the double hospital room:
"Five people found burned beyond recognition in an abandoned SUV in an area of Arizona frequented by smugglers were likely the victims of one of the same drug cartels that have ravaged parts of Mexico with their rampant violence, the local sheriff said today.

A border patrol agent noticed a white Ford Expedition stopping around 4:30 a.m. Saturday in Vekol Valley, a desert area that's a well-known smuggling corridor for drugs and illegal immigrants from Mexico. Suspecting the car stopped to pick up drugs, the agent tried to make contact with the vehicle, but the vehicle fled.

When the sun came up, the agent noticed car tracks leading off the road and followed them for a couple of miles into the desert. The agent found a smoldering vehicle and called for back-up. When other agents arrived, they used fire extinguishers to put out the fire and found five charred bodies inside the car, say the police.

"This is pretty significant," Pinal County Sheriff Paul Babeu said. "Given all these indicators, you don't have to be a homicide detective to add up all the information."

One victim was found in the sedan's rear passenger seat and four others in the back cargo compartment, their bodies burned beyond recognition.

Investigators have not yet determined whether the bodies were bound, the sheriff said.

Babeu told ABC News that it's likely others fled the scene.

"There wasn't anyone in the front driver's seat or the front passenger's seat and the position of the bodies lead us to believe that it's most likely that other people were aboard it," Babeu said.

Babeu said the deaths are being investigated as homicides.

"The vehicle was stopped in an open area. It did not crash into something. Clearly whoever murdered these people did it intentionally," he said. "They brought them there either alive or dead and torched the vehicle to conceal the evidence."

Babeu said the incident is likely a case of drug cartel violence.

"This is more than likely connected to drug smuggling," he said. "It's most likely not human smuggling because most of the time if the illegal person is no longer of use or too slow for the rest of the group, they're left to fend for themselves or die. We don't see many cases where illegal people are killed. They're usually only killed if they put up a fight as they're being robbed.

"This is more likely either punishment on criminals who tried to steal from the cartels or some competing interest in a criminal element."

Babeu said investigators will try to determine whether the victims were dead before the fire was started or whether they were alive when the SUV was set ablaze.

RUDE BUAY VOL. III

The Vekol Valley is located 70 miles north of the U.S.-Mexican border. Babeu called the area a "hotbed for human and drug smuggling."

The federal government put up 15 billboards that read: "Danger Warning, Travel Not Recommended, Drug Smuggling, Active and Armed Gunmen" in the area along Interstate 8.

Last year, the Vekol Valley was the site of the largest drug bust in the history of Arizona.

Seventy-six members of the Sinaloa cartel were arrested in the bust, known as Operation Pipeline Express. The suspects had 108 weapons, including scoped rifles, AK47s and two weapons from the U.S. government's Fast & Furious program.

The controversial program, run by the Bureau of Alcohol, Tobacco, Firearms, and Explosives, was designed to track guns bought in the United States by straw men and delivered to drug cartels in Mexico, in an attempt to catch the cartel higher-ups. Begun in 2009, it was shut down after the December 2010 murder of U.S. Border Patrol agent Brian Terry, who was killed with a weapon sold through the program.

Babeu said, the fact that the Fast & Furious guns were found in the possession of the Sinaloa cartel members, is a sign that the program is "criminal."

"We will be back with more in a minute."

The attending nurse walks in and signals five more minutes. She then departs.

Tate looks across at Alberto Gomez, so do Denise and Shelly Hall as they reminisce on this previous Associated Press report:

Ten suspected gangsters were killed Thursday morning during a running gun-battle in the Mexican border town of Nogales, just one week after the U.S. State Department warned of growing violence among narcotics rings.

Mexican media said Sonoran justice officials confirmed the number dead and reported that several police officers were injured by shrapnel when fleeing suspects tossed grenades at them. No law enforcement agents were reported dead.

The events in Nogales were part of a bloody day along the nearly 2,000-mile Mexican border, where 21 people died in 24 hours of violence involving drug traffickers and other criminal syndicates.

In Ciudad Juarez, along with the Texas reporter, the Associated Press reported four men were shot dead in front of a crowd at an amusement park and a toddler died when the car he was in crashed during a gun-battle. Also, a businessman was murdered after leading a protest against violence.

This is a very, very dangerous time to be a drug agent, said Beth Kempshall, special agent in charge of the Drug Enforcement Administration in Phoenix. The stakes are greater right here in Arizona than I've ever seen them.

Kempshall said the situation in Nogales was still unfolding Wednesday afternoon, and information was sketchy. The number of bodies, it was still in chaos, she noted. It wasn't a good situation down there.

| RUDE BUAY VOL. III

The Tucson Citizen reported that shootings began around 6 a.m. as police stopped a pair of vehicles containing suspected gangsters. It was not immediately clear whether that incident was preceded by fighting between narcotics groups or something else. Officers pursued the suspects along major Nogales streets, with at least two battles occurring a few miles from the border.

Four suspects reportedly died after officers shot out a vehicle's tires, causing it to crash. Others were killed by gunfire. Three civilians also suffered minor injuries during the fighting, according to the Citizen.

Last week, D.E.A. officials said violence in Sonora is growing because outside narcotics organizations are challenging the so-called Sinaloa cartel, which for years claimed dominion over smuggling routes into Arizona. Kempshall said a crackdown by the Mexican government and increased pressure by U.S. agents had added friction: They're fighting over the routes into the United States, and over control of the border area.

Brian Levin, a spokesman for Customs and Border Protection, said U.S. entry ports are always prepared for violence, so no additional security measures are in place.

The State Department alert said Nogales is among several border cities that have recently experienced public shootouts during daily hours. Conflicts involving heavily armed gangsters claimed about 3,000 lives in Mexico this year. In September, there were at least five public gun-battles, including the murder of a man next to a school. Last week, gunmen fired hundreds of rounds into the home of a Nogales reporter, who was not injured.

On Wednesday in Ciudad Juarez, four men were shot inside an amusement park where teenagers were riding bikes through obstacle courses, skating, and rappelling.

Elsewhere in the city, a used car salesman was shot to death while driving down the main boulevard hours after leading hundreds of other business owners in a protest against kidnappings and extortion. The demonstrators had threatened to close their businesses or stop paying taxes because so many were being targeted by extortionists demanding up to $500 a week for protection against crime.

In Tijuana a 1-year-old boy was killed, when the car he was riding in crashed, as the driver tried to flee a gunfight late Wednesday between the police and three armed men, officials in the state prosecutor's office said. The toddler had been sitting in his mother's lap.

"There is no more Rude Buay to interfere and whoever Michael Ortiz puts in his place is not ready for such a force as us. Neither is the Sinaloa Cartel. The bozo heading it up doesn't even know his left hand from his right."

Miles Tate proclaims.

"As for Rude Buay's replacement, there is no one to put in Rude Buay's place as far as I know. Heidi Hudson is not ready for such a task. He was her strength, a shoulder she leaned on. Those Jamaican agents are nothing, very incompetent. Michael Ortiz would not take us on by himself. I doubt he would use them."

Adds Denise Gomez.

The nurse returns to the room. They abruptly adjourn the meeting. Alberto Gomez kisses Denise on her lips. He then quickly departs with ex-agent and now ally, Miles Tate.

5

Methamphetamine, cocaine, heroin along with other narcotics pour into Nogales - Arizona, El Paso, San Diego, Canada, Miami, China and the Jamaican cities of Tivoli Gardens, Kingston and Port Antonio - originated from Nogales, Mexico. Truckers carefully unload their cargo in these major drug smuggling cities. The dealers arrive and pick up the drugs in their high-end automobiles. They distribute them to buyers at parks, grocery stores, clubs, parking garages, yachts, and airplane hangars. While some deliver at more secret locations like back alleys and business offices.

Getting high on the streets from cocaine, meth, and other drugs have become the thing to do as if drugs have been legalized. You could walk down most any street and buy narcotics just like you would candy or bottled water. For so many drug addicts their new long-lasting high comes from the drug Methamphetamine.

On the street; this brain and body killer drug Methamphetamine or Meth; is more commonly sold under names as crank, speed, crystal or ice. This whitish or pale yellow crystal-like powder is normally chewed, ingested, injected, snorted or sometimes smoked.

Methamphetamine, sold in large quantities, is a powerfully intense stimulant that creates a euphoric and energetic feeling. It releases high levels of the neurotransmitter dopamine, which stimulates brain cells, enhancing mood and body movement.

While cocaine high lasts about 15-20 minutes, a meth high lasts 2-14 hours. The *Dragon Drug Cartel* uses this opportune sales pitch to push Meth like none other.

Drug users and pushers alike trading on the streets seems to have no respect for law enforcement. The plea of most drug users is: "legalize drugs so the price would drop." Many even say: "Legalize drugs so people can have easy access without interference from the police."

On the other hand, most Jamaican law enforcement authorities have seen enough living through the *Tivoli Gardens* riots and with the streets in Kingston being blocked off recently. They wouldn't fall for that legalization phenomenon. In Jamaica, the police beef up their operation and arrest many narcotics offenders including several young adult drug smugglers.

IN THE INTERIM; WHILE DENISE GOMEZ AND SHELLY HALL recuperate from their injuries; profits from Methamphetamine around the globe, soar at an amazing pace. Unfortunately, though, these profits do not flow to the *Dragon Drug Cartel*; they had previously focused their efforts on the profits from the drug cocaine in Colombia.

Alberto Gomez realizes that despite all of their worthy plans and past successes, they have been only been playing from the periphery of the game. Miles Tate and Gomez concentrate on playing "catching up" to the *Sinaloa Drug Cartel,* who outshone them in every way possible.

Hence Gomez decides to revert to the young, the innocent, and the gadded to move meth expediently from Mexico across the U.S. borders, to catch up with his competitors.

MEANWHILE, ACROSS THE U.S./MEXICAN El Paso border, a stand-off ensues as U.S. Border Patrol Officers confront and seize over 500 pounds of Methamphetamine, a street value of over $20,000,000.00 (20 million dollars) in Miami.
Several smugglers transporting the substance in cars were detained and arrested as they tried to illegally transport them across and into the U.S. Even as these smugglers were placed in handcuffs by U.S. border patrols, the *Dragon Drug Cartel* sent in over 2 dozen pre-teenagers, recently trained at a firing range to combat the attacks made by the border patrols on those smugglers.
In the interim, while the El Paso border patrols were busily conducting their investigation of the smugglers, those same over 2 dozen kids ages 11-12 stormed through the Mexican city of Nogales and across the U.S. border into the Arizonian city of Nogales, demanding a release of the smugglers and their seized narcotics.
Armed with AK47s they confronted the investigation focused border officers, shooting and killing many. It was said that the El Paso border patrols did not even the score. Instead of retaliating those officers choose not to return fire because they realized that they were

dealing with a bunch of minors or what some may call *Generation K2-10*.

By the time those border patrol officers reverted to tear gas to restrain the kids, many of them were already gunned down by the antagonistic pre-teenagers.

The arrested smugglers were then released by the efforts of the minors who stormed into the border's detention center. Using keys found at fallen border patrols desks they unlocked the handcuffs of the detained and set them free.

Upon their release, the smugglers continued on their trafficking routes throughout the U.S., as well as Canada.

After the vicious shoot-out; which left many border officers dead; the kids were reinforced with other minors as back-ups penetrating the Mexican city of Nogales in SUVs, spraying bullets like rain from the machine and sub-machine guns.

It wasn't until their bullets ran out that the still alive officers stationed at the border and those who were rushed in to defend as well, were, able to catch up with many of these pre-teenagers trying to flee back into Mexico. At the end of this standoff between the minors and border patrols, over one dozen minors were arrested.

The others took flight and fled into the hills of the Mexican desert. For days, later on, the Mexican Police combed through the desert equipped with tear gas in search of those remaining kid shooters. Days and days of searching, unfortunately, produced negative results as the police returned empty-handed.

The kids, on the other hand, had returned safely to the base camp of the *Dragons* in Southern Nogales and sought refuge. There, they continued their combat training under the auspices of Drug Czar Alberto Gomez, leader of the infamous *Dragon Drug Cartel*.

6

Greg Bascombe an African Jamaican in his mid-40s is the dad of two daughters. Greg lives in Jamaica with his family. His wife BRENDA BASCOMBE is Caucasian and in her late 30s. Together the Bascombe family is raising their twin teenage daughters, GLENDA and THELMA.

Greg is one of Jamaica's finest at the Port Antonio Police Department. His tenure in law enforcement dates back almost a decade. He is also a leader in his church, revered by the young and old alike. Greg is the youth pastor as well as the church treasurer. His wife Brenda is a church elder who sits on the church board and is part of every major decision that the organization makes.

At fourteen the girls are straight "A" students. Thelma wants to become a doctor and Glenda a missionary. Additionally, they are the talk of their church and the community. They excel in just about everything they touch. Putting it subtly, the girls are evolving into Port Antonio's Model Citizens.

Lately, though, Greg has diverted into a slump. His ways are uncanny. Not only has he been missing important appointments, but he has been hanging out with his high school buddies at regular freebasing and meth consumption sessions.

Brenda, noticing Greg's unaccountability suggests that they start attending counseling with their senior pastor Douglas Cambridge. Greg has a big ego and refuses, not wanting to submit his ego to another man. At church, although the Bascombe's put on a façade of a tight-knit family with all of their ducks in a row, at home the family is falling apart at the seams.

One Sunday afternoon after church, Greg leaves his car at home and asks one of his high school buddies to pick him up. Together they drive to a house where three of their other ex-school mates join them for a freebasing session.

In the interim, Glenda visits her dad's car parked on the street. She rummages through the car. In the glove compartment, she discovers not only almost one gram of cocaine but methamphetamine, along with freebasing utensils. She is ecstatic and indulges.

Narcotics usage has been an evolving habit for young Glenda. For several weeks she has been sneaking into her dad's car every time he's away and subsequently acquiring her fix. Additionally, some of her peers had on several occasions brought meth to school. To say the least, the young teen has gradually become an addict and would often join her classmates for their regular get-high sessions during lunch breaks. Then they would return to class flying on cloud nine.

This time around, her high gives her the cravings for more and more methamphetamine. She finds herself licking the foil paper clean of all residues with her tongue not fearing if her dad would realize his product has been tampered with.

Gradually and oblivious to Glenda, the meth intake had been wearing on her brain and body over time, causing both to deteriorate.

Later, Glenda walks the streets solo in high spirits. She enters the ramp and onto the major highway. Several vehicles are traveling at high speed. The driver of the oncoming eighteen-wheeler tractor trailer sees her staggering across the road. He applies brakes. Even so, unable to stop the trailer he runs her over, crushing her under the vehicle's wheels.

Other vehicles crash into the trailer creating a multiple-vehicle collision. Many injuries occur. Lives are lost in this multiple-vehicle accident including the driver of the trailer. As the vehicle slams into the median upon impact, the driver is tossed from inside the truck and onto the street. It is a massive automobile pile-up with multiple vehicles colliding and forming a heap.

There's pandemonium in the chicest community of Port Antonio as neighbors rush to the scene. Brenda and Thelma making dinner get the sad news and hurry to the scene on foot and in tears.

In the meantime Greg, bathed in remorse; after hearing the sad news; gets dropped off at the house in a taxi. His colleagues, so high on meth were unable to drive him home.

Greg gets to his car and decides to drive to the scene. He notices the foil paper on the seat and clues in on the scenario: His narcotics which he had confiscated during a recent drug bust and which had intentionally not been transferred to the station had been tampered with by his daughter. He races to the scene of the accident still under the influence.

Upon arriving at the scene, and noticing the mayhem, Greg Bascombe armed on his off day reaches inside his gun holster. He removes his gun and shoots himself in the head.

The sound of the gunshot alerts those at the scene including his wife and daughter, along with his neighbors and other attending police officers.

It is too much not only for his family but for the small community of chic Port Antonio to unravel on that Sunday afternoon. There are wailing and lamentation of the community. Brenda and Thelma are discombobulated. Many cries go out on their behalf. Their church members show up in droves providing comfort during the moments of double grief.

7

Through the upscale Port Antonio community, traffic is at a standstill as funeral-goers by the hundreds proceed to the cemetery. Some mourners, traveling in buses, cars, on motorbikes and others on foot are still saddened with the shock of the double narcotics-related suicide.
Leading the procession is a motorcade of Jamaican police officers displaying the Green, Black, and Gold,

on motorbikes, followed in tow by two wreath covered hearses. Spectators, sitting on their porches, verandas, and patios are bathed in tears as the procession passes the village. Motorists yield and give way to the saddened procession in a tear- shedding homage to the dead.

Meanwhile, the regretful multicultural, multiethnic, multiage procession with songs of praise wipe their crying eyes as they travel along the streets of Port Antonio.

Even while the news media in Jamaica are lashing out against the Mexicans for infiltrating their country with Methamphetamine, multiple kilos of coke and other drugs rapidly continue to contaminate the Jamaican community. Getting high has radically become the "thing" to do. Not doing it says that you are square or have a serious problem with the most important person – YOURSELF.

While some maintain the stance that if there are no customers to buy drugs, no drugs would get sold. Something no drug dealer wants to hear knowing fully that the buck stops with the client.

The funeral procession arrives at the cemetery. Glenda Ann Marie Bascombe is laid to rest. While the grave diggers fill that grave with soil, the minister prepares for the burial service of her dad Police Officer Greg Patrick Bascombe, the cousin of agent Randy Bascombe, adjacent and a few feet away.

The black, green and gold Jamaican flag covering his casket is removed by a fellow Jamaican police officer. His casket is then lowered into the grave.

It is a dual solemn occasion as more tears are shed by mourners. Glenn's wife Brenda and daughter Thelma standing at the head of the gravesite breakdown once again and are comforted by a group of consoling women.

At the end of the ceremony, the gravediggers fill this other grave also with soil as the mourners amble away from what will go down in history as the most tragic twin burial in Jamaica.

8

A black BMW pulls up outside a house in MO' Bay. TAMARA ROSS, the stunningly eye-catching-mid to late twenty-year-old beauty steps out. She proceeds to retrieve her keys to unlock the house door. Her cell-phone rings at the same time. She answers it. The call creates a sense of urgency as she heads back to the car and takes off speedily. The automobile screeches around the bend in the road as Dr. Ross puts the pedal to the metal.

From many miles away the sound of a speeding ambulance siren echoes. Meanwhile, a Chinese Private Jet makes its presence felt as it takes off to the skies from MO' Bay airport. Earlier a passenger on a gurney was seen deplaning from that aircraft.

The early morning traffic is now bumper to bumper as the BMW navigates its way through the huge traffic gridlock.

Suddenly, the driver of a tailgating minivan loses focus and rear-ends the BMW. This mayhem brings traffic to a standstill; as the drivers of both vehicles involved are now caught up in accessing the damage done to their vehicles. After the settlement with the exchange of information the standstill traffic proceeds. Tamara continues her journey.

Dr. Tamara Ross' car pulls into the parking lot of MO' Bay Hospital's, ER entrance. She races to the emergency room. The nurse on duty says to her, "He's in room #26!"

Dr. Ross rushes upstairs to that room. The patient lying in bed is no stranger to her, but this is the first time that she has been entrusted with the responsibility of possibly doctoring him back to health.

Agent RANDY BASCOMBE better is known as **RUDE BUAY** aka "Rude Boy" is of Jamaican descent. He opens his eyes and smiles at Dr. Ross. Rude Buay, in his early forties, is adorned with a scorpion tattooed to his bald head, with its fangs upstaging his forehead, and a tail extending towards his right earlobe. He is also badly bruised and battered. Dr. Ross returns the smile.

"How are you felling agent?"

She asks coyly.

"How soon can you get me out of here?"

Rude Buay asks.

"I am going to have to diagnose your condition first before I can determine the length of your recovery. From what I can tell: you seem to have been badly hurt. I don't know how you survived. In so far as I know, there isn't a quick-fix recovery method in medicine, for a building falling on someone. I saw that collapsed building. You got out of there alive, that's a miracle in itself!"

Rude Buay smiles again.

"So how soon?"

Asks Rude Buay.

Dr. Ross continues.

"Why didn't you get fixed up in Shanghai or the United States? They can rush the healing process. Are you here for treatment or some TLC?"

"I picked Jamaica because of your expertise... I wouldn't trust anyone with putting me back together again."

Tamara is flattered. She leans in and kisses Rude Buay on the cheek.

"Don't worry. I'll get you out of here in record time."

She assures Rude Buay.

Tamara checks the chart and begins attaching I-vies to the agent's body. As Rude Buay begins to fall asleep, she administers to his many wounds.

At the Emergency Room, a patient is wheeled in suffering from gunshot wounds. Dr. Tamara Ross gets the call. She concludes the dressing of Rude Buay's wounds and heads to the E.R.

FLASHBACK:

At the *Wood House*, Rude Buay finally wakes up. He rolls over and realizes that he's been trapped beneath the rubble. He immediately embarks on setting himself free. It is a tedious task as multiple wood timbers press their weight against his body. He twists and turns continuously.

Finally, Rude Buay manages to squeeze his way out of the rubble. He sees a lighted area and crawls to it. He hears a neighing sound and reflects his first encounter with the horseback at *The Lodge*. To Rude Buay's surprise, the horse is also trying to remove objects with its mouth to gain access to the interior of the collapsed building where he is trapped. It finally gains access.

Rude Buay, in pain, climbs upon its back and rides across the street. Two Chinese Policemen guarding the structure notice him drenched in blood and rush to his aid.

Later, upon Rude Buay's request, they put him on a private jet bound for Jamaica.

BACK TO PRESENT:

Dr. Ross re-opens the door to Rude Buay's room. She notices he is still fast asleep. The doctor smiles, closes the door and departs.

9

Later, at MO Bay Hospital, agent Rude Buay sits up in bed gleaning through the newspaper *Jamaican Gleaner*. The headlines read: **Jamaican Police Officer Glen Patrick Bascombe and Teen Daughter Commit Meth Related Suicides In Port Antonio.** Rude Buay gives the page heading multiple second looks. He knows Glen. Not only are they related cousins, but they also went to High School together. As he reads the front page news horrified, Rude Buay can't help reflecting on the death of his brother Clifford, over a decade ago in a drug-related incident outside their tenement yard in Jamaica. He can still see his mother holding his blood-drenched brother in her arms before the Jamaican police conducting their investigation and him standing next to her along with his godmother Maude Davis.

Rude Buay tosses the newspaper aside and focuses on the I-vies still attached to his body as he tries to roll onto his side but feels trapped. Suddenly, the screen opens and Dr. Tamara Ross enters. Looking at Rude Buay she says,

"How was your rest?"

"I guess my thoughts were so centered on getting out of here, I don't recall resting except that it was a mixture of dreams and nightmares."

Says Rude Buay.

"You've got to follow the doctor's orders. Rest is a must if you want a speedy recovery, my dear."

Tamara encourages.

She continues,

"So what was the dream?"

"I had a dream about you but then woke up and began reading the front page of the *Jamaican Gleaner*. There, unfortunately, I learned about my cousin and his daughter's drug-related suicide."

"Which copy was that?"

Asks Tamara.

Tamara picks up the paper and stares at the headlines.

"No wonder, and you missed his funeral. I had no idea you all were related."
"Good guy, bad situation."
"Yep. I am glad that you survived."
She comments as she puts down the newspaper. As she cleans and dresses Rude Buays' wounds she probes,
"The dream? ... and about me?"
Asks Tamara,
"I'll save that for when I can stand on my own two feet."
Says Rude Buay,
"Why do men always want to make women wait?
Asks Tamara,
"Why? Because ... you all do the same thing to us."
Says Rude Buay.
"I am not sure that is medically correct."
Responds Dr. Ross.
"I want to let you know that as your physician, my duty is two-fold. I still don't trust any nurse taking care of you."
Adds Tamara Ross.
Rude Buay admires Tamara as she unfolds her thoughts.
"I don't blame you, after that previous dilemma with the nurse and Axel James several months ago at the Port Antonio hospital; one never knows who is connected."

RUDE BUAY VOL. III

Tamara reattaches the life support to Rude Buay and reaches inside her purse. She removes her cell phone and shows Rude Buay pictures of Jamaican Policemen guarding the corridor as well as the checkpoint at the hospital's entrance.

She then retrieves a semi-automatic gun from her larger purse and hands it to Rude Buay.

He checks the gun and sees that it is silencer attached as well as fully loaded. He puts it carefully underneath his pillow.

Dr. Ross answers her cellular pager. She has to go. She blows Rude Buay a kiss and departs.

10

Tamara ambles through the parking lot. She gets inside her car and drives up to the hospital's security checkpoint. There she is stopped, although still attired with the stethoscope around her neck; she is detained, her car is also searched thoroughly by two Jamaican Police Officers. She is later given the *green-light*. Tamara views the situation as just a routine check and continues on her way unaffected. Several miles up the road, she notices something through her rearview mirror and senses being followed. This vehicle has been tailing her BMW for more than a mile. She speeds up. Her perpetrator does vice versa. She accesses her car phone and immediately dials 911. A rookie officer picks up the call at Montego Bay Police Station.

Tamara reports the fact of the matter to the officer, who asks:

"What is your location, Miss Ross?"

"Heading west on Overlook Way,"

She responds.

"What is the make and model of the vehicle trailing you?"

Asks the still wet behind his ears police officer.

"It's a black SUV. No front license tags."

Responds Dr. Ross.

"What does the driver look like?"

Asks the officer.

"It looks like two men wearing dark sunglasses and dark suits."

Dr. Ross responds.

"Where are you now?"

The officer asks.

"At the peak of Hilltop Road, I pulled off from the regular route going to my house and they are still in pursuit. You need to send in a response team right away!"

Explains Dr. Ross.

"Miss Ross ..."
Responds the officer.
Dr. Ross interrupts,
"Why... all of these questions? Don't you get it that I am being followed for several miles by a pursuer who will not let up?"
A female officer interrupts and intercepts the conversation.
"Miss Ross, Don't panic, drive normally. We are on our way. That is a lonely stretch of road. However, there is a shopping center two miles up the road you may want to pull into that busy mall. We will be there soon."
Dr. Ross speeds up and sees the huge shopping mall beckoning in the distance. Before she could make that exit to the mall, the trailing SUV speeds up, passes and appears in front of her BMW.
Dr. Ross stops her car and attempts to make a U-Turn. Before she could position her car for that getaway turn, the two armed men jump out and surround her vehicle. The doctor makes sure her doors are locked. One of the men breaks the driver's window using a crowbar.
The Doctor yells for help. Her cries are not heard by anyone except the two men as she is still a great distance away from that mall.
The two men drag her out of the car. They tape up her mouth. They bind her with ropes and throw her in the back of their SUV and re-board their vehicle. The

RUDE BUAY VOL. III

speeding SUV departs from the scene continuing on its recent path.

11

A Jamaican Police Officer sneaks into Rude Buay's room. The officer looks around the room. Rude Buay's eyes are closed. The officer attempts to remove the life support attached to the agent's wrist. Rude Buay opens his eyes and senses the officer's motive. Realizing that the agent is helpless and unable to defend himself the officer removes the life support attached to the monitor and reaches for the one attached to the agent's arm.

In the interim Rude Buay reaches underneath his pillow and retrieves his gun. Before the officer could bring out and engage his pistol Rude Buay shoots him in the face with the silencer-attached weapon.

Some time elapses as Rude Buay tries to make his way out of bed. The other officer realizing his partner has not returned barges inside Rude Buay's hospital room. Rude Buay hears his footsteps and sees him coming.

Rude Buay, though in pain arms himself and slumps back in the bed. He fires off a round that hits the police officer in his head. The officer topples over to the ground dead. Now two officers are lying bloodied and dead on the floor of his hospital room.

Rude Buay makes another effort to get out of there. He is not even focusing on the detached life support which hangs from the machine. Even so, it seems like he is trapped inside that room.

MEANWHILE, A NURSE filing away papers in her office notices a stack of fresh sheets undelivered to room # 26, the same room in which Rude Buay resides. So, she checks the housekeeping records.

Additionally, she checks the records more in-depth and realizes that Dr. Tamara Ross has not reported for work in some time.

"If she did show up those bedsheets would not be sitting in that room."

Says the nurse, as she picks up the bedsheets, and heads swiftly to room # 26.

Upon entering the room, she notices a silhouette sitting on the agent's bed with a pointed gun in his hand. Not only is the gun pointed at her, she also notices the two dead bodies on the floor. The site of the blood-drenched uniformed police officers makes her quiver. Retracting the curtain she notices agent Rude Buay sitting up in bed with his gun pointed at her. She screams out.

"Help!"

She drops the bedsheets on the ground and darts out of the hospital ward and back to her office. She goes to her desk and calls in hospital security.

There is a male patient in another bed in that hospital ward with his leg propped up in a cast. He hears the cry for help. He tries moving off the bed to assist in the situation.

In the meantime, Rude Buay looks out the window then back inside the room. The distance between his room and the ground level descends many stories. In a state of panic, he grabs the blood-stained bedsheets off the floor, picks up his gun and ties it around his neck using the pillowcase.

He gets out onto the ledge of the window. Finally, he ties those sheets together like a rope and attaches one end to the window's bar. Holding on to the strung-together sheets he makes his descent.

Inside the hospital, security guards are alerted. They emerge racing to his room followed by the same nurse. The patient with the leg in cast aches as he hurts his leg in the process of getting up to assist. By this time the security guards arrive at Rude Buays' room and look through that opened window, Rude Buay has already made it to the ground level of the hospital. They race out in pursuit.

Rude Buay sprints to the morgue area. He sees a hearse parked next to the *dead house*. He tries the driver's door. It's open. The agent looks inside for the ignition keys. There are none. His bullet wound in the leg begins to bleed severely. He runs inside the morgue. There is nothing to stop the bleeding. A dead man lies on a gurney with a sheet wrapped around him. Rude Buay removes the sheet. The dead man is dressed in black trousers, a white shirt, and a bow tie. He rips the sheet and uses a portion of it to wrap around his wound. He then removes his hospital attire, throws them on the floor and rids the dead man of his clothing, He puts them on. He finally discovers a pack of bandages while getting dressed. He grabs it and returns to the hearse.

Rude Buay pulls the vehicle's hood lever. The hood pops open. He hot-wires the vehicle and makes his getaway through the back streets of the hospital and merges with the flow of the main street traffic.

RUDE BUAY VOL. III

Meanwhile, the security guards at the hospital return to their posts unaccomplished on their pursuit of Rude Buay.

RUDE BUAY VOL. III

12

Rude Buay pulls up across the street from a church. He parks the hearse and walks to the hotel up the block. He gets a hotel room. Once inside he begins to attend to his wounds using the bandage. His phone rings. It's Michael Ortiz, his boss in Miami.
"Rude Buay, how is the recuperation process?"
"My wounds are being attended to as we speak."
Says Rude Buay.
"Can you speak now?"

"Yes. I am by myself."
"Really?"
"Go ahead!"
"How soon can we expect you back in Miami?'
"Are you asking me to return to Miami or are you suggesting that I return. While I am still...?"
Rude Buay notices that his wound is bleeding more than before.
"Medical conditions here are superb. Plus we have drug-related issues here in the U.S. too, you know."
Says Ortiz.
"Boss, I still have dual citizenship and always will. The drug crisis here has expanded tremendously. Methamphetamine is on the rise. I recently lost my cousin and his daughter. The *Dragons* are not letting up. We are in a situation where this country needs a lot of help to fight this war on drugs. What is the availability of agent Hudson?"
"Rude Buay, I am afraid that you've gotten in way too deep. You were only on loan from the U.S. remember? And now you are asking to have agent Hudson join you again? Since you took on this Caribbean vacation, we have lost three agents. Two of them you shot and killed yourself and one who has recently deflected."
"Boss, if you were to ask agent Hudson if she would rather be working in the Caribbean over Miami, I can bet she will say the Caribbean any day. Plus, it's

ludicrous I must say, to blame me for the misdeeds of others. They were traitors…"

"Apparently you've brainwashed her enough that she will cover for you as she has always done, Rude Buay."

"If the war on narcotics is ever going to be won, at our level I would say we need the best fighters, those who would not whimper but fight to the … end. You have read it in the news: The cartels are now getting their guns from the *Fast & Furious* program. What's next?" States Rude Buay.

"I will ask her tomorrow and get back to you. But I am not going to twist her arm."

Rude Buay hangs up the phone expecting agent Hudson for sure to buy into his concept.

He continues to freshen up and administers to his wounds. That same evening a rental car company drops off a car for the agent. He picks up a pair of shoes at a nearby store and drives through the city hoping there's a chance he would run into Dr. Tamara Ross. His search for her is in vain. So the agent returns to his hotel room unaccomplished.

Rude Buay calls Chelo his Colombian counterpart to see if he could be of any assistance in tracking down Tamara's whereabouts using his spy gadgets.

13

Chelo, in his mid-30s and of Colombian descent is fiddling with his multiple spy gadgetries. He takes a break and answers the phone.
"Rude Buay! Man, it's sure good to hear from you. Sorry about that satellite failure in Shanghai. Anyway, I heard you survived according to Ortiz. How can I help you?"

"The *Dragon Drug Cartel* has possibly kidnapped Dr. Ross. She has been missing from the hospital for several days now. I need some help to track her whereabouts."

Says Rude Buay.

"You know how tough it is transmitting signals out of Jamaica. Too many ... interceptions! Plus since Miles Tate gave the 411 regarding our operation to the *Dragons*. They could clue in on our whereabouts easily. Try Walter Banks he might be able to assist better in the present circumstances."

Rude Buay hangs up that call and dials.

WALTER BANKS, the veteran agent is reading about a Mexican drug account in the *Jamaican Gleaner*. Banks is an African American man with salt and pepper hair and in his fifties.

"Good to hear from you Rude Buay. I thought the doctor was looking after you. At least that's what Mildred conveyed to us before our planned meeting with the Commissioner to honor you with a eulogy."

"Mildred always seems to know where I am. Doesn't she?"

States Rude Buay,

"The Commissioner and I had already discussed the tragedy and felt there was no way you would survive the collapse of the *Wood House*. Now that you are unbreakable like that "Six Million Dollar Man", I know

it won't be long before we teamed up again." I'll see what I can come up with through my existing local connections. As you may have already learned our main satellite source has become problematic."
Says Banks.
"Let's do it sooner than later."
Says Rude Buay.
"Nothing from Chelo, huh?"
Asks Banks.
"It has become very problematic for him since they took out our Colombian satellites in Bogotá."
Says Rude Buay.
"Okay, I'll see what I can find."
Says Banks.
"I will be counting on you!"

RUDE BUAY VOL. III

14

Later Rude Buay is alerted by an email on his laptop. He checks it. The email is from Tamara. He is somewhat relieved.
Until he starts reading it,
It states:
Dear Rude Buay,
I hope you have stopped pursuing the Dragon Drug Cartel. It's a waste of your time. Any day now I could be hanged and fed to vultures. I miss you, Rude Buay. Thanks for the times we've shared. All the best with your recovery.

RUDE BUAY VOL. III

XOXO Tamara.
Sandals, MO' Bay.

Rude Buay is confused. This is not like Tamara. He ponders:

"Is that all she wrote? Was she pressured by fear tactics by the kidnappers; forcing her into writing this twisted style of email?"

These questions and other similar ones riddle his mind. While he applies a fresh bandage to his wounds and gets dressed. He takes up the gun which Tamara left him at the hospital. He looks it over. He is satisfied; the gun is still loaded minus the two used bullets. He straps the gun underneath his pullover jacket. He retrieves another gun that belonged to one of the fallen officers at the hospital and straps it around his leg underneath his trousers.

Rude Buays' phone rings. Walter Banks is on the line. Banks alerts Rude Buay that Tamara was reportedly seen at *Sandals* in Montego Bay. With that confirmation of her location, he ensures his weapons are intact. He heads out speedily and asks Banks to cover as back up. Banks agrees.

RUDE BUAY PULLS UP outside *Sandals*. This famous Hotel and restaurant are buzzing with activity. Parking attendants valet cars in rapid succession. Patrons mingle all over the compound. He moseys inside the resort with caution. As soon as he enters the lobby an armed man approaches him and sticks a gun in the back. Still, he manages to bring out the gun underneath his pullover in confrontation.

The man proceeds up through the hotel's stairway. Rude Buay follows looking for another good aim to blast the perpetrator.

Before he could make his way up the second set of stairs, a door from that floor level opens, he tries to reach for the other gun under his trousers. Another man grabs him from behind and wrestles the gun away from him. The man manages to *floor* Rude Buay. Instantly the other perpetrator runs back down the stairs. Together they drag him back outside through the exit door. They have a hard time restraining the agent who is valiantly putting up a fight. One of the men lets up and reaches inside his jacket pocket and pulls out a syringe. He sticks a needle in his arm and injects fluid into that arm.

Unknown to Rude Buay the two men were also involved in the authoring of the email sent by Tamara earlier.

They escort Rude Buay to the parking lot. Before getting to their vehicle he is partially knocked out. They drag him and toss him inside the trunk of their vehicle and drive off. Rude Buay struggles to stay in a conscious state of mind. But all he can see is a flashback to almost a year ago when Axel James and Ian Baynes, two members of the *Dragon Drug Cartel* tied him up and put him inside the trunk of their car and then drove him through the hills of Jamaica for the kill.

Finally, the drug sets in and the agent snaps into a semi-unconscious state.

15

During the night Rude Buay sleeps like a baby in the private Jet aircraft manned by the *Dragon Drug Cartel*. The following morning, he wakes up in Nogales, Mexico. The airplane in which he was transported, touched down and taxied to a private hangar. They transport Rude Buay to a guest house strapped inside a customized van. This wooded building is located deep inside the rugged hills of Nogales, Mexico and overlooking the city.

Later, one of Alberto Gomez's guards drags Rude Buay from the guest room and, into the makeshift meeting room. There is a big table set in the middle of the room surrounded by six chairs. The aura inside that room is so tense; you can cut it with a knife.

Seated at the head of the table is Drug Czar Alberto Gomez. On his right in the anti-clockwise direction is his wife Denise Gomez. Next to Denise is seated, Shelly Hall. Marcus Ranks sits to her right. Next to Marcus and facing Alberto Gomez, is Miles Tate! Sitting next to Tate is Grace McCloud. And seated next to Grace is Sammy Chin.

The guard escorts Rude Buay to that vacant seat at the table next to Alberto Gomez. He plops the agent down on the chair.

The door, in two halves, swings open in unison. Two Hispanic men in male nurse attire enter, closing the door effortlessly behind them. One guard places a tray on the table in-front of Rude Buay and grinds his enormous bicuspids teeth. The other places a pair of pliers and a washcloth next to the tray and grunts *doh, ray, me, fah, soh, la, te, doh*. As if to say this is my song, soon we are going to kill you if …,

Alberto Gomez presides:

"Welcome Agent Rude Buay!"

Rude Buay is still groggy but can still hear the echo of the last *doh!*

Alberto Gomez slaps Rude Buay in his face.

Rude Buay feels it. He evolves into an alert stance.
"Are you with us Rude Buay?"
Asks Alberto Gomez.
Rude Buay stares at him as his intellect drifts in and out like a rolling tide.
"It is imperative you remain alert during this meeting as this could determine if you should live or die."
Rude Buay nods in unconscious agreement.
"While we have your undivided attention, Rude Buay I might as well cut straight to the chase. I must let you know that you are a very lucky man, to still be alive. We could have had you killed but instead, we brought you to Nogales to allow you to team up with the fastest-growing cartel ever orchestrated. You are hardworking: meaning you get the job done. It would be beneficial to you and us both if you would team up with the organization as part of our extension program.
You would benefit from an unmatched salary. Plus receive bonuses from our annual profits. In the first year a whopping 5% will go to you, the second year 10%, the third year 15% and the fourth year 20%. I know how much you make as a U.S. D.E.A. I would say it's peanuts compared to what you can earn just on salary alone in the narcotics trade.
Rude Buay is hearing Alberto Gomez but he isn't assimilating nor digesting the team player mindset strategy or the Czars' monotonous trade philosophy.

"Basically, you will be working along with the border patrols acting as if you are completely on their side. We need an inside man on our side. You will let our dealers into the U.S. unscathed. If ever there is a sticky situation involving our men you will work it out in our favor. Of course with you being the head honcho you will step in and put out the fire. Our men are well trained they know the border lingo, even dealing with the meter maids on the other side they are adept. With you as the "top dog" we will be a force to be reckoned with.

It's no happenstance that the lead *Border Patrol Officer* position is open. With your credentials, you shouldn't have a problem nailing that prestigious job. The U.S. government would not turn you down; all you need to do is to apply. Look at what you've done for them. Your résumé speaks for itself, agent."

Rude Buay is somewhat flattered.

"You will fit in so well no one would even know you are working for us. After 5 years you can feel free to walk away, no strings attached!"

There is silence. All eyes are now focused on Rude Buay anticipating his acceptance of the deal. Instead, he composes himself but remains silent.

Alberto Gomez quickly states:

"If you refuse the job we'll have no choice but to execute you by hanging based on charges of treason, along with all the trouble you have caused us in the past. So while the noose waits to dangle for your neck at the gallows, those two gentlemen standing over you have been instructed to extract one of your fingernails daily, leaving your pinky fingers for the last days leading up to your hanging."

Once again all eyes are focused on Rude Buay expecting him to give in. Finally, he composes himself. *"The things I've been through give me fortitude. I'm not easily broken. Not only have I seen too much but I've been through too much. Selling out is not in my character. You may hang my body on that gallows but you will never hang my character!"*

States Rude Buay.

"I'll give you ten hours to think it over and come to an intelligent decision. The initial nail removal process could begin at sunrise tomorrow. First, they would start with your right thumb and then your trigger holding finger the next morning."

The meeting adjourns. Not before the *Dragon Drug Cartel* performs its freebasing *get-high* ritual.

16

It's almost sunrise the following morning and almost ten hours since the *Dragon Drug Cartel* wrapped their meeting with Agent Rude Buay. The agent still doesn't accept the offer to team up with the *Dragons*. So to put seasoned salt in Rude Buay's wounds the *Dragons* put Dr. Tamara Ross on a Jet bound from Jamaica to Nogales, Mexico. The objective: to arrange for her hanging before Rude Buay's trip to the gallows.

Dr. Ross has no idea what their plot is about. The flight crew speaks using codes. None of which is familiar to her.

BACK IN JAMAICA Banks shows up at *Sandals* as backup for agent Rude Buay. The traffic heading to *Sandals* was full of nothing but gridlock and bottlenecking. Somewhat slowed he arrived there late. Now he is surprised that he didn't get a progress report from Rude Buay.

Upon arrival on the hotel compound, Banks learns from his inside source at *Sandals* that Dr. Ross had been moved to a facility in Nogales, Mexico. His source an elderly woman had heard them speaking in Spanish and heard their planned destination for Dr. Ross. Also, that agent Rude Buay was seen accompanying two men to their car hours before.

Upon returning home Walter Banks gets a phone call from Chelo informing him that the *Dragons* had moved operations from Colombia and set up base in Nogales, Mexico; to better facilitate their Meth trade. Chelo and Walter Banks later pack up some of their spy gadgets in boxes and suitcases. They head out separately to the Arizona, Mexican border town of Nogales and later to Nogales, Mexico.

IMMEDIATELY AFTER SUNSET the following day, the door to agent Rude Buay's makeshift prison cell opens. The room is exactly 10 feet by 5 feet. Inside, there is a cot on one side against the wall. On the other side is a small wooden table on the other side. Next to the table is a small trash can. The dangling light bulb on a hanging electrical cord in the roof is illuminated. The two men, seen before dressing in a nurse's uniform, barge inside.

Rude Buay is lying on the cot with both hands and feet tied with nylon ropes.

One of the men is carrying a tray along with a large pair of pliers. The other man holds in his hands a small damp towel and a box of latex gloves. He is also wearing an apron. He passes a pair of transparent latex gloves to his partner, who puts them on methodically as if he's a surgeon getting ready to perform a special surgical operation.

Moments later the apron-wearing man grabs agent Rude Buay's hands. Together they tie down Rude Buay's right hand on the table, securing the ropes around the wooden table's legs.

Rude Buay knows what's about to go down any minute, he flinches not only in his mind, so does his body. The agent's right thumb is the main focus of the pair of pliers.

One attendant presses down on Rude Buay's right hand using both of his hands, while the other brutally removes the agent's right thumbnail using the pair of pliers. Rude Buay yells out as the pain surges through his entire body.

The thumbnail, with some flesh attached to it, gets deposited in the trash can. The attendant then uses the damp rag to wipe the blood from the table including the vast amount flowing from the agent's bleeding right thumb.

From inside his apron pocket, the attendant grabs a piece of bandage and wraps it around the nail-less thumb, tying it around the agent's other four fingers on that hand and tying it around the wrist.

Rude Buay is then escorted to the cot in his room. The two men finish cleaning up of the blood residue and depart.

The following evening at sunset they return and extract the thumb on his left hand. Each day for ten days, these men remove one of Rude Buay's fingernails leaving those on his two pinky fingers for last as ordered by Alberto Gomez.

17

With the ten-day fingernails removal ordeal completed, Rude Buay remains all drenched with blood, as blood from his ten fingers drains into a cloth bag wrapped around both of his hands like a muzzle. The bag is tied at the wrists. The two men dressed in bloodied nurse uniforms strap Rude Buay onto a truck. Before they send Rude Buay to the gallows they ask the agent what he would like before he dies.

"I would like to see Dr. Tamara Ross again."

RUDE BUAY VOL. III

Says Rude Buay.

Attempting to get the agent to buy into the team concept of the *Dragons* for one last time and avoid being hanged, Alberto Gomez requests a laptop computer brought to the truck with video clips of Tamara. The two male attendants bring out the laptop and show Rude Buay video clips of Tamara being beaten and spat upon by several Mexican maids.

The videos, very horrifying and are more than what the agent wanted as a dying wish. He tugs at the ropes to escape but is restrained by the two men.

In the interim, the driver arrives and checks the truck along with the ropes, which binds Rude Buay, to ensure the agent is securely tied up.

The truck departs during the wee hours of the morning as the clouds begin to give way to the sunrise in Nogales hills. Alberto Gomez, Denise Gomez, Miles Tate, Shelly Hall, Marcus Ranks, Grace McCloud, Sammy Chin, and the two male attendants celebrate during an intense freebasing event in the upper room of the *Casa*. At this meeting, Alberto Gomez also introduces newcomer Victor Crip a Mexican native in his mid-30s to head up operations in Nogales - the position which Rude Buay had recently turned down.

As part of Victor's initiation, the *newbie* pulls out a glass pipe, similar to a crack pipe. He pours in about 0.2 grams of methamphetamine. Holding the pipe on his lips, he starts to gently heat the bottom part of the pipe to allow the drug to vaporize. He slowly inhales. He passes the pipe along with the crystal meth folded in an aluminum foil. The others partake in the *chasing of the white dragon*, a term used amongst drug dealers for meth smoking. They all are now as high as kites. They laugh and cut up detailing what Rude Buay will say and do as the noose tightens around his neck.

Rude Buay couldn't help but hear and notice their taunting from the window across the way as he is driven to his hanging by the Mexican truck driver. In a celebratory and festive mood, the drug lords synchronize their watches; as the hanging was set for 9:00 AM sharp.

CHELO HAD ARRIVED IN NOGALES, MEXICO on the afternoon of the previous day before the scheduled hanging and set up his spy operations in that city. After working tirelessly rigging several antennas from his wooden hut, he was able to pinpoint the location where agent Rude Buay was detained by the *Dragons*. On foot, he hustled to the area. Everyone was still asleep at the *Casa*.

Later the truck took off and subsequently made its way through the rolling hills and dirt roads of Nogales, Mexico. The journey continued as multitudes of vulture swarmed overhead sweeping down momentarily to feed on the remains of human bodies littered like a mass execution through the hills. Rude

Buay had never been to war in this country but imagined that at least they buried the bodies. The milieu was horrific! The hissing musical sound of maggots indicated that no graves were prepared for those who perished, not even trenches. The stench is overbearing, to say the least.

The truck finally stops on top of the hill close to the gallows. From that vantage point, one could see a swinging noose awaiting the agent. Two men dressed in coveralls await his arrival: One to hang him and the other standing next to the grave to bury him in that seven-footer open shallow trench. The driver steps out focused on the task at hand.

 Chelo takes a portion out of the page from the book by Walter Banks who had rescued him when he was driven to the gallows in Colombia over a year ago. Chelo promptly unties himself from underneath the truck's chassis and swiftly kicks the driver in his lower stomach region. The driver falls over gasping for air. As a result of the blow, the driver's rifle falls and is lying on the ground. Chelo kicks the rifle in Rude Buay's direction. Both of Rude Buay's hands are still muzzled in that bloodied cloth sack. Using his teeth the agent speedily unties the sack and crawls on his stomach and elbows towards the fallen rifle.

The barefooted Chelo kicks the driver one more time. This time he kicks him hard in his stomach. The driver once again crouches and gasps continuously for air.

Forgetting how painful it could be losing all ten fingernails in less than two weeks, Rude Buay picks up the rifle, forces his bloodied swollen trigger finger inside the trigger slot. It bleeds as he pulls the switch. He blasts the driver.

The hanger and the undertaker both hear the sound of that single gunshot and depart speedily from around the hanging site. The undertaker drops his shovel in the process. It falls into the trench. They race to the truck which transported Rude Buay to the *set*.

Rude Buay shoots again and kills both men while Chelo positions himself as a decoy. Chelo and Rude Buay hurry on their feet.

Moments later, after their departure, the truck in which Rude Buay was transported explodes at exactly 9:05 AM into a ball of fire.

Now free, Chelo and Rude Buay continue on foot for many hours through the rugged hillsides of Nogales.

CHELO, EARLIER before the truck was scheduled to leave for the gallows, ever alert; while under the truck's chassis, and waiting for it to depart from the *Casa*; was fortunate to eavesdrop on the conversations of the two male attendants. They had mentioned Tamara's whereabouts about two miles away from the *Casa*. Also, that she was next on the list to be hanged and that she was supposed to be hanged before Rude Buay but Alberto Gomez had wanted to welcome in

Victor Crip with the hanging of Rude Buay on the following day instead. They had even articulated about her beauty and implied doing a twosome or a *watch while I do it* with her if time permitted. They even joked about the latter and suggested tossing a coin upon arrival for supremacy. Immediately after their conversation, Chelo was able to pick up this house where Tamara resided on his pen radar.

Now, he and Rude Buay move swiftly in that direction through Southern Nogales.

The terrain is a rough one through the hills, more so for Rude Buay not exposed to that mode of getting around since his days in elementary school when he sometimes went to school barefooted. Chelo, though on barefoot can deal with the blisters and bruises to his feet. Rude Buay still in those shoes, he wore to locate Tamara back at Sandals in Jamaica, has at this point almost worn them out. Their soles give way leaving him with not only multiple calluses but severe bruises and blisters as well. The thorns from failed cactus add their punch to the feet of both men.

While traveling through the hills they discover many chopped up dismembered bodies as vultures continue to feed and the unpleasant odor surfaces. The stench remains unbearable, coming from the corpses made up of men and women and children and celebrated by maggots. Even so, they must hurry as time elapse and the already high stakes increase. Rude Buay falls

RUDE BUAY VOL. III

between some waist-high shrubbery but gets up and continues tirelessly.

RUDE BUAY VOL. III

18

Nearing the house a small dog begins barking as Rude Buay and Chelo closes in on the domicile. A guard keeping watch is alerted and trains his weapon on Rude Buay and Chelo for several minutes accompanied by dogs. The guard's gun runs out of bullets after an extensive cat and mouse ordeal. Now, the switch flips. Rude Buay, on a foot race, is in pursuit of the guard. The dogs cool it wagging their tails. Using his rifle he cuts down the guard whose dodging skill and agility on foot-speed runs out. He enters the house in take-down style with Chelo in tow.

Inside he discovers Dr. Tamara Ross. She is tied up hands and feet kneeling at the bedside. Chelo finds a kitchen knife and quickly cuts the ropes. Together the trio journey into the city and takes refuge in a hotel after sundown. The following morning at sunrise Chelo says his goodbyes to Rude Buay and Tamara.

TAMARA PROCEEDS TO BANDAGE-UP Rude Buay's ten nail-less fingers and attends to his gunshot wound suffered in Shanghai. The regular program on the TV is interrupted as the reporter comes on with breaking news:

"Almost two dozen kids under the ages of 12 and involved in the trade of Methamphetamine were involved in yet another standoff with border patrols in Nogales, Arizona earlier today. As a result, many officers were left dead and more than half of those kids were captured and their AK47s confiscated. However, the other kids fled to safety through the Mexican, Nogales hillsides. Mexican police are now combing through the desert looking for these bandits. More news to come on this evolving story."

Rude Buay asks,

"What's up with these kids?" They have no epiphany as to what they are into."

"Not only that,"

Says Dr. Ross.

"What's your take on Meth?"
Asks Rude Buay.
Dr. Tamara Ross voices her concern:
"You lost your cousin and his daughter."
"Don't remind me,"
Says Rude Buay.
She continues,
"According to the National Institute on Drug and Abuse, National Institutes of Health in regards to how Meth affects the Brain and the Body:
No matter how methamphetamine is used, it eventually ends up that it can affect lots of brain structures but the ones it affects the most are the ones that contain a chemical called dopamine. The reason for this is that the shape, size, and chemical structure of methamphetamine and dopamine are similar. Before I tell you more about dopamine and methamphetamine, I'd better tell you how nerve cells work.
Rude Buay is all ears.
The human brain is made up of billions of nerve cells (or neurons). Neurons come in all shapes and sizes, but most have three important parts: a cell body that contains the nucleus and directs the activities of the neuron; dendrites, short fibers that receive messages from other neurons and relay them to the cell body; and an axon, a long single fiber that carries messages from the cell body to dendrites of other neurons.
Axons of one neuron and the dendrites of a neighboring neuron are located very close to each other, but they don't

touch. Therefore, to communicate with each other they use chemical messengers known as neurotransmitters. When one neuron wants to send a message to another neuron it releases a neurotransmitter from its axon into the small space that separates the two neurons. This space is called a synapse. The neurotransmitter crosses the synapse and attaches to specific places on the dendrites of the neighboring neuron called receptors. Once the neurotransmitter has relayed its message, it is either destroyed or taken back up into the first neuron where it is recycled for use again."

Rude Buay senses that Dr. Ross is on a roll and chooses not to interrupt the flow of such vital information but nods to assure her that he's still listening.

"There are many different neurotransmitters, but the one that is most affected by methamphetamine is dopamine. Dopamine is sometimes called the pleasure neurotransmitter because it helps you feel good from things like playing soccer, eating a big piece of chocolate cake, or riding a roller coaster. When something pleasurable happens, certain axons release lots of dopamine. The dopamine attaches to receptors on dendrites of neighboring neurons and passes on the pleasure message.

This process is stopped when dopamine is released from the receptors and pumped back into the neuron that released it where it is stored for later use.

Usually, neurons recycle dopamine. But methamphetamine can fool neurons into taking it up just like they would dopamine. Once inside a neuron, methamphetamine causes that neuron to release lots of dopamine. All these dopamine causes the person to feel an extra sense of pleasure that can last all day. But eventually, these pleasurable effects stop. They are followed by unpleasant feelings called a "crash" that often lead a person to use more of the drug. If a person continues to use methamphetamine, they will have a difficult time feeling pleasure from anything. Imagine no longer enjoying your favorite food or an afternoon with your friends!

Methamphetamine has lots of other effects:

Because it is similar to dopamine, methamphetamine can change the function of any neuron that contains dopamine. And if this weren't enough, methamphetamine can also affect neurons that contain two other neurotransmitters called serotonin and norepinephrine. All of this means that methamphetamine can change how lots of things in the brain and the bodywork.

Even small amounts of methamphetamine can cause a person to be more awake and active, lose their appetite, and become irritable and aggressive. Methamphetamine also causes a person's blood pressure to increase and their heart to beat faster."

(She pauses for breath and then continues)
Long Term Effects of Meth:

Scientists are using brain imaging techniques, like positron emission tomography (called PET for short), to study the brains of human methamphetamine users. They have discovered that even three years after long-time methamphetamine users had quit using the drug, their dopamine neurons were still damaged. Scientists don't know yet whether this damage is permanent, but this research shows that changes in the brain from methamphetamine use can last a long time. Research with animals has shown that the drug methamphetamine can also damage neurons that contain serotonin. This damage also continues long after the drug use is stopped.

These changes in dopamine and serotonin neurons may explain some of the effects of methamphetamine. If a person uses methamphetamine for a long time, they may become paranoid. They may also hear and see things that aren't there. These are called hallucinations. Because methamphetamine causes big increases in blood pressure, someone using it for a long time may also have permanent damage to blood vessels in the brain. This can lead to strokes caused by bleeding in the brain.

Tamara **adds:**
Researchers are only beginning to understand how methamphetamine acts in the brain and body. When they learn more about how methamphetamine causes its effects, they may be able to develop treatments that prevent or reverse the damage this drug can cause."
"Really?"
Asks Rude Buay as he picks up his car keys and automatic rifle.

"That's why Glenda at an unconscious level and state of mind walked onto the Freeway and committed suicide by having that eighteen-wheeler run her over and Glen later blew out his brains,"
Says Rude Buay.
"She must have been so brain-dead, her body had to follow its leader,"
Informs Tamara Ross.
"Thanks for the research. Maybe someday you'll make the next breakthrough."
Says Rude Buay.

He kisses Tamara on her lips as he walks towards the door.
"They can't stop you! You're **UNSTOPPABLE**, you're **UNTOUCHABLE** but most of all … Randy, you're *SHATTERPROOF!!!*"
Proclaims Tamara to Rude Buay.
He slips two pairs of ventilated gloves provided by Tamara over the fresh bandage on his five fingers of both hands. Rude Buay makes his exit from the hotel room door in terminator style.
"I'll get you out of here soon!"

19

The Methamphetamine trade continues to expand rapidly, not only in Mexico and Arizona but has also diversified to Jamaica, Asia, Los Angeles, New York as well as the U.S./Canadian border. Several dominant cartels including the *Dragons* and the *Sinaloa Cartel* compete viciously for drug territory resulting in many killings, particularly in Mexico.

Many traders in Mexico distribute the drug on multiple levels of trade. Chelo, one day while collecting video feed through his high tech satellite equipment discovered what Rude Buay later described as one of the most successful and amazing ways, though on a small scale, to smuggle drugs across the border.

The *Dragons* smuggled narcotics through these tunnels from Mexico to Arizona every day including Saturday, Sundays and Holidays.

Methamphetamine smugglers in the border town of Nogales, Mexico continue to bring drugs into the U.S. through Nogales, Arizona, as some would say *for the cost of a quarter*.

They habitually use parking meters on International Street, which hugs the border fence in Nogales: These meters cost 25 cents. So the smugglers in Mexico would tunnel under the fence and wind up under the metered parking spaces. There they would carefully cut neat rectangle type manholes out of the pavement. Their associates in Nogales would park false-bottomed vehicles in the spaces above the holes, feed the meters, and then wait while the underground smugglers stuffed their cars full of Meth and other narcotics from below. This was done multiple times per day.

As soon as this exchange was finished, the smugglers use jacks to put the pavement *plugs* back into the manholes. The cars then drive away loaded with a variety of narcotics, mainly methamphetamine.

Additionally, some smugglers were caught on video using catapults which launched bales of drugs across the border fence. If it was going to get across the border those Mexicans found a way.

Methamphetamine became very popular also in Jamaica even though the effects of Glenda Bascombe's death were still felt and talked about by many during their daily routines whether on the street or in their homes. To many concerned parents, it stuck out like a sore thumb.

IT IS WELL KNOWN INSIDE the drug world that the cartels control the trafficking of drugs from South America to the U.S., a business that is worth an estimated $13billion (£9 billion) a year. Their power grew as the U.S. stepped up anti-narcotics operations in the Caribbean and Florida. A U.S. state department report estimated that as much as 90% of all cocaine and methamphetamine consumed in the US comes via Mexico.

Meanwhile, many are killed both in Mexico and neighboring U.S. border towns like Nogales by the *Dragon Drug Cartel*, not only as of the demands for narcotics increase but also because smugglers fail to carry out their assignment and creditors fail to pay up for their drugs.

The Mexican government issued partial figures on 11 January 2012. These showed that 12,903 people had been killed in violence blamed on organized crime from January to September 2011. Added to the previous overall total, this

means that 47,515 people had died in the five years of Mr. Calderon's presidency. Although there is no breakdown, the victims include suspected drug gang members, members of the security forces and those considered innocent bystanders.
Reported one source,
While another source stated:
Violence was first concentrated in Mexico's northern border regions, especially Chihuahua, as well as Pacific states like Sinaloa, Michoacán and Guerrero. Ciudad Juarez (just across from El Paso in Texas) was the most violent city. In 2010, some 3,100 people were killed in Juarez, which has a population of more than a million.
But since 2010, violence has spread to other regions, including Nuevo Leon and Tamaulipas states. One of the focal points for violence has been Mexico's third-largest city, Monterrey.
The year 2011 also saw new areas hit. For example, VeraCrip on the eastern coast saw a series of mass killings.
The Government of Mexico feels the police cannot be trusted. Drug cartels with massive resources at their disposal have repeatedly managed to infiltrate the underpaid police, from the grassroots level to the very top. Efforts are underway to rebuild the entire structure of the Mexican police force, but the process is expected to take years.

RUMORS SPREAD QUICKLY in Jamaica amongst Rude Buays' peers that the agent was still alive and stationed in Mexico fighting the war on drugs. Meanwhile, many Jamaicans, as well as meth users, were becoming mentally paralyzed from the use of Methamphetamine. Jamaica was rising rapidly in the meth using stats.

Commissioner Richard Baptiste, in his 50s, and Mildred Simms, who had previously teamed up with Rude Buay in Jamaica and China against the *Dragons*, for a while believed that the agent Rude Buay had turned his back on his people.

Mildred Simms and the Commissioner also accused Rude Buay of forsaking his Jamaican people when they faced similar drug problems. *Tivoli Gardens* stated: was like a simmering volcano and could erupt again spewing out many more Johnny *Too Bads*.

Not sure how to handle this dilemma, they even took things a step further to discuss the elimination proceedings of Rude Buay with the Governor-General of Jamaica Bradford Wiley.

In this plot they would secretly deliver Rude Buay into the hands of the *Dragon Drug Cartel,* just like the Philistines, in the *Bible* days did to Samson.

Even so, Governor-General Wiley, a man of peace and tranquility saw things differently and suggested to both the Commissioner and Mildred Simms that they team up with Rude Buay to fight against the *Dragons*. His wisdom led him to believe that Rude Buay was about "One Love for Jamaica."

Was that enough to change their perspective on the Rude Buay's situation? At least they let it rest for a while as they came to grips with convincing themselves that if Rude Buay was involved it had to be a worthwhile cause not only for Jamaicans but the whole world.

20

A dark-colored jeep speeds through the dirt road surrounded by trees and shrubbery in the hillsides of Nogales, Mexico. A blanket of dust follows it in tow. Finally, the vehicle comes to a halt on top of a hill overlooking Nogales close to the Mexican/U.S. border. Another jeep is parked on top of that hill.

Out of the newly arrived vehicle, step out Denise Gomez, Shelly Hall, and Grace McCloud. The three women are dangerously armed with rifles. They move towards the other parked jeep.

Inside that parked vehicle is Victor Crip the newly appointed drug lord to oversee trade between the twin cities of Nogales. Using his binoculars Crip surveys the border. Noticing the three *femme Fatales,* Crip discards his binoculars and picks up his semi-automatic. He senses some rivalry. The women continue to aggressively pursue Victor Crip with aimed rifles. He now senses more than ever his life being threatened. He notices their dragon tattoo signature. He knows them.

"*¿Cómo eta?* What's up, ladies? We are on the same team."

Crip addresses,

No one responds verbally, neither in Spanish nor English. Instead, they maintain their stance with weapons pointed at him.

"Mistaken identity? We work for the same boss. Are you *locas*?"

He questions.

"What's up with the Nogales shipment?"

Asks Denise.

"That's right! The Nogales shipment?"

Restates Shelly Hall,

"*Muchos problemas señoritas.* The Blackman! The Blackman! Let me explain."

Says Victor Crip.

"Explain?"
Asks Grace McCloud.
Denise continues,
"Do you see all the cars parked on meters over on Independence Street? They have been there all day. If those drivers run out of quarters to feed those meters, do you know we could come up against the *policia*? If we fail in getting them to accept a bribe, they will instantly shut down our tunnel meter operation."
"That's right! Los Angeles and Canada are still waiting for their supply of Meth. You are pissing off Miles Tate. Who thinks we are dropping the ball!"
Says Shelly Hall.
Victor Crip looks at his pair of binoculars on the floor of the jeep with its driver's door still ajar. He then looks at the women still maintaining their offensive stance.
"You are causing problems on Independence Street, Victor Crip."
Says Grace McCloud,
"What were you looking at inside that gadget when we showed up? *Shades of...*? You are not doing your job. Goddammit!"
"*Dios* made the man and he made the woman. If you all will let me speak, I can certainly explain."
"And your name is JESUS?"
Asks Grace McCloud.
"No. I was looking through those binoculars for a black man carrying a rifle and sporting a scorpion tattoo.

Didn't you hear? Last night they said he shot up the tires on all the eighteen-wheelers heading for the parking lot and then called in the police who made several arrests. We don't have his full identity. The only evidence is that he is black and had a rifle according to one of our drivers who made his getaway."

"Why the heck weren't we notified? Did you inform Alberto Gomez?" We could have already caught the bastard. On the other hand, I think you are dreaming." Says Shelly Hall.

"I just got the word so I decided to find that man before he strikes again. I want to kill him myself."
Says Victor Crip.

The women re-board their jeep and drive back down the hill and on their way back into the hills and into Mexico.

MOMENTS LATER, Rude Buay on the other side of the hill, oblivious of the fact that Victor Crip has visitors in the form of Hall and Gomez kept crawling on his stomach toward the summit. He finally gets a glimpse of Victor outside his jeep looking through the binoculars. Victor's back is turned in the direction of the agent as he is focused on binocular surveillance.

Rude Buay whistles out and then throw a rock at Victor Crip. As soon as the drug lord turns around and is now facing Rude Buay, the agent caps him with several rounds while still lying on his stomach. He then gets up out of the fetal position and rummages through Victor Crip's jeep. Rude Buay discovers at least 30 pounds of Meth, two rifles, stacks of U.S. one hundred dollar bills, freebasing utensils, along with twenty kilos of uncut cocaine.

Additionally, agent Rude Buay confiscates Crip's binoculars and his jeep.

Using his elbow to steer the vehicle the agent departs speedily down the hill.

21

While returning to the base of the hill Rude Buay's phone rings. He fumbles to retrieve it from inside the pocket of his pullover jacket and does. It's Heidi Hudson. He immediately senses a sparkle in her voice. She is upbeat. Was she looking forward to once again connecting with her true partner in crime?

"Rude Buay, where the heck are you?"
She inquires.

"Nogales, Mexico,"
He responds.
"I will be joining you shortly even if it costs me my J O B. Ortiz was not happy with me asking for the time off. He suspected I was going to be teaming up with you and didn't look too happy."
Says Hudson.
"Very Interesting. Hit me up when you land."
Says Rude Buay, as he hangs up.

THE FOLLOWING MORNING Heidi Hudson arrives in Nogales, Mexico and meets the battered Rude Buay near his hotel across the way from Independence Street.
Noticing his swollen hands, and most noticeably the fight inside of him not being realized brings tears to her eyes. She gets on the phone after shedding some tears and connects with their other Jamaican allies.

IN MEXICO AND ITS BORDER TOWNS, the word spreads that a black man using a rifle shot up several tractor-trailers carrying Meth to be distrusted through the border tunnels. The cartel senses that it is Rude Buay but doubts that he could have escaped the hanging much less the vehicular explosion. Alberto Gomez, Miles Tate, Denise Gomez, Shelly Hall, and the others are very confused as it has been reported that the man sports a scorpion tattoo like the one displayed by Rude Buay.

Also, upon learning about the death of Victor Crip, yet another mystery is created for them; they recently discovered Crip's corpse in the Nogales hills.

While the *Dragons* look for the mysterious Blackman, the Mexico *policia* looks for more evidence regarding the tunnel drug transporting operation. They not only tow away several vehicles from Independence Street but discover that these vehicles were equipped with a manhole in the floor to pick up drugs from suppliers through underground tunnels with manholes and deliver them to dealers ready to transport them across the U.S., Canada, and China. Several arrests were made.

The following day city workers in Nogales embark upon sealing off those manholes and tunnels used as conduits for smugglers to transport drugs across the Mexican border into Arizona.

LATER THAT EVENING, Mildred, the Police Commissioner, and Banks; who have been searching tirelessly in Mexico for Rude Buay; arrive in the Mexican city of Nogales. They finally meet up with agent Heidi Hudson, Chelo, and Rude Buay in a small hotel suite and orchestrate a plan of attack to further counteract the *Dragon Drug Cartel*. At this meeting which, in more ways than one is like an ally reunion,

RUDE BUAY VOL. III

Rude Buay talks about the harmful effects of Methamphetamine on the human brain and body. Some key points in the research delivered by Tamara bear weight in his speech. Additionally, also how they were going to stop the *Dragons* by destroying their Mexican strongholds. The main objective: to decrease the number of drugs flowing out of Mexico to the U.S. and other countries as well. In the words of Rude Buay: "We will not only cripple but we will freeze the trade." So they divide, and team up, to conquer. Agent Heidi Hudson teams up with the veteran agent Walter Banks, Mildred Simms teams up with the Jamaican Police Commissioner Richard Baptiste and Rude Buay teams up with Chelo.

Walter Banks and Heidi Hudson were paired up not too long ago in Jamaica so that chemistry was tight. Mildred Simms and Richard Baptiste had also worked together when Rude Buay first fought against the *Dragons* in Jamaica. They had also worked together for the Jamaican government in Port Antonio. So they all were in sync.

Rude Buay felt obligated to mentor Chelo and pass the baton to the man who risked his life to save his. Everyone had been in this warfare before except for Chelo; he had never used a gun.

In three separate jeeps, all six officials pack up multiple guns and other weapons of mass destruction.

Immediately they take to the streets of Nogales, Mexico.

22

With the death of the newly appointed Victor Crip, the *Dragon Drug Cartel* was now without a key person to head up their drug smuggling operation at the Mexico/Nogales border. Plus, the word was out that agent Rude Buay could still be alive except none of the Dragons had seen him. So they turned down the rumor about his existence.

Alberto Gomez their leader was already heavily taxed with the global expansion of the *Dragon Cartel*, so he required a quality replacement in Mexico.

RUDE BUAY VOL. III

IT IS NOW 10:15 PM IN CHINA. Exactly 15 minutes after the lockdown at the Shanghai Central Prison. All heads are accounted for except Salvador. The Colombian chemist and Drug Lord who worked previously for the *Dragon Drug Cartel* and imprisoned less than 3 months ago is missing. He was initially arrested, charged and sentenced after over ten thousand cans of milk packed with uncut cocaine were discovered inside a submarine down the Chinese river bound for the Caribbean. The estimated street value of the cargo was over $10M. Salvador was already serving a portion of that 10-year sentence.

Outside the prison gate and up the street, Salvador, in a warden uniform, boards a waiting taxi. The taxi takes off.

About over an hour before prison lockdown and a few minutes after dinner, Salvador whisked away from the prison yard to the men's room.

Earlier that day after a phone conversation initiated by Alberto Gomez, Salvador accessed the warden's office and stole a uniform carelessly sitting inside the warden's closet. He placed it inside a black plastic trash bag and stored it at the bottom of the men's restroom trash can.

Before lockdown and after dinner, Salvador changed into that uniform and boldly walked out of the prison. The guard on duty waved to Salvador as he exited.

Oblivious that he was not the warden whose name tag was prominently displayed on his jacket.

Alberto Gomez had already arranged to have a taxi waiting for Salvador after lockdown.

Salvador was whisked away to the airport. There he met a woman who handed him a plane ticket, fake IDs and a duffel bag. Salvador went to the men's room and changed into civilian clothing, breezed through security and boarded an aircraft heading to Mexico. The following day he arrived in Nogales, Mexico.

Upon Salvador's arrival Drug Czar and leader of the *Dragon Drug Cartel*, Alberto Gomez quickly appointed the Colombian chemist, better known as Sal to head up the Nogales/Mexico border. The position which agent Rude Buay had turned down.

Sal had been known for creating the Dragon X brand of cocaine in Colombia. This brand was the result of a glitch. One mixed with cyanide and responsible for killing several Jamaican kids almost a year ago. Sal was also the point person who assisted David Lee, the Chinese drug lord in the packaging of cocaine wrapped in Ziploc bags and shipped in milk cartons. This narcotics shipment strategy caused the death of many, including little Leticia the 3-year-old Jamaican girl.

As the man in charge of the Methamphetamine operation in Mexico, the *Dragons* had put in place not only a chemist but a hard-working individual in the

person of Salvador. He was not only loyal to Alberto Gomez but dedicated to his cause: growing the cartel into a global operation. On several occasions Alberto Gomez reminded Sal: *We will not only expand across the five oceans but will cause some of the most devastating recalls that country* (referring to the U.S.) *has ever experienced.*
Salvador bought into that concept.

CHELO, USING HIS LAPTOP connected to his satellites and hidden cameras, which was recently set up in Nogales along the Mexican border and elsewhere. By doing so he was able to eavesdrop on the *Dragons*.

The cartel also positioned itself in Vermont close to the U.S./Canadian border. At that location, they used an old warehouse as a depot. The eighteen-wheelers would pull up, bound from Mexico. Then transfer their cargo inside waiting vans.

These were customized vans usually manned by two or three people. They would load up their Meth supply onto the vans and head for the Canadian border. The border patrols on the Canadian side would do minimal checking of these vehicles operated by Canadians. So these Meth smugglers got away scot-free. It was said that the ex-agent Miles Tate, a Miami native, had this drug smuggling operation locked down. Meth sales soared in Canada as a result of his involvement.

RUDE BUAY VOL. III

Grace McCloud has filled the void left by the deceased Frankie O'Neal, Johnny *Too Bad*, Amanda Kingsley and Agnes Richards in Miami. This city situated in south Florida serves as a hub not only for the southern states but the Caribbean as well. Their shipments came through the Mexico/El Paso border on eighteen-wheelers. Products were unloaded and stored in a warehouse similar to the previously owned *Milky Way*. Marcus Ranks headed up the Tivoli Gardens/Port Antonio operations in Jamaica. Their shipments came through the Mexico/El Paso border on eighteen-wheelers via Miami and were sent out in small ships into Jamaica via Port Antonio and Ocho Rios.

Ever since Rude Buay, and most recently his team, began concentrating on combating the trade of narcotics in Mexico, Ranks had some room to trade freely and became stellar at smuggling Meth along with other narcotics products into Jamaica. He was too clever for Jamaican law enforcement. In other words, he was slippery. A relative of Johnny *Too Bad*, Ranks had a vendetta not only against the U.S. but against Drug Enforcement Agencies as well.

OVERSEAS, IN CHINA Sammy Chin tied the knot with the imprisoned widow of the deceased drug lord David Lee. With Lee's empire shattered and now in the rebuilding stage, his widow Chu Ling became a great fit for Sammy Chin. The only downfall was: even though she was an adept drug dealer who unfortunately got busted, she had to operate from behind prison walls. Palladium on Chu Ling was very tight. Serving mostly as a referral source for Chin, was her main contribution to the trade. Chu Ling was determined to be in the thick of things very soon. Thus, giving China that clout it once had when her previous husband David Lee was alive and ran the narcotics trade.

RUDE BUAY AND CHELO followed in tow by Walter Banks and Heidi Hudson, accompanied by Mildred Simms and Richard Baptiste, pull up outside an abandoned warehouse in Mexico a few miles from Nogales, the neighboring town in Arizona. The agents are poised. They, survey from their vehicle and gather satellite feed posted at the border.

23

While the agents waited undetected in their vehicles parked between the trees located above the warehouse, several tractor-trailers pull up and enter the warehouse. The agents waited for them to exit the building but they never did. So the agents moved in ensuing an investigation and a possible drug sting. Upon arrival, the more than six eighteen-wheelers had all vanished. The loading docks were empty as well as the back parking lot. Rude Buay familiar with disappearance tactics used by the *Dragons* reflects on the disappearances of Johnny *Too Bad* and

RUDE BUAY VOL. III

Frankie O'Neal at a Manor in Miami several months prior. So the agent perceives and pursues a possible underground tunnel getaway.

Moments later all six agents find themselves driving through a long extended tunnel. In less than 15 minutes they wind up in another warehouse, this time across the borderline into Nogales, Arizona. That fleet of eighteen-wheelers is still nowhere to be found, not even a trace.

Rude Buay is also very cognizant of the fact that this tunnel had been used by the *Dragon Drug Cartel* to transport narcotics from Mexico into the U.S. He had seen the underground tunnel which was built underneath that manor in Miami.

Moments later Rude Buay gets on the phone with Michael Ortiz. Both men discuss the possible ways of freezing tunnel narcotics traffic to the U.S. Later that day U.S. Border Patrols surround that same warehouse in Nogales and with the aid of heavy-duty equipment they put up roadblocks to stop further tunnel traffic into the U.S.

As the news spreads, U.S. Border officials beef up border security to curtail any other tunneling from Mexico into the U.S.

THROUGH THE CALCULATED surveillance efforts of Chelo, Rude Buay learns that Salvador had arrived in Mexico and was filling the void left by the executed Victor Crip. So he and the agents embark on a mission

RUDE BUAY VOL. III

to find Salvador. Rude Buay and Chelo cover the Mexican side of the border while Banks, Hudson, Simms, and Baptiste cover the town of Nogales, Arizona. With the disappearance of those eighteen-wheelers, they decide that they would beef up their security as well as their investigation.

Rude Buay and Chelo later return to Mexico through the same tunnel. On their way back they meet with an eighteen-wheeler coming straight ahead at them as if pursuing a head-on collision. Rude Buay manages to shoot at the driver and blowing out the front windscreen. The driver is untouched by that round. However, he tiers the truck on the right side of the tunnel while Rude Buay's jeep squeezes by on the left.

Rude Buay's jeep comes to a stop. The driver of the eighteen-wheeler truck gets out and starts shooting at Rude Buay and Chelo. They retaliate with several rounds of their own. The cat and mouse duel continues for several minutes inside the dark unlit tunnel. Finally, the driver takes off on foot through the tunnel and heading towards Mexico.

Chelo, excellent on foot leads the way in the foot race with Rude Buay following closely behind him.

The driver shoots again at the two agents. This time once again, only training his weapon.

Rude Buay get a shot off that sends the driver to the ground, another round finishes him off. After a search of the driver, his truck was searched, over 100 kilos of uncut cocaine was discovered in addition to large quantities of Methamphetamine and other narcotics inside the trailer. After calling in the *Policia* Rude Buay and Chelo leave the scene in pursuit of more *Dragons*.

LATER THAT DAY after receiving the news, Salvador consults with Alberto Gomez about the roadblocks placed by DEA inside the tunnel and impeding the flow of drugs to the U.S. along with the sting carried out on the now-deceased truck driver. Alberto Gomez, not only wondered who was behind this operation but set out to capture them. First, he thought it was the border patrols but knew he had been operating this way for several months and they had not caught on. So he ruled them out.

He thought about the U.S. DEA. But he knew without the experienced agent Rude Buay in their camp, they were playing major catch up. Although he had heard that a black man took Victor Crip's life, in his mind he knew that he had sent Rude Buay to the gallows. Additionally, to ensure the successful execution of his task, he had also backed up that expedition with a bomb attached to the truck carrying the agent to the gallows. So he ruled out the Rude Buay comeback scenario.

Could it have been Rude Buay's allies? Alberto Gomez knew they were not as efficient without the man who he so badly wanted on his team. So he sent Salvador on a rampage to bring in whoever it was that was raining on his Mexican global parade.

Rude Buay had previously equipped Chelo with a semi-automatic gun but was concerned about the barefootedness of the man who had saved his life. Knowing how treacherous the search for the *Dragons* could become through the rugged hills of Nogales. So he pulls up at a shoe store and steps inside to purchase a pair of comfortable shoes for his sidekick. Planning to surprise Chelo, later on, he puts the pair of moccasins in a shopping bag and returns to his jeep. To his surprise, the jeep is there but Chelo and the laptop are missing.

24

When ex-agent Miles Tate learned that Chelo had been captured by the *Dragons* in Mexico, he travels from Vermont, where he had been stationed to be a part of the interrogation. He had already passed on U.S. D.E.A. secrets to Alberto Gomez, leader of the *Dragon Drug Cartel*. This opportunity would not only make him look good in Alberto Gomez's eyes but give him a chance to get some firsthand information from the man who had spied on the cartel from Colombia for many years. Tate was stoked!

Upon arriving in Mexico, Tate was met by Sal, the newly appointed Drug Lord to head up that region, also the man responsible for capturing Chelo. Alberto Gomez wanted to be in on the proceedings so he immediately flew into Mexico from China.

The interrogation was set for an office inside an abandoned warehouse in Nogales, Mexico. Chelo who looked somewhat battered was brought into the room that morning bound with ropes. Accompanied by two guards, they seat him on a chair in the middle of the room. Tied to the wooden chair which permitted him any but no movement or else the chair moved with him, Chelo sensed that his fate was going to be decided. He was not sure if they knew he was responsible for Rude Buay's escape. If they did, he envisioned not escaping, and being either hung from the gallows or executed.

Alberto Gomez and Salvador looked on while Miles Tate began with the *digging* process.

"Good morning Chelo!"

"Morning,"

Responds Chelo.

"Where do you live Chelo?"

"Bogota, Colombia,"

Replies Chelo.

"What brings you to Mexico? You've been here for some time now."
"D.E.A. business,"
Reveals Chelo.
"Who is your affiliation?"
"The U.S. government,"
Chelo responds.
"So you were brought in from Colombia to spy on the *Dragon Drug Cartel*?"
"I was brought here to work…"
Counters Chelo.
"Who brought you into Mexico?"
Interrupts Miles Tate.
"The D.E.A.,"
Says Chelo.
"Who…? Banks? Ortiz? Who do you report to?"
Asks Miles Tate.
"The D.E.A.,"
Answers Chelo.
"Is Rude Buay alive?"
"I don't know."
"You are such a liar. Which of those men, that I've just mentioned, do you report to?"
Asks Miles Tate.
"None of them. I report to the headquarters,"
Says Chelo."

"Every spy is accountable to someone even if that person is part of a group. So who are you accountable to? Who are you protecting?"

"The D.E.A."

Tate punches Chelo in the stomach.

"Give me the truth man! I don't need the D.E.A. bullshit. I have worked for the organization, you have to report to someone. Come on!"

That blow strikes Chelo hard. He coughs up blood as a result. Alberto Gomez looks at him as if to say: *don't waste my time. I did not fly in from China to be lied to.*

"Who was with you when you were captured?"

At this point, the *Dragons* are still unaware that Rude Buay has escaped death once again and is well alive and that he was with Chelo before being captured.

"No one. Why don't you ask Sal? He is standing right across from you."

Responds Chelo very calmly.

"Where are the rest of your guys?"

Questions Tate.

"I am not my brother's keeper. I work for the Drug Enforcement Agency."

Responds Chelo.

"Where is your satellite located?"

Asks Tate.

"That's a D.E.A. business."

Responds Chelo.

That feels like a slap on the face, to Miles Tate. He realizes that he is not going to get anything out of Chelo. Alberto Gomez and Salvador are all of the same opinions.

"How would you like to work for us?"

Interjects Alberto Gomez.

Chelo doesn't answer.

Alberto Gomez presents an attaché case filled with stacks of crisp U.S. One Hundred Dollar Bills.

Chelo looks them over.

"We'll pay you well. You sure know how to keep secrets."

Says Alberto Gomez.

"No thank you."

Responds Chelo.

"Give him a day or two to think about it. In the meantime prepare the gallows to hang his ...."

Says Alberto Gomez.

Tate ceases his questioning.

Salvador removes Chelo from the room. He puts him inside his pickup truck and escorts him back to the *small house* where he is kept under confinement.

25

While Rude Buay drives through the neighborhood looking for the missing Chelo his phone rings. It's his boss Ortiz on the other end. Rude Buay looks at the number on the caller ID and delays answering the call. After several rings, he accepts the call.
"Bascombe this is Ortiz. Would you like me to call you back?"
Asks Michael Ortiz.
"We can talk now."

Says Rude Buay.
Ortiz feels it in his agent's voice.
"You don't sound too…"
"Chelo is missing. Possibly captured!"
Informs Rude Buay,
"You are kidding me. Without him, we are dead in the water. Was it the *Dragons*?"
"Most likely! They have not claimed responsibility yet but…"
"Bascombe I told you, you've gotten in way too deep. Without him, it's over. Your entire team of agents could be wiped out at an instant. If you don't know where they are, it's like walking through a minefield. You need him to monitor those bastards especially at the border."
"That I know very well,"
Responds Rude Buay.
"I'm aware that Hudson recently joined you. She could have told me what her objective was instead of saying she wanted some time off."
States Ortiz.
'Really? Boss, I am not up on what Hudson does …"
Says Rude Buay.
"My suggestion is that you tell your team you are packing up and, return to Miami where at least it's not so bad and we have more control."
Says Ortiz.

"No thanks. I am not a quitter. There isn't a quitting cell in my makeup. I will fight them in the desert, I will fight them in the mountains, I will fight them in the tunnels, I will fight them amongst the cactus, I will fight them at the border, I will fight them in the air, and on the water ... I will fight them everywhere. I am not giving in. All it takes for evil to prevail is a bunch of men with no backbone."
Declares Rude Buay.
"You are putting the lives of your teammates at risk, Bascombe. Maybe you should ask yourself the question. Why are we in Mexico? Additionally, what does the U.S. have to gain? They are our neighbors, not our friends. They bring us more harm than good. Why don't they sell it to their people? Their governmental views are opposed to ours. It is time to get out."
Says Ortiz.
"I hear you, boss. I am not going to quit so they can feel they have won. Plus, the man who saved my life from the gallows has probably been captured. And if there is even the remotest possibility that he is alive, then, I've got a job to do, and that is to find him. Quitting is not an option. *When the dream is strong enough, the facts don't count.* I need your support. If I can't have it, that's okay, I will fight this war alone till the end. I may lose some battles but I will not lose this war."
States Rude Buay.

"This is not the Winston Churchill era, Bascombe. He had Britain behind him. What do you have? Plus Chelo's understudy Bruce is very wet behind the ears."
Says Ortiz.
Rude Buay continues,
"*Until one is committed, there is hesitancy, the chance to draw back, always ineffectiveness. Concerning all acts of initiative (or creation), there is only one truth, the ignorance of which kills many ideas and splendid plans, that the moment one definitely commits oneself, then Providence moves too.*

All sorts of things occur to help one that would otherwise never have occurred. A whole stream of events issues from the decision, raising in one's favor all manner of incidents and meetings and material assistance: which no man would have believed would have come his way.

Whatever you think you can do or believe you can do begin it. Action has magic, grace, and power in it.' So said Goethe,"
Quotes Rude Buay.
Ortiz removes the phone receiver from his ear and stares at it, thinking Rude Buay has got to be crazy. He is fighting a Mexican war as long as the river Nile. Not only is he shorthanded but he's fighting with two injured hands.
"Hello,"
Says Rude Buay.

There is no answer coming from Ortiz on the other end of the phone. So Rude Buay hangs up on his end. After digesting the interlude between him and Ortiz, he reaches over on the front passenger seat. There sits the package with the pair of moccasins which he purchased for Chelo. He opens it and retrieves the shoe box. Rude Buay stares at the pair of moccasins.

"Requesting D.E.A. presence at an abandoned warehouse in Nogales just outside the Mexican border and across from Independence Street. Officer down! I repeat! One Border Patrol Officer down ...!"

It is the voice of Bruce Chavez, Chelo's Mexican understudy.

Rude Buay makes a U-Turn in his jeep and heads speedily in that direction.

26

Rude Buay approaches the warehouse where the eighteen-wheelers were first seen. He had thought about using the tunnel but changes his mind and opts for the local street instead. In less than fifteen minutes he's at the border into Nogales. Moments later he pulls up at the warehouse once used as a clothing depot.

Flashing ambulance lights welcomes him along with busy medics surrounding the corpse of a uniformed border patrol officer.

Immediately after Rude Buay arrives on the scene, Mildred Simms, Richard Baptiste, Walter Banks, and Heidi Hudson pull up. They jump out of their jeeps and join in the investigation.

According to the eyewitness report of an elderly Mexican man:

Several cars were in line at the U.S. border crossing. Border patrol officers after detaining several Mexican motorists proceeded to search their vehicles. While rummaging through their cars, several teens arriving on foot from Nogales, Mexico emerged at the border crossing. In a confrontation, they demanded the release of those arrested. These kids armed to the max carrying AK47s opened fire on investigating border patrol officers as well as border workers.

When it all ended not only were several border patrols killed but the kids attempted to takeover border operations there in Nogales.

It was right about then that agent Rude Buay arrived on the scene.

The leader of the pack, a feisty Mexican kid, of dwarf stature and adorned in a bandanna. Yells out:

"We are the young "Dragons" and we are in control."

Rude Buay looking at him from a distance in his jeep says to himself:

"A minor is in control, he's got to be kidding. He could still be wetting his bed."

But looking at the waving AK47 in the kid's hands and the army of kids rallying for his support, the agent realizes that this is serious business. Plus there were no border patrols in sight except for those dead bodies lying around.

So Rude Buay decides to negotiate after summoning his backup of agents.

"Hey Kid! My name is agent Bascombe, D.E.A. You are indeed a tough kid. But whoever set you up to this is such a weakling, a coward. They should have done these acts themselves. You have no doubt so much potential and all your life ahead of you. Whoever set you up to this has nothing to live for…"

Interrupting the kid responds,

"Your name is not Bascombe, it's Rude Buay … aka Rude Boy. We don't need a sermon because we are not in church and today isn't Sunday. Plus, I dislike Sunday school. You are the man with the scorpion tattoo and causing a lot of trouble at our borders. You think this is Jamaica…! You've killed Johnny *Too Bad*, David Lee, Ian Baynes, Axel James, Desmond Scott, Jose Mendez, and Ricardo Herrera. You are not going to do the same for me!

The kid shoots off a round at Rude Buay. It misses.

"Look! Behind you coming through those hills are 10 eighteen-wheelers. We want their safe passage through this border which has for too long been like an iron wall to us Mexicans. When we feel they are safe

we might be willing to discuss our plan B. I won't miss the next time around."
"What's inside of those trucks?"
Asks Rude Buay.
"None of your business!"
"Kid. Ever since 9/11, any vehicle entering the U.S. has to be checked. If I allow your trucks though, as an agent I would not be doing my job and could cause harm to many Americans."
The kid shoots at Rude Buay. Again he misses. The agent dodges out of the two rounds.
"That was just a warning. I want what I say, and I get what I want."
Says the kid.
"You are spoiled! What do your friends think? Are they in with you on this?"
Asks Rude Buay who would not let up off his aimed rifle at the kid.
"We don't have to listen to you. Look around you. The trucks are coming."
Says the kid.
Rude Buay peripherally sees another group of kids forming a circle around him.
"The choice is yours! In a minute over 30 bullets could be penetrating your body. Only one of mine... Do you want war or do you want peace?"
Yells the kid.
"Okay. I will let the trucks through, but one at a time."

RUDE BUAY VOL. III

Says Rude Buay,
The kid radios,
"Come on through, only one by one!"
Before the trucks could descend across the border, two jeeps emerge racing alongside them and raining tear gas onto the border compound.
Rude Buay grabs his mask and protects himself. Many stray bullets scatter from wielding AK47s, the experienced agents in both jeeps are unscathed. Caught up in the tear gas deposit the kids fall to the ground. The eighteen-wheelers are stalled in their tracks. Mildred Simms, Richard Baptiste, Walter Banks, and Heidi Hudson emerge from their vehicles. Along with agent Rude Buay, they pounce on the gassed kids, confiscating their weapons.
Moments later not only is the border reopened and manned by replaced border patrols, who are flown in, but 30 kids are arrested and detained along with 10 tractor-trailer drivers.
After a search of the eighteen-wheelers over 300,000 pounds of methamphetamine is seized along with 100,000 kilos of uncut cocaine.

27

After this seizure, it became official news that not only was agent Rude Buay alive but that his team of agents was conducting U.S. D.E.A. duties in Mexico at the U.S border. Alberto Gomez now knew for sure that someone was covering Rude Buay when he was sent to the gallows or the men trusted to hang him, set him free, instead. So he put out a countrywide search in Mexico to have Rude Buay once again captured; so he could pull the trigger and take agent Rude Buay's life for good if he refused to team up. Rude Buay quickly learned of the Drug Czar's objective by signs placed on telephone poles. Hence, not only was he in pursuit of Rude Buay; for the possible kill, but Rude Buay was also in pursuit of him; and his entire team for *Operation Clean Sweep*.

It wasn't long after that, Bruce also discovered Alberto Gomez's plot, by tapping into a hotel phone line during his conference call with Salvador, Shelly Hall, Denise Gomez, Miles Tate, Marcus Ranks, Sammy Chin, and the remaining young *Dragons*. Bruce tipped off by an informant at the hotel was granted brief access to that Hotel's phone communication system. The informant made his side money that way.

Rude Buay, meanwhile, knew that no matter the many "what ifs" that surrounded Chelo's possibility of being still alive, he had to try his best to search and rescue him out of the grasp of the *Dragon Drug Cartel*. Rude Buay now waits outside his car at a local multicolored pottery shop in Nogales. He was informed by Bruce that Alberto Gomez, Denise and Shelly Hall frequented that block to shop and dine the *delicioso* local cuisine, known to awaken one's taste buds.

ONCE AGAIN THE VOICE of Bruce Chavez transmits through the D.E.A. radio circuit.

"Requesting D.E.A. presence at a food warehouse in Campillo and Belto Juarez. Two agents down."

There was no information on exactly who the fallen agents were. So, Rude Buay takes off in that direction. As do Banks and Heidi Hudson. Mildred Simms and Richard Baptiste also respond to the call. Three identical jeeps are now racing through Nogales, in Sonora, Mexico. Rude Buay's jeep is first to arrive at the scene, followed by Bank's jeep and then Mildred's. It's a bloody scene as two American agents lie on the street bathed in their blood and killed execution-style.

Rude Buay jumps out of his vehicle with his hands still bandaged. Walter Banks and Heidi Hudson using latex gloves gather information on the deceased agents by searching through their pockets and wallets.

"He is one of ours!"

Yells Hudson after viewing the first agent's ID. She views the second ID now handed to her by Walter Banks. Mildred Simms and Richard Baptiste yellow tape the area as they keep their eyes open for perpetrators.

Removing her gloves Hudson says,

"Both U.S. agents IDs are from New Mexico."

"What are they doing here by themselves? They should have known better than to be operating independently."

Says Rude Buay.

"What if Ortiz sent these men in to derail our progress? Heck, I wouldn't put it past him."

Says Hudson.

"Really?"

Asks Mildred.

"He is up for a promotion and needs people on his side."

Informs Rude Buay.

"Anything he can do to rank up, huh?"

Says Richard.

Rude Buay then calls in the Mexican *Policia*.

"Let's get out of here!"

Says Rude Buay.

As they get inside their vehicles and depart, Rude Buay senses being followed. His instincts are right on target as bullets instantly ring out raining on top of their vehicles.

BEFORE THE TWO AGENTS were gunned down. Both agents showed up at the warehouse: The purpose was for striking a deal with Denise Gomez and Shelly Hall for the purchase of 200 pounds of methamphetamine. The two men claimed they were from Los Angeles, California and were unable to acquire the product in the big city.

A drought had emerged in LA since those eighteen-wheelers were seized; loaded with narcotics, and bound for San Diego.

Conversely, those two agents from New Mexico were sent in by Michael Ortiz and Al Cortez. The latter was the head D.E.A. in New Mexico and wanted to help win support for Ortiz (to be known for) fighting the *Dragons* in Mexico. Both Special Agents were aware and concluded that Rude Buay and his team were taking the matter in Mexico into their own hands. More so, most Americans were now more tuned into what went on in Mexico and the drug trade because of the huge amounts of killings that ensued. They wanted to make sure their borders were intact and protection beefed up against the Mexicans. In a nutshell the reason for Ortiz's involvement; he woke up smelling the coffee and was now looking for shoulders that he could lean on. So he reached out to his ally, Cortez, in New Mexico.

As those two agents from New Mexico, posing as Drug Lords were led to the van loaded with drugs. They then returned to their car to hand over the attaché case filled with cash and collect the van's keys from the drug dealers. They had planned on one agent driving the vehicle to LA while the other followed in their car bearing California tags. Denise Gomez and Shelly Hall became suspicious. They wasted no time and snuffed them out with multiple rounds.

When Rude Buay and his team arrived, Shelly Hall and Denise Gomez were immediately interrupted as they attempted to reclaim possession of the 200 pounds of Meth aboard that van. Rude Buay and his team had passed the parked van and the car up the street not too far from where the two agents were gunned down.

They searched the van and not only was it loaded with meth but evidence indicated there could have been a chase of the two agents before they were shot and killed.

WITH THE DARK COLORED JEEP pursuing Rude Buay and his agents, the street race continued from Campillo onto Avenue Alvaro Obregon. Gaining some advantage and way ahead Rude Buay and his team pull off the road and into a secluded rest stop. The pursuing jeep continued and passed the rest area along the Avenue at high speed.

Moments later the three agent vehicles merged onto the Avenue in pursuit of the dark-colored jeep and its unknown occupants.

28

The three jeeps continue along the Avenue, moving at high speed to catch up to Shelly Hall and Denise Gomez's who's inside that vehicle. Inside the lead jeep is agent Rude Buay, followed by Walter Banks and behind Banks is Mildred Simms.

Meanwhile, Shelly Hall and Denise Gomez are still oblivious that they are being followed by these D.E.A. agents. In their mindset they have no idea that who they are in pursuit of, are now their followers. Finally, it dawns on them that the agents took a detour. So instead of continuing on the Avenue they too take a detour through the hillside. They embark on a downgrade. As their vehicle makes its descent Rude Buay still in pursuit spots it.

Rude Buay radios Banks' and Simms' vehicle.

"That car is about a mile away going through the hills, step on it!"

Says Rude Buay.

"We are right on your tail, Rude Buay,"

Says Banks.

"We are covering you, Banks,"

Says Mildred.

Richard Baptiste, the Commissioner concurs.

The three agent's vehicles are now gaining ground on Denise Gomez's and Shelly Hall's vehicles.

Shelly Hall looks in her rearview mirror and discovers they are being followed closely. How she wished the table had turned right about then. The winding treacherous hills and valleys beckon along with this now desolate two-lane highway. Shelly Hall speeds up but right about that time Rude Buay's jeep is speedily catching up to hers.

The agents arm themselves in preparation for an imminent showdown with the two women. Rude Buay with one arm on the steering wheel and the other holding on to that rifle he has grown so accustomed to. The passenger window in his jeep is now rolled down as he places the barrel of his rifle on that door so it protrudes outside and points towards the vehicle ahead.

Banks' jeep is on Rude Buay's vehicle's tail. Heidi Hudson sitting in the passenger seat equips herself with her loaded semi-automatic. At this point, Hudson relives those taunting memories she suffered under the hands of oppression by Shelly Hall and Denise Gomez. Banks looking across at Hudson knows she is focused and ready for battle.

Inside Mildred Simms' vehicle, which tails Banks', is Baptiste the Jamaican Police Commissioner. He is armed with a semi-automatic weapon. Mildred maintains command of the road and is also armed with the same type of weapon. Baptiste could sense the tension but unfortunately not the extent of Mildred's vendetta against the two *femme Fatales*. He rolls down the window and cues his gun in the same manner as Rude Buay's, as if by design.

At the same time, Shelly Hall's vehicle picks up speed. Her gun sits between her seat and the passenger seat. Denise occupying that passenger seat prepares for battle with her gun in hand. The agent's vehicles also pick up the pace.

Rude Buay get a few shots off. Unfortunately, nothing connects. Denise responds with a few of her own. Same result, *Zilch, Nada,* Nothing Connects!

Rude Buay's vehicle is now so close it's almost rear-ending Shelly Hall's. The road opens up providing a shoulder. Rude Buay speeds up and takes it. He is poised to get a good shot off at Shelly Hall. Shelly Hall drives out of the shot which sails into space.

Shelly Hall's vehicle is now in full view to agent Banks and Hudson as Rude Buay tries to make up for that missed opportunity to shoot Shelly Hall.

Heidi Hudson blasts several rounds at the two women. While Rude Buay and Shelly Hall jockey for position, Hudson tries passing on the other side and is almost at even keel with Denise's raised gun. Shelly Hall speeds up oblivious to the fact that she has derailed Rude Buay's focused gun on her. Now she drives leaving room on the left. Rude Buay tries positioning parallel with her vehicle so he can get a great aim at Shelly Hall. Instead, Shelly Hall tries forcing his jeep into the gutter.

Hudson's round of bullets connects with the two rear tires on Shelly Hall's vehicle and punctures both tires. Shelly Hall's car is slowed as it wobbles. Hudson manages to get another round-off, which blows out the rear windscreen.

In the meantime, a shot from Hudson's gun strikes Denise Gomez. Rude Buay also gets a shot off which hits Shelly Hall. Not only is Shelly Hall hit, but she also loses control of the vehicle. As a result, her vehicle nosedives over the steep embankment, rolling several times. It stops after crashing into a huge tree.

The agents get out of their vehicles and assess the damage from the roadway up above. From their vantage point, the two doors are ajar on this totaled vehicle. Mildred Simms and Heidi Hudson finish it off with several rounds, setting it ablaze. The agents depart I haste.

29

Rude Buay and his agents are combing the city of Nogales, Mexico. They are looking for any lead in finding Chelo.
"Requesting D.E.A. presence at the Nogales, Arizona border! Five border patrol officers down. They are at the scene where two illegal trailers are trying to cross into the U.S. from Mexico. They could be loaded with narcotics." The voice of Bruce echoes over the radios inside the three jeeps manned by the D.E.A. agents. Bruce conducts his survey from the hills of Nogales,

Mexico in a small house overlooking the U.S. border with Mexico.

Rude Buay, Walter Banks, Heidi Hudson, Mildred Simms, and Richard Baptiste take off towards the crime scene. Upon arrival they catch one of the drivers who later revealed his name as Javier, searching through the pockets of one of the fallen border patrol officers. The other driver waited inside the cab of his eighteen-wheeler in anticipation of getting the go-ahead from Javier. That decision to drive his trailer across the U.S. border was halted by the agent's presence.

During their investigation, the agents discover three border patrol vehicles parked on the street: Vehicles which probably served as impediments to the trailer's crossing into the U.S. Next to those means of transportation, are three dead officers and two on the pavement outside the border compound.

Upon the arrival of the agents, Javier and the other driver did not surrender but fired several rounds at them. The agents before they could get a shot off, they heard gunshots from both the men:

"Click! Click!

Those were the sound coming from the two drug smugglers guns. The two men try fleeing the scene back into Mexico but are caught by the agents and placed in handcuffs.

Rude Buay questions Javier about his involvement sensing that he was the ring leader. Rude Buay asks him what he was looking for in the officer's pocket. Javier tells the agent he was looking for keys. He also tells the agent that he is from Nogales in Sedona, Mexico. He further discloses that he has two daughters, 10 and 11. Also, Javier says that his wife Nora was killed in a drive-by shooting several months prior leaving him a widower. The other driver only reveals that his name is Jesus when asked by Rude Buay. Besides, he doesn't say very much. Rude Buay asks Javier for his two daughter's pictures. The smuggler has none to present, neither does he have any photos of his deceased wife.

Rude Buay asks him why he took the lives of the Border Patrol Officers. Javier said bluntly:

"They stood in our way. They block the street, asking what's inside the truck. I said none of your … business! They shoot … first. I had to defend."

Rude Buay wants to believe him but Javier doesn't look him in the eye.

Meanwhile, the accompanying D.E.A. agents discover large quantities of narcotics inside both trailers. Rude Buay asks the men why they were smuggling drugs into the U.S., to whom, and who they were working for? Javier tells Rude Buay they were paid to drive the trailers from Nogales to El Paso because there was trouble at the El Paso border. There in El Paso, they would transfer the trailers and drive back to Mexico. Javier discloses that they were hired by the *Dragon Drug Cartel*. When asked who in the organization they reported directly to. Javier informs they reported directly to Salvador.

Rude Buay then questions Javier about Salvador's whereabouts. Javier says he couldn't say, he didn't want to be any snitch, or else the *Dragons* would kill him by hanging him from a pole.

After pressuring Javier further to disclose Sal's whereabouts Javier attains a comfort level with agent Rude Buay. So, Javier tells Rude Buay that Salvador stays at the Cactus Motel in Nogales.

Rude Buay feels that he has gotten the info he wants. Before departing with the other DEA agents additional border officers show up at the border. They take Javier and Jesus into custody and charge them with murder and drug smuggling.

Rude Bauy says to his other agents, departing.

"Let's get ... out of here!"

30

Upon arriving at the *Cactus Motel*, the huge cactus plants on the premises very much compliment the signage. The hotel parking lot at mid-afternoon is almost empty. Many guests are checking in and out.
Javier had lied so much when questioned by Rude Buay, he felt this could be nothing but a hoax. Even so, he goes inside the motel lobby. Walking up to the

counter Rude Buay tells the receptionist he is a U.S. D.E.A. and that he is looking for Salvador.
"He no here,"
The middle-aged woman says nervously.
"Where is he now?"
Asks Rude Buay.
"Nobody here right now. New people check-in."
Replies the woman.
Looking out at the almost empty parking lot Rude Buay asks,
"Did he check out? I don't see his pickup truck. What color was it again?"
Rude Buay points his rifle towards the woman's head.
"Green!"
Says the woman.
"Where's his room?
The agent asks.
"He left, *señor*."
She responds.
"Is he coming back?"
Rude Buay asks,
"I don't know. No speak English!"
Rude Buay get the message. She knows but would not divulge. So Rude Buay waits along with his agents. While they wait for Sal to show up, breaking news airs over a Jamaican TV station and is transmitted through to the agent's vehicles:

"Two Jamaican Police Officers were gunned down earlier this morning by drug dealers in Tivoli Gardens using weapons from the Fast & Furious program. It was said that police was informed about an alleged drug deal of Methamphetamine.
One source said: When police arrived on the scene, members of the Dragon Drug Cartel, aligned with Jamaican Drug Lord Marcus Ranks, prowled on the two officers. Their arsenal instantly outmatched that of the police. The officers died suddenly.
Meanwhile, Methamphetamine in large quantity continues to pour into Tivoli Gardens, Port Antonio and Kingston. It was also claimed that many teens who have used the drug in the past continue to suffer from the slowness of both their brain and body."
States the reporter.
Moments later vehicles started pulling into the driveway sporadically. The guests continue to check-in. There is no sign of Salvador. The other agents look at Rude Buay as if they weren't sure this motel raid is going to go down.
Finally, the green pickup pulls into the parking lot. Sal appears, dressed in skinny jeans along with with a rolled-up sleeves white shirt unbuttoned at the top, a straw hat and a pair of black and white alligator boots. Sal prepares to enter his room on the hotel's ground level.
Rude Buay steps out of his jeep armed with a gun in hand. He is covered by Walter Banks, Heidi Hudson,

Mildred Simms, and Richard Baptiste. As soon as Sal turns the key inside the door lock and pushes it open, Rude Buay in pursuit yells out:

"Don't move Sal, U.S. Drug Enforcement Agents!"

Sal is alerted and tries closing the door on them. Instead, Sal abruptly aborts his entry to make his getaway. Rude Buay pushes him inside using the barrel portion of his rifle before Sal can get a shot off.

Sal's room is now filled with DEA agents. The atmosphere looks like an extended stay by its occupant Sal, instead of a weekend getaway. The odor says he's been staying there for a while; his BO and the room have blended.

Sal remains crouched on the floor with agents guns pointed at him. Rude Buay moves pass Sal's Meth lab which is set up inside a cubicle. He couldn't help but notice the test tubes inside this well-structured laboratory.

Additionally, he hears a moaning in the other room. He investigates.

Rude Buay's attention is drawn to a man tied up on a chair with his back turned. Rude Buay pushes the chair around with his feet. Surprisingly enough it is Chelo, tied up on that chair with multiple nylon ropes. Additionally, Chelo's right thumb and index fingers are bandaged and bloodied, indicating that some of his fingernails have already been removed. Rude Buay reminisces about the nail removal process he underwent at the hands of the dragons. He glances at his hands still bandaged. Even so, he senses difficulty untying the nylon ropes. So he summons Heidi Hudson:

Hudson darts into the room. She pulls out a switchblade from inside her boots under her jeans. She cuts the ropes which bind Chelo. The battered Chelo gets up from the chair somewhat lethargic and discombobulated. Hudson helps him out to the living room.

"Let's move it!"

Commands Rude Buay.

They get ready to leave. Salvador is still on the floor face down. He tries to get up in retaliation. Even so, he notices three guns are pointed at him. His shirt is now unbuttoned. Visible on his body are multiple second-degree burns. Rude Buay senses that their origin comes as a result of Sal's involvement in Methamphetamine preparation.

Rude Buay asks Salvador,

"Where is Alberto Gomez?"

Sal doesn't reply.

"Sal, where is your boss Alberto Gomez?"

Once again Sal doesn't respond.

Rude Buay shoots Sal in his right leg.

Still, Sal does not inform Rude Buay regarding his boss' whereabouts. So he shoots Sal a second time this time in the other leg.

RUDE BUAY VOL. III

In pain, Sal responds.

"Jamaica!"

Rude Buay pumps two more rounds inside Sal's body putting him out of his misery. The agents depart from the motel room.

While the agents went up to Salvador's room. The woman attendant at the front desk had called some of Sal's contacts alerting them that D.E.A. agents were after Sal and had headed over to his motel room.

As the agents arrive at the front parking lot of the *Cactus Motel,* they are greeted by a group of armed men. The men of Mexican descent are in a huddle waving machetes and cutlasses towards the D.E.A. agents. One of the men says to the leader of the pack:

"Let's chop them ... up."

Rude Buay hears and proceeds towards them with his rifle in hand. "Let's chop Rude Buay up to pieces."

Echoes the leader of the pack,

"I will take them on solo."

Says Rude Buay to his agents.

"You are crazy, *mon*! You don't know who you are dealing with."

Says Banks to Rude Buay.

"I wouldn't stop him if he thinks he can avoid getting chopped up by these Mexicans."

Says Baptiste.

"Get them Rude Buay!"

Says Heidi and Mildred in touché fashion.

"That's okay. Their asses are mine."

Rude Buay thinks about taking them on with some sweeping rounds but at the same time the leader of the pack Julio, holding on to an extended *one seamed cutlass* invitingly signals Rude Buay into a duel. Rude Buay never passes up a challenge and he was not about to pass this one up. So he advances towards Julio in confrontation. Julio separates himself from the rest of the crowd for leverage. He sucks Rude Buay into the duel.

To the amazement of the other D.E.A. agents, Rude Buay takes on Julio one on one with his rifle in hand. They begin sparring at each other. Julio's posse is now transformed into spectators as well as the other agents. All onlookers were now transfixed as the cutlass was swung at Rude Buay on many occasions. Rude Buay threw a few flying kicks at Julio for a while, none of which connect.

Finally, a kick from Rude Buay catches Julio in his stomach area. Julio tries to catch his breath. His cutlass soars and hits the pavement "CLING! CLANG!" as the kick from Rude Buay catches him unexpectedly. Rude Buay tosses his rifle in the direction of the agents and goes at Julio barehanded.

Julio ingeniously recovers his cutlass and swings at Rude Buay. Mildred and Hudson tremble like a leaf. Unfortunately, the swing from Julio misses Rude Buay.

Julio swings at him again. This time Mildred has her finger on the trigger ready to blast Julio.

Rude Buay does a 360 and plants a flying kick in Julio's neck area. Julio spins around and falls to the ground, in pain. Julio struggles to get up and falls back to the ground. He clenches tightly to his neck. Julio's posse comes charging at Rude Buay with cutlasses and machetes.

Rude Buay retrieves his rifle and blasts the entire lot of Julio's posse.

Rude Buay and the DEA agents re-board their vehicles and depart forthwith.

Meanwhile, the woman attendant at the reception office takes stock of the bloodbath from behind the hotel lobby blinds.

31

The next morning the agents arrive in Montego Bay Jamaica on the heels of Dr. Tamara Ross who has just reported for duty at the Port Antonio General Hospital. Dr. Ross was immediately put in charge of over a dozen patients, mostly teens, suffering from Methamphetamine overdose.

After exiting the airport terminal, the agents were met and greeted by a *Distinguished Gentleman*. He is dressed in white clothing and also sports a well-manicured beard.

"Mr. Rude Buay, it's good to see you again. If you survived the Villa, Tivoli Gardens, Shanghai, and Nogales, you can survive this. Although I must inform you that the man you will come up against Marcus Ranks, is more dangerous than Axel James, Frankie O'Neal, Ian Baynes, Ricardo Herrera and Johnny *Too Bad*. His skills outmatch theirs. Plus, he could very shortly be joined by Alberto Gomez. Here are the keys and directions. It is filled with gas. It has only been driven once. Your toys from the *Fast & Furious* program are in the trunk. You are going to need them."
"Thanks, but I love my rifle. I've grown accustomed to it. Plus…"
Says Rude Buay.
The other agents look on at the exchange between the two men.
"Agent Rude Buay, you must match your firepower to the new weapons used by the *Dragon Drug Cartel* or you and your team would be outmatched by Marcus Ranks in Kingston. You must conquer your comfort zone. This is the age of the *fast and furious*. Your country needs you."
The *Distinguished Gentleman* mounts his white horse and departs.
Rude Buay and his agents board the extended SUV and head speedily for Kingston.

The following morning the agents arrive in Kingston. Walter Banks questions if they should divide to conquer. Rude Buay, on the other hand, feels that unity is strength. He feels like they are about to bring in Marcus Ranks. With him leading the quest, accompanied by Banks, Simms, Baptiste, Hudson, and Chelo, Rude Buay feels whoever they came up against at this point had no chance.

As they drive through the busy streets of Kingston, a youth no more than seventeen crosses the street amid the traffic. Not only do many motorists, including Rude Buay, apply brakes but honk their horns. The retard does not heed any warning. Luckily he escapes being run over. He crosses the street and joins a weed-smoking huddle across the street. Hudson in the rear of the SUV shakes her head in dismay.

Later they pull up at *The Cave*. This hole in the wall was first on the list received from the *Distinguished Gentleman*. This was known as a possible hang out spot for Marcus Ranks.

The SUV pulls up and parks in-front of *The Cave*. Rude Buay sees a youth leaving the spot.

"Hey youth man! You saw Marcus Ranks lately?"
Asks Rude Buay.
"I don't talk to no police."
Says the youth.
"What you have against us?"
Asks Hudson.

"Nothing, I mind my own business. He just left an hour ago. Try the shooting range."

Rude Buay sticks a hundred dollar bill inside the youth's hand. They take off hurriedly through Kingston.

32

The agents pull up in front of the shooting range nestled in a backlot of a slum in Kingston. They quickly exit the SUV. Rude Buay, Banks, and Hudson barges in while the others cover. Inside a group of shooters hone their skills. They were later identified as Marcus Ranks' posse. These shooters are all hitting their targets as they are all going for the shooting target's head.

Rude Buay, Walter Banks and Heidi Hudson all *sign up* as guests to investigate the posse.

Unfortunately by the time the D.E.A. agents are finished, fitted and set to begin their shooting workout, the posse had already returned their weapons and made their exit through the back parking lot.

The agents return the following day. Except for this time they show up an hour earlier. Rude Buay, Walter Banks and Heidi Hudson are now involved in their shooting exercise. They are accompanied by Chelo undergoing an intense training session directed by agent Rude Buay. Chelo very early on is very much on target hitting the bulls-eye. His shots land in the head and stomach regions successively. The agents applaud his efforts, especially Walter Banks with an extended version.

Marcus Ranks still doesn't show up. The agents return the gear and head out. On their way to the parking lot, Marcus Rank's posse comes barging in. This time Rude Buay approaches them with his drawn *F & F* gun as soon as they exit their cars.

"Hold it right there! Drug Enforcement Agents!" Announces Rude Buay.

Before the posse of four men and two women could arm themselves, they find themselves surrounded by all six D.E.A. agents armed with *F and F* program weapons.

The other agents cover while Rude Buay, Banks and Hudson search their vehicles. The agents discover inside the trunks several pounds of Meth and kilos of

cocaine. Baptiste accommodates several pairs of handcuffs retrieved from inside the rear of the SUV.
Moments later, the posse is sitting on the sidewalk in handcuffs and being questioned by Rude Buay. The agent continues:
"I understand you are affiliated with the 'Wanted Marcus Ranks.' Not only that, but you were also caught in possession of illegal drugs as well as illegal firearms. Crimes like these could keep you in a Jamaican prison for a serious time. You can get those times reduced substantially however if you choose to cooperate by leading us to Marcus Ranks."
One of the women says,
"We don't know any Marcus Ranks!"
"Yes, you do Megan Holt."
Says the Commissioner looking at her straight on,
The Commissioner continues after Megan Holt looks away:
"Our records indicate that you provided Officer Bascombe with a constant supply of Methamphetamine. That drug which not only caused the death of his daughter Glenda but also caused the officer to take his own life. That supply was traced to Meth prepared by the *Dragons* and sold in Jamaica by you along with Marcus Ranks as the middle man."
"How much time is going to be knocked off of this deal?"
Asks the other woman.

All eyes are now on Rude Buay.
The woman continues,
"Because ..."
"Shut up bitch ..."
Says the leader of the pack, a midget, adorned in a black, gold and green tam, covering up his dreadlocks hairstyle.
The Commissioner remarks,
"We will be willing to negotiate on your behalf."
"Look for the ship *Marc I*. He docks at the pier at nights."
The rest of the posse looks at Megan Holt as if she was crazy to rattle on their boss.
Once again, the leader of that pack addresses,
"What makes you think these PIGS are going to help you get your time reduced?"
In the interim, the Commissioner calls in the Jamaican Police. They have just arrived on the scene. They quickly take the six members of Marcus Ranks' posse into custody.

33

The agents swarm the dock at Kingston later that night in search of Marcus Ranks. This stakeout by the agents results in a no show once again by Marcus Ranks.

The following morning agent Rude Buay receives a text message from Bruce still stationed in Mexico that the *Dragons* were meeting in South Beach, Miami. Attendees at that meeting are supposed to be Alberto Gomez, Miles Tate, Grace McCloud, Sammy Chin, and Marcus Ranks according to the text message. So the agents later board a plane bound for Miami.

RUDE BUAY VOL. III

IN SOUTH BEACH, MIAMI: Hip-Hop and Rap music reverberates from sidewalk bars, restaurants and night clubs on a busy evening. Some even entertain with House music and R & B from underneath their tents. Hot women, some of them attired in tight jeans, others in miniskirts and some in cheeky shorts parade the streets during the early evening hours. The men salivate, casting multiple double-takes.

Drug dealers and buyers conduct business managing to avoid Law Enforcement Officers, as they use their two-way radio feature on their cell phones to alert each other of danger zones. Street after street is crowded with pedestrians. The vibe is like that of a Memorial Day weekend in South Beach. Buses even avoid making stops along some of those pedestrian crowded streets. The sidewalks are roped off and barricaded, thus allowing a steady easy flow of pedestrians.

The nearby restaurants, bars, stores, and clubs are buzzing with activity. Never before has South Beach drawn such a crowd except on a Memorial Day weekend. Miami police walk the beat as a routine. The drug pushers and buyers cleverly escape their surveillance as narcotics trade hands.

Meanwhile, in a South Beach hotel suite, a meeting is in session: five members of the Dragon drug Cartel convene to save the depleting *Dragon Drug Cartel*. Some of the topics being discussed are:

1) Eliminating Rude Buay and his agents to allow free trade between Mexico and the rest of the world if he will not agree to sign onto the team.
2) Adding new members to the cartel.
3) Sabotaging the efforts of competing cartels in Mexico like the Sinaloa Cartel.

Alberto Gomez chairs the meeting. Additionally, he displays pictures on a TV monitor:

1. Several closed and out of business Nogales local banks.
2. Mexican drug smugglers reverting to making pottery and other handcraft products.
3. Border patrols surveying the drug tunnel operations between Mexico and Arizona.
4. The discontinued drug activity at many abandoned warehouses in Mexico.
5. Pictures of Rude Buay's duel with Julio as taken from the woman at the hotel's POV.
6. Pictures of Sal's corpse.
7. Pictures of Victor Crip's corpse.
8. Government workers in Arizona sealing up the manholes at the parking meters on Independence Street.
9. Eighteen-wheelers carry drugs across the U.S. border seized by border patrols.
10. The overturned car once occupied by Denise Gomez and Shelly Hall

At this point, Alberto Gomez turns off the monitor. He has seen enough. He is not the only one who is frustrated so do the other members of his team.
He articulates,
"Guys we need to act now not only to recapture those D.E.A. agents but to hold our cartel together. Let's not forget, we are *The Dragons*. We Rule! I will not let another Mexican cartel thrive on what we have put in place for so many years."
"How soon will a new Chemist be reinstated…?"
Asks Miles Tate.
"Same question."
Interrupts Marcus Ranks.
"We have many orders to fill in New England and neighboring cities."
Says Miles Tate.
"Miami is going to be dry after this weekend. Plus I can't keep my Cuban customers waiting much longer. Their patience is running thin."
Says Grace McCloud.
Before Sammy Chin can speak, Grace follows up by saying:
"It is the first time we have ever had a shortage of supply here in Miami. Pushers have doubled their prices for both Meth and Cocaine. We are in no position to compete with members of neither the Sunshine Cartel nor the Sinaloa … in this marketplace."

"If anyone has an extra supply of Meth let me know. I will have to smuggle it into China myself. Shipping it would take too long. Chu Ling's clients are waiting. Don't want to piss them off."
Says Sammy Chin,
"I have found a new Chemist, His name is Chico Rubio. The first mixes could be a little harsh until he gets seasoned. We'll just have to market our product anyway."
Says Alberto Gomez.
"What about possible recalls?"
Asks Sammy Chin.
"No recalls. I don't like that dirty word."
Says Alberto Gomez.
"That's a hard pill for Jamaicans to swallow."
Says Marcus Ranks.
He is not clearly understood. So he clarifies.
"Could we buy from another source until Chico Rubio gets a hang of this?"
"I would not endorse buying from the Sunshine or Sinaloa Cartel. They are part of what got us in this glut. If they had not tried sending so many eighteen-wheelers loaded with the product across the U.S. border we would not be in the glut we are in. Never rush the Americans. They get you all the time. Slow and steady wins the race. This meeting is adjourned. If anyone runs into Rude Buay, I have my gun loaded with bullets initialed RB."

RUDE BUAY VOL. III

Alberto Gomez exits and boards a waiting limousine. The others board individual taxis as they leave the South Beach hotel.

34

Rude Buay, Chelo, Banks, Heidi Hudson, Mildred Simms, and Richard Baptiste embark upon South Beach with a vengeance. Once again they pair up for battle with the *Dragon Drug Cartel*. Agent Rude Buay reunites with Chelo in the first car. Walter Banks and Heidi Hudson are in the second car and Mildred Simms and Richard Baptiste in the third.

The agent convoy moves through the streets of South Beach in a surveillance style. With many of the main boulevards blocked off with barricaded sidewalks, the agents take a detour using the open side streets. They pull up at the hotel where the *Dragons* had just wrapped their meeting. After parking their vehicles they barge inside armed to the maximum. A hotel employee but who is also an inside informant directs them to the executive suite.

Rude Buay knocks on the door, no one answers. Using his gun he blows out the lock. They enter. A few pens and scrap paper residue is evidence a meeting was in session. The delegation, on the other hand, is absent. The agents depart to the outside re-board their vehicles and head off through the streets of South Beach.

The streets, although only accessible to minimal vehicular traffic has become more traffic-laden than when the agents arrived on the strip. The gridlock traffic creates a bottleneck for South Beach exiting traffic. The agents are now caught up in that going-nowhere, very slowly, dilemma.

Rude Buay as if equipped with the eyes of a hawk spots the getaway SUV with Miles Tate in the driver's seat. He alerts his other agents via radio and pursues Miles Tate. Rude Buay's vehicle weaves in and out of traffic as he tries to catch up with Tate's. His other agents follow suit in tow.

Meanwhile, inside Tate's SUV, Tate with the use of his side mirrors sees the aggressively pursuant. Rude Buay's vehicle has now passed several cars and aligned itself three cars ahead making it the fourth car behind Tate's. Not only does Tate notice the pursuing Rude Buay, but he also notices, the other two cars accompanying Rude Buay. In an instant that vehicle careens around those three cars using the shoulder of the street and is now exactly behind Tate's SUV.

The pressure is now building on Tate's end as the only exit from Beach Street is the beach exit. The buses transporting passengers to and from South Beach have all clogged up the boulevards. Not only that, he knows that Rude Buay wants his head on a platter for deflecting and being a snitch. He also notices Chelo accompanying the agent and occupying the front seat. Two men who should have been dead are following him along with four other survivors.

Tate reaches for his gun as he opts to exit on the street leading towards the beach. The agents are right up behind him tailgating. Tate's vehicle is slowed by the sand on the beach, but more so, the vehicles of the agents in pursuit. The sedans finally split from the convoy and form a periphery around the SUV.

Tate jumps out and fires off a few rounds at the agents before making his plunge into the water. Not only do his rounds miss their target but Rude Buay is only a few feet away in pursuit. Tate tries to swim away into the deep but Rude Buay is about to have him cornered. The agent yells at Tate as he tries to dive:

"Tate there isn't anywhere to run to. I told you if you ever became a snitch we would go fishing. Even so, you are too big a *bait* for Jack Fish. Plus, they only thrive in the Caribbean, not in Miami. The sharks would be happy though. They are always drawn to human blood.

Tate tries to get a kick, aimed at Rude Buay. He misses. They have now squared off waist-deep in the water. Rude Buay throws a left jab and a right uppercut. Tate is hit by the jab to his face but as he ducks in the uppercut escapes him.

Rude Buay throws him a right jab which lands in his mouth causing him to spit out blood as a result.

Banks standing on the beach with the other agents, yells:

"Let me shoot the bastard. No need to get saturated with *his* blood! Nothing but a ... traitor!"

The water rises as they are drawn in deeper by the tide. Rude Buay pushes Tate under and refuses to let up. Tate begins kicking for his existence. Yet, Rude Buay does not let him up. Tate drinks until he can drink no more. Rude Buay releases him to his death and returns to the beach. Before Tate's body submerges Chelo fires a round at the ex-agent. It connects to his head. Tate goes under.

As they get ready to re-board he gets a call from D.E.A. headquarters requesting his presence at the Miami harbor. The call is regarding a ship alleged to be loaded with narcotics. Without a chance to change out from the wet clothing, Rude Buay and his agents rush, to the Miami port accompanied by sirens and flashing lights.

35

The agents pull up in their BMW's at Miami Harbor. They notice the harbor saturated with multiple ships. With the use of binoculars, they try to determine the target ships carrying out the narcotics transfer. Rude Buay zooms out and locates their targets. He alerts the other agents.

The agents quickly board a speedboat heading in that direction. The speedboat takes off navigating its way through the crowded port, leaving an extended trail of white water behind it.

As they are nearing the ship which made the transfer, that ship raises its anchor and takes off. The other ship named *Marc 1* is about to do the same. Banks at the helm of their speedboat pulls up in front of the *Marc 1*'s bow. The man lifting the anchor alerts the rest of the crew. Bullets from *Marc 1* begin to rain onto DEA the agent's speedboat. The agents manage to dodge out of those bullets. Before Richard Baptiste, now in command of the ship, abandons it he attaches a rope to *Marc 1* using a lasso.

Rude Buay and Walter Banks have already jumped aboard the suspected *Marc I*. Two men aboard the *Marc I* see the agents approaching and train their weapons on them. The sight of the agent's *F & F's* weapons has the two men with their backs up against the wall. Another man armed approaches from the hull. Rude Buay yells out:

"D.E.A.! Hands on your heads."

The three men comply with the agent's request.

"Where is Marcus Ranks?"

Asks Rude Buay.

"He is not here."

Says the last man to exit the hull of the ship dressed in a dreadlocks hairstyle.

"Where is he?"

Asks Rude Buay.

"No idea."

Says the man.

"You are under arrest for drug smuggling."
Says Rude Buay.
Banks, Hudson and Baptiste put handcuffs on the three men while Rude Buay and Chelo descend inside of the hull. Rude Buay and Chelo discover several bags of marijuana, over 500 pounds of methamphetamine and about 300 kilos of cocaine in addition to an assortment of weapons and U.S. currency.
On the outside, the *Marc 1* lifeboat's engine starts up. Helming it is Marcus Ranks who had previously emerged from under some tarpaulin on the other side of the *Marc 1*. He is about to make his getaway.
Inside the hull Rude Buay sees Ranks trying to make his getaway from through the porthole. Rude Buay takes off with Chelo. Passing through the deck Banks joins them. The three agents board the speedboat in pursuit of Marcus Ranks.
Meanwhile, Michael Ortiz is standing on the bridge across the way overlooking the harbor and watching the unfolding of events through a pair of binoculars. Rude Buay, Banks, and Chelo continue to go after Marcus Ranks at full speed.
Ranks sees them rapidly approaching and fires off a few quick rounds, tragically catching nothing, but air.
Banks is at the helm of the speed boat. Chelo is now on the phone with Ortiz talking about their next plan of attack on the *Dragons*. Rude Buay get a good aim at Ranks and blasts him. Marcus Ranks is hit in the chest.

He falls over into the lifeboat. His boat continues and crashes into a pillar upholding the bridge.

The agents return to the *Marc 1* and wrap up their narcotics seizure. They depart in the speedboat as Miami police now on the scene arrest the three drug smugglers and confiscate the seizure of narcotics.

36

The agents pull up in front of the club *Dynasty* dressed to the nines. Even so, Chelo is the only one not part of the group. They pull up outside and enter flashing their badges. Inside the club, it's a party as usual. The agents mingle. The vibe on the inside puts South Beach in the evening, on a whole other level. *Go Go Dancers* dance from inside huge glass cases. Hot babes saunter throughout the club. Surfer type males interact with these Hotties. Some are fortunate to get a number. On the other hand, the more passive men wait at the bar to make their approach. The agents survey and have a few drinks.

RICHARD BAPTISTE'S WIFE Christine calls. Richard answers.
"When are you coming home, Richard? I miss you!"
He tells her that the Miami situation has become very demanding. He also reminds her that he would be home on time for her birthday in two weeks.
Christine, after ending the conversation looks at the calendar hanging over the fridge, and then plops down on the couch and continues playing her game of Solitaire and enjoying a glass of Merlot.

AT THE CLUB Mildred approaches Richard and signals him to the dance floor. The DJ had just put on a dancehall tune. The DJ mixes it with a soca beat. Mildred goes wild putting Richard under severe pressure to keep up with her on the dance floor. She is now center stage with Richard. The other agents cheer them on. So do the heavily gathering party crowd.
The band gets ready to set up for their musical performance. Rude Buay signals time to leave. They head towards the backstage.
Behind the curtain is the new look Chelo, dressed in a sharp business suit, a tailored shirt with a smashing tie. On his feet, he wears the pair of moccasins which Rude

Buay bought him back in Mexico on the day he was captured by Salvador. It is a spit shine. This wardrobe upgrade gives him the look of a Cuban businessman, enhanced with a hat and a cigar.

Through the back exit door walks Grace McCloud. The *femme fatale* is carrying a duffel bag in her hand. Back there Chelo waits for solo but with a certain degree of confidence. McCloud presents the bag to Chelo. He opens it and inspects its contents. He is satisfied. Chelo hands over the attaché case to McCloud. To her, it is the right amount of cash for the 15 pounds of Methamphetamine and the 5 kilos of cocaine. The case is closed quickly and McCloud walks towards the exit door to the parking lot. Chelo picks up the bag of narcotics heading towards the stage.

Before McCloud could get to the door, Rude Buay, Walter, Heidi, Mildred, and Richard have her cornered.

"Hold it right there McCloud! D.E.A., nobody moves!" Chelo stays put to accommodate. The four agents pass him by and hold McCloud at gunpoint. McCloud calls them bluff and heads through the door, quickly dodging rounds of bullets, before boarding the waiting limousine.

They pursue and shoot up the trying to get away limousine. McCloud showing resilience opens the moon roof and fire off several rounds at the agents. The agents run out of bullets in their semi-automatic

RUDE BUAY VOL. III

weapons as a result of the onslaught on the limo. McCloud is hit but continues to shoot back at the agents.

From underneath the table, Chelo speedily wheels out an open trunk filled with *F & F's*. Rude Buay, Walter, Heidi, Mildred and Richard once again return fire on McCloud and her limo driver, this time from the state of the art weapons. The limo gets demolished with McCloud and the chauffeur inside.

The agents depart while the patrons rush to the back parking lot.

37

As the agents leave the club and merge with the boulevard traffic. Rude Buay's phone rings. It's a familiar number as revealed by his caller ID. On the other end is his boss Michael Ortiz.
Rude Buay did you get them?"
Agent Ortiz asks.
"Yes. I did!"
Says Rude Buay.
"Both of them?"
Asks his boss.

"Yep!"
Says Rude Buay,
"McCloud and Chin?"
Asks Ortiz.
"Chin wasn't there."
Says Rude Buay.
"He followed McCloud to make the drop for Chelo and then he went to fill up at the gas station."
"Really? What is he driving?"
Asks Rude Buay.
"A Cadillac Escalade, ivory in color. Do not let him get away, Rude Buay,"
Says Ortiz.
Rude Buay is *gamed*.
The agents speed up.
Moments later Rude Buay notices the Escalade speedily moving in the direction to the club. He and his team make a U-Turn and follow that vehicle. As they close in, on it, he recognizes Sammy Chin under the driver's seat. The blue lights on his dash begin to flash and revolve. The other agents follow suit as he is now tailgating Chin's vehicle.

Chin would not let up. An intense chase ensues. Chin seems like he is about to make a getaway on the open roads. He continues to pursue Chin with his agents following in tow. The chase continues through the back roads of South Beach. Rude Buay is now close enough to the Escalade and gets a shot off at Chin. The bullet hits the front left fender of the vehicle. Chin begins to fight back with several rounds. Rude Buay and his agent begin to shoot up the Escalade with an onslaught of bullets. Chin is hit. As a result the SUV slams into a retaining wall. Rude Buay searches the SUV and discovers at least 50 pounds of Methamphetamine inside a duffel bag.

Rude Buay goes through Chin's wallet and discovers two hotel room keys and a check-in receipt billed to Gomez's credit card.

38

Rude Buay, cognizant of the fact that where there is smoke there is Alberto Gomez still at large. So he heads for the *South Beach Casa Nora Hotel*. It isn't long after departing the scene that his phone rings. Once again it's his boss.
"We are down to the last man. They say he's invincible. Whatever you do I want him alive. This is like your Holy grail"
"Let me call you back,"
Says Rude Buay.

Rude Buay ponders the statement. In his mind, he knows Alberto Gomez's life has been spared many times, at his own hands. He knows what he has lived through at the hands of the most notorious Drug Czar to ever run a cartel, Gomez. Chelo sitting in the passenger seat senses Rude Buay's confusion.

Rude Buay calls back Ortiz.

"Sorry boss, no can do. When I catch Alberto Gomez I am going to kill him. Whether that pleases you or not, this man has been a menace to society. He has caused many innocent kids to die by his actions. It's like asking me to spare a thousand *Osamas*. Do you know what we are in for if he continues to breathe any longer."

Ortiz on the other end of the phone is not giving up and persists in his demands to Rude Buay.

"Just bring him in, Agent Bascombe."

"I am sorry you will have to come and get him yourself if you want him under those conditions."

Rude Buay puts Ortiz on speakerphone. He radios the rest of his agents:

"When we catch up to Albert Gomez, no matter what's the condition let me have him. I want to be the one to drill his skull."

Rude Buay hangs up the call with his boss and pulls up outside the hotel.

He speaks to the manager sitting behind the desk. The MOD is a middle-aged woman of Cuban descent. The woman focuses more on Chelo than on Rude Buay.
"I am looking for Alberto Gomez," says Rude Buay disclosing his badge.
"No."
Responds the woman nervously.
"That's okay. There is no need to be afraid of him. Gomez can't harm you."
Says Chelo.
"You all got to be crazy,"
Responds the woman.
"We are not. We just need to talk to him,"
Says Rude Buay.
He reaches inside his pocket, pulls out a money clip and peels off 5 one hundred dollar bills. The woman's eyes light up.
"Executive floor on the 23rd floor but I forgot he has tight security. Do you want your money back?"
"That's okay keep it."
Say Rude Buay.
He leaves in haste to his car and picks up his *Fast and Furious* ammunition; Chelo also arms himself as well. The other agents are also armed and ready.
The MOD is alarmed as Baptiste is stationed in the parking lot, Mildred is in the lobby, Hudson heads for the elevator, Chelo takes the stairwell. Banks takes the stairs to the 23rd floor covering Rude Buay. Upon

arriving, Rude Buay and Banks see the two guards pacing the 23rd floor. Rude Buay pops one while Banks pops the other.

Rude Buay knocks on the door to Gomez's suite. There is no answer. Although they can hear the TV playing no one answers the door. Rude Buay kicks in the door. On the table in the room, there are used freebasing utensils along with Alberto Gomez's *F & F* gun. Rude Buay grabs the gun and charges in with both guns; his and Gomez's

Alberto Gomez dashes out of the bathroom wearing a white bathrobe. He launches for his weapon on the table. Rude Buay shows it to him while balancing his on the other hand.

"Those guards just lost their jobs."

Rude Buay senses that Gomez is trying to make small talk so he could arm himself or buy time. Gomez looks peripherally for a substitute weapon. At this point, even a table knife would do in Gomez's mind. Just some kind of defense but there is none.

"I don't think you have the balls to shoot me Rude Buay."

"How about a fingernail every day for the next ten days?"

Asks Rude Buay,

Banks edges closer.

"Or how about both your eyes right now?"

"FYI, I am here to torture you before the vultures have you for their delight."
Says Rude Buay.
"So you are into Moses' law."
Banks is animated and ready to end Gomez's life.
"*An eye for an eye or a tooth for a tooth*? I thought you were all about the Messiah. Who said, *Forgive and it shall be forgiven you.*"
Continues Gomez.
"There is nothing to talk about. Let's shoot the bastard!"
Says Walter Banks,
Rude Buay shoots Gomez in the right leg with his gun and blows it off. The residue of that round leaves a huge hole in the wall.
"I am trying to be like the Messiah, It's a tough job. He walked on water, didn't he? Then he turned water into wine. He even healed the sick. He also made the lame man walk."
Says Rude Buay.
"Shoot the sucker; don't let him break you down,"
Says Banks.
Rude Buay shoots Gomez in the other leg, this time with the Drug Czars' gun. Gomez is now on the floor, both legs severed from the knees down. He is undergoing tremendous pain.
"Jesus also knelt and prayed, didn't he?"
Says Rude Buay.
Alberto Gomez is groaning and in pain.

Rude Buay looks at Gomez's two jumping legs while the Czar continues to suffer.

"Cuff him Banks!"

Banks lays his weapon on the table and place handcuffs on the bleeding Alberto Gomez.

Rude Buay takes out his cell phone and dials his boss Ortiz.

"We've got him. He is now yours. FYI, he is going to need a pair of crutches."

"Great job! I'll get some to him soon."

Says Ortiz.

Rude Buay and Banks exit the room and team up with the other agents in the parking lot. **They drive to D.E.A. Headquarters.**

About The Author

John A. Andrews, screenwriter, producer, and author of several books, founded Teen Success in 2009. Its mission statement: ***To empower Teens in maximizing their full potential to be successful and contributing citizens in the world.*** As an author of books on relationships, personal development, and vivid engaging stories, John is sought after as a motivational speaker to address success principles to young adults. John makes an impact in the lives of others because of his passion and commitment to make a difference in the world. Being a father of three sons propels John even more in his desire to see teens succeed. Andrews, a divorced dad of three sons ages 17, 15 and 13, was born in the Islands of St. Vincent and the Grenadines. He grew up in a home of five sisters and three brothers. He recounts: "My parents were all about values: work hard, love God and never give up on your dreams."

Self educated, John developed an interest for music. Although lacking the formal education, he later put his knowledge and passion to good use, moonlighting as a disc jockey in New York. This paved the way for further exploration in the world of entertainment. In 1994 John caught the acting bug. Leaving the Big Apple for Hollywood over a decade ago not only put several national TV commercials under his belt but helped him to find his niche.

His passion for writing started in 2002, when he was denied the rights to a 1970's classic film, which he so badly wanted to remake. In 2007, while etching two of his original screenplays, he published his first book "The 5 Steps to Changing Your Life" Currently he's publishing a string of novels, coaching two of his sons who are writing their first novel, bringing some of his work to the big screen, while working on empowering teens worldwide.

In 2008 he not only published his second book but also wrote seven additional books that year, and produced the docu-drama based on his second book; *Spread Some Love (Relationships 101).*

See Imdb: http://www.imdb.com/title/tt0854677/.

RUDE BUAY VOL. III

FOR MORE ON
BOOKS THAT WILL ENHANCE YOUR LIFE ™
Visit: **A L I**
www.AndrewsLeadershipInternational.com
EMAIL US
john@johnaandrews.com

Website
www.JohnAAndrews.com

*Rude Buay is a drug prevention chronicle about teens caught up in the war on drugs and contains content for adults; parental discretion is advised for children.

A 2012 Books That Will Enhance Your Life. All Rights Reserved.

Resource:
Methamphetamine:
http://www.nmtf.us/methamphetamine/methaphetamine.htm

News Report: ABC News

THE MACOS ADVENTURE

RUDE BUAY VOL. III

RENEGADE COPS

CROSS ATLANTIC FIASCO

BLOOD IS THICKER THAN WATER

JOHN A. ANDREWS
RENEGADE COPS
Creator of
The RUDE BUAY Series
&
The WHODUNIT CHRONICLES

RUDE BUAY VOL. III

WHO SHOT THE SHERRIFF?

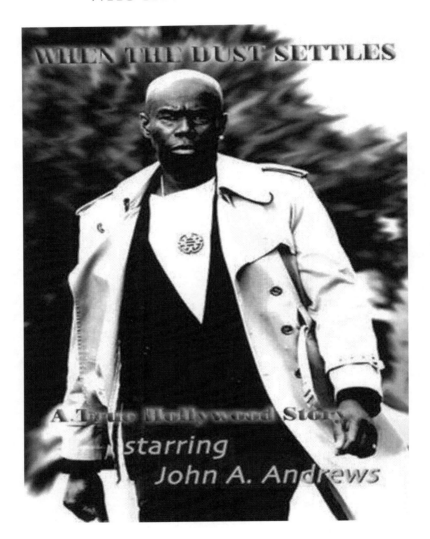

RUDE BUAY VOL. III

RUDE BUAY ... THE UNSTOPPABLE

RUDE BUAY VOL. III

RUDE BUAY VOL. III

CHICO RUDO

| RUDE BUAY VOL. III

CHICO RUDO II

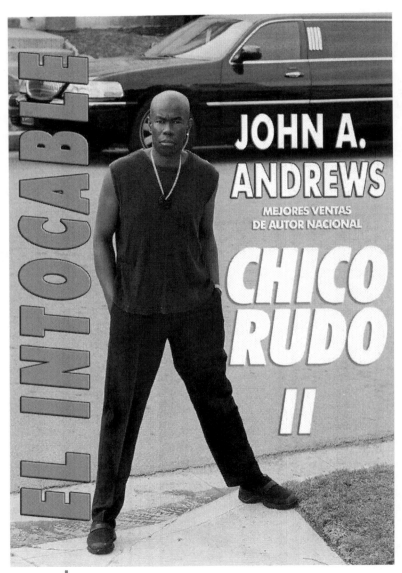

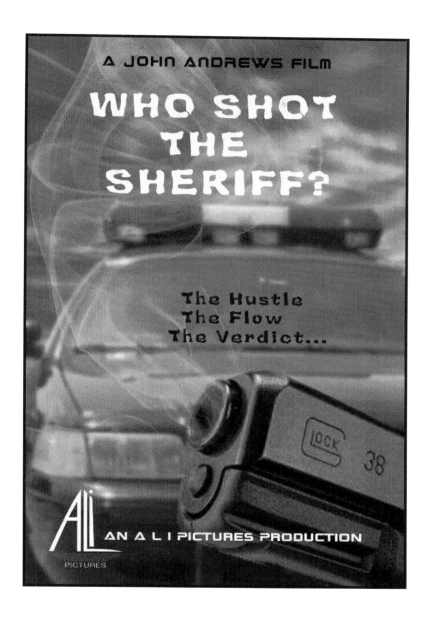

RUDE BUAY VOL. III

QUOTES UNLIMITED II

RUDE BUAY VOL. III

RUDE BUAY VOL. III

National Bestselling Author of
Rude Buay ... The Unstoppable

THE 5 STEPS TO CHANGING YOUR LIFE

BY: JOHN A. ANDREWS

RUDE BUAY VOL. III

RUDE BUAY VOL. III

DARE TO MAKE A DIFFERENCE

SUCCESS 101

FOR

ADULTS

#1 INTERNATIONAL BESTSELLING AUTHOR

JOHN A. ANDREWS

RUDE BUAY VOL. III

RUDE BUAY VOL. III

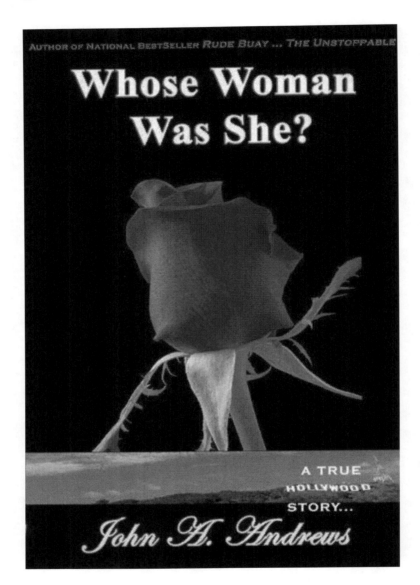

RUDE BUAY VOL. III

RUDE BUAY VOL. III

RUDE BUAY VOL. III

VISIT: WWW.JOHNAANDREWS.COM

NEW RELEASES

NEW YORK CONNIVERS ©

FROM THE CREATOR OF *WHO SHOT THE SHERIFF?*

JOHN A. ANDREWS

UNTIL DEATH DO US PART

A NOVEL

ONE FOOT IN *NEW YORK UNDERCOVER*
THE OTHER IN *ALFRED HITCHCOCK PRESENTS*

NEW RELEASES

NEW RELEASES

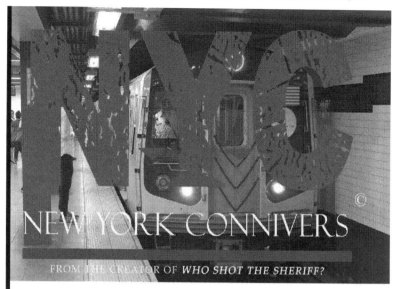

NEW YORK CONNIVERS

FROM THE CREATOR OF *WHO SHOT THE SHERIFF?*

JOHN A. ANDREWS

NEW YORK CITY BLUES

THE UNDERGROUND OPERATION

A NOVEL

ONE FOOT IN *NEW YORK UNDERCOVER*
THE OTHER IN *ALFRED HITCHCOCK PRESENTS*

NEW RELEASES

NEW RELEASES

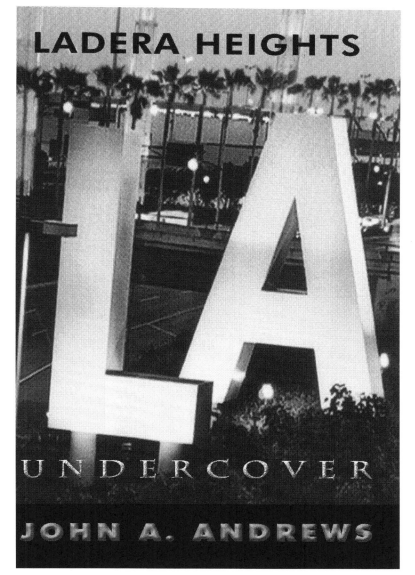

NEW RELEASES

Climbing Up From The Bottom AUTHOR

JOHN A. ANDREWS

Dare To Make A Difference (Success 101)
Spread Some Love (Relationships 101)

The 5 Steps To Changing Your Life

THE SUCCESS TRIANGLE™

Three Books In One Volume
Including **DARE TO MAKE A DIFFERENCE**

NEW RELEASES

Made in the USA
Middletown, DE
29 April 2024

53620665R00392